Stranger

in my

Arms

Doubleday

New York London Toronto
Sydney Auckland

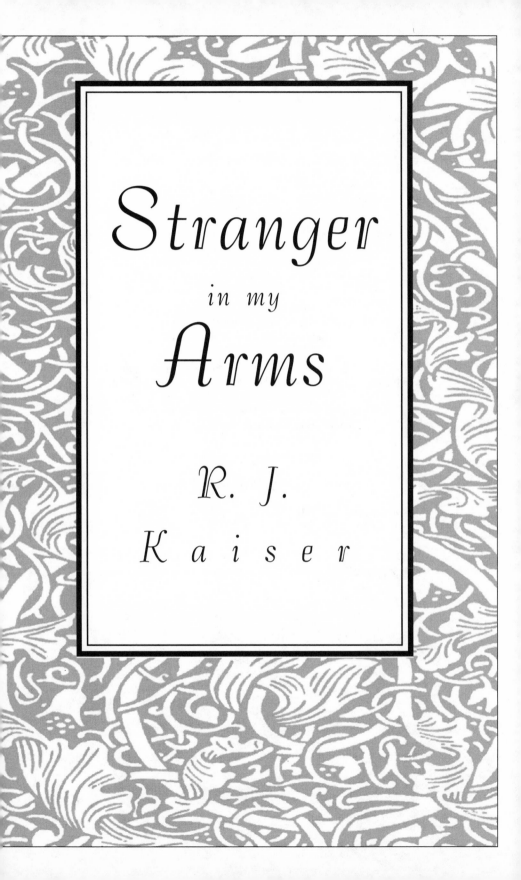

Stranger
in my
Arms

R. J.
Kaiser

PUBLISHED BY DOUBLEDAY
a division of Bantam Doubleday Dell Publishing Group, Inc.
1540 Broadway, New York, New York 10036

DOUBLEDAY and the portrayal of an anchor with a dolphin are trademarks of
Doubleday, a division of Bantam Doubleday Dell Publishing Group, Inc.

Book design by Cathy Braffet

Library of Congress Cataloging-in-Publication Data
Kaiser, R. J.
    Stranger in my arms / R. J. Kaiser.
      p.   cm.
    I. Title.
PS3561.A4152S77   1993
813'.54—dc20   93-19917
                                                                   CIP

ISBN 0-385-46966-7

August 1993
First Edition

1   3   5   7   9   10   8   6   4   2

*F*OR OUR PARENTS:

Ruth Small Kaiser
Al Kaiser
Edris Smith Bender
and
Harold C. Bender
(1904–1988)

Acknowledgments:

WE WISH TO THANK Robin Rue for her faith,
Beth de Guzman for her guidance,
Nita Taublib for her support,
Marie and Bernard Henry for their knowledge,
and a special thanks to Sherie Posesorski
for showing us the way.

Stranger
in my
Arms

IT'S STRANGE THE way the mind can shield itself from the harsh reality of sin. It can erase whole lives, whole worlds, so that the only truth left is innocence. I discovered this for myself when I awoke in a place I did not know, among people I'd never met.

But even before my eyes opened I was aware of a scent, the musky smell of roses. The perfume filled my lungs, evoking a powerful emotion. My heart began to pound and I heard myself moan, though I was unable to focus my thoughts. I was still clinging to the gauzy unreality of near sleep.

When I finally opened my eyes, all I could see was a blank wall. Then I became aware of my bed and the other walls defining the room. Another moment or two passed before the nurse, a homely creature with a large nose and bulging jowls, put her face in front of mine and said, *"Madame, vous voilà revenue à vous!"*

I blinked, not understanding her. The scent of the roses was comprehensible, but not this woman. "Where are the roses?" I murmured.

Her eyes lit up, then the face vanished as quickly as it had appeared. I thought her reaction bizarre, absurd even. Had I awakened in some sort of film—one by Fellini perhaps? It was a curious thought and later, when I was describing those first moments of consciousness to the psychiatrist, I couldn't tell him how I knew about Fellini.

The medical doctor, a smallish man with pinched features and a wispy mustache, arrived then and peered into my eyes as though he were looking into a petri dish. He, too, seemed pleased by what he saw. "Hello, madame," he said in strongly accented English. "How do you feel?"

I did not relate to his words. I had sensation, yet I was a total stranger, even to myself.

"Where am I?" I said, my voice hoarse and weak.

"You are in hospital at Toulon."

"Toulon?" The name meant nothing.

"I'm afraid you've had a very bad knock on the head, madame. Do you remember?"

I shook my head. I remembered nothing, except smelling the roses. The recollection of that was strong, but it had been only a few moments earlier. The nurse was standing nearby. Her face was familiar, but I'd only just seen it too. I turned my head, aware how terribly stiff my neck felt, and peered about the room.

The ceiling was high, the walls painted white. The French windows were tall and I could see sunlight filtering through the billowing sheer curtains. On the bedstand were the roses, perhaps two dozen long-stemmed red ones. I noticed the fragrance again.

I turned back to the doctor, who seemed calmly concerned. The half smile was intended to tell me everything was all right, but I knew it wasn't. "I don't understand what's happening," I said.

"You're disoriented, Madame Bass. This is to be expected. Soon it will start coming back to you. You've suffered a very serious trauma."

That made sense. But why did he call me Madame Bass? It was at that moment that I first realized I didn't know who I was. I tried searching my memory, only to discover I had none. It was as blank as the wall across from me.

The discovery was disquieting, to say the least. I had a strong sense that I should know who I was, that it was urgent that I do so. My eyes filled with tears. I felt like a child without its mother. "I don't know who I am," I murmured.

The doctor patted my hands. "You must relax, madame. It will all come back to you soon. Your disorientation is not uncommon. Yesterday we notified your husband that you may be regaining consciousness soon. He is on his way. I should think he will arrive by this evening. There is nothing direct from London, of course. So it takes time."

My *husband*? I was *married*? That did not seem right at all. Somehow I could accept the fact that I didn't know who I was, but it upset me to think that I was married and didn't know it. I had absolutely no sense of knowing anyone that well. "Are you sure?" I asked.

"Well, no, madame, I cannot be certain when he will arrive. He simply said he'd come as soon as possible."

"No, I mean are you sure that . . . I'm married." The last words faded to a mumble. Of course he was sure. One didn't say such a thing unless one knew.

The doctor understood that my question needn't be answered. He put his small, cool hand on my forehead. "I think you should rest, madame. We should get some solid food in

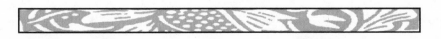

you. The neurologist will want to examine you. And the psychiatrist, Dr. Thirion. For now, please try to relax. Nurse will be here if you need anything." He smiled a thin-lipped smile and left my side.

I had an urge to call out to him not to leave, but I said nothing. Instead I looked at the nurse, who beamed benevolently. I made an effort to smile back.

I tried to gather my thoughts, but my brain wouldn't cooperate. It was as though my memory were a maze and I a rat within it. I tried this route and that, then another, but each led nowhere—every course that should have taken me back in time led to a dead end. I was stuck in a life that had begun only minutes earlier with the roses, the nurse, the doctor, and the room.

I looked at the woman, feeling a determination to get to the bottom of this bizarre situation. "Why am I in France?" I asked.

"You live here, madame. Some of the time anyway, I think. And in England, as well."

That seemed strange. "My husband is rich then."

The nurse looked embarrassed for me. *"Oui, madame."*

That discovery brought me no particular satisfaction. I lifted my hand to see if I had a ring, to learn what I could about my taste and his, but my fingers were bare. Undoubtedly my jewelry had been removed.

I closed my eyes and tried hard to remember, but nothing came to me. Nothing. This Fellini film I'd awakened in was taking on a Hitchcockian quality, and that was beginning to intrigue me.

Not knowing who I was, I felt a certain courage that a normal person most likely wouldn't. "My name is Bass," I said to the nurse. "Is that right?"

"Oui, madame."

"What is my first name?"

4

"Hil-air-ee."

The accent was strong, but I understood her to say Hillary. "Hmm . . ." I considered the name. Hillary Bass. Hillary Bass. It was completely devoid of meaning. Bass. I could dismiss that. A married name was assumed, one that could be dropped or replaced. But Hillary, the name I'd had my whole life, should have sent a spark of remembrance through my bones. It didn't. Not even a twinge.

"Perhaps you should rest, madame, like the doctor says. Do not upset yourself. You have been asleep for a very long time. You must begin slowly, *n'est-ce pas?*"

Maybe they were right. I did feel tired. I barely had the strength to move my limbs. And my head felt strange. It wasn't a pain, exactly, but it felt very full and yet at the same time very empty. Maybe the cloud would lift if I let it. A little relaxation might do the trick.

But if I was to rest with the quiet of my own thoughts, I wanted a bit more to work with. "A few more questions first," I begged.

"*Comme vous voulez, madame.*"

I wrinkled my nose, not understanding. "Do I speak French?"

"We were told that you did. *Vous ne comprenez pas?*"

I shook my head.

"*Tiens.* How strange. Nothing I say?"

I shrugged. "Perhaps a little. It sort of sounds familiar."

"You see. It will come back, madame. I promise you."

I was not reassured. Why was I having no trouble with English? Did a loss of memory affect only second languages? It was a question I was to put to the experts without getting a satisfactory answer. My case, as it turned out, was a bedeviling one—for them as well as for me.

"How was I hurt?" I asked. "What happened to me?"

"I do not know if it is good to speak of this," she said.

5

"Why? Is it bad?"

"Tragique."

A chill went through me, a dread. "Is it my child?" I asked. "Do I have a child?"

"No, madame, you do not." She shook her head emphatically, seemingly distressed.

I don't know where the question came from. I had no vision of a child, no memory of one. Perhaps tragedy and children—or childhood—were somehow associated in the inner recesses of my mind. "What is the tragedy, then?" I demanded. "What happened to me?"

"There was an accident on your boat, madame. You were found unconscious on the—how do you say it—the floor. You were adrift at sea off Nice."

"I was alone?"

"Alone when you were found." The woman lowered her head, her jowls resting on her corpulent chest. She was clearly embarrassed.

"What aren't you telling me?" There was obviously more and I figured I should know what it was.

"It is not my place, madame."

"Tell me," I said. "I'm entitled to know."

"No one can say what happened for sure, but the . . . gentleman's body was found in the sea the next day."

"What gentleman?"

"I do not know monsieur's name. This is not my affair," she insisted. "Truly."

"Well, who was he? What relation to me? Tell me that much."

She lowered her eyes and shook her head. "I cannot say."

"A friend?"

She gave a Gallic shrug, refusing to say more.

A lover, I thought. It was obvious. Good heavens, I was

having an affair. I did color at that. I believe I must have turned beet red.

Evidently a sense of propriety and shame did not dissipate with one's memory. I had discovered that much. Here I was, a woman married to a man I did not know, and I had been unfaithful to him with another man I did not know. What kind of woman was I? What other surprises did Hillary Bass have in store for me?

The nurse withdrew to a chair in the far corner of the room, afraid, probably, of what else I might ask. I, for my part, felt humiliated, stunned. No wonder I'd taken refuge in amnesia. I was far better off as a blank slate. I tried to move, but my muscles were so stiff the slightest motion made them ache. I stared at the ceiling, feeling miserable, patently unhappy.

"How long have I been here, Nurse?" I asked.

"Three weeks, madame."

Three weeks! I did have a clunk on the head. "How serious are my injuries?"

"You were badly burned by the sun. That's how they knew it was hours before you were discovered. But it was your head they worried for. At first the doctors were of the opinion you would die."

I closed my eyes again, trying to recall something that would confirm the story she was giving me. Nothing provided even the slightest hint of validation. I could conjure no impression of my husband—not a sense of the sort of person he was, whether I liked or hated him, whether he was a victim or a villain. That he was a victim seemed more likely, considering my behavior.

"Do you know my husband?" I asked the nurse.

"No, madame."

"Have you seen him?"

"Only briefly and at a distance. He came to visit you once, soon after the accident."

That said a lot about our relationship. My marriage was not a happy one. "What is his name, his first name?"

"Monsieur's *prénom* is Car-tair."

"Carter?" I said.

"Oui, madame."

Carter Bass. It was an unusual name. "What nationality is he?"

"Why, American, like you, madame."

So I was an American living in France married to an American living in London, or at least coming from London to see me. Where had I lived in America? I wondered. Strangely I had a sense of the physical place. I could visualize a map in my mind, but I could not locate myself on it. How could I not have a home, a childhood, a family? And yet there was nothing, no past, no events, no history, no reality before today.

When I breathed deeply, the scent of the roses filtered into my brain. They enkindled something, though it was difficult to tell whether it was good or bad. Yet the emotion was strong, and it made me vaguely anxious.

"Where did these roses come from?" I asked.

"Why, from monsieur, madame. They arrived yesterday."

Perhaps he didn't hate me after all, I thought. Maybe he even loved me. Why did that thought sound good, even though I hadn't the faintest idea who the man was? Need, perhaps? Or guilt? Carter Bass. What sort of man had I married?

—

All afternoon they trooped in to see me, like customers at a carnival awaiting their chance to gaze at the latest freak in the sideshow. There was a neurologist, a psychiatrist, an intern or two, and the first little man who had seen me, a physician by the name of Guy Lafon.

The psychiatrist, Gerard Thirion, was a tall, hoary-headed man with a narrow face and the eyes of a wolf. He had an aloof manner and cold eyes. In the few minutes we talked he told me that my problem might be psychological as well as physiological, but predicted there would be improvement within days, if not hours.

Seeing my husband would undoubtedly help, he said. After all, I had not arrived on earth that morning fully formed. The hospital staff might be strangers to me, but my husband would not. Carter Bass would be like the first room in a large dark house, the psychiatrist said. When I saw him a light might come on, leading to the next room, then the next, until my entire past was revealed.

I told Dr. Thirion about the roses and how they alone seemed to register with me, though I still couldn't figure out why.

"This could be important, Madame Bass," he said. "It could be a chink in the protective armor you've placed around your mind. Work with the roses and let them work for you. It is also something you might discuss with Monsieur Bass."

I awaited my husband's arrival with a mixture of hope and fear. What if he wasn't the least bit familiar? Presumably we'd been intimate, but could I be a wife to a man I didn't know, especially when he wasn't similarly disadvantaged? It seemed so inequitable. I could only hope I would recognize him and it would all come back.

That afternoon I was having my first full meal in weeks when Dr. Lafon came in with the news that Carter had been detained in Paris and would not come to see me until the next morning. I was disappointed, though relieved in a way. "Did you tell him about . . ."

"Your loss of memory? Yes, I told him about your condition. It is up to Dr. Thirion to provide the detail."

"How did he react?"

"He is concerned, of course."

How bizarre this conversation was. I was worried about the feelings of a man who was, for all practical purposes, a stranger. "Doctor, what if I never remember?"

"You will."

"But suppose I don't."

"Then I suppose you must start your life afresh, madame."

I shivered to think what it would be like to live with a man I didn't know . . . as his wife. I would be at his mercy, just as I was now at the mercy of everyone in the clinic. "Is it paranoid of me to think this might be some kind of a grand conspiracy?" I asked.

Lafon smiled, smoothing his mustache with his finger. "It is entirely normal to feel insecure, but don't worry, madame. The fog will lift. I am sure of it."

By the time I went to sleep that night I'd experienced dramatic improvement in my physical condition. I'd had a session with the physical therapist who had massaged and articulated my limbs during my big sleep. I walked a few steps with a nurse on each arm, and I saw myself in a mirror for the first time.

To my profound relief, my face was familiar to me. I recognized it, just as I had recognized the fragrance of the roses. My dark, straight hair was blunt cut just below my jaw. It was limp and badly in need of washing. My skin had been scrubbed clean, though I knew instinctively this was not the way I ran about in public.

I stared into my dove gray eyes, expecting a flash of remembrance, but looking into them was like peering into a murky pool. I could not visualize the woman staring back at me in any other context than the present. I could not say how she normally dressed, what colors she liked, what perfume she wore, nor anything else about her. She was familiar, and yet she was unknown. In that sense, I was alien even to myself.

When Dr. Lafon checked in on me that evening I asked if he knew anything about my background—my family, my hometown, my education, my friends.

"I'm afraid I know very little, madame. The amnesia was not anticipated, so we did not discuss these things with your husband." He patted my hands. "But don't worry, Dr. Thirion will speak with monsieur."

I nodded, disappointed.

"Sleep well tonight," he said. "With luck, tomorrow it will all return."

I thanked him and watched him head for the door, his white lab coat hanging on his slight frame. "Oh, Dr. Lafon . . ." I called to him.

"*Oui, madame?*" he said, turning.

"What was the name of the man who died?"

He arched a brow. "You were told about that?"

"I demanded to know about the circumstances of my accident."

"I see." He put his finger against his chin thoughtfully. "The gentleman's name was Michel Lambert, I believe."

"He was French."

"*Oui,*" the doctor said, clearly in no mood to discuss the matter.

"One last question, Doctor. Does my husband know about Michel Lambert?"

The physician shifted uncomfortably. "I am certain he does. But I am neither a personal friend nor a confidant of Monsieur Bass. I am afraid I have told you all I can on the subject. *Bon soir, madame.*" With that he nodded politely and left the room.

I was alone then, and I used the time to search my

11

empty mind. I played for a while with Michel Lambert's name, trying to glean from it what I could. To my dismay, something about it was vaguely evocative, though I couldn't say of what. An emotion perhaps, or some event. The accident, maybe? Was the horror of that day so great that I was forced to seek refuge in amnesia?

Later a nurse's aide looked in on me. She was a young girl with an innocent round face. "*Ça va, madame?*"

I nodded. She came to the table by my bed to check on the water in my pitcher. I watched her sniff the roses my husband had given me. "Would you hand me a bud so I can smell it?" I asked.

"*Bien sûr.*" She pulled one of the long stems from the vase and gave it to me.

I took a deep breath with the bud pressed against my nose. Again a flood of emotion followed, but no specific memories. The scent was lovely, and it set my pulse to racing, just as it had when I'd first awakened. This time, though, the effect was even stronger. And suddenly, inexplicably, I began to cry.

THE NEXT MORN-
ing found me physi-
cally stronger, though
my mental condition
was unchanged. It didn't surprise
me that I still had no memory. I
sensed it would be a long time before I returned to normal.

After breakfast the nurses allowed me to shower and shampoo
my hair. Then they gave me a
suede cosmetic pouch that someone had brought to the clinic
from my home. I examined the
pouch with trepidation. Presumably I had used the contents on a
daily basis and I wondered if
something I found inside would
spark a memory.

The nurse attending me was
a plain, round-faced young woman
with fine blond hair. She stood
behind me and I looked up at her
in the mirror above the dressing
table. I unzipped the pouch and
dumped everything out. Nothing
looked even remotely familiar.

The gold case with three shades of eye shadow was half used, the powder worn with distinctive grooves. The application brush seemed large and heavy. I peered into a jar of lip gloss. Could my fingertip really have carved out that gouge? I looked at the nurse again. "Are you sure these things are mine?"

"Mais oui, madame."

Her indignation was assurance enough that there was no grand conspiracy to deceive me. My things did not evoke the familiar because they were as unfamiliar to me as the rest of my life. They might as well have belonged to another woman.

I tried to ignore my disappointment, but I felt cheated. Something should belong to me, some little something I could hold on to.

I began opening the various bottles and jars. Most of the products were French and I couldn't always tell what was inside. Discovering some moisturizer, I applied it to my skin. Next I picked up a bottle of base, examined my skin in the mirror, and set the bottle aside.

I contented myself with a smudge of eye shadow, liner, and mascara. Then I did my lips, using what seemed the most used of the pencils. I checked the result. The tones were certainly right for my coloring. The effect was natural, though I'd used only a fraction of the cosmetics.

The nurse's aide showed me the clothes that had been delivered along with the cosmetics. The under things were lacy, bordering on risqué—the lingerie of a woman with a lover. The dresses were chic and expensive. Again the colors and fit were perfect, but I could not relate to them.

I selected a cream silk day dress. Because I was still weak, the nurses helped me put it on. Afterward, they walked with me to a small sitting room where I was to wait for my husband. The room was furnished in antiques and opened onto a private garden through a set of French doors. The blond nurse sat on the edge of the chair across from me.

14

I gazed out at the garden. There were flowering shrubs, a spot of lawn, more greenery, and then a stone wall. The trees beyond were olive, an orchard, apparently.

The air wafting in was pleasant, distinctly Mediterranean. I did not know either the month or year, but I judged it was late spring or early summer.

I tested the scent of the air and for a brief instant I thought a chord had been struck, a flicker of remembrance, but then it left as quickly as it had come. I was reminded of my roses.

"Could I ask a favor?" I said to the girl.

"Bien sûr, madame."

"Would you bring the vase of roses from my room and put them there on the side table?"

She complied at once. I thanked her and told her she needn't stay. I was content to sit alone until my husband arrived.

"Votre mari est sur le point d'arriver, madame."

She had been reluctant to speak English, though she clearly understood me. I was fairly certain she'd said Carter was coming soon. It pleased me to discover there was some French in my brain after all. Perhaps it was slowly coming back to me. A sign of things to come.

After the nurse had gone I surveyed the room, aware of my growing nervousness. I was in a private clinic, and not a cheap one. Carter was not just well off, he was discernibly wealthy. It hadn't occurred to me till then, but I had no idea what age my husband was. Could he be elderly? Had I married him for his money perhaps?

Why did that notion bother me? If marrying for money struck me as mercenary now, then surely I couldn't have done such a thing before. A clunk on the head could not change one's values, could it?

Just then there was a light knock on the outside door. I tensed. "Yes? Come in," I said.

15

A nurse opened the door. *"Monsieur votre mari est arrivé,"* she said, announcing him as though he were a person of great importance.

She turned and faced up the hall, then backed away as the sound of footsteps drew near. He appeared then, pausing for a moment in the doorway. I was surprised, even shocked at how good-looking he was.

Carter Bass was a tall, elegantly proportioned man of forty or so, with a confident yet stern air. I stared at him, mouth agape, disbelieving. He didn't say anything. He was sober-faced and did not seem pleased to see me.

Carter stepped into the room, casually slipping his hand in his pants pocket as the door closed behind him. He was in a double-breasted blue blazer, maroon tie, and beige slacks. He had thick brown hair, streaked blond. His skin was deeply tanned, giving him the natural, healthy look of a sportsman, though his sophistication was undeniable. On balance he was quite handsome, in a rugged, square-jawed way. What struck me most was his prominent brow and deep blue piercing eyes.

"Hello, Hillary," he said matter-of-factly. "Glad to see you up. How do you feel?"

Some sort of perfunctory response was called for, yet I couldn't bring myself to speak. Instead I stared at him. After a moment I shook my head and murmured, "I don't know you."

The faintest smile formed before his expression turned ponderous. "They said you were having problems with your memory."

"Problems?" I said as I studied him. "That's an understatement, if I ever heard one. I can't recall a thing before yesterday."

Carter unbuttoned his jacket and dropped into the armchair across from the love seat. He rubbed his chin and looked into my eyes. There was skepticism on his face, and maybe a

16

touch of accusation. I was certain he didn't believe me. "What do you remember?" he asked.

I shook my head. "Nothing. Absolutely nothing." We contemplated each other. "I was hoping you would look familiar, but I can honestly say I feel as though I've never laid eyes on you in my life."

He smiled broadly, his strong white teeth showing. Carter Bass had an air about him, a presence that I found thoroughly unnerving.

"This could turn out to be rather amusing," he said.

I hadn't known what to expect, but his lack of compassion annoyed me a little. I glared.

"Well, don't you agree?" he said.

"No. I don't find it funny in the least."

"I see you haven't lost your bite," he replied, "even if your memory's abandoned you."

My eyes flashed, but he was unmoved. I knew right then that he shared neither my uncertainty nor my confusion. "How can you be so uncharitable?"

"So it's charity you expect."

"Am I that bad? *Really?*"

He turned from me with a sigh and looked out at the garden. I traced his profile with my eye, feeling surges of anger and resentment, but also a fascination with what was happening. It was obvious we were not on friendly terms, and yet I found myself attracted to him. That troubled me. I did not want to feel ambiguous about my husband. I wanted either to like him or not.

After several moments of silence, he said, "If it's not one thing with you, it's another."

Incensed, I started to rise, but I couldn't have walked far, not without risking a fall. It was pointless to try to make a grand gesture, so I decided we might as well have it out. "Can't you see I'm lost, Carter?" When he did not react I plunged ahead. "The only reason I'm even talking to you is because they told me you're my husband. If we'd passed in the street, I'd never have known you."

My voice was full of anxiety. I was so frustrated that I felt near tears.

He stared at me, stone-faced.

"Until you walked in the door I had no idea if you were eighty years old or thirty," I said, explaining. "I didn't know what you looked like, if you were cruel or kind, a friend or an enemy." I was beginning to harangue, but couldn't stop. "Can you imagine what it's like to wake up and have someone say to me, here, this man is your husband?"

I was on the verge of losing control. And I felt like a fool on top of everything else. I took a breath to calm myself. When I looked into his eyes I saw no softening whatsoever.

"If we have no marriage, just say so," I said. "I see no point in having to sit here and endure your hatred."

"It never bothered you before."

"Well, it does now," I snapped.

He contemplated me, letting silence be the accuser.

"Look, Carter, why put me through this? It's apparent we don't have a good marriage. I accept that, even though I don't fully understand it. Maybe it's my fault, maybe you're completely innocent. But I have to tell you I feel unjustly accused. I'm not even sure, exactly, what I've done."

"Well, forgive me, Hillary, but that's pretty damned convenient."

Tears flooded my eyes. I was cursed by a past I couldn't recall, punished for sins for which I felt no responsibility. "I can see you don't believe me," I said, wiping my eyes, "so there's no point trying to convince you. If you want to hate me, be my guest."

18

Carter got to his feet and paced across the floor. "Well, I'm sorry you don't remember anything. I'm sorry that you were injured. I take no pleasure in your suffering, but I'm not sure what you expect of me at this point."

"Please," I said calmly, "I know this must seem bizarre, but you can't imagine how frustrated I am. The people here know virtually nothing about me. I don't know a thing about my family, where I came from, what my maiden name was, where we met, how long we've been married. I don't even know my age."

Carter returned to his chair, looking at me more benevolently than before, as though he was actually beginning to understand the magnitude of my problem. My resentment began to abate. Maybe there was hope.

"It's all really a blank? You can't remember any of that?"

I shook my head.

The corner of his mouth bent slightly and he regarded me with different eyes. I wanted to reach out to him. I wanted to act on the impulse, the attraction, but I was afraid.

"What have they told you?" he asked.

"The little the staff said upset me terribly. I can tell you that."

He waited for an explanation.

There was no point in being coy, so I said, "There was a man who died in the boating accident. Michel Lambert. Who was he?"

Carter's expression turned cold. "Do you really want me to spell it out for you?"

"Then he was my lover," I said, shivering at the words.

I expected a stinging rebuke, but Carter kept his silence. His utter disdain was obvious, though.

"I was afraid of that," I said glumly. "I have no memory of it, nor of him. All that's been blocked out too."

19

Carter Bass sat there motionless, a sober, uncharitable expression on his face. I had the same sinking feeling as before.

"The thought that I did that to you horrifies me," I said. "I'm terribly embarrassed, even though I can't remember anything about it."

I waited for a comment, but he didn't even blink.

"I don't know the man," I went on. "I couldn't even tell you what he looked like, and yet I feel so guilty." I took a deep breath, searching for courage. "I'm sure you feel nothing but contempt for me, and I understand that. I'm truly sorry for any pain I've caused you. But I'd hope you'd have some compassion for me. It's very difficult apologizing for something you have no recollection of doing. Can't you understand how hard that is?"

Carter continued to regard me, his chin resting on his folded hands. Finally, he said, "This bump on the head has turned out to be rather timely, hasn't it? You can profess your guilt while shirking moral responsibility."

I was stung. "What else do you expect of me? I can't undo whatever it is I've done! I feel terrible about it and I've told you so. I've apologized."

He nodded, acknowledging the point. "It's an improvement on your attitude in the past, I'll say that much."

What had I said in the past? I sensed it wasn't wise to ask. Carter was struggling to remain civil, which probably told me all I needed to know at present. "I hope that you accept the fact that I'm sincere," I told him.

"If it's forgiveness you want, Hillary, I'm not sure this is the time or place. You're fortunate you can't recall what's happened. I wish I could say the same."

Everything suddenly seemed hopeless. Nothing I could do or say would make a difference. I wiped my eyes.

Carter was unmoved. He gazed at me for a while, then got up again and went around behind his chair, leaning on it as he looked at me. "I had a brief conversation with Dr. Thirion," he said. "He thinks it's only a matter of time before you'll come out of this. They'd like for you to stay here a few days longer. I have business in Rome. When I've finished, I'll take you home to Montfaucon. I hadn't planned on staying in France, but depending on your condition, I may arrange to stick around for a while. We can discuss things then. And if your memory hasn't returned by that time, you can ask me anything about the past that you wish."

"Can't we talk now?"

"Dr. Thirion said I shouldn't upset you. As it is, I'm afraid I have already."

"Please don't leave me in limbo, Carter. Please."

He drew an impatient breath. "All right. What do you wish to know?"

I thought for a moment, realizing there was so much. "How long have we been married?"

"Nearly eight years."

"And we have no children?"

"That's right."

"We didn't want any?"

"*You* didn't."

"I see." My mind was spinning. How could I not know this? A woman's feelings about children were so basic. "Where am I from? Where is my family?"

"You're from New York. Westchester County. Your father was an investment banker. He's been dead for some time. Your mother died last year."

My parents were dead. I tried to get a grip on the fact. I searched for the emotion one associates with such a thing. There was nothing. "Do I have brothers and sisters?"

"No, you were an only child. Your parents were older when they had you."

How strange it seemed to be hearing these things. He might as well have been talking about somebody else, another

21

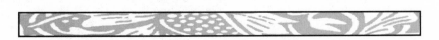

life. I tried to picture New York City. There were images in my head, but they were vague. Westchester County meant absolutely nothing to me. I didn't even know where it was.

Carter was not enjoying our conversation, but I had to take advantage of the opportunity while I had it. "Where did we meet?" I asked.

"In Paris. I'd done business with your father in New York and had seen pictures of you. He had them all over his office. Even though I'd never seen you in person, I was very aware of you. Then when I heard you were in Paris, I looked you up. You were a photographer's model, just in from New York and all the rage in the European press."

"I was a model?"

"Yes. Your career really took off once you landed in Paris. For a year and a half you were everybody's favorite cover girl. Your face was on newsstands all over Europe."

My mouth sagged open. "I never would have guessed."

"You apparently haven't looked in the mirror."

It was the closest he'd come to a compliment and it made me blush. Carter didn't acknowledge my reaction. I searched for another question.

"Were we ever happy?" I asked.

That half smile returned. "What difference does it make?"

I had no answer.

"The past can't be changed," he said.

His words hung heavily. I'd been damned for all eternity. My own husband was pronouncing me a pariah. We stared at each other for a long time and I sensed another reluctant flicker of compassion in him. He frowned, apparently to signal his indignation with my ability to cull charity from his heart.

Carter went to the door, indicating the interview was over. "Take it easy, Hillary, and get some rest. That's probably the best thing you can do if you want to find your old self."

I didn't want him to leave. This was hardly enough
. . . not considering all that had happened, all I needed to
know.

"Please," I said, stopping him before he could leave,
"tell me one more thing. Do roses have any special significance
to me?"

He reflected. "Well, I used to send them to you when
we were first married. I like them myself. Frankly, I didn't think
you could be bothered with them one way or the other. They
were just something else you got. Why do you ask?"

"Maybe I like them more than you realize."

Carter pondered my comment, then, without a word, he
turned and left the room.

—

Our meeting left me anxious and unhappy. It was not
easy to accept that there would be no forgiveness. And despite
fleeting signs of compassion on Carter's part, I was not hopeful.
There was a lot of history between us—perhaps too much history. Yet something inside me refused to accept the fact that my
husband was my enemy. Still I didn't have many options. To
understand my marriage, I had to understand myself. That was
the first order of business.

The two days of Carter's absence were devoted to my
recovery. My body became reaccustomed to solid food, my
limbs started regaining their strength and flexibility. Yet my
mind stubbornly remained in a fog.

Dr. Lafon and I chatted a few times, but the important
work was done with Dr. Thirion. I went to his office, sat in the
buttery leather chair his patients used, and together we probed
the nebulous depths of my mind.

The cool-mannered psychiatrist found it interesting that
Carter was fond of roses, that he'd sent them to me over the

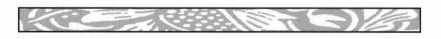

years, and that they were the one thing that stirred a promise of remembrance. "This may be the way you've found to reach out to him," Dr. Thirion suggested. "You can't bring yourself to assume responsibility for your actions just yet, but by reacting to the roses you are holding out promise, making a gesture."

"But I had no idea Carter liked roses when I woke up. I didn't even know he existed. And I still don't know what it is about them that's so compelling."

"That may be the point, Madame Bass. You know there is something to be dealt with, but you aren't yet ready to face it."

"But I'm aware of the awful things I've done. I know I was unfaithful to Carter. What else is there to hide from?"

"Evidently something. Otherwise you wouldn't be here, would you?"

"I do have a feeling," I admitted. "It's difficult to describe, but it's an uneasiness about something."

"Are you afraid?"

"Yes, but it's more than that. It's . . . I don't know . . . like I have a secret, and I can't spit it out."

"Of course you have a secret. Your past."

"No, it's something much more specific."

He laid a finger against his jaw. "You know it's specific yet you can't say what it is."

"That's right. But I don't think it has anything to do with my affair."

"Why not?"

"It's different, somehow. This is . . . I don't know how to put it . . . something terrible . . . and unresolved."

The doctor studied me.

"Do you think I'm crazy?" I asked.

"Of course not, Mrs. Bass. You're in the midst of a psychological crisis and are coping the best way you know how."

His words were meant to reassure, but I felt he didn't truly understand. And how could I possibly explain it to him when I didn't comprehend the nature of my torment, either? All I could say with certainty was that it was somehow bigger than me, that it was more than this woman I was, more even than her dead lover and ruined marriage.

"Let me ask you a very direct question," Dr. Thirion said. "What was your reaction when you first saw Mr. Bass? What did you think of the man you saw?"

I considered the question. "Well, I was surprised."

"How so?"

"Carter struck me as very attractive, handsome."

"You didn't expect that?"

"I guess not."

"Can you tell me more about your inner feelings toward him after you talked?"

"He's obviously an intelligent, sophisticated man, but I didn't like it that he was brusque with me. He was severe and rather intolerant."

"So you disliked him."

"Well, I also understood that he had his reasons. To be fair, I may have detected some charity in him."

"And now that you know Monsieur Bass is your husband, when you stop to tell yourself, I am his wife, how do you feel inside?"

It was not an easy question. As I thought of how to answer him, I looked out the window. The view from the psychiatrist's office was a sweeping panorama of the hills above Toulon, a serene perspective that Cezanne might have painted. For several moments I was lost in it, thinking of my husband, picturing our encounter.

"To be honest, I'm fascinated by the idea," I replied. "In a way the notion is arousing."

"Sexually arousing?"

"Yes."

Dr. Thirion nodded. "So can you imagine loving your husband?"

"I can imagine it, of course. But how could I love him? We've only just met."

The doctor smiled. "Well put, Madame Bass. Let me ask you if you feel you can open yourself to Monsieur Bass, and tell him what's on your mind, your deepest feelings."

"I didn't feel constrained when I talked to him," I said. "I imagine Carter might even have found me outspoken."

"Are you an outspoken person?"

"I think I am . . ." The last word died on my lips. I smiled. "You tricked me."

"Ah, madame, it was not a trick. I merely illustrate that there is a good deal more of you in your mind than you realize. You have a sense of self. You have a conscience, a moral code. It is only the events in your life that are missing."

"But why are they missing?"

"The blow to your head, to begin with. And we both know there is something more. That is what we shall discover, *n'est-ce pas?*"

It seemed so ominous, the discovery of one's own life. Yet I found myself intrigued by the notion, even though a part of me refused to believe all the things that had been said about me. But my marriage had captured my imagination, and I was fascinated by the prospect of getting to know my husband. Maybe I even wanted to love him as I surely had before.

WHILE MY BODY recovered, I did battle with my mind, trying—unsuccessfully—to coax a recollection from the past. I conjured up images from my imagination, hoping that one of them would prove to be an actual memory.

I pictured myself as a child playing in the snow, as a schoolgirl sitting in a classroom, as a young woman waiting to be picked up for a date. I imagined myself in elegant clothes, modeling, being photographed, attending lavish parties with Carter, sailing on a yacht. Nothing worked. Everything my mind produced was as flat and unreal as the pages of a magazine.

By the afternoon of the second day, when Carter called from Rome, I had regained my strength and was eager to leave the hospital. "When will you be coming for me? In the morning?" I said hopefully.

"I'm afraid not, Hillary. That's why I'm calling, to let you know I'll be tied up here until tomorrow."

I was disappointed. I wanted to go home, though my desire was based on what a home was supposed to be. I was certain familiar surroundings would speed my recovery. "That means I won't be getting out of jail then," I said.

"I can have Polly pick you up in the morning, if you'd rather not wait for me," Carter said.

"Polly?"

"Oh yes, you wouldn't recall. Polly is your secretary. She went to England to visit her mother when it looked like you'd be in the hospital for an extended period. I sent for her when you regained consciousness, thinking you would be needing her."

So I had a secretary as well as a husband. "That's very thoughtful of you," I told him.

"She can reacquaint you with everything at Montfaucon. Shall I make the arrangements?"

"Yes, please."

"All right," he said. "I'll see you at Montfaucon then." He hesitated. "I take it you're still unable to remember anything."

"As the doctor says, my condition is unchanged."

"I'm sorry."

I wasn't so sure he was sorry. My present condition gave him all the advantages. On the other hand, Carter's attitude seemed somewhat improved. He was more open than before.

"There's one other thing, Hillary. Have they told you yet about the police?"

"The police? No, what about them?"

"The authorities in Nice are eager to talk to you about what happened on the boat."

"But I have no memory of anything."

"Yes, I know, but Dr. Lafon informed me that they wish

28

to speak with you anyway. I imagine you'll be getting a call. You're their only witness."

Witness? To what? Did something happen I wasn't told about? "What can they be thinking, Carter? I'm useless to them."

"Well, someone has died. They'll need to document the event for their files. I'm sure it's routine. I wouldn't worry about it."

"I suppose you're right."

He was silent and I sensed he was more concerned than he was letting on. "Well," he said at last, "I'll see you tomorrow."

"Yes." I hung up, realizing the situation was more complex than I had been led to believe. I didn't know whether I should be concerned about the police or not. But Carter was a different matter. Dealing with him was not a temporary problem.

I had been aware of this for a couple of days, but every so often I would tell myself it was all a terrible mistake—that I wasn't Hillary Bass and that this wasn't my life. How could I possibly have made love with the man and still have no sense of him? Would we have to be intimate again before my memory of him would come back?

When Dr. Thirion came to my room that evening to say good-bye, I mentioned this to him.

"Don't prejudge what will happen, madame," he said. "Let time tell you how you feel about your husband. "The important thing is to relax. Let things evolve as they will."

"If they evolve at all."

"It's possible you'll never remember, but highly unlikely. I had a case similar to yours many years ago, a young gentleman who'd been in an automobile accident soon after his wedding. He could remember nothing. His young wife was a complete stranger to him."

29

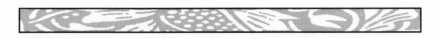

"How long before he got back his memory?"

"A few weeks, as I recall. Now they have three children."

"Then there's hope."

"If it's children you want," he said with a laugh.

The serious-minded psychiatrist had a sense of humor after all. "I was referring to regaining my memory."

He smiled. "My feeling is you will be back to your old self in short order."

"Considering what I know of Hillary Bass, I'm not sure that would please me."

He shook his finger. "That will not help, madame. It will not help at all."

—

In the morning, when a nurse brought Polly Frampton to my room, I was standing at the window, looking out at the garden. I turned as she entered.

"Good morning, Mrs. Bass," she said.

I studied her, and of course I didn't recognize her. Polly was wearing a white silk blouse, a dark skirt, and high heels. Though she was petite, she was quite full-breasted. She had short blond hair that was swept back, prominent eyes, and a rather small pinched mouth. She was not pretty, but she had a presence that was attractive.

I had learned that I was thirty. I guessed Polly to be around the same age. Though she smiled at me, I did not discern any genuine warmth.

"Good morning," I said.

"How are you feeling, ma'am?"

"Physically, I'm fine." I walked over to her and casually extended my hand. "But I've got amnesia. It's like I'm meeting you for the first time."

30

She took my hand. Her fingers were cold. "Yes, I know. Mr. Bass explained."

"The doctor thinks it will all come back to me soon," I told her. "In the meantime I may be relying on you to tell me who I am."

A hint of a smile touched her lips. "I understand, Mrs. Bass."

Polly took my small case and we left the room. She said nothing to me as we made our way toward the entrance. Dr. Lafon and the nurses were waiting at the front door. I told them good-bye with a certain degree of emotion.

A black Bentley was waiting for me. The chauffeur, a handsome young man in dark trousers and an open-necked white shirt, held the rear passenger door for me. He had a head of dark curly hair, broad shoulders, and a boyish smile. Polly introduced him as Antonio, and I decided there must be some Italian in his blood.

"*Bonjour, madame,*" he said solicitously and with panache. He gave my hand a little squeeze as he helped me into the car. I wondered about the gesture, then dismissed it as an affectation.

Antonio took the case from Polly and put it in the front seat. She climbed in beside me, and when Antonio was ready, I waved to the hospital staff and we pulled out the gravel drive, through the wrought-iron gate, and onto the road.

It was odd, but I felt as if I were embarking on an odyssey, not returning from one. My companions were strangers, not trusted members of my crew.

We headed toward the hills, passing through a semirural residential area of modest cottages surrounded by orchards and vegetable gardens. Soon we came to a more heavily traveled highway that wound through the hills toward the village of Montfaucon.

It was a sunny day and I surveyed my surroundings

31

with the eye of a tourist—curious, yet wary. Everything was new to me. I had not seen this country before.

There was so much I had to learn that I felt completely at a loss. Polly was not eager to engage me in conversation, leaving the initiative to me. I had no appreciation of what a personal secretary did, how I utilized her, and what I could expect. I'd gathered that there was a certain formality between us, but that could be attributed to the fact that she was English. I turned to her and asked what she did for me.

"Whatever you require, Mrs. Bass," she replied. "I run the household, organize your social calendar, handle your correspondence and business affairs, see to your personal needs— everything you wish not to deal with yourself."

"How long have you worked for me?"

"Nearly three years, ma'am."

"You must know me pretty well, then."

"I believe so."

There was a reticence in her voice and maybe even a tinge of disapproval. It was under the surface, cautious and disguised, but it was there. I decided that should not be surprising. I hadn't yet found a lot in myself to like.

If I'd sensed more rapport between us, I'd probably have deluged her with questions. It would have been nice to know what kind of person I was—whether I was cold and thoughtless, or decent and considerate. I wanted to learn everything I could about Michel Lambert, and of course more about Carter. The list seemed endless. But I didn't feel comfortable raising those issues with her. At least not yet.

"Do I spend most of my time in the south of France?" I asked, starting on safer ground.

"About half of each year . . . since I've been in your employ in any case. You spend a fortnight in Paris two or three times a year, plus the occasional weekend. Before your mother passed on you went to New York twice a year, but not for very long. Most of the rest of the time you traveled, Mrs. Bass. You like skiing with your friends, that sort of thing."

My friends. There had been no mention of friends before now and I was relieved to learn I had some. "You'll have to tell me about them," I said. "It would be rather embarrassing not knowing who I'm speaking to, should someone call."

"There's a stack of cards and notes waiting for you at the villa, Mrs. Bass. Also flowers and phone messages. I sorted through everything quickly after I arrived to make sure there was nothing urgent. It seems everyone you know rang up to pass on their best wishes for your recovery."

Polly's tone was matter-of-fact, but the news made me feel better, even though I was sure none of the messages would mean a thing to me. My expectations had changed to the point where I now anticipated that nothing would be familiar.

"Does Carter spend much time in Montfaucon?" I asked.

Polly seemed a little uncomfortable with the question. "In the past year virtually none, ma'am."

The past year seemed pivotal in so many ways. My mother had died and I was now getting the impression that the year had witnessed the disintegration of my marriage. Michel Lambert was probably the critical factor. "Where does my husband spend his time?"

"Mostly in London, but also Paris. When you saw him, it was usually there. Before this year, he would come to Montfaucon in the summer."

Before this year. She might as well have said, "Before Michel Lambert." I wondered how much Polly Frampton knew. Based on what I'd seen so far, I guessed we didn't discuss anything intimate, but surely she'd been aware that I had a lover. "Do you travel with me?"

"Usually to Paris and London. Seldom anywhere else."

"You didn't know my mother, then."

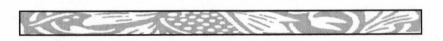

"No, ma'am. I never went with you to the States."

I looked out at the unfamiliar countryside. We were in the hills now, occasionally passing through a village. There seemed to be one every few miles. At a crossroads, we turned onto a secondary route. It was narrow and very twisty.

I searched my mind for questions, things I would need to know. "You said earlier you helped me with my business affairs. What do they consist of?"

Polly looked at me with surprise. "Mr. Bass hasn't discussed that with you, ma'am?"

I had a feeling I'd ventured into a sensitive area. "No, should he have?"

"I'd have thought he'd have done so, Mrs. Bass."

"Well, he hasn't. We've talked very little, actually." I appraised her taciturn face. "What, exactly, are my business affairs, Polly?"

"You own half of Mr. Bass's investment company. In your own name. It was your father's originally. He and Mr. Bass were partners, and when he passed away, the share came to you, though part of the income was held in trust for your mother. Now that she's gone, it all comes to you."

"So Carter and I are partners."

"You aren't involved in the operation, of course. Actually, you want nothing to do with it."

"So you handle it for me?"

"I talk to your accountants and solicitors for you, ma'am. And keep your personal accounts. There's not a lot to be done."

That scrap of information gave me new insight into my relationship with Carter. No wonder my husband hadn't pitched me out on my ear. He was stuck with me, at least financially. The news wasn't particularly gratifying. In fact it left me feeling empty.

34

I stared out the window without registering much. The little optimism I'd felt before evaporated. But there wasn't anything I could do about it. "Tell me about the staff, Polly."

"At the villa, ma'am?"

"Yes."

"Well, there's Yvonne, the cook and cleaning lady who works full hours, two part-time gardeners, and Antonio, who is part-time as well."

The chauffeur looked at me in the mirror at the mention of his name. He also smiled, but I turned my attention to Polly. "Do I spend most of my time at the villa or do I go out a lot?"

"It depends whether you're alone, ma'am."

I sensed it wasn't a subject to pursue.

"Oh, there's one other thing, Mrs. Bass. There have been a few calls from the police officials in Nice wanting to make arrangements for an interview."

"Yes, Carter said they'd be calling."

"A detective rang up again this morning. It seems there's been a new development and he wanted to speak with you most urgently."

"What sort of new development?"

"I really couldn't say. He didn't explain. I told him you would be home today and that if he wished to make an appointment, he should call this afternoon."

That feeling of uncertainty gripped me again. Something was going on. And as with so many other things, I was the one in the dark.

We entered Montfaucon. The main street was narrow and cobbled. It was the sort of rustic village that hadn't changed much over the past couple of centuries. In places the road was so narrow that a bicycle could be parked in the street and still lean against the front of a building.

We left the village as suddenly as we entered it. Barely

had we passed the last house when Antonio spoke up, pointing out the side window. *"Voilà la maison, madame,"* he said. *"Là-bas. Vous voyez?"*

I looked in the direction he was pointing. I could see a large house on a hill in the distance and assumed he was indicating the villa. French was not coming easily to me, though I vaguely understood most of the simpler things said.

"Yes, I see. Thank you." I leaned toward Polly. "Does he know what happened to me?"

"Yes. He and Yvonne both were very concerned and asked for news of you as soon as I arrived from England."

"Good. I wouldn't want to have to explain."

We were soon winding our way up the long drive to the villa, going through a very ancient-looking orchard as we went. There were several rows of grapevines on the slope of the hill, though it hardly qualified as a vineyard. Polly saw me looking at them.

"Mr. Bass bottles his own wine," she said. "It's his hobby. Before this year he came to supervise the harvest."

Again there was a hint of reproach in her voice. It was subtle, but I had little doubt that some things that had been happening in my life did not meet with my secretary's approval.

As we mounted the hill I surveyed the perspective, finding it lovely, pastoral. "I evidently enjoy the country and solitude," I said.

"You're not alone much, Mrs. Bass. Seldom does a fortnight pass in which there isn't a guest or two in residence. And you frequently take your friends to Cannes and Monto Carlo. You also spend some time at your flat in Nice."

"We have an apartment down here too?"

"It's yours, not Mr. Bass's."

It was so strange having my life explained to me this way. Polly had showed no signs of smugness or condescension, no hint of glee at my disadvantage. And yet my morality seemed

36

to be at issue and questions about it hung heavily in the air. It didn't matter that the facts were stated without judgment. Through Polly's eyes, I was coming to see the kind of person I was.

The car entered a courtyard through a gated wall, giving me a first close-up view of my home. I was nervous, somewhat like a small child on her way to a new school. Would something suddenly click, making everything come tumbling back—my memories, my life, my understanding of myself?

I stared through the car window. The house was a lovely two-story yellow stucco villa with an ancient red tile roof. Bougainvillea covered a fair portion of the main structure, and part of one of the wings. There was a very large tree in the courtyard. The beds around it were filled with flowers. Opposite the house and some distance from it were the garages and out-buildings. The wall enclosed what otherwise would have been open space between the buildings, thus giving the place the feel of a fortified castle when viewed from the perspective of the courtyard. It was a most pleasant, comfortably rustic-looking Mediterranean, but it wasn't the least bit familiar. Antonio stopped in front of the entrance, where the heavy oak door was already ajar and a woman in her fifties, wearing a gray dress and white apron, stood, a discreet smile on her face, though no particular joy.

"That's Yvonne," Polly said unnecessarily.

Antonio was quickly out of the car and came around to open my door. He helped me out, his hand firmly gripping my arm, his smiling eyes peering into mine.

I turned from him as Yvonne moved forward to welcome me. We exchanged a few words, then I stepped inside, feeling tense and apprehensive. I glanced about eagerly, discovering at once that the interior of the house was as alien to me as the exterior. The public rooms were bright, airy, and contemporary. There were bold paintings on the white plaster walls. I contemplated the one over the sofa, a composition of large geometric shapes in primary colors.

"Did I select this, Polly?"

"I believe you did."

I stared at it, knowing that even if I couldn't remember it, there should have been some sort of emotional attachment—a reaction akin to the one that had drawn me to it in the first place. There wasn't. "Funny. I don't relate to it at all."

"Don't you like it?"

"I can't decide. Isn't that strange?"

"The house isn't familiar to you at all, Mrs. Bass?"

I shook my head. Stepping to a table, I ran my hand over the smooth polished wood, hoping that the feel would be familiar. I inhaled the scent of the room, thinking surely that would do something for me. I was disappointed again.

Polly led me upstairs to my bedroom suite. I stood in the doorway, my heart aching to recognize the room I slept in, what should have been the most personal room in my home. I liked what I saw, but it was as foreign to me as all the rest. The decor was similar to the downstairs, except the colors ran more to pastels, which I liked better. There was a good deal of clutter. Magazines were piled on a table. The writing desk was covered with books and stacks of letters. Could this really be mine?

My eye searched out the more personal items, the photographs, objets d'art. There was a picture of Carter and me on the dresser, which made my heart skip. At last, something I could connect to myself. I picked it up, glad for a rare opportunity to glimpse into my past.

Carter was standing on what looked like a dock, and I was at his side, hanging on him actually, clowning, being silly. He looked dignified in his sailing attire. That slight smile of his seemed to indicate a vague embarrassment. I was in shorts, my shirttail tied up so that my midriff was bare. I had on a baseball cap with the brim turned up. I'd struck a coquettish pose with one shoulder angled toward the camera, one knee drawn up and in front of Carter's legs. I knew the camera well. That was evident.

I put down the picture, opened a drawer, closed it, and opened another. Things seemed to be jammed in them haphazardly. I glanced around the room, feeling frustration rather than the comfort I'd hoped for.

"Do Carter and I share this room?" I asked Polly.

"No, ma'am. Mr. Bass takes one of the guest rooms."

"Has it always been that way?"

Polly's look darkened. "Only for the past year or so."

"And before that, he slept here?"

"Yes, ma'am."

I don't know how I could have expected it to be otherwise, yet it came as a relief to discover that Carter and I were sexually estranged. Had he expected to sleep with me, I don't know what I would have done.

I wandered into a smaller room off the master suite that had been made into a gigantic walk-in closet. It had probably been intended as a crib room originally, and it contained so many clothes I was startled. I don't know why it seemed overwhelming, they were mine.

There were racks and racks of shoes, dozens of suits, dresses, evening gowns, casual clothes and sportswear, shelves of sweaters. I took a few dresses down and examined them. Everything had designer labels, many obviously made to order. Nothing was inexpensive. Some of what I saw struck me as a bit outré, though everything was in good taste. Yet I had trouble relating to the opulence and didn't feel comfortable with it, in much the same way I was affected by the extravagance of the entire house.

I wondered why that should be. What was I afraid of?

Walking along the row of suits, I thought again about the police and their desire to talk to me. I'd tried not to let it upset me, to dismiss it as routine, but my suspicions were growing. I sighed and left the closet. Polly stood waiting in the center of the bedroom.

I felt the need to assert myself. I invited her to sit in one of the two armchairs by the window. I took the other. "I want to ask some questions," I told her. "It may not be pleasant for either of us, but you're the only one I can turn to."

"I understand, Mrs. Bass."

"What can you tell me about Michel Lambert?"

Polly's reaction was surprisingly composed. She drew a breath, then said, "I didn't know Mr. Lambert personally, of course. He was your friend."

"My lover."

"Yes, your lover, Mrs. Bass." There was challenge in her eyes, but it didn't linger long. Her look soon returned to indifference.

"Did I see him often?"

"Yes. He came here to dine on a couple of occasions, and he was a frequent guest at your parties. But you usually met him elsewhere. He had a home near Cannes. You spent a good deal of time with him there."

"I see." I tried not to appear as embarrassed as I felt. "Did I seem to care deeply for Mr. Lambert, or was it a more superficial relationship?"

"If it's a personal view you'd like, ma'am, I suggest you talk to Lady Nyland. She's your best friend and privy to your personal thoughts."

"Lady Nyland?"

"She was Jane Goodson until she married last year. She acted as your agent when you modeled, and you've been friends ever since. She stood up for you at your wedding. Since she married James Nyland she no longer works, but she still lives in Paris and comes here often. More than anyone."

"She's married to a Brit but lives in Paris?"

"Lady Nyland's mother was French, ma'am. She's perfectly bilingual and prefers Paris to London. Lord Nyland is a Francophile himself and is content to visit her in Paris. I suppose you could say it's a modern marriage."

"Does Jane know about my . . . condition?"

"Oh yes. She's rung up regularly. The messages are by the telephone. I spoke with her again this morning, as a matter of fact, and she said she'd ring back this afternoon."

I glanced out the window at the sunbathed hills, realizing I hadn't yet taken the time to fully appreciate the lovely setting. It seemed too good to be true. How long would it take for me to feel comfortable here again?

I looked at my secretary, feeling exhausted. I'd been back from the brink of death for only a few days and the doctor told me I would have to take it easy for a while. He'd prescribed frequent rests and naps. Polly seemed to read the fatigue in my eyes.

"Are you feeling all right, Mrs. Bass?"

"I'm a little tired."

"Would you care to rest before lunch?"

I glanced over at the large bed with the flounced pillows and decided it did look inviting. "Maybe I will." When I stood, I felt a little shaky, surprised at how quickly my strength had failed. I went to the bed and kicked off my shoes, sitting heavily on the soft mattress.

I heard a meow and looked up to see a cat sitting at the door to the closet and looking at me. I felt a start of recognition inside, and I very nearly called out her name, but it evaporated from my mind before I could get it out.

"That's Poof, Mrs. Bass," Polly said. "Do you recognize her? She's your cat."

"Poof," I repeated, finding the name unfamiliar even if the cat herself struck a chord. She was black with white stockings.

41

I leaned over, holding out my hand. Poof walked to me nonchalantly. She sniffed my hand briefly before rubbing her body against my legs. I picked her up and hugged her, feeling my first real joy since arriving home.

"Yvonne says Poof hasn't been the same during your absence, ma'am. I think she's happy to see you."

"I'm happy to see her," I said, stroking her head.

Polly got a cashmere throw from an armoire and placed it on the bed beside me. "There's a buzzer on the nightstand, ma'am. If you require anything, just press it and Yvonne or I will come."

"Thank you, Polly."

She left the room. I put the cat down and removed my dress, laying it carefully over a straight-backed chair. Then I went to the closet and found a summery robe to wear while I slept. Poof was back up on the bed, so I lay on the cool peach satin spread beside her and pulled the throw over my legs. She curled up against me and I stroked her.

As the lightly perfumed scent of the room filled my lungs, I closed my eyes. I was now resigned to being estranged in a foreign land where everybody professed to know me, but where I knew no one, except perhaps my cat.

I DRIFTED INTO A dreamy trance, one that enveloped me as I floated between sleep and wakefulness. It was disconcerting because I knew that it was happening, yet I accepted it, hoping to find refuge in the spell.

The initial sensation was of being in a misty cloud, without clear delineation between earth and sky. In time, shapes formed and turned into rosebushes, heavy with blooms. I could smell their perfume and I became infused with emotion, though I didn't know exactly why.

Then a person appeared, an ephemeral female figure. Sometimes I could see her and at other times she faded into the mist. She was older and very dark. I was calling out to her, hoping to touch her. But she stayed beyond my reach, amid the roses.

I fell into a deep sleep then, full of disturbing dreams. Hours passed before I was awakened by the sound of persistent knocking. I sat bolt upright, my heart pounding as if I'd just run up a flight of stairs. I was terrified, but it wasn't the knocking that upset me, it was my dreams. They still had me in their grip.

I looked at the door, my eyes wide as I struggled to comprehend. I pushed back damp strands of hair at my temples, confused by the knocking, not knowing who it was. Then I heard Polly's voice.

"Mrs. Bass, are you all right?"

I swallowed hard, struggling to come fully awake. "Yes," I said weakly. "I'm okay."

"May I come in?"

"Yes."

The door opened slowly, and I saw Poof dash out from some hiding place and exit through the gap in the doorway. Then Polly appeared. I lay back on the pillow, still trying to recover. She made her way to the bed and looked at me with concern.

"You were crying out," she explained. "I was worried."

"Was I? It must have been my dream."

The clutch of emotion was still with me, the sensation vivid. I had been with a strange man. We were on a sailboat, a yacht, and we were fighting. He had struck me, though I felt no pain, and he was clawing at me as I was trying to shove him overboard.

I was strangely detached from the action, though the emotion was strong enough. It was like a film, and I was watching myself battle this man. I could see the expression on his face as he teetered on the rail.

I glanced at Polly, relieved by her presence. The dream had been so real. I couldn't get the image out of my mind—that terror-stricken face, my own desperation.

"It was a very bad dream," I said to her.

"You sounded upset."

44

"I was." I rolled my head toward the window and stared at the cloudless sky, finding reassurance in that as well. I was finally coming back to earth.

"Lunch is ready, Mrs. Bass, if you're hungry. We didn't want to awaken you, so Yvonne has been keeping it for you."

"What time is it?"

"Half past one."

"I did sleep a long time."

"Yes, ma'am."

The semireality of my dream still haunted me, its implications starting to take perspective. If I'd been on a sailboat, could the man with me have been Michel Lambert?

"Yvonne will serve lunch on the terrace, unless you'd prefer to eat here," Polly said, oblivious to my turmoil.

I sat up and ran my fingers through my hair. "I'm a bit groggy, but I'll dress and come down."

"Very well, Mrs. Bass." She turned for the door, but I stopped her.

"Tell me, is there a photo of Michel around anywhere?"

"I believe there may be one in the dressing-table drawer. I saw you put one in there once, if I'm not mistaken."

"Would you mind getting it?"

"Certainly." She found the photograph and brought it to me, a faintly disapproving grimace marring her countenance.

I took one look at the photo and gasped. He was the man in my dream. My hand trembled.

Michel was attractive, genteel, moneyed-looking, and very French, all of which was to be expected. He was posed on what appeared to be a sailboat, mine perhaps, his dark, gray-streaked hair had been blown slightly by the wind. He had a thin mustache and a narrow, masculine nose and a full lower lip. A vague, suggestive smile was forming at the corner of his mouth.

45

Could my dream have been real, an actual event I was able to face only in my sleep? I could think of no other explanation. Unlike everyone else, Michel was no stranger to me. I studied the photo again and had to admit he looked familiar. I knew Michel, but why not Carter?

The answer was evidently related to the trauma that had shut out my past. Did that mean Michel might trigger other recollections? Dr. Thirion had told me one memory regained would lead to the next. It was something I needed to discuss with him.

Polly, who had noticed my reaction to the photo, asked if I'd remembered seeing it before.

"Not the picture, no, but I do remember Michel."

That brought no response. Had I been unwise to be so candid? After I glanced up at her she said, "That reminds me, the police rang up while you were sleeping."

"Again?"

"Yes. They wanted to make an appointment, but I insisted you couldn't be disturbed. The inspector I spoke to wasn't at all gracious. He'll ring back, I'm sure."

I looked at Michel's picture, wondering if the fight in my dream had really happened, or if it had been a product of my imagination. I shivered at the thought that there could have been violence, that the police might be aware of something I hadn't been told about.

"There were a couple of social calls as well," Polly said, "but nothing important. Just the usual wishes for a speedy recovery."

"It's nice to know people care."

"You have many friends, Mrs. Bass."

"What about Lady Nyland? Did she phone back?"

"Not yet."

I had no sense of what Jane was like, even though she

was my best friend. I wondered if a photo of her would kindle a recollection, as it had with Michel Lambert.

Polly shifted uncomfortably as I continued to stare at Michel Lambert's Gallic face. "Would there be anything else, ma'am?" she finally asked.

"I'm sorry," I said, "I'm afraid I'm still numb. This picture has opened the door of my memory a crack."

"Are you beginning to remember then?" she asked.

"A little. Not much. Maybe I should look at more photographs. There must be others."

"Yes, you have scads, lots of albums."

"After lunch I'll leaf through them then. I also want to go through my address books and correspondence, appointment books, whatever else there is so I can reacquaint myself with the people in my life."

"Yes, ma'am."

I put the photograph down on the bedside table. "Well, I think I'm okay, Polly. I've gathered myself. I'll dress and be downstairs shortly."

When she had gone I sat on the edge of the bed, waiting for my strength to return. The nap had helped, despite the anguishing dreams.

I padded off to the bath. The face in the mirror was puffy. I peered into my eyes, still hoping for a miraculous awakening, a sudden awareness. When I finally did remember, would the whole business seem amusing? Would I laugh about it with my friend Jane? Or with Carter?

I sighed. Somehow I couldn't visualize chuckling about it with him. Even without concrete recollections of our marriage, I sensed we weren't likely to laugh about anything together.

I washed my face, splashing it with cold water to get rid of the puffiness. After drying it, I opened the medicine cabinet. There was the usual assortment of patent medicines, toiletries, and the like, though the brands were mostly French and unfamiliar.

On the bottom shelf was a large bottle of Calèche that I immediately opened. The fragrance sent a ripple of remembrance through me, much as the roses at the hospital, my cat, and the picture of Michel Lambert had. I inhaled it again. The scent was very familiar. It was me!

This little victory gave me a rush of excitement. I closed my eyes and tried to pull more from my mind. There was something there, something just beyond my reach, but I couldn't quite grasp it.

Frustrated, I dabbed some perfume on my throat, returned the bottle to the shelf, and left the bath. I intended to put on the dress I'd worn that morning, but decided instead to have another look at my wardrobe.

I slipped out of the wrap I'd slept in, hung it on a hook, and began going through my summer dresses. I pulled out several, finding each one not quite right. The colors were all lovely, but for the most part I found everything too elegant, too chic. I persisted, managing at last to find a T-shirt dress in French blue. It was short, but the simplicity appealed to me. I was taking it off the hanger when there was another knock on my bedroom door. "Yes?" I called out, assuming it was Polly.

I heard the door open. "Polly?"

"No, it's me." Carter suddenly appeared. He was in the bedroom, looking at me through the doorway.

"Oh!" I said, flinching. I clutched the dress to my throat.

"Sorry if I startled you," he said. He moved toward the closet, stopping at the entrance, where he leaned against the doorjamb. He was in a suit, his collar unbuttoned, his tie loosened. He looked a little tired.

I was so shocked at the sight of him, I backed away,

dumbfounded that a man should walk in on me while I was in the middle of dressing.

Carter's eyes moved down over my partially covered body, a curious grin forming on his lips. "What's the matter, Hillary, did that thump on the head make you shy too?"

"I wasn't expecting you."

"It never bothered you in the past if I came in while you were dressing—or anyone else for that matter. I could have been Antonio and you wouldn't have cared."

My eyes flashed with indignation. "Well, I do care and I don't appreciate the remark."

Carter appraised me. "I just arrived," he said soberly. "I haven't had lunch and they said you were coming down. If you'd rather eat alone, I'll go back downstairs and eat by myself." There was an edge to his voice that cut right through my indignation.

I considered putting the dress down and showing him I didn't give a damn if he looked at my body, that I could play the role of indifferent wife. But I wasn't able to. "Carter," I said, "I'm sorry. I didn't mean to be curt."

He straightened, peering directly into my eyes. "Well, I probably owe you an apology too. I'm not making allowances, and I should. It's hard thinking of myself as a stranger to you."

"Imagine how I feel."

He nodded, letting his eyes drift down me once more.

"Why don't you go sit down?" I said. "I'll slip this on and be with you in a minute."

"All right." He turned and went to the chairs by the window.

I was able to see him from the closet, but he was gentleman enough not to look my way. He casually glanced out the window, pulling back the sheer curtains for a better view of the

49

rolling countryside. I quickly stepped into the dress, feeling safer somehow for having a bit of fabric covering me.

"I take it there's been no change in your condition," he said, fingering the curtain as he continued to peer out the window.

I'd been watching Carter continuously. He fascinated me. It was more than his rugged good looks and serious, almost ponderous demeanor. I was attracted to the idea that I was married to him, yet at the same time I found it horrifying. "Nothing major," I said in answer to his question. "Little flashes, but no sudden recollection of who I am." I started searching through the rack of shoes for a pair of sandals.

"What sort of flashes?" Carter asked.

I was reluctant to bring up Michel Lambert just then, so I mentioned my reunion with Poof.

He smiled. "That's one thing that's never wavered—your love for your cat."

"I was happy to see her," I said, noting his evident sarcasm. "Very happy."

"The house didn't do anything for you?" he asked.

"No, I feel like today is the first time I've ever been here." I dropped some sandals on the floor and slipped my foot into one, noting the place on the leather insole that had been worn by my great toe. That gave me more of a sense of connection to my personal effects than anything yet.

I put on the other sandal, and when I glanced up, I noticed that Carter was no longer in the chair. I went to the door and found him standing by the bedside table, the picture of Michel Lambert in his hand. He looked up at me.

"Have any flashes over Michel?" he asked cuttingly.

My cheeks burned. "Not the way you're thinking."

He gave me a sardonic look. "Evidently he's not the stranger I am."

I shook my head. "No."

50

"Well, Hillary, you always did have your own priorities and your own agenda. That shouldn't be surprising."

"It's not like that," I said weakly. "I don't know Michel any more than I know you or anyone else." I hesitated. "I just have one recollection of him."

"Really? And what's that?"

I lowered my eyes. "I took a nap after I got here this morning, and while I slept I had a dream. In it Michel and I were on a boat, a sailboat."

"That's credible. You certainly spend a lot of time on the *Serenity*. I'm sure plenty of it was with him."

I could feel Carter's hostility, perhaps even hatred. His eyes were hard, his expression resolute. "I can't help the past," I said. "There's nothing I can do to change it."

"No, I suppose that's true. Let's just hope you don't end up paying for it." He gave me a look and headed for the door. "Yvonne's been holding lunch so long it's probably spoiled."

For a moment I didn't budge. The comment about paying for it was still ringing in my ears. Carter didn't say so, but I knew he was referring to the police. Tears filled my eyes and I felt dreadful, wondering what I might have done. What dark secret was I hiding, even from myself?

I heard Carter going down the hall. "Come on, Hillary," he called to me, "let's have our lunch."

—

He waited for me at the bottom of the stairs. We walked through the house together. Neither of us spoke until we stepped out onto the terrace. "If it's too warm for you out here, we can eat inside," he said.

"No thank you, this will be fine."

We went to a table, protected from the rays of the sun

51

by a large blue umbrella. Carter held my chair for me, a gesture that struck me as false. He obviously felt contempt for me, so why did he bother with the little courtesies, unless it was simply to rub in my failures of virtue?

He removed his suit coat and tossed it on a side chair, then sat across from me, taking his napkin and laying it on his lap. He looked out at the remarkable view of the valley, seeming to me a bit the lord of the manor in modern clothing.

Despite the ill will between us, I couldn't help finding him attractive. I had a very strong sense of Carter, the physical man. I was aware of the way his shirt molded his chest, the breadth of his shoulders, the way he held himself in my presence. And whenever his eyes passed over me, I noticed how they seemed to be painting disapproval one moment and signaling sexual awareness the next.

I looked at his long fingers, aristocratic yet strong, and tried to imagine his touch. Was he a gentle lover or brusque? Realizing the danger in my silly game, I looked away, gazing out at the view.

I was able to see a couple of villages in the distance, though not Montfaucon itself. There were orchards and vineyards, white-washed farmhouses with red tile roofs. The air was dry but fragrant with blossoms. It was lovely, but it engendered no particular recollection, no nascent familiarity.

When I turned to Carter, he was leaning back in his chair, contemplating me. It was a critical appraisal, but not so hostile as I had come to expect.

"How was Rome?" I said. "Did you have a successful trip?"

He smiled. "That's the first time you've asked a question like that in five years, Hillary."

"Well, if you hadn't said so, I'd never have known. Or do you prefer that I be inconsiderate?"

He chuckled. "The amnesia is an improvement."

"Don't go getting the idea you can knock me on the head every time you don't like my attitude."

My husband nodded appreciatively. "Rome was hot and the trip successful. Thank you."

Carter observed me. The sexual energy emanating from him was more intense than ever. It seemed obvious he was thinking of me in physical terms, perhaps recalling how he'd caught me in the closet, undressed. What might he have done earlier in our marriage, if he'd happened upon me that way? Was Carter the type to take liberties when he chose? Was I the type to let him?

"Why didn't you tell me we were partners in your business?" I asked, hoping to get my mind onto a less dangerous subject.

"I wasn't keeping it a secret," he said calmly. "It just didn't come up." He measured me. "Why? Don't you like the idea?"

It was an interesting question. I let it roll through my mind, speculating on the implications. Did I like the idea? I wasn't sure. There were too many unknowns for me to decide. "I'm not sure. I was just curious why you didn't say anything earlier, and now I know."

Carter considered that without signaling his conclusions. He picked up the bottle of mineral water and poured us each some. Then he took a long drink from his glass. He put it down and gave me a half smile. "Warm today."

I nodded. "So we're investment bankers?" I said.

"Yes, Hillary, *we're* investment bankers."

His sarcasm stung. "I know I don't have anything to do with the business, I only wanted to make sure my assumption was correct."

"It is."

I sipped my water. "Do we fight over the business?"

"No, you don't give a damn about it—as long as you have enough money to live your life as you like."

"You make me sound so frivolous."

"You *are* frivolous. Without apology, I might add."

I gave him a tight smile. "That's nice to know."

"It's a fact," he said.

"And so I should put any thought of business from my mind and stick to the things I care about, like clothes and cruises and lovers. Is that what you're suggesting?"

He gave me a hard look. "The books are open, Hillary. Your solicitors check up on things regularly, and you're welcome to come by and have a look anytime you wish."

"That's not what I was getting at."

"What were you getting at?"

I hated this tension—animosity I truly didn't feel and certainly didn't understand. It seemed whichever way I went there was a pitfall. "Nothing," I said. "Never mind. It's not important."

"You must have intended something."

"Carter, I'm just trying to understand our relationship, who I am. Okay?"

He looked chastened. "I'm sorry, I didn't mean to be snide." He glanced toward the house and Yvonne, who was approaching with a tray.

The housekeeper served our first course, a broth made with chanterelle mushrooms, and some bread. Carter said a few words to her in French as he poured us each more water. Yvonne reacted positively, her regard for him obvious. After a brief, not altogether approving glance at me, she withdrew.

"Is it my imagination," I said, "or am I unpopular with the staff?"

"You mean Yvonne?"

"I mean everyone. Polly has been polite, helpful, and entirely proper, but I know she doesn't approve of me."

"You're paranoid."

"No," I insisted, "it's subtle, but I sense it."

"In the past you wouldn't have noticed and couldn't have cared less if you had. I imagine they just aren't used to this newfound sensitivity of yours."

"You say it with such disdain."

"I didn't mean to," he replied.

I drew an anxious breath and looked at my soup plate, not having much of an appetite. But I had to eat. Dr. Lafon said I had to rebuild my strength. I tested the broth and found it good, though the distinctive flavor was new to me. How bizarre. My house, my husband, and even the food I ate were alien and unfamiliar. Now I really understood how Alice felt in Wonderland.

We ate for a while without talking. I managed to work up an appetite after all. Carter ate more deliberately, breaking off chunks of bread in the European fashion and dipping them in the soup. I watched him until he seemed aware of my scrutiny and looked up at me. I turned my attention to the view.

The hills were bathed in sunshine, the air was warm. I could see how this might be a very pleasant life. It seemed a shame, in a way, that Carter and I were so estranged. It would have been so much better if we had loved each other, though I suspect no less bizarre for me. It might even have been harder. At least this way something besides my amnesia was keeping us apart.

"What are you thinking about?" Carter asked.

I looked at him with surprise. "Huh? Oh, sorry, I guess I'm a bit distracted."

"Are you liking what you've found here, or not?"

"You mean do I like my life and who I am?"

"Yeah, something like that."

"The house is very pleasant. I like it. I've already told you how I feel about myself."

He pondered me, his lips eventually curving into a smile. "I still find that remarkable. It's hard to imagine you being anything but self-satisfied. You're a complete surprise to me, Hillary. Amazing, actually."

"Is that good?" I asked, more hopefully than I wanted.

He was amused. "It could be worse."

"There are no guarantees about the future, I guess."

"No, I suppose not."

"I don't know if I should be more afraid of remembering or not remembering," I said. "Each has its down side."

"You probably won't have much choice. A few things are starting to seem familiar," he said. "It's probably just a matter of time."

"I'm holding in some very intense emotion," I told him. "Something ominous. It's fighting to get out, I can tell. It frightens me."

"Like what?"

"This morning as I was falling asleep, I fell into a kind of trance, a semidream state. I was in a rose garden and an older woman was there. I don't know who she was, but I felt deeply about her."

"Maybe it was your mother."

"I don't know my mother, though. I have no mental picture of her whatsoever."

"There are photos of her in your albums."

"I'll want to see them."

Yvonne came out and removed our soup plates. She said nothing. I watched her retreat. My eyes met Carter's, then. A moment of awareness followed, unspoken messages passed between us—anguish, hope, regret. In spite of the longstanding rancor keeping us apart, I felt something else, something intangible, drawing us together. I sensed it when I looked at Carter, and I had a feeling he was aware of it as well. He continued staring at me, seemingly reluctant to end the connection. I finally looked away.

"Was my mother dark?" I asked, finding the courage to look at him again.

"No," he replied, "she was blond. She colored her hair toward the end, but she was always fair."

"Then my father was dark."

"More so than your mother, yes." Carter steepled his fingers, watching me over them as he had a few moments earlier. His blue eyes were softer than when he'd been angry, but they were questioning. I judged he was trying to make sense of me, just as I had been trying to make sense of him and our marriage. It seemed as though he wanted to say something, but he was holding back.

"I wish you wouldn't look at me that way," I said, searching for a means to make him express what was on his mind.

"Why?"

"I can't tell what you're thinking."

"That never bothered you before."

"Well, it does now, Carter. Just because I did something or felt something or thought something in the past, doesn't mean I do or feel or think the same way now. I wish you'd give me the benefit of the doubt."

"I didn't mean to offend you," he said. "It was an observation. I can see you're frustrated, Hillary. But I'm not quite sure what you expect of me."

Again we peered into each other's eyes as though nothing had changed. I was at a loss as to what to say.

Thankfully, Yvonne came with another tray, sparing me the trouble of finding a response. The sight of Poof, trotting along at her heels, made me smile. She was obviously very interested in what Yvonne was carrying. When it turned out to be a seafood salad, I understood why.

When the housekeeper left, Poof stayed behind and immediately began culling my favor by rubbing against my legs. I examined the dish, noticing what appeared to be tiny tentacles among the chunks of fish and vegetables.

"Is there squid in this?" I asked.

"Yes, there is," Carter replied.

I felt my stomach quiver. "Does Yvonne fix this often?"

"It's one of your favorites."

"Strange. It must be an acquired taste that my stomach can't recall acquiring."

He laughed. "I can have Yvonne bring you something else, if you don't want it."

"No, no. I don't want to offend her."

Carter's eyebrows rose. "Since when does it matter whether or not you offend the help?"

I sighed with exasperation. "Please don't even tell me. I'm tired of hearing what a shrew I am. Like I said, I'd rather be judged for the way I am now." I picked at my salad with my fork.

"You *are* different," he said. "It's very noticeable. I don't see the same woman anymore when I look at you. You're softer. It's strange."

I stared at him, trying to understand what he was implying. Did he really mean to compliment me? Maybe he read the question in my eyes because he didn't stay with that line of conversation.

"I like your hair shorter, by the way," he said. "It's attractive."

This was an unequivocal compliment, but a far safer one. "Don't I always wear it this way?" I fiddled with the ends. "This length seems normal. But then, what is normal?"

58

"You wore it short like that when we met," he said. "You'll be able to see in the photographs."

"How long has it been since you last saw me?"

He put down his fork. "I guess the last time was in Paris, six or eight weeks ago."

"I must have had it cut since then."

"I'm sure Polly could tell you when and where."

I ate some of the marinated vegetables, then forced myself to take a bite of the squid. It was palatable, but I had no desire for more. I sneaked chunks of it under the table to Poof.

"You don't have to feed the cat surreptitiously, Hillary," Carter said. "It's your lunch and your cat."

I flushed. "I didn't want to hurt Yvonne's feelings by leaving the squid, that's all," I said, trying to justify myself. Even as I said it, I knew I wasn't sounding like Hillary Bass.

He beamed at me, chewing his food.

"Like it or not, this is me, Carter."

He gave an innocent shrug. "You don't hear me complaining."

After glancing toward the house, I pointedly gave Poof two more chunks of squid, then stroked her silky fur. "Have I changed a lot during our marriage?" I asked. "Was I a bitch from the beginning, or is it a character trait I acquired?"

He laughed, wiping his lips with his napkin. "Hillary, I never would have believed that comment coming from your mouth in a million years."

"Well, answer the question."

"I suppose people don't change all that much when you come right down to it. Let's just say I didn't fully appreciate the diversity of your qualities when we first married."

"Don't patronize. I hate that."

"Do you?"

I realized it was a very good question. I'd said it with such assurance, as though I knew that about myself. But how

59

could I? Or did one's attitudes remain, even if memory was lost? "Maybe I should ask you, Carter. Do I hate being patronized?"

He pushed his plate away. "I didn't think you analyzed things that closely, if you want to know the truth. If you didn't like something someone said to you, you just told them to fuck off."

"Oh, God." I blushed and it embarrassed me that I did. I tried not to show how flustered I was. "So when did our marriage go wrong?" I took my glass and sipped from it while Carter considered my question.

"I suppose things were never quite the same after you got pregnant."

I nearly choked, putting down my glass. "I was pregnant? What happened, did I lose the baby?"

"You had an abortion."

The words cut right through me. "Why?"

"Because you didn't want to be a mother."

I was horrified.

"You turned the crib room into a closet and filled it with clothes," he went on. "I took that as a rather definitive statement of your feelings. You've always been selfish, Hillary, and rather self-righteous about it. The truth is you've never given a damn about anybody but yourself."

Tears welled in my eyes as we exchanged looks. I knew nothing of what he was saying, but I deeply felt the emotion flowing between us, the bitterness, the hurt—above all the hurt.

Soon the tears started flowing. I wiped them away, but they kept coming. I could hardly look at Carter, yet I wanted to know if what I saw in his eyes was disdain or hatred. I had to know how the abortion had affected us. "Did you want me to have the baby?"

"You really don't remember?"

"Of course not!" I cried. "I don't remember anything!"

60

"There's no need to discuss it," he said.

"But I want to know!"

"I was upset because you had the abortion without even discussing it with me. I know it was your body and all that, but I felt you could have at least talked it over with me."

I felt sick.

"Soon after that we each went our own way," he continued. "It took a while for the break to be complete, but eventually we were married in name only."

I sniffled and drank some water. "Well, at least now I know why."

Carter fell silent and I could feel all the hurt that had been between us over the years. I felt absolutely miserable.

Yvonne came out again with a basket of fruit and a plate of cheeses. As she cleared the table she glanced at me, evidently seeing that I had been crying. Carter sat motionless. No words passed among any of us. The housekeeper went back inside.

I offered to cut Carter a piece of cheese, but he declined. I started to cut some for myself before realizing I'd completely lost my appetite.

Down the valley a tractor was moving slowly through a distant field. I watched it, though my insides were aching. I felt pain for both of us.

"Why haven't we divorced?" I asked. "Is it because I own half of your company?"

He avoided my eyes and said nothing.

"Aren't you going to answer me?"

"You could have divorced me as easily as I could have divorced you," he replied.

"Yes, but you know why you haven't divorced me, Carter. I have no idea why I haven't divorced you."

"It's no great mystery," he said. "Maybe just simple inertia."

Inertia, I thought. That was what was keeping us together?

The silence was broken by the ringing of the telephone. Yvonne came to the French doors.

"It's for you, madame," she said. "It is the police."

I exchanged looks with Carter.

"Maybe I should take it for you," he said.

"I wish you would." I didn't feel up to dealing with the police, particularly if there was a language problem. I watched my husband go into the house.

It was still warm out, but I shivered anyway. Between the emotion of our conversation, and the call from the police, I was a bundle of nerves. Poof was still at my feet and I invited her to my lap. She licked her paw as I petted her. Then I noticed a hawk of some sort circling overhead. It seemed to be looking down at me. I prayed it wasn't an omen.

The news that I'd had an abortion was a real shock. Carter had said I didn't want children, but even allowing for the fact that I was both selfish and thoughtless, I had trouble imagining I had actually done such a thing. It wasn't as though I'd been raped, or had some sort of medical problem. Yet as I questioned my actions, I couldn't say what my moral convictions were.

Carter returned to the terrace after about five minutes. He looked glum as he made his way to the table. I searched his eyes as he sat down in his chair. Evidently the news was not good.

"They wanted to come out right away," he said softly, "but I put them off until tomorrow morning. I didn't want you to have to face that this afternoon. Not your first day home."

"Why the urgency?"

"Apparently the situation has changed. It is no longer a routine matter."

"What do you mean, changed? What's happened?"

62

"The inspector said witnesses have come forward."

"Witnesses? Witnesses to what?"

"I don't know," Carter said, "but it doesn't bode well."

It was obvious he was troubled. "You're saying it's serious."

"I'm afraid so, Hillary."

His words sent a jolt through me. My God, did they think I was responsible for Michel Lambert's death? That I'd killed him? Was that what Carter was thinking?

When I considered the possibility, I realized there was nothing I'd learned about myself that said I couldn't have done such a thing. My eyes glistened and I wanted badly to tell Carter it wasn't possible—not me. But the terrible truth was, I did not know. I simply did not know.

I PACED BACK AND forth across my room. For the first time since I'd awakened as Hillary Bass, I was on the verge of panic. There had been anxious moments, but now I felt trapped, alone, and in danger. What if they arrested me for murder? What if I went to prison?

The notion that I might be a murderer seemed inconceivable. I would have dismissed the idea as a misunderstanding, a mistake, were it not for my dream about Michel.

As I thought about it, I began wondering if I was losing my mind. Dr. Thirion hadn't shown any particular concern along those lines, but the good doctor didn't know about my dream.

I decided the thing to do was to talk to him, so I used the buzzer to summon Polly. A minute later she knocked on my door.

"I'd like to phone Dr. Thirion," I told her. "And I'd

like to speak to him in private. Can you get him on the line for me?"

"Yes, Mrs. Bass. Your husband is using the telephone at the moment. He's had a call from London. When he's finished I'll ring up the clinic for you." She left the room.

I was still agitated, but the thought of speaking with Dr. Thirion calmed me some. I glanced over at the telephone, sitting on the bedside table, and hoped Carter wouldn't be long. Finally I decided to check. I picked up the receiver and heard voices. Carter was speaking to a man with a strong upper class English accent. They were discussing interest rates. I carefully replaced the receiver and sat on the bed.

I tried to convince myself that the police would not actually arrest me. If that was their intention, surely they would have come for me before now. More likely they would be probing for information. At least I didn't have to fear that. There was nothing I could tell them, and therefore nothing I could hide.

Several minutes passed before Polly was at my door again. She came with a stack of photo albums in her arms. "I rang up the clinic, ma'am," she said. "Dr. Thirion is unavailable now, but he'll ring you back. In the meantime, Mr. Bass suggested I bring these albums in case you'd like to have a look." She carried them to the table by the window.

I got up and went to where she stood. "That's very thoughtful of Carter," I said, running my fingers over the smooth leather cover of the top album.

"He said he had some other calls to make, but he'll try not to keep the telephone engaged too long."

Carter's thoughtfulness continued to confound me, especially coming on the heels of a virtual announcement that I was a murder suspect. "Is it his nature to be kind?" I asked.

Polly looked at me with surprise bordering on alarm. "Mr. Bass is a gentleman, ma'am."

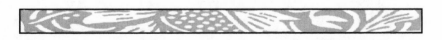

"You like him, don't you?"

She averted her eyes. "I have the utmost respect for Mr. Bass."

"But you don't feel the same about me, do you, Polly?"

She took my question as an affront, her eyes flashing before she regained control. "Mrs. Bass, I have always tried to meet my responsibilities and serve you to the best of my abilities."

"I didn't mean that as an accusation," I said. "I was simply trying to understand our relationship."

"I assure you, you've never complained."

"I'm sure I haven't."

"If there's anything I've done to offend . . ."

"No, Polly, please don't take offense. I'm just not comfortable yet with who I am. Maybe I read more into people's reactions than I should."

"I don't regard it my place to judge, Mrs. Bass."

"Just forget it."

Polly drew herself up, trying to maintain an even demeanor. "Will there be anything else, ma'am?"

"Yes," I said, "I'd like for you to stay with me while I look through these albums. You can be my guide, perhaps answer my questions."

"If you wish."

We sat down and she pulled a rather dated-looking album from the stack. "We should begin with your baby snaps, I suppose," she said.

I was curious and a little apprehensive as I began leafing through the folder. I didn't expect the baby in the snapshots to be familiar, but I'd hoped the pictures themselves might be. They weren't. My anxiety escalated when I finally came to a photograph of my mother holding me.

I stared at the woman's face, longing to recognize her.

She was fair, as Carter had said, but she was a stranger. It was the same with my father. "How can I recognize Michel Lambert, but not my own parents?" I said aloud.

"Maybe some of the more recent snaps will be familiar," she said.

I went on to the next album, recognizing the little girl in the childhood photos to be me. Yet I was unable to recall either the occasion, the other persons, or having seen the picture before. How could that child, that teenager, that young woman who was so clearly me, have lived without my being aware of it?

I closed the last of the albums and sat back in my chair. Polly could see my disappointment.

"There are several others covering the period since your marriage," she said. "I put them together myself, as a matter of fact. It was one of the first jobs you gave me." Polly handed me one. In the pile of folders she'd brought there were some scrapbooks and portfolios, as well.

I was discouraged, but didn't say anything. I opened the first album chronicling my married life. My expectations were not high, but I was very curious. I wanted to see myself with Carter.

The photographs proved to be a pictorial confirmation of the marriage he had described. I saw a serious man and a frivolous woman behaving as though they belonged together. I saw the false joy on their faces. And as the years passed, I saw them discovering their mistake.

It is amazing what one can see in a photograph, if one is looking for it. A smile can be painted on, but the truth in body language cannot be defied indefinitely.

I saw nothing in the pictures I had ever seen before with one possible exception. There were three photos of Carter and me on the sailboat. The occasion, the way we were dressed, held no special significance, but the name of the craft, *Serenity*, plainly visible in two of the pictures, touched a nerve.

"Tell me about the sailboat," I said to my secretary.

"It was Mr. Bass's originally. As I understand it, he more or less gave it to you. You fancy sailing and took the boat out two or three times a week when the weather was good. Some of your friends enjoy sailing and you'd make a do of it whenever there was a group." She'd recited the facts blandly. Her earlier hostility was now hidden, though I surmised it was still there.

I studied the photo. It made me terribly uncomfortable. I tried to reassure myself that simply because I dreamed that Michel and I had fought, it wasn't necessarily so.

The last album that Polly handed me contained photos of my social life, my friends, my trips and parties. This was my life apart from Carter. In the photographs I saw the libertine I truly was. I saw myself topless at the beach, in a party hat, sitting on some strange man's lap, my skirt hiked up as far as it would go. I saw myself dissolute and debauched, often drunk, always self-indulgent, the egoistic bon vivant.

At first I asked the names of the people in the photos, but after a while the exercise became meaningless. Polly did point out Jane Nyland, though.

Jane was surprisingly ordinary in looks, handsome in a way the English often are. The photos of her revealed a certain flair and panache, from her French side, perhaps.

Many of the photos were loosely stuck between the pages. Among the more recent ones were numerous pictures of Michel. The shots of us together showed us to be lovers. It was obvious I cared for him.

As I closed the album, one of the loose snapshots fell to the floor. I picked it up. It was a picture of me in a bikini with a large, well-tanned and well-built man of twenty-eight or thirty. He was bare-chested, had a full beard that was trimmed short, tousled windblown hair, and his arm was around me. We looked happy in each other's company.

"Who's this?"

"Bob Whitford, Mrs. Bass. He looks after your sailboat. I should say, formerly did. He no longer does."

"What happened?"

"You discharged him shortly before the accident."

"Why?"

"I'm not certain."

I studied the photograph, my intuition telling me there was a story behind the smiles on our faces. The notion was disheartening. I almost didn't want to know.

"What nationality is he?"

"American. I believe he first went to work for you the year after I arrived. That would make it roughly two years ago."

"Is it common to have someone look after a boat?" I asked.

"Mr. Bass says with a yacht the size of yours, ma'am, it's essential. There's a great deal of maintenance required."

"I see. And does someone look after the boat now?"

"Yes. Mr. Bass engaged an Englishwoman who lives in Toulon. As I understand it, the arrangement is temporary, subject to your approval, since the boat is essentially yours."

"An Englishwoman, you say?"

"Her name is Erica Maxwell. She's been out here for years and knows all there is to know about sailing."

"Do you know her?"

There was a slight pause. "We've met."

"Then she's someone else I should meet," I said.

"Considering the time you devote to sailing, yes, ma'am."

I studied the photo. "Do these people go along when I take out the boat?"

"Mr. Whitford lived on the *Serenity*, which I'm told is common. He went with you when you sailed, or didn't, according to your wishes. Miss Maxwell lives in a flat in town."

"I see."

I turned my interest back to the photo album, looking at the pictures of me with my friends, particularly studying the ones of Michel. After a few minutes, I set them aside and sighed like someone who'd just learned a harsh, unpalatable truth. Despite the opulence and gaiety, I didn't have a pretty life. I glanced at Polly, who sat mute beside me. "I seem to enjoy my friends and my pleasure."

"Yes, ma'am."

I proceeded to leaf through the scrapbooks with the tear sheets from fashion magazines, chronicling my career. These were more benign than the last bunch of photos and I was intrigued by them, amazed even by the camera's magic. But I found nothing helpful to my quest for rediscovery, except that, as Carter had said, my hair had once been very much in the style I wore now.

A thought occurred to me. Could I have cut my hair because I wanted to recapture that earlier time? If I'd fought with Michel, could it have been because I wanted to give him up? Perhaps I'd realized I belonged with Carter after all.

The notion gave me hope. Polly must have seen it on my face because she looked at me curiously.

"Polly," I said eagerly, "how long have I been wearing my hair this way? When did I get it cut?"

"You know, I was wondering about that, ma'am. The past few years you've been keeping it a bit longer. When you do get a cut it's usually in Paris." She paused for a moment. "Now that you mention it, I suppose you must have decided to try a new salon in Nice. You were there for a couple of days before you were hurt."

"I like it, Hillary," came a deep voice from across the room, "so maybe you ought to continue using that hairdresser." It was Carter, standing in the doorway. He sauntered into the room and over to where Polly and I sat at the table.

I happened to catch a glimpse of the admiration on her face as she gazed up at Carter. But he was looking at me, smiling slightly. I took it as a gesture of peace.

I now had a clearer sense of the history of our marriage. It wasn't a happy story, but I was beginning to understand my husband better. Were it not for Michel, I was sure we would be having a much easier time of it now.

"Find any pictures that did anything for you?" he asked.

"Only the ones with the sailboat," I replied.

He nodded. "Considering that's where the accident occurred, I guess it's not too surprising."

"Thank you for calling it an accident."

"I don't set myself up as a judge and jury, Hillary."

Polly fidgeted. "Perhaps I should leave," she said.

"Yes, Polly," Carter countered, "step out for a few minutes, if you don't mind. I would like to talk to Mrs. Bass in private."

"Yes, sir."

Polly left and Carter sat in her chair, looking at me. I was uncomfortable under his scrutiny, not knowing what to expect. His expression was not severe, though I wouldn't have described it as warm. As he glanced down at my legs, I realized that Carter was evaluating me in sexual terms, and I didn't quite know what to make of it. Was this part of our relationship, or was it something new?

I would have thought our disaffection had extended to the sexual realm, and shuddered to think I was wrong—that I might be expected to engage in perfunctory sex. But that notion flew in the face of what Polly had said—that Carter scarcely came to Montfaucon anymore. That would mean that we were estranged. And until now he had said nothing to make me think otherwise. Yet I kept picking up signals, signs of interest. Were they unconscious, or was I reading something into the situation that wasn't there?

Once again, my terrible disadvantage came into play. Carter knew all about our sex life, and I knew nothing of it. I had no idea when we'd last made love or what it was like. Did I entice him and play sexual games, or had I rejected him entirely for Michel?

"I've got a business problem that needs tending to," Carter said, interrupting my thoughts. "I'm going to have to run into Cannes. There's a brokerage firm there with facilities I sometimes use. I'll be gone several hours, but I intend to be back in time for dinner." He hesitated, and I felt another flicker of awareness pass between us. "I want to say something before I go, though," he added. "I know you're upset by the police. I am too. I won't pretend otherwise. We won't know what they have until they get here, so there's no point in jumping to conclusions. We'll just have to wait and see."

"I appreciate you saying that," I said, "but it's fairly obvious you have your suspicions, even if you aren't jumping to conclusions."

"I have no idea what happened on that boat," he replied. "And I guess you don't either. So in that sense we're on equal terms."

He was being diplomatic, and I appreciated it, but he wasn't proclaiming my innocence, he wasn't reassuring me that everything would be all right. And what was so frightening about that was that Carter knew me much better than I knew myself.

"When I get my memory back, we'll know," I said.

He stared into my eyes for a long time before nodding. "Yes, I suppose that's true."

Carter could see how anxious I was. It must have bothered him because he reached over and patted my knee. It was a small gesture of compassion, but it meant a lot to me. When he didn't remove his hand immediately I became aware of the feel of it on my skin. A shimmer went through me. This was the first time he'd touched me. The connection wasn't as troubling as I might have thought. It was affection, and I rather liked it.

He stood, and I gazed up at him. I realized what I would have liked just then was for him to hold me—not because of the physical attraction, but simply because I needed to connect with him. I needed more than words, more than a simple touch.

"I'd better get going," he said. "I've got a lot to do."

My heart sank as he walked away. He'd shown me kindness and I was grateful for that, but I was sure it was more a reflection of his decency than his faith. Deep down Carter had no confidence in me. At the door he stopped.

"I'll send Polly back in so that you can finish looking at your albums."

He went out the door. I was soon in tears, more fearful than ever that there was a monster I didn't know inside of me. I began hating my past again.

Polly had scarcely returned when the telephone rang. She went to answer it.

"It's Lady Nyland calling from Paris, Mrs. Bass."

I wondered if I dare put off the call. I hardly felt up to social conversation, but it *was* an opportunity to interact with one of the most important people in my life. I went to the phone. Polly handed me the receiver and left the room.

"Hello?"

"Hillary, love, is it true? You've really lost your memory? I rang up the bloody hospital and when they said you had amnesia, I thought it was a joke. It can't be true. Is it, Hill?"

"I'm afraid so."

"You can't remember a thing?"

"No."

"Then you don't even know me?"

"Polly explained who you were and I've seen pictures of you, but that's it."

Jane laughed. "What a hoot!"

"I wish I could say I found it amusing."

"Oh, Hillary darling, I didn't mean to be insensitive. Honestly. It's just so bizarre when you think about it. What a way to expurgate one's sins!"

"I've been discovering that." There was an uncertain silence, so I said, "Jane, I apologize for sounding weird, but I don't know anyone. Even Carter is a stranger."

"You've seen him, have you?"

"He arrived from Rome this afternoon. And he also visited me briefly in the hospital."

"Has he said anything about Michel? Uh . . . you do know about Michel, don't you?"

"Oh yes. The police are interviewing me tomorrow morning about the accident. And I know all about the affair. I've been sick over it."

"Sick? Whatever for?"

I could tell by her manner that we were indeed friends. But Jane was talking to the old Hillary Bass. How could I explain that I neither liked nor respected the friend she thought I was? In any case, I didn't want to get into the business about Michel having been murdered and me possibly having been the culprit. "Let's just say it's put me in a terrible mess, Jane."

"You poor dear. You've had a rough time, haven't you? Is there anything I can do? Anything at all? I realize I'm a voice

74

out of the blue, but I'm at a loss what to say. Should I come see you? Would that be a help?"

"I don't know. Nothing has triggered my memory yet. Maybe it would help to see a friend."

"I'm scheduled to spend the weekend with James, but I could pop down at the beginning of the week. Would that do?"

"If you don't mind."

"Of course not. What are friends for if not to help relive the sins of the past?" She let off a peel of laughter. "Sorry. I'm being insensitive again. I'm having trouble relating to this amnesia business."

"So am I. But tell me something. How do I sound to you?"

"Well . . . you sound like you . . . considering what you've been through. You seem subdued, I suppose, but then you are talking to a stranger, aren't you?"

"Yes, but I'm trying my best to relate to people as they expect me to, Jane."

"At least you're alive, thank God."

"Sometimes I'm not so sure that's a blessing. I feel so guilty about . . . everything. And with Carter I'm at a complete loss. I just don't know what to think about our relationship."

"I shouldn't think that would be so dicey, love. What difference does it make? It's a marriage of convenience and has been for years. Why worry?"

"A marriage of convenience?"

"Yes. Hasn't Carter said anything?"

"I know we're estranged. No announcement was needed for that," I said.

"I suppose it's the money that's kept you together. I shouldn't expect this business with Michel will help matters, though. There was talk in London that Carter was planning a divorce, but didn't want to do anything until you either died or came out of the coma."

I shouldn't have been shocked by her words, but I was —or maybe hurt was more accurate. True, Carter had been less than compassionate at the clinic, but he'd been somewhat friendlier since then. Only a few minutes earlier he'd shown true kindness, leaving me with a feeling of hope. And now this? "He's actually said he's going to divorce me?"

"That's the gossip, Hill. You've speculated about it yourself. You used to joke that Carter could never decide which he wanted more—his freedom or your half of the business. We've had a laugh over it more than once. Don't you remem— No, of course you don't."

"Carter hasn't intimated anything like that . . . but then why would he?"

"Don't make anything of it, love. You didn't mind. Honestly."

"What did I want, Jane? A divorce?"

"Oh, you considered it, especially after you and Michel became involved. But after a while you began seeing your marriage as an asset. You told me once the married mistress is the happiest mistress."

I gasped. "I didn't."

"Oh, but you did, Hill. You didn't like being taken for granted, and you felt your marriage kept Michel on his toes."

"That's disgusting," I said.

"Well, perhaps I'm being a bit glib, but what I've described is you, love."

"Carter hasn't said a word to me about divorce," I said. "Could he have changed his mind, or is he too kind to kick me while I'm down?"

"Well, the way I heard it, he was really cheesed off after that incident in London with Michel."

"What incident in London?"

"Oh, damn, of course you don't know. How can we have a decent conversation with me having to explain everything I say? Well, where do I begin?"

I sat on the bed. "You may as well tell me everything. I know almost nothing about Michel."

"Well, he adored you. Michel was absolutely, madly in love with you."

"Yes, but who was he?"

"Michel was *le tout Paris*. Very social, if a bit nouveau. Had scads of money, but wanted more. A lot more. He was a charmer, Michel was. I always liked him."

"Then you knew him well."

"The three of us knocked about some, especially at first when I was your alibi, though as it turned out you didn't need one. Carter didn't seem to care how you spent your time as long as you didn't embarrass him."

"Did Carter have someone else?"

Jane laughed. "If you mean anyone serious, I think not. At least we weren't aware of anyone."

I was relieved, though any jealousy I felt was ironic, to say the least. But what had I wanted? How serious had I been about Michel? That's what I needed to know. "You said Michel loved me. Did I really love him?"

"After a fashion, yes. But I think part of it was the flattery. Michel gave up his family for you. And he claimed to have made a lot of sacrifices in his business for the sake of your relationship, though you didn't buy that one for a minute. You claimed Michel loved your body, but your money even more.

"He owned the French equivalent of Carter's investment banking firm and felt he could double his operation in a merger with you. You used to torture the poor man by sharing

77

Carter's successes whenever you received a report from your accountants. It would infuriate Michel, but you said it did wonders for your sex life."

"How clever of me," I said glumly. I couldn't help a shiver. "What about Michel's family? What did you mean when you said he gave them up for me?"

"Divorced his wife of nearly thirty years. Claudine was even more social than Michel, and believe me, it was a bitter pill to swallow when he left her. For a time there were circles in Paris that broke into warring camps over you and Claudine. I've been snubbed at more than one party, just by virtue of my friendship with you, ducks."

"Wonderful."

"In the last several months things had cooled down considerably," Jane said. "The social turmoil surrounding *affaires de coeur* always pass. But it was a hoot while it lasted."

"Did Michel have children?"

"Two grown sons. They sided with Claudine."

I groaned. "So, what was the incident in London you alluded to?"

"Michel decided to take matters into his own hands. He went to see Carter. Michel had this annoying habit of behaving like an eighteenth-century nobleman, especially when he got his dander up. It was his worst trait, in my opinion."

"What happened in London?"

"Michel announced that he intended to marry you and suggested the decent thing for Carter to do was step aside. I wasn't there, mind, but the scene must have played like something out of *Don Juan.*"

"Good Lord."

"You were furious. You called me the morning you left for Nice and said you had some important business to tend to, and while you were there you were going to give Michel the what-for. I guess coming on the heels of that business with your boatman, it was just too much."

"What business with a boatman?"

"No, I don't suppose anyone would have told you about that either. You're aware of the hunky chap, Bob, who looked after your sailboat, aren't you?"

"Yes, I've heard. Apparently I fired him."

"Then you do know."

"I know that much. But what does that have to do with Michel?"

"Michel was the reason you discharged the fellow, Hillary. Michel found out Robert occasionally serviced you, as well as the boat."

"Oh, God," I muttered.

"I don't think you used him much the last year, but Michel was terribly jealous and insisted Bob had to go."

"What about Carter? Did he know about me and the boatman?"

"He must have suspected, but he had to know it didn't mean anything. Besides, love, Carter is well beyond caring about you trifling with the help."

That stung, but I was coming to understand that was the way things were between us. "Evidently Michel wasn't so broad-minded."

"Precisely. You finally gave in to his demands, but you resented it. Then, when Michel went to Carter, it was the last straw. You were absolutely livid and I couldn't calm you. That was our last conversation."

"No wonder I've blocked everything out. I couldn't get along with my husband or my lover. I'm not surprised Carter wants to divorce me. I can't really blame him."

There was a long pause. "Hillary, you haven't had one of those religious conversions, have you? Where's the girl who was always determined to live her life to the fullest, convention be damned?"

"Well, I can only behave the way I feel, and at the moment I feel chastened. Not only have I betrayed my husband, I may even be responsible for Michel's death."

"Rubbish."

"Maybe you can dismiss it, but I find it a difficult burden."

Jane Nyland hesitated. "This remorse, or whatever it is, Hillary, won't help matters. I suggest you try to regain your former perspective as rapidly as possible. All the parties to the affair were adults. You played the game by the same rules as the others involved."

"Unless, of course, I killed Michel intentionally."

"Killed him intentionally? What in God's name are you saying?"

My lip quivered. "It's possible."

"You wouldn't kill anyone. Don't be daft."

Jane's response was reassuring. It was nice to know I wasn't thought of by my best friend as someone who would kill. "When there are allegations, and you have no memory of events, it becomes very difficult to be sure of yourself," I said, my voice trembling slightly. "I wish I were as confident about it as you. I have to admit, I'm not."

Jane Nyland said nothing.

"I hope you aren't beginning to doubt too, Jane."

"I'm not."

"Why the silence?"

Her voice took on a more sober tone. "Earlier you asked if you sounded like yourself and I told you that you did, except more subdued. Well, now I'm not sure that's quite right. It's your voice I hear, Hillary, but you're not the woman I know. You are different. Unquestionably."

"I hope that doesn't disappoint you."

"No, ducks," she said, "I'm your friend and I'll stand by you. But I have to be completely honest. I always have been. That's my style."

"I wouldn't want it any other way."

"Still want me to pop down at the beginning of the week?"

"Of course."

"I'll ring you after the weekend then."

"Fine."

"Stiff upper lip, Hill." She laughed devilishly. *"Ciao,* love."

After I'd hung up I sat there for a long time, thinking. Jane had given me an intimate picture of myself. But it troubled me that I continued not to like what I saw, and I think it troubled her too.

If anything, I felt worse about what had happened with Michel than before. Without knowing it, Jane had given me a motive for being upset with him—perhaps even a motive for murder! The realization stabbed at my soul. Was I really capable of such an act? I prayed not, but I didn't know.

AFTER MY CON-
versation with Jane, I
lay on my bed, trying
to bring everything into
perspective. I was beginning to
hate my amnesia. At first it had
been weird, even surrealistic, but
it was rapidly becoming perni-
cious, a curse.

Dr. Thirion telephoned a
short time later and I was glad for
the opportunity to share my misery. I got right to what was troubling me.

"I have to know, Doctor,
am I capable of having murdered
that man?"

"Under the right circum-
stances almost anyone is capable of killing, madame," he replied.

"Yes, but I'm afraid that in
my case it may be true."

"Why?"

I told him about my dream
of being on the boat with Michel.
I explained that of all the

photos I'd seen, only Michel and the sailboat sparked remembrance.

"That's hardly proof of murder," the psychiatrist said. "Tell me, what were you feeling as you fought with Monsieur Lambert in the dream?"

"Well, it was terrifying, of course. But . . . there was a certain detachment. I was as much an observer as a participant."

"This is not uncommon. In the world of dreams, associations are often vague. You cannot take them too literally."

"In other words, there's no way to tell what happened for sure."

"Not from a dream alone," Dr. Thirion replied. "We can be fairly certain that the incident on the sailboat is at the heart of the amnesic episode. Anything beyond that is speculation."

Speculation, I thought. I wished I could be so cool and detached about what had happened. But for me it wasn't a subject to be analyzed analytically. What had occurred on the boat had been torturing me almost from the moment I'd awakened.

"So tell me," Dr. Thirion said, "how are things going with monsieur?"

"I'm not sure," I said, feeling ill at ease.

"Not sure?"

"Well, Carter's being kind to me. I appreciate that. There haven't been any arguments, if that's what you mean."

"I wasn't thinking so much that, Mrs. Bass, as feelings of familiarity, perhaps a twinge of recollection of your past life."

"No, there's been nothing," I said. "Well . . . nothing concerning Carter. He remains a stranger. My cat is more familiar to me, though I can't say I remember her."

"At least you're getting along with monsieur," Dr. Thirion said.

"Considering that for all he knows I'm a murderer, I guess you could say that."

83

"Surely there's been no suggestion that . . ."

"No, nothing formal. But the police are coming to interview me. There's been something new about a witness. I know that's not an accusation, but I'm worried and I believe Carter is too."

"There's an expression that applies to this situation, I believe," Dr. Thirion said. "Something about borrowing trouble."

"Yes, you're right."

"So, your spirits are getting better and you're stronger," he said.

"Yes, but it's very, very difficult to try to live your life with no memory of the past. I feel like a rat in a maze. I keep walking into walls."

"*C'est normal, madame,* but still I'm encouraged."

"While we're talking, Doctor, there is one other thing. You said before that I still had a sense of self, a moral code and values and so forth."

"Yes . . ."

"Is it possible for me to come out of this amnesia with new attitudes and values?"

"What do you mean?"

"I don't like who I am, Doctor. The things I've done distress me. My husband and best friend both say I'm not the same woman I was. Even my taste in food is different. It's as though I've rejected everything I've learned since coming to Europe."

"This is most interesting," he said. "Your case is a bit unusual. There are people who undergo sudden transformations —criminals who become saints, misers who become philanthropists, and so forth. The change often follows a traumatic experience."

"What are you saying, that I'm taking this opportunity to reform myself?"

"You may be rejecting parts of your past in the same way the religious convert rejects his sin. Saul became St. Paul, madame. His experience is different from yours only in that he could remember his past and you cannot."

"Perhaps you're right. But I'm deeply afraid of going back to being the woman I was. My husband didn't love me before, but at least now, despite his doubts, he feels some compassion for me."

"The subconscious may be wiser than we think," Dr. Thirion said with a laugh.

I hoped he was right.

—

Before I'd left the clinic, Dr. Lafon had told me to take it easy for a few days, but with Carter gone, I felt restless. I wanted some air.

I changed into a pair of black French terry walking shorts and a white cotton shirt. Polly was working on accounts in the study, and I asked her where I might go for a stroll. She told me that I often took a path that meandered about the grounds. Carter had it built just for that purpose. It sounded perfect and I welcomed the chance to see more of the estate.

I went out into the courtyard. Antonio was polishing the chrome on the Bentley. He looked up, watching me pass by. There was something suggestive in his manner, the way his eyes followed me, that made me uncomfortable. I nodded vaguely in his direction, then tried to ignore him, but he called out my name. When I hesitated, he sauntered over.

Antonio had a smile that was boyish and uninhibited. His flirtatious manner would have been insulting if it wasn't so natural. I dismissed it as a product of youth and naiveté.

"Bonjour, madame. Et votre tête, ça va?"

"I'm sorry, Antonio, but I haven't been able to speak or understand French the way I could before the accident."

"Oh, that's okay," he said in a heavy accent. "We talk English, eh?"

"Until my French comes back anyway."

"I only say to you, how's the head? *La tête,*" he said, pointing to his head, "it's okay?"

"Oh, I see. Yes, my head's fine, thank you. I'm feeling better."

He looked at my legs pointedly, smiling again. "Good, good. That's pretty good," he said.

It was hard to know if he was referring to my head or my legs. I decided to give him the benefit of the doubt.

Antonio swelled his chest a bit, absently scratching the hairy mat at the opening in his shirt as he contemplated me. It was evident he functioned at a physical level.

"I was going for a walk," I said as a prelude to leaving, "to see the grounds."

"Oh," he said. "It's very pretty here. Nice, very nice."

I smiled and turned to go.

"A moment, madame," he said, reaching out and all but taking me by the arm. "Can I say something?"

I hesitated. "Yes, what is it?"

"The English one," he said, tossing his head toward the house. "Polly. Be careful, eh?"

The comment, clearly a warning, surprised me. "What do you mean?"

"Don't trust her."

"Why do you say that?"

"She is not . . . how do you say, *dévouée?*"

"*Dévouée?*"

"*Oui, dévouée.* It means . . . oh . . . *fidèle.* You know?"

"Loyal?"

"Ah, yes. Loyal. The English one is not loyal."

I was immediately leery of what smelled like some sort of palace intrigue. "Why do you say that, Antonio?"

"Sometimes in the car I hear her tell Monsieur Bass about you and Monsieur Lambert. I tell you this before, *madame, n'est-ce pas?* Remember? You only laugh. And this morning, before we get you at the *clinique* in Toulon, I take the English to the town. She tell me to stay in the car, but I follow to see, *vous comprenez?* She go to a café. She talk to a lady."

"What lady?"

"Je ne sais pas, madame. I was in the street, don't see them so good. The English stay maybe five minutes."

"That's all quite interesting, Antonio, but I don't see how that makes Polly disloyal."

He grinned, touching his nose. "I know this, madame. The English thinks I just drive the car. She doesn't know I see many things. I know she's in love with Monsieur Bass." He smiled his boyish smile and took another languorous look at my legs.

I did not like the tenor of the conversation, but the last remark piqued my curiosity. "Polly may be fond of Mr. Bass, but that hardly means she's in love with him. Nor does it mean my husband was interested in her." I said the words, but there wasn't as much conviction in them as I would have liked.

"Monsieur Bass has a beautiful wife and he's a very rich man, madame. He doesn't need the English for love. For him, it's conversation. But the English, Polly, she's in love." He beamed.

"Perhaps you spend too much time watching other people, Antonio," I said. "Maybe it would be better if you just drove the car."

He acted wounded. "I don't say these things, madame, for another bottle of champagne." A little smile played at the corner of his mouth. "Don't you remember? We are friends."

"I gave you a bottle of champagne?"

He flickered his eyebrows. *"Oui, madame.* Because you like me. You don't remember this?"

I shook my head. "No, I don't remember anything."

"Ah, c'est vrai!" I forget. You have the *amnésie.* But it's okay. I can tell you. You are always very kind with me. And to you, madame, I am *dévoué.* Loyal."

"Thank you," I said, uncertain what he might be alluding to. Antonio made me uncomfortable. And, as always, I felt at a terrible disadvantage. It seemed best to leave. "Well, I must go," I said. "I think we should forget the past. Things are completely different now."

He seemed disappointed, but was in no position to protest. *"Comme vous voulez,"* he said with resignation.

I walked briskly across the courtyard, shuddering at the notion that I might in some way have been involved with the chauffeur. I'd already learned that I "availed myself," as Jane Nyland put it, of the man who had looked after my sailboat. To fool around with the chauffeur as well was simply inconceivable. On the other hand, I wondered if Antonio might be trying to take advantage of my loss of memory. All I knew for certain was that anyone could tell me almost anything about myself and I couldn't dispute it. I was at the mercy of the world.

I went through the gate and had only to go a few yards down the drive before I came to the beginning of the path. I stopped for a moment, viewing the valley and the surrounding hills.

It was still warm. I inhaled, testing the air for familiarity. The eight years I'd spent in Montfaucon had to have left an indelible mark on my brain. The land did not seem alien, but neither did it suggest the accustomed surroundings of home. Each step, each new sight, every vista, was a fresh experience, a new discovery.

How many times had I breathed this air, traced with my

eye the line of the hills, savored the hues and tones and light of sky and earth? As I reflected, I was sure there was a special piece of ground I cherished, but somehow I had doubts that it was this place. I belonged somewhere, but did I belong in these clothes and in this skin?

Dr. Thirion had convinced me that my amnesia was my way of coping with my considerable problems. It enabled me— at least for a while—to defer responsibility, giving me a fresh start, another chance. But that didn't explain why I so thoroughly rejected Hillary Bass. I rejected her tastes, her values, her identity, virtually everything about her. I would have thought the whole business a bad joke, except for the fact that my memory was blank, and I had no one to cling to but her.

As I started down the path, my mind drifted back to my conversation with the chauffeur. Antonio might well be a troublemaker. The explanation could be as simple as that. And yet, one thing in particular did ring true. When he said that Polly was in love with Carter, I believed him.

The path wound down the hill to a small wood that traced a creek at the bottom of the valley. A stone bench had been placed there and I sat on it to rest. I was fatigued. Those weeks in the clinic had sapped my vitality. But the setting was tranquil and I regained some of my strength.

Sitting there, protected by my solitude, I lamented the terrible state I was in. If only I could remember. I decided to meditate in hopes of coaxing something back from the past.

I emptied my mind, putting myself at one with the tranquil setting. Then, much like that morning when I lay down for my nap, I went into a sort of trance. I saw the rose garden again. It came as a kind of vision. The fog was not so thick this time, but there was a vastness, an open endless space beyond the rosebushes. To look out was to peer beyond the edge of the world.

The vision frightened me, but when the elderly woman

89

appeared I was reassured. I could see her face more clearly this time. She had a kindly demeanor and I felt a curious love without feeling I truly knew her. I wanted to reach out, but she drifted away and I was left alone.

I tried to bring her back, but she wouldn't come. Instead I heard the sound of distant voices, children's voices. It was as if I were standing in the middle of a school yard with my eyes closed. The sound comforted me even though I didn't understand it. Why children? And what were they to me?

Children, roses, that woman who haunted me. They were alien to the world of Hillary Bass, yet in a sense they seemed more a part of me than my life at Montfaucon. How could that be?

I sat on the bench for a long time, struggling with reality and unreality, truth and fiction. My mind's stubborn refusal to free me was vexing, yet I was reluctant to go back and face the only world I knew, the only one I could touch and feel.

Knowing I couldn't stay away forever, I got up and continued along the path. The outing had been more challenging than I had anticipated. I became dizzy and had to stop several times. Once I actually sat down on the ground for fear I would faint.

Eventually I came to the last steep climb leading to the villa. My heart pounded from the exertion. I paused every ten yards or so to catch my breath, discovering much too late how weak my injury had left me. When I got to the courtyard I saw an unfamiliar car, a Peugeot sedan. The Bentley and Antonio were nowhere to be seen. I moved toward the house, my brow damp with perspiration, my legs shaky as I leaned against the front door.

Taking a deep breath, I went inside. I'd no sooner closed the door when Yvonne came hurrying across the foyer, a stricken look on her face.

"Madame," she said breathlessly, "you have a visitor."

A visitor? "Who?"

"A gentleman from the press in Paris. Mademoiselle Frampton had Antonio drive her into the town on an errand. When the gentleman came, I told him you were out walking. He asked to wait. He says it is very important. I didn't know what to do. Do you wish to speak to him, or shall I tell him to go away?"

"Where is he?"

"In the salon, madame."

"Does he speak English?"

"I don't know, madame," Yvonne said, wringing her hands. "He has a slight accent. I don't think he is French, but I don't know what he is."

"Tell him I'll be with him shortly. I'll just freshen up."

"Oui, madame."

The adrenaline gave me new energy. As I climbed the stairs I wondered why a reporter from Paris would want to interview me. Would a boating accident really be newsworthy this long after the fact? Or did he know something I didn't, something about the witnesses the police had mentioned? There was only one way to find out.

I sponged my face and neck, put a few more drops of Calèche on my throat, then ran a brush through my hair. I was still weak, but I wanted to find out why a reporter would want to speak with me.

Yvonne was waiting in the entry hall. "I asked to him," she said. "He speaks English. He's American."

"American? Don't worry then," I told her. "I'll take care of this. You can go back to the kitchen."

"Are you sure, madame?"

"Yes, go on."

I stepped to the entrance of the salon where I found a

shaggy-haired man in a light blue wash and wear suit standing at the fireplace, examining the array of porcelain on the mantel. His back to me, he was resting his hands on his hips, under the open flaps of his jacket. I cleared my throat and he turned around.

He stared at me for a long moment before breaking into a grin. He appeared to be in his early thirties, and about average height, thin, but with wide shoulders. His suit hung on him. "You're Mrs. Bass," he said. "I recognize you from your photo spreads in the glossies." He walked toward me, still smiling. "Name's Todd Halley. I'm with the *New York Press Enquirer*." He extended his hand and I took it.

"I thought you were from Paris."

"I am. I'm the paper's chief correspondent in Europe." He chuckled. "And the only one. I also free-lance for a paper in London and one in Paris, *Le Beau Monde.*"

"That's quite a résumé, Mr. Halley. Why would someone like you wish to speak with me?"

"Your boating accident off Nice was in the papers, just a short blurb." He held his fingers inches apart to illustrate his point. "No big deal. Routine. If Michel Lambert hadn't been so socially prominent Paris wouldn't even have noticed."

"So?"

"So, there are rumors kicking around that there might be a little more to the story. I wanted to ask you about them."

His words belied my fears. He did know more than I. And although he'd made the comment in an almost offhanded way, I heard it as an accusation. My knees began to shake.

"Why don't we sit down?" I said as evenly as I could. The truth was I wanted to ask him to leave, but I was so light-headed that I was in danger of fainting. And that was the last thing I wanted to do.

We went to the seating group near the fireplace. I gestured for the reporter to sit. He took a wing-backed armchair. I sat on the sofa. I took a couple of deep breaths. Halley watched me.

"You'll have to forgive me," I said. "I've been walking and I overdid it a little."

"It's a hot day."

"And I haven't fully recovered. I was in a coma for a couple of weeks."

"Yeah," he said. "That's what I understand." He clasped his hands and leaned forward, resting his elbows on his knees. "All right, Mrs. Bass. I'm here because I'd like to know what really happened on the boat. It's pretty obvious it wasn't an accident, so I'd like to hear your version of events."

I blinked. "What do you mean, 'It's pretty obvious it wasn't an accident'? What right do you have to say a thing like that?"

His grin was so wide it seemed to bend around his face. "Anybody can make an observation. Or ask a question."

"That doesn't mean you're entitled to an answer."

"What are you saying? That you've got something to hide?"

"Of course not."

"Then what's the problem? If you're innocent, then why not answer?"

"Innocent of what?" I shot back, hoping my indignation was coming through clearly.

"Let's not beat around the bush," he said. "The police are checking into Lambert's death as a possible homicide. And they're looking at you as the possible murderer. If you're innocent, I'd think you'd like to get out your version of the facts. Make a statement for the record."

"Listen, Mr. . . ."

"Halley."

"Mr. Halley. I'm suffering from amnesia. I can't remember anything that happened before four days ago. Even if I wanted to help you, I couldn't."

"Yeah, I heard about the amnesia story. Frankly, I find it a little convenient."

"I don't care how you find it." I got to my feet. "As far as I'm concerned, this conversation is over. I'd like for you to leave."

He didn't budge. "Come on, Mrs. Bass, nobody's accusing you of anything. At least not me. I just want to know what gives."

"What makes you think anything gives? And where did you get your information anyway?"

"That's not important," he said. "What matters is that this story is going to break soon and it would be in your interest to beat your accusers to the punch."

"What accusers?"

"The police, for starters."

My knees shook and I had to sit back down, even though I wanted this over with and him out of the house. "I can't believe the police would talk to you."

His only response was a smile.

"I want to know where you got your information!" I was getting shrill, but I couldn't help it.

"Lambert drowned, according to the autopsy. Did you push him overboard?"

I just stared at him.

"Was it a spur of the moment thing? I mean, you didn't plan to kill him, did you?"

"No, of course I didn't. It was an accident."

"Mrs. Bass, I thought you said you didn't remember. Is your amnesia selective, or is your memory coming back now?"

"That's enough!" I shouted, getting to my feet. "I want you out of here. Now!"

"What about the witnesses?" he said, refusing to move. "My sources say there are people who could break this case wide open. What do you say to that? Still maintain it was an accident?"

I began trembling. "They obviously didn't witness a murder, otherwise there'd already be an arrest."

"Then what did they see?"

"I have no idea."

"Come on, Mrs. Bass. You can do better than that."

Tears of frustration welled in my eyes.

"You've got to have some idea," he went on. "You must have some kind of feeling deep down. It was a lover's quarrel, wasn't it? You were his mistress. What did he do that made you want to kill him?"

"Leave!" I sobbed, barely getting out the word.

Halley reluctantly got to his feet. "You're making a mistake," he said, shaking his head.

I heard the front door opening. Todd Halley seemed not to notice until there was the sound of footsteps. We both turned toward the entrance.

Carter appeared, his jacket over his arm, a bouquet of roses wrapped in tissue in his other hand. He stared at the two of us.

"Carter," I cried, "make this man leave."

He came into the room, putting the flowers and his jacket on a chair near the entrance. "What's going on?"

"Mr. Bass," Halley said, straightening himself, "I just came to ask your wife a few questions. She misinterpreted my intent."

"What intent? Who are you?"

The reporter took a couple of steps toward Carter, extending his hand. "The name's Halley," he said. "I'm with the *New York Press Enquirer*. I just came by to get Mrs. Bass's side of the story."

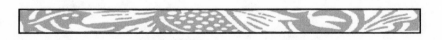

Carter ignored the outstretched hand and looked at me. "Hillary, did you let this guy in the house?"

I wiped my eyes. "He was here when I came back from my walk."

Carter's expression turned furious and he pointed toward the door. "Get out of here."

My heart was beating like a jackhammer. I felt faint. I started sobbing, unable to control myself.

"Sure, sure, I'll go," Halley said, "but I won't be the last. The press will be all over this place." Carter took Halley's arm but the reporter jerked free. "Keep your hands off of me, Jack."

"Listen, you slimeball, get out of my house before I throw you out."

Halley stomped toward the door. As I watched, my head started to spin. He paused, pointing back at Carter. "You can toss me out, mister, but you can't cover up the truth. If what I hear is true, your wife is headed for the slammer." He smirked. "And as far as I'm concerned, good riddance."

He disappeared into the entry and Carter turned to me. I reached out to him and tried to speak, but everything suddenly started spinning. My knees buckled and I was unconscious even before I hit the floor.

I HAD A HAZY REC-
ollection of Carter lifting
me into his arms and carrying me up the stairs. I
sensed the coolness of the satin
bedspread and its enveloping soft-
ness. I knew there was a world
beyond my closed lids, but I
yearned for the comfort of the
land of dreams.

I was told later that Yvonne
undressed me, but I had no clear
remembrance of anything until I
heard Guy Lafon's voice and felt
his cool fingers on my cheek.

"Mrs. Bass," he said softly,
his voice coaxing, "please wake
up. Time to open your eyes."

My lids fluttered open. I
stared into his narrow-set eyes, illuminated only by the light of the
setting sun coming in the window.
His wispy mustache twitched with
delight.

"Eh, voilà!" he said. "There
you are!"

For a moment I thought I

was back in the clinic. The scent of rose blossoms was strong. I glanced around the room. There were red roses on the writing table, but I was not in the hospital. And the woman standing at the foot of the bed was not a nurse. It was Yvonne.

Unlike the last time I had been unconscious the events of the afternoon came tumbling back through my mind. "Where's Carter?" I said.

"He was downstairs speaking with a policeman when I came up."

"The police?"

"A local gendarme. Would you like to see your husband?"

"Yes, I think so."

Lafon signaled for Yvonne to get Carter. Then he sat on the edge of the bed. "They tell me you went on an expedition against my orders." He gave me a stern look, making me smile.

"It was just a walk."

"Such things are for next week, madame. You must take it more slowly."

"But if I sit around the house, I'm likely to be set upon by a crazed reporter."

He chuckled. "You have your sense of humor. This is good."

But it wasn't good. All the horrible things that man had said came to mind. It was official, apparently. I was about to be branded a murderer. Maybe they were there now to arrest me. "I almost wonder if I wouldn't be better off dead," I said.

"Mrs. Bass, you can't think that."

"You don't know how hard it is, Doctor. Considering what I might be facing, I'm not sure I ever want to remember."

"*Du calme,*" he said, patting my arm. "Don't get yourself excited."

Tears filled my eyes and I fought to hold them back. What if I had killed Michel? His poor family. A tragic accident was one thing, but murder was another entirely. "Think how many lives I have ruined," I murmured. "I'm not surprised people hate me."

"You live a very interesting life, Hillary." The voice came from across the room. It was Carter at the door. He walked over to the bed, put his hands on his hips, and stared at me. The last rays of the sun cast shadows over his face. He looked handsome, despite his obvious fatigue. "God knows what's coming next."

I didn't know whether to laugh or cry, so I did neither. Guy Lafon patted my hand.

"I'll leave you some capsules to help you sleep, madame." He got to his feet. "Shall I look in on the patient tomorrow?" he said to Carter.

"Ask her."

The doctor turned to me.

"I don't think it will be necessary," I said, "unless in the meantime an angry mob tries to burn me at the stake or something."

He chuckled. "I shall leave you, then. Rest as much as you can." He stepped from the room, leaving Carter and me alone.

I stared up at my husband—ashamed, miserable. I was grateful that he didn't look angry, though he didn't seem particularly pleased, either.

"You gave me a scare," he said. "When we couldn't wake you up, I thought you'd decided to take another long sleep."

I tried to smile but couldn't. A tear ran down my cheek. "I'm afraid, Carter. I'm afraid of what I might have done."

Carter sat beside me on the edge of the bed. He seemed torn, unsure whether to be exasperated or sympathetic. "Well, you haven't lost your knack for getting into trouble," he said. "What am I going to do with you?"

"Shoot me."

"Hillary, I have trouble putting down a horse with a broken leg, so that's out."

"Then why don't you divorce me?"

He gave me a strange look. "Is that what you want?"

"It's what *you* want, isn't it? I mean, isn't that what you've been planning to do?"

He didn't answer.

"I've been unfaithful," I said, "a cause of embarrassment to you. Apparently everybody's talking about us, and what I've done is probably going to hit the newspapers soon. If I were in your shoes, I'd get a divorce."

"Who have you been talking to?"

"Nobody."

"Nobody?"

"Well, Jane."

"I might have known."

"Well, what I said is true, isn't it?"

"Lady Jane is a profligate," he replied. "And she's a lady in name only."

"I take it you don't like her," I said.

"Jane and I have never seen eye to eye. But then none of your friends particularly appeal to me. Nor I to them."

"What she said, though, is true, isn't it? You plan to divorce me."

"People say things when they're angry or unhappy or under stress, Hillary. I don't see any point in hashing it out now. We've got enough to worry about already."

I wondered why he didn't want to talk about divorce. Was he being kind, trying to spare me? Or did he have an ulterior motive? "I have to know how you feel about me."

That clearly upset him. Carter didn't answer immediately. Instead he looked off toward the window, his jaw working. "You're lying here, seemingly innocent. How do I explain something so complex to someone who doesn't even know herself?" he said.

"Is it that hard? Or am I that bad?"

My question brought a faint smile and nothing more.

I followed an impulse and put my hand on his. He felt so warm. I looked into his eyes, finding surprise in them. "Was it the baby?" I asked. "Is that why we grew apart?"

Carter got up and moved to the foot of the bed, putting his hands on his hips and looking impatient. "I think we should change the subject."

I hadn't intended to upset him, but apparently I had. "Don't be angry," I said.

"I'm not angry."

But he was, despite his words. And there was something more too. I sensed a concern—a concern he didn't feel comfortable with. Carter was fighting himself as much as he was fighting me, and I didn't understand why.

"I had another dream this afternoon," I said, trying to find a way to connect, to reach out to him. "A vision, actually, of the rose garden. The woman was in it again, but this time there was something new. Children. I didn't see them, but I heard their voices."

Carter didn't say anything.

"The sound was a comfort," I said. "I'm sure I don't hate children, Carter. In fact, the opposite is true. I think I like them."

He didn't react.

"I'm only saying it because I want you to know it's true!" I insisted. "I can't help what I've done in the past. But I can tell you how I feel now."

Still nothing.

"Won't you give me the benefit of the doubt?" I pleaded.

He continued to stare.

101

"Carter, say something. Please!"

"I don't understand you, Hillary."

I turned my head away. It seemed so hopeless. Out of the corner of my eye I saw him shift uncomfortably.

"What did that jerk Halley say to you before I arrived?"

I drew an uneven breath. "He was trying to provoke me. I shouldn't have spoken with him. It was stupid of me."

"I discussed the matter with the local gendarmes. They'll do what they can to keep people like him away in the future. Don't worry about him. He's a whore."

"He knew about the witnesses." My voice grew unsteady. "He talked like he knew I was guilty."

Carter was silent. I saw he was trying to put it all in perspective. What would he think if he knew about my dream of fighting with Michel? But he wouldn't know, because I'd never tell him. It was far too damning.

And yet, in my heart, I didn't believe that I could kill. I couldn't conjure up hatred toward Michel—the very concept was alien to me. Still I knew I was no angel. I'd done things to hurt Carter, probably even before the abortion. But what? I had no idea, and he obviously was in no mood to discuss it.

"It's very difficult for me to live like this," I said. "I feel besieged and helpless."

"Let's not jump to conclusions before we've talked to the police," Carter replied. "Halley may be blowing smoke or exaggerating."

I didn't hear much conviction in his voice. "Did the police say anything when you spoke with them?" I asked.

"They were strictly local. The people who are coming tomorrow are inspectors from Nice."

I shivered involuntarily.

Carter returned to the side of the bed. "Hillary, you're capable of a lot of things, but I don't think murder is one of them."

The comment was meant to reassure me, and I was grateful. I sensed that underneath it all he felt something for me besides hostility. But what? There wasn't any love between us, at least not now. Yet I found myself wanting to believe that there had been.

"I'm not trying to flatter you," he added. "It's true."

I swallowed hard. "Jane said the same thing."

"Well, maybe she and I agree on some things, after all."

His blue eyes seemed darker in the fading light, his expression softer. I liked his face. There was a benevolence about it.

Carter did something unexpected then. He leaned over and brushed my cheek with the back of his fingers. His affection seemed incongruous, and I wasn't quite sure how to react, what to say.

"I wish I could undo what's happened," I finally murmured. "I wish I could set things right."

"First we have to deal with tomorrow."

I turned toward the window, unable to look at him anymore. The curtains billowed gently in the breeze. The quality of light was remarkable, even magical.

"It's a nice evening," he said.

"Maybe I'll get up."

"Do you think you should?"

"Yes, I'd like to sit by the window and enjoy the air." I sat up, and when the sheet that had been covering me fell away, I discovered I was in a rather low-cut nightgown. Carter didn't seem to notice until I lifted the sheet to cover my chest.

"Would you like a dressing gown?" he asked.

"If you don't mind."

He went to the closet as though it was routine. Had he frequently gotten a robe for me in the past? I wondered. I thought again of having made love with him. It was a peculiar thing to have been intimate with a man and yet have no memory of any sort of tenderness whatsoever. I could not say what his lips felt like or conjure up the taste of his mouth or the feel of his hands on my body.

He returned with the summery robe I'd worn that morning. He offered his hand and helped me from the bed, then held the robe so I could slide my arms in. I wrapped it snugly around me.

Carter had a strange, wistful look on his face. He was remembering, calling on a catalog of memories I no longer shared.

"What are you thinking about?" I asked.

He seemed reluctant to answer at first. "I was remembering the early days."

It was a surprising admission. "Fondly?"

He nodded. "Yes, fondly."

We sat at the table where Polly and I had leafed through the photo albums that afternoon. Most of them were stacked on the floor under the window, but one of our marriage still lay on the table. Carter opened it randomly.

"Was there anything in here that pleased you?" he asked.

"Not a lot."

"There's something obviously sad about our marriage, isn't there?" he said.

"Yes."

The twilight illuminated our faces, but the rest of the room seemed dark. The air was soft. I turned from Carter to look at the lights in the villages and farms that dotted the tenebrous landscape like earthbound stars. In the distance a cow mooed. A hush of wind lifted the curtains against our arms.

"I like this place," I told him. "It's not yet my home, but I can picture how it could be."

"It's your home, Hillary. Amnesia doesn't change that."

I contemplated him. "When we divorce, will you take it from me?"

"You seem more concerned about divorce now than you did before your accident," he said.

"I feel insecure."

"Do I make you feel insecure?" he asked.

"Sometimes. But sometimes you're nice to me."

"I'm sorry things aren't as clear and straightforward as you'd like." He flipped a page or two of the album and pointed to a photograph. It was of the two of us sitting at a table in an outdoor café. As usual I appeared giddy and vampish; he seemed solemn. "I remember that day," he said. "I recall wanting to love you and not being able to anymore. Not the way I would have liked."

The sorrow in his voice enveloped me like a shroud. "Why have we stayed together so long?"

He closed the album. "People don't undo things as lightly as they do them, whether they're partners in a business or not." He got up then, pulling the curtains open all the way. The last of the daylight was dying beyond the hills. The air was cooler and taking on a dampness. We could hear some clamorous old vehicle rattling along a distant road.

Abruptly Carter turned to me. "Will you have dinner with me, Hillary, or would you prefer that Yvonne bring something up here?"

"I'll dine with you, if it's okay."

He nodded. "Of course it's okay." The light had grown so faint that I could barely see his features. He distractedly tapped the cover of the album. "How long do you need?"

"I'd like a shower," I said.

"Shall I come for you in half an hour? An hour?"

105

"Half an hour would be fine."

Carter looked as though he wanted to touch me. He restrained himself. "I brought you some roses," he said, gesturing toward them.

I glanced over at the vase on the writing table. "Yes, I saw them. I meant to thank you. They're lovely."

My hand was on the table. He lightly drew his fingers over it. Then he went out of the room.

—

I found a simple black cotton dress at the back of the closet and was ready by the time Carter returned. He had changed into a white linen sport coat with navy trousers and navy tie. He looked very debonair.

Each time I saw Carter his effect on me came as a surprise. We'd talked enough that I was starting to think of him as my husband, yet he also confounded me. I never quite knew what to expect, how he would react to what I said and did. I suppose the anticipated visit by the police was weighing on us both. But thinking about that got me upset, so I tried to banish it from my mind.

"Are you feeling stronger?" Carter asked as he went with me to the door.

"I'm all right."

"Take my arm," he said. "There's no point in falling down the stairs on top of everything else."

I took his arm, realizing we were going to play the roles of husband and wife. I wondered if this was something I normally did, if Carter and I ever pretended. It must not have happened frequently in the past year. According to Polly, we hadn't seen each other much.

We went down to the dining room. There were candles

106

at either end of a long table where our places had been set, and a candelabra on the sideboard. Carter helped me with my chair.

I took my napkin and he stood there for a moment rather than going to his place. I glanced up at him, but he was staring at my hands.

"Hillary, where is your ring?"

I looked at my bare fingers. "What ring?"

"The diamond I gave you as an engagement ring. I've never seen you without it before."

"I haven't had a ring on, not since I awoke in the hospital."

"They must have taken it off there. But didn't they give it to you when you left?"

"No. Unless they gave it to Polly."

"They must have done so. You normally wear all kinds of jewelry—rings, bracelets, earrings. I just haven't paid any attention until now." He turned toward the kitchen door. "Yvonne!" he called.

The housekeeper appeared. *"Oui, monsieur?"*

Carter rattled off some words in French that I couldn't quite follow, though I did gather it was something about Polly. Yvonne left and Carter went to the other end of the table. "We'll clear the mystery up," he said confidently.

We peered at each other up the long table. I felt a bit like someone who was playing at being the lady of the manor, yet there was something about it I liked. Carter's scrutiny continued unrelentingly.

"What are you looking at?" I said.

"I was thinking you look quite nice. This new image of yours is . . . appealing."

"What new image?" I asked self-consciously.

"You look different, Hillary. Softer, simpler. I don't quite know how to put it."

"Maybe it's my hair."

"Maybe."

"Am I at all like I was when we first met?" I ventured.

"In the early days you weren't as confident. But you've always been brash and it's grown over the years—that is, until now. Your accident seems to have subdued you."

"I must have been this way at some point in my life. I didn't invent my nature while I was unconscious."

He stared at me over the flickering candle. "You'd have to be an awfully good actress for that, wouldn't you?"

I didn't know whether to take that as a casual observation or an accusation. But it occurred to me that the swings in his attitude might be a product of his doubts. Was he suspicious, or was he merely testing me?

While Yvonne was pouring our wine, Polly arrived. She was dressed in a velour jogging suit, looking very different from the proper young woman in skirt and heels. She apologized for her appearance.

"I'm sorry to bring you from your rooms, Polly," Carter said, "but Mrs. Bass seems to have been separated from her engagement ring somewhere along the way. Did the clinic turn her jewelry over to you when you picked her up?"

"No, Mr. Bass, there was no mention of her personal effects, and I neglected to ask. I'm sorry."

Carter tapped his head. "How stupid of me. I completely forgot. When I went to Nice to see Mrs. Bass at the hospital, the police gave me her purse. They'd found it on the boat and felt it needed safekeeping, so I brought it here to the villa. I glanced at the contents, but didn't really examine them. Maybe the ring is inside."

"You mean you think they removed the ring and put it in her purse?" Polly asked.

"I don't know, but we ought to check before we declare

108

it missing. Would you mind getting the purse, Polly? I put it in Mrs. Bass's closet, on the shelf with her other bags. It was a white cloth thing, small, rectangular, about the size of a paperback book."

"I know the one," she said. "I'll just be a moment." Polly went off.

"I hadn't thought about a purse," I said. "Maybe it'll be a good thing for me to see."

"There wasn't a lot in it as I recall. A few odds and ends. You aren't the type who carries her life around with her all the time, as some women do."

It again struck me as strange to be told what I was like, and yet be unable to relate to it. It was unsettling, yet it was becoming routine.

Yvonne entered with our soup as Polly came in the other door. She started to hand the purse to Carter, but he gestured for her to give it to me. Predictably, it did not look familiar.

Inside there were only a few items, just as Carter had said—a comb, a small mirror, a lip pencil, three one-hundred-franc notes, an American Express card, a handkerchief, and an identity card, all of which I spread out on the table. I turned the purse upside down. There was no ring.

"That eliminates that possibility," Carter said.

I thanked Polly. She stepped back, her hands folded in front of her, ever respectful.

I picked up the identity card—a driver's license, it appeared—and opened the cover to see my face, bangs slightly mussed, peering out vacuously at the camera. If there was any emotion at all, it was boredom or mild annoyance. Neither the feeling I had that day I was photographed, nor the picture itself, were familiar. More of the phantom me.

Yvonne set down my soup plate.

"Well, it was an oversight, I'm sure," Carter said. "Ring them up at the hospital in the morning and inquire, will you, Polly?"

"Certainly, sir."

"Mrs. Bass was transferred from the emergency hospital in Nice, so they must have removed any jewelry there and passed it on to the people at the clinic. But normally they give you back your clothes and things when you leave, don't they?"

"I believe so, sir. That certainly is the procedure when one is in hospital at home."

"Check it out then, please. I don't imagine her other personal effects are important, but that was a five-carat diamond on her finger."

"Yes, sir."

I scooped everything back into the purse and set it aside. Polly and Yvonne both left. When we were alone, Carter picked up his glass of wine, the candlelight playing on his face. "Well, *à la tienne*," he said. "Cheers."

I sipped my wine.

"Like it?" he asked.

"It's good," I said. "Is it yours? Did you make it?"

"Yes."

I reflected. "Am I knowledgeable about wine?"

He grinned. "This gives us an interesting opportunity for an experiment," he said. "Does one lose one's technical knowledge with a case of amnesia? Evaluate the wine, Hillary."

I shrugged. "I said it was good. I like it. It seems fine to me."

"Spoken like a true viniculturist," he teased.

"I'm being honest."

"Hillary, that's not you talking. You're a wine snob. You like to think you know more than you do, but you can toss off the jargon and you're not afraid to put something down. You refuse to drink what I make, for example. The cellar is full of expensive labels just to please you."

I put down my glass, shaken.

"It wasn't a criticism. You're actually more pleasant as a neophyte."

"Thank you, I guess."

Carter seemed rather amused and I wondered if this was some sort of test. Maybe he didn't believe me. Maybe he thought I'd begun preparing my case for the police. The notion upset me.

I considered challenging him as I tasted the soup, but decided against it. The situation was complicated enough already. But then I recalled my conversation with Antonio about Polly. If Carter could test me, then why shouldn't I test him?

"Do you consider Polly competent?" I asked.

Carter put down his soup spoon and peered up the table at me. "Yes, I would say so. I don't think that business with the ring was an intentional mistake. The worst that can happen is that the clinic would have to have someone bring it by. Why? Do you have some doubts?"

"No, she strikes me as very efficient."

"Why did you ask, then?"

"It's hard to understand the motivation for her loyalty," I said. "I'm not a very pleasant person to work for."

"You shouldn't feel that way," he said.

"Would you trust her with a confidence?"

"One appropriate to her position, yes." He seemed perplexed. "I don't understand what you're getting at, Hillary."

I was either too subtle, or Carter wasn't about to tip his hand. Then, too, Antonio could have fabricated his story. Polly might be innocent, and I'd raised the issue for nothing. I deflected his question. "I'm just trying to get your insights," I explained.

111

Yvonne served the main course, some sort of braised chicken with a very aromatic sauce. I watched her solemn face as she moved around the table. Once she'd left the room, I asked Carter about Antonio, seeing what there was to be learned there. "Do you think he's trustworthy?" I asked.

"I wouldn't run around without your underwear on, if that's what you're getting at."

"What do you mean by that?"

"Antonio seemed to appreciate your proclivity for nude sunbathing."

"Good God," I said. I was so humiliated I couldn't look at Carter.

"This is France," he said. "People do sunbathe in the buff. And I'm no prude, but at times you can be a little cavalier, even for my taste. If you want to know the truth, Hillary, I think you went out of your way to titillate Antonio."

I felt sick. Now I understood the chauffeur's attitude toward me.

"Yvonne didn't approve," he went on. "I think primarily because she doesn't much care for Antonio. I didn't want dissension in the ranks, so I put a stop to it, mainly for her sake."

"What about for *your* sake?"

Carter smiled sardonically. "With all due respect, I had other things to be concerned about."

I wasn't sure if he meant other things concerning me, or other things in his life. But since so much dirty laundry had already been aired, I thought I might as well get it all out. "Jane said I had a fling with Bob, the guy who took care of the boat. Did you know about that?"

"I knew you liked him, and I assumed it wasn't only for his seamanship."

"You're incredibly open-minded."

112

"I'm a realist, Hillary. It's been some time since I've had any illusions about you."

I dabbed my lips with my napkin. "You are talking about Michel."

"Not the way you're thinking." He gave me a long, weary look. "Maybe this isn't a promising line of conversation. The meal hasn't gone too badly so far. I'd like us to get through it on reasonably friendly terms."

We finished the main course. Carter talked a bit about his wine making and the various improvements he'd made to the villa, but it was small talk. We were having cheese and fruit when it occurred to me that we were talking about mundane concerns, like any other married couple.

There must have been a note of wonder on my face, because he asked if I was feeling better.

"Yes, eating's helped."

"You aren't too tired?"

I shook my head.

"Are you sure? Dr. Lafon seemed to think it was important that you rest."

"I'm enjoying sharing this meal with you, if you can accept the honesty."

"I never reject honesty. Especially when it includes flattery." He rewarded me with a smile.

Yvonne brought us coffee and little cakes. I ate the strawberry off the top of the pastry, noticing that Carter watched me lick my lips. The awareness between us had grown very strong.

"What haven't we talked about yet?" he asked. "Do you have any questions that haven't been answered? Anything Polly couldn't tell you?"

"Yes, as a matter of fact. I know very little about you."

"Me?"

"That's right. All I know is that you're an investment banker, that you make wine, and that you spend most of your time in London."

"That pretty well sums me up."

"Tell me who you are, Carter, where you came from, about your past—everything."

He complied, giving me a modest summary of his life. He'd started his career in New York and formed a partnership with a British firm in London. When his partners suffered financial difficulties, he convinced my father to buy them out. Altogether he'd been in Europe for twelve years.

Carter was forty, ten years older than I. He'd been born and raised in Virginia, where his parents still resided. He'd attended Dartmouth and the Harvard Business School. In addition to the villa he had a house in Kensington, a flat off the avenue Bosquet in Paris, and a small farm outside Charlottesville, Virginia.

After completing his discourse, he leaned back and sipped his coffee. I watched him while Yvonne cleared the table.

Carter Bass was an attractive man with sophistication and class. He was well-spoken, educated. But mainly he appealed to me because I felt a connection with him, tortured though it was. We'd been dancing around each other since he'd appeared on the scene, our history at war with our more immediate and intangible feelings toward each other.

I could only assume that the allure he held for me had to do with the fact that he was both a stranger and my husband. My body, in effect, remembered Carter as my mind could not.

I picked up my coffee cup, but paused with it at my lips. Something had been troubling me for some time and I decided to blurt it out. "Do you have a mistress, Carter?"

He blinked. "What kind of a question is that?"

"A serious one. You know all about me, it's only fair I know about you."

"I don't have a mistress."

"Are you lonely?"

He smiled indulgently. "Hillary, we have an unspoken agreement. You don't ask and neither do I."

"Then you don't want to talk about it? I should mind my own business, is that what you mean?"

He contemplated me. "Maybe we should step out onto the terrace for some air—sort of clear our mental palate."

"If you like."

Carter came round and helped me up. "Could I interest you in a brandy?"

"I don't think so. I enjoyed the wine. That's really all I'd like."

He took my arm and we went through the salon and onto the terrace. He kept his hand on my elbow, though I was no longer shaky. His attention was flattering, and I decided I liked the changing chemistry between us, even though I had so many doubts.

It was a clear night and there were countless stars. I inhaled the pleasantly cool air and looked at my husband. Carter let his hand drop away.

"I miss this place," he said.

"Did I drive you away?"

"No, I've stayed away by choice."

"It's all so sad," I said, staring off down the dark valley. "I think we're a tragic pair. People shouldn't be as unhappy as we seem to be."

"You're talking about the past. Amnesiacs aren't supposed to do that, my dear."

I smiled at his teasing.

"I'm learning all about myself, about us, very quickly."

"I wonder if you're better off not knowing," he said, a trace of sadness in his voice.

"I can't run away from who I am," I replied.

"No, I suppose you can't."

"You'd like for me to change, though, wouldn't you?"

"What difference does it make? Your condition is temporary. It's probably better in the long run to treat you as the person I know you to be."

His words seemed cruel—or at least unkind—though what he was saying was not only obvious, it was also reasonable. Why should he assume the burden of my sins? I sighed and looked away.

"I'd like to believe in you, Hillary," he said. "But it isn't as simple as just giving you the benefit of the doubt."

"If I could erase the past, I would." My eyes shimmered. "But even if you were willing, *they* wouldn't let me."

Carter knew whom I was referring to. "They" were coming for me in the morning, though their purpose was still somewhat vague. "They" were the whole issue, it seemed to me —maybe the final arbiter of who I really was. My past not only defined me, it was my destiny.

"I don't think you should jump to any conclusions," he said. "Let's wait and see what they have to say."

He reached out and took my bare arms, seemingly to savor the feel of my skin. His hands were quite warm, and he gripped me firmly as he searched my eyes. I was sure then that he had brought me to the terrace to touch me, to connect with me physically. He had wanted to be close to me. And maybe I'd come along because I wanted to be close to him.

There were signs of desire in Carter's eyes. Heat. My heart picked up its beat when he lowered his mouth toward mine. His kiss was tender and it aroused me. I'd hungered for this—for the affirmation, for the affection—more than I knew. But still I wasn't prepared for it. I didn't expect to want him as much as I did.

I kissed Carter every bit as deeply as he kissed me. Then, at exactly the same moment, we pulled apart, retreating as swiftly as we'd come together. When I looked into his eyes I saw the reflection of my own feelings—the same doubt, distrust and fear that I myself felt.

And when he released me, I realized that the issues separating us remained unresolved. The past, like the future, was undeniable. The morning would come. It would come much too soon.

I SEARCHED CAR-
ter's face. He seemed mo-
mentarily unnerved, though
he quickly regained his
composure and eased away from
me. As he stared off into the night
I told myself the kiss didn't mean
anything. I'd surrendered to him
because I was vulnerable and
needy. I didn't even want to think
about the sexual implications.

Still, I did wonder about
Carter's motive for reaching out
to me. He had no excuse that I
could see—unless he'd been
overcome by compassion. Yet that
didn't seem quite right either. He
was too complex for such a simple
explanation. I could only assume
that he was as confused as I.

"I'm a little chilly," I said.
"If you don't mind, I'm going
back inside."

"Certainly. I'll take you in."

He walked me to the house.
The light inside seemed especially
bright, and when I glanced

at him, I could see he, too, was self-conscious and un-easy.

"Sure you wouldn't care for a cognac?" he asked.

"No thank you. I'm already tired. I think I'd better get some rest."

"Let me walk you upstairs. It won't do you any good to faint, then fall and hurt yourself."

We went up the staircase. Carter, ever the gentleman, took my arm. He released me when we got to the top. We went along the hallway and stopped at the door to my room. An uncomfortable moment followed. He seemed to want to say something. Finally he spoke.

"I'm sorry about what happened out on the terrace, Hillary. It wasn't fair for me to kiss you."

I appreciated the apology, even if it did seem a bit odd —a husband normally didn't express regret for kissing his wife. But then, there was nothing normal about our relationship. "You don't owe me any explanations," I said.

"Just so long as you don't feel I took advantage of the situation."

"I don't." I looked at him then, wondering if this would be a good time to ask the question that had been on my mind all day. I took a deep breath to fortify myself and said, "I have to ask you something, Carter. Something embarrassing."

"What?"

I lost my courage briefly before regaining it. "When was the last time we made love?"

A flicker of amusement touched his lips. "Why do you ask?"

"I want to know what it's been like between us, what your expectations are."

"I have no expectations." He studied me in a way that suggested he might be replaying our kiss over in his mind. "So, do you still want an answer to your question?"

119

"Yes," I said.

"It's been the better part of a year and a half since we've made love, except for once eight or nine months ago when we were both drunk and had been arguing. The sex was an extension of the argument more than it was lovemaking."

I lowered my eyes. "That's sad."

"Yes, it is."

I started to reach for the door handle, but Carter took my arm.

"Hillary, it's been three or four years since we've spent an evening as pleasant as this one. I can honestly say I enjoyed being with you."

I was touched by his seeming sincerity. "Thank you for saying that."

"Living without your memory must be very difficult," he said. "I can see how vulnerable you are, how dependent. I know you must be awfully scared about tomorrow, and I feel badly about that. You've been very brave. I want you to know I admire the way you've handled things."

"You say that, knowing tomorrow or the day after I could wake up and become the person I was?"

"I've decided the only fair thing to do is to deal with you as you are. The difficult question is how it's going to be once you regain your memory."

There was no way I could answer that. How could I speak for the Hillary Bass I did not know? I was a bit like Cinderella at the ball, aware the fantasy couldn't go on forever. But Carter was right, I'd had this dance. We'd connected and I was grateful for that.

"We have no choice but to wait and see," I said.

"Yes, I suppose that's right."

I extended my hand. "Good night, Carter."

The formality of the gesture amused him, but he took my hand, holding it for a moment before leaning over and

120

kissing my cheek. We exchanged a silent look, then I turned and retreated into my room.

—

When I awoke it was still dark. The first thing I thought of was Carter. Had I been dreaming about him or was I simply recalling the hours I'd lain awake thinking about our kiss and the conversation that followed?

My first day at Montfaucon had been an emotional roller coaster ride. Carter had given me a reprieve of sorts, yet in the back of my mind I knew I was on probation. I'd been shown kindness because Carter was decent, but our problems remained, not the least of which were the apparently widespread suspicions about my role in Michel Lambert's death.

By thinking about my situation, I could easily become desperate. In the middle of the night things always seemed worse than they were. Still, knowing that didn't make me any less anxious. I got up, resigned to being awake for a while.

As I passed by the window, I heard a sound coming from outside. I listened carefully. There were voices, the faint murmur of people talking on the terrace. I crept closer and peered out. Carter and Polly were sitting at the umbrella table. I was surprised to see them together.

I looked back at the face of the clock glowing on my bedstand. It was after midnight. I recalled Antonio's warning about Polly's disloyalty. Could she and Carter be conspiring?

I strained to hear them, but I couldn't. Neither could I see Polly's face, but I suspected it was full of love and admiration. Carter's attitude toward her was harder to envision. He appeared to be relaxed, his legs were casually crossed, his hand was resting on the table. A glass was in it. He took a sip. Cognac, probably.

Were they sharing a nightcap? Was Polly having the

drink I'd declined? There was no glass in her hand. Maybe she had happened by while he was sitting on the terrace, sipping his brandy. Maybe they were discussing accounts or the ring that hadn't made it home with me. Maybe I wasn't witnessing a clandestine meeting after all.

I leaned as close to the open window as I dared. I thought I heard Carter mention Antonio. Was he warning her about the chauffeur or simply discussing some administrative matter? My name passed his lips a couple of times. They were discussing me also. But in what regard?

I couldn't help but be suspicious. I doubted if they normally conducted business in the small hours. Something was going on. I wondered if that conversation I'd had with Carter had been a ruse, a smoke screen, to throw me off guard. I hated it that I couldn't hear what they were saying.

The tenor of their voices changed; the leg of a chair scraped on the stone of the patio. I peered out the window again. I heard Polly say, "Good night," but not the rest of her sentence. How had she addressed him? "Carter" perhaps? Or had it been "Mr. Bass?"

I watched Polly, still in the jogging suit, make her way to the house. Carter did not look after her for long. He sat down again and stared out over his domain, enveloped by the hush of night.

I peered down at him, buffeted by contradictory feelings. My suspicions were stronger than my sympathies. How could I know who to trust?

It was then I heard a soft purr and felt the brush of fur against my leg. I looked down and saw Poof in the darkness. I picked her up and clutched her to my breast.

She was my friend. Her love was unconditional. I kissed her head, feeling the comfort of familiarity. Poof meowed rather loudly and I shrank into the shadows, afraid that Carter might hear and look up, but he didn't. I stared down at him as I stroked my cat.

My feelings for Carter, I decided, were definitely confused, yet I also felt a very powerful curiosity. He fascinated me. I could understand why I'd married him, and yet the fact that he was my husband seemed totally bizarre.

Carter appeared so serene sitting there under the night sky. I wondered if he was thinking about me now. Or was Polly on his mind? Or tomorrow's meeting with the police?

Poof meowed again and I rubbed my cheek against her, my eyes still on Carter. Could I trust him? I didn't know. Maybe I was truly on my own. How ironic that was. Alone and dependent on a self I knew no better than the rest of this alien world.

After another minute or two Carter got up and went into the house. There was nothing more to see, so I carried my cat back to the bed and lay down.

I stared at the ceiling, stroking Poof, as I agonized. In time I managed to banish my troubles from my mind—the police, Michel Lambert, Polly, and Carter slowly, grudgingly, faded away, and sleep finally came.

—

I slept so deeply that in the morning Yvonne had to come into my room to awaken me.

"You sleep like the dead, madame."

It was an unfortunate choice of phrase, though I knew she didn't mean anything by it. I rubbed my eyes and sat up. I glanced around but Poof was nowhere to be seen. "Good morning," I said.

"Monsieur says you have only an hour before the police. He wanted you to have time for breakfast."

I quailed at the mention of the authorities. The moment of truth was not far off now. "Thank you, Yvonne."

The housekeeper gave me a thoughtful look. "It's nice you use this word, madame. Before you never bother."

"What word?"

"Thank you."

I was astounded. "Not even *merci?*"

"No, Madame Bass. Not often. Certainly not kindly."

"I'm sorry for that," I said. "I haven't been as considerate as I should. I'll try to do better."

The housekeeper shook her head. "I never see a blow on the head do so much good before. I hope you don't forget when the memory returns," she said.

"I hope not too."

When she'd gone I sat for a minute in my bed, testing my memory, but found it unchanged. I couldn't recall anything before awakening at the clinic. The events since then were vivid, however. I ran through them in my mind—my return to Montfaucon, Carter's arrival, our dinner and the kiss on the terrace. But there was Todd Halley too, and the pressing calls from the police. I needed no reminding of them.

I knew I'd drive myself crazy if I dwelled on the negative, so I got up, showered and washed my hair. Then, as I penciled my lips, Poof showed up, rubbing against my legs. I took her into my arms, wanting to remember something specific about her—an incident, a sensation. Nothing came to me.

Setting the cat down, I quickly put on a pale yellow silk day dress. It was quite short, shorter than seemed natural and comfortable, but I liked the color. It cheered me.

I went downstairs and found Carter out on the terrace. He was having a cup of coffee and reading his papers. By the light of day he seemed much more benign than he had at midnight, talking to Polly. He got up when he saw me approaching.

"Good morning, Hillary." He smiled.

"Bonjour," I said brightly as I approached the table.

He swept his eyes down me. "Your French coming back?"

"A few words, anyway."

He held a chair for me, then retreated to his place. "Yvonne said you were sound asleep when she went up to awaken you. Did you have a good night?"

"Fair. I feel better."

He folded his paper and set it aside. "Good." He seemed genuinely pleased. Carter was in a beautifully tailored stark white dress shirt with large gold cufflinks and navy slacks. The shirt was open at the neck. He looked fresh and sophisticated and very sexy. "Coffee?" he said, picking up the Limoges coffeepot.

"Please." I pushed my cup and saucer over so he could reach it. When he'd put the pot down, I said, "What were you and Polly babbling about in the middle of the night?"

"Did we disturb you?" he said smoothly.

"No, but it seemed a strange time to conduct business."

"It's been a while since I talked to her," he said with perfect composure. "She was up, so we went over some things together."

"Did you discuss me?"

Carter showed surprise for the first time. Then he smiled. "Yes, we discussed you."

I sipped my coffee. "And what did you say?"

He glanced up at my window. "Couldn't you hear?"

"No, you were talking very quietly, like someone who didn't want to be heard."

"Or like someone who didn't want to disturb the household," he said.

"Is that what it was?"

He grinned. "Yes."

I regarded him. "So, what did you have to talk about?"

"We mainly discussed household matters."

"I mean about me."

Carter gave me a bemused look. "Are you jealous or just nosey?"

I thought for a moment. "Nosey."

"Well," he said, "among other things I asked what she thought of you since your return."

"And she said?"

"That she's noted a definite change."

"I'm not the harridan I was, right?"

He nodded. "More or less."

I wondered if he was telling the truth. I was inclined to believe him, more because I wanted to than for any other reason.

I drank some more coffee, watching Carter over the rim of the cup. "Yvonne made the remark this morning that in the past I wasn't very polite. Am I really that bad?"

"You've never been particularly sensitive to other people's feelings."

"A bitch on wheels, in other words."

Carter's silence was the answer.

"How did you stand me when I had my period? I must have been unbearable."

His expression went blank. Then he looked embarrassed. I wondered if my remark had been that offensive.

"I didn't mean to embarrass you," I said, my cheeks coloring.

"I'm afraid there's a piece of information that somehow wasn't brought to your attention, Hillary. At the same time you had your abortion, you had a hysterectomy. You'd had some health problems and told the doctor to go ahead and take care of it all at once."

126

I was stunned, dazed. I couldn't speak. It was a most bizarre way to discover such a personal thing. I thought about my shower that morning. I hadn't noticed a scar, but then the surgery could have been done vaginally, requiring no outside incisions. I shivered. How odd, to remember that an operation could be performed that way, yet not to recall that I'd had one.

"I should have wondered why I didn't find any tampons in the bathroom," I said, trying to smile. In fact, I was feeling pain at the news.

Carter regarded me sadly.

"So," I said, trying to sound brave, "I'll never have any children."

"No."

"Funny I should give it two thoughts," I said, reaching for the bread in the basket. "It happened a long time ago."

He nodded, watching me.

"Did I mind?" I asked. "This didn't upset me, did it?"

"No, Hillary, it was what you wanted."

I recalled the dream I'd had about children, the strong positive feelings toward them. What could have happened? Was my conscience rebelling? Maybe I'd been at war with myself and only now, because of the amnesia, did I begin to realize that.

"Don't you believe me?" he asked, perhaps reading the skepticism on my face.

"I'm sure it's true." I broke off a piece of bread and put some butter and jam on my plate. Smearing a little of both on the bread, I stuffed it in my mouth. I glanced up at Carter as a tear rolled down my cheek.

"Then what's wrong?" he said.

"I guess there are some things about me I don't like very much," I replied, struggling to keep my emotions in check.

His eyes were glistening too. He managed a faint smile. I did as well.

"Good jam," I said, chewing. "Do we make this here on

127

the farm?" Tears streamed down both cheeks and I tried to wipe them away with the backs of my hands.

Carter took out his handkerchief and handed it to me, looking as though he might shed a few tears himself.

"No, darling," he said, "we don't. It's from the store."

I nodded and took another bite of bread, glancing out at the sunny countryside that rolled away so splendidly from our villa. I tried to appreciate what a lovely morning it was, but it was difficult. My heart felt as though it were breaking in two.

—

The detectives from Nice arrived while we were still at the breakfast table, though we'd finished eating. Carter told Yvonne to show them into the salon.

When she'd gone, he gave me a long questioning look, as if to ask if I was ready for the ordeal. Then he reached over and patted my hand.

"Are you okay?"

"I guess so."

"Unless there's something you know that I don't," he said, "I suppose the best policy is honesty."

"That will be easy in this case. I don't remember a thing."

"Then let's get this over with."

I took his arm as we walked across the terrace. My insides started to churn. I had no idea what the police would say or do.

The two men in our parlor were French to be sure, but cops the world over were the same. I couldn't say if it was the way they used their eyes, or the way they evaluated what they saw. Skepticism, paranoia, perhaps even a measure of self-righteousness must have been stamped into their characters when they first put on their badges. One look at them and I knew I was in for a rough time.

The senior man was named Debray. He was in his late forties, dark complected, on the short side, and stocky. His hair looked wet and was combed impeccably. His eyebrows were bushy and ran together over the bridge of his nose.

The other man, Lepecheur, was ten years younger and six inches taller. He had brownish blond hair and a neatly trimmed red beard. His bearing was not as magisterial as Debray's, but he did regard me more as a man does a woman. I shook hands with them both.

Carter motioned for the officers to be seated. They waited for me to slip into the wing-backed chair before sitting on the sofa. Carter stood beside me.

"Mrs. Bass," Debray began, "we are told your injuries have harmed your ability in the French language, so if you will bear with my English, we shall try to ask our questions and leave you to your affairs."

I smiled faintly at his misuse of the idiom. And I was greatly relieved that they were there only to ask questions. Or was this a trap, an attempt to lure me into complacency? "You speak English very well, Mr. Debray," I said. "I'm sure we'll understand each other."

"My thanks in advance, madame," he replied. The courtesies out of the way, his eyes hardened. "I understand you suffer from amnesia," he said.

"Yes. I can remember nothing before I awoke five days ago at the clinic in Toulon."

"I have spoken with your doctors, Mrs. Bass. They have confirmed this."

Carter spoke up. "Hillary was unconscious for three weeks, Monsieur Debray. This obviously is not something a person could fake."

129

"Indeed, monsieur, I do not suggest by my words that Mrs. Bass is a fake. I only wish to confirm what are the facts." He turned to me. "We must have the words from your mouth, madame. Then, when your memory returns, we can compare your new recollections with the old."

"I understand."

"From your own memory, what can you tell me about the day of the accident?"

"From my own memory, nothing."

"Nothing at all?"

"No."

Debray tapped his index finger against his chin and reflected. Lepecheur, who had not said a word, jotted a note on a small pad lying on his knee. "Madame, again from your memory, what can you tell me about Monsieur Michel Lambert?"

"Nothing from my memory. But when I saw his picture, I recognized him."

"Recognized?" He was having difficulty with the meaning of the word.

"*Il était familier, connu,*" Carter said.

"*Ah, oui. Merci, monsieur.*" Debray turned his gaze back on me. "Michel Lambert was, as you say, familiar to you. What caused this, in your opinion, Mrs. Bass?"

"Dr. Thirion thinks that Michel is a major factor in the cause of my amnesia."

"Because of the incident on the boat, do you mean?"

"Yes. The other thing that is familiar is the sailboat. When I saw a photograph of it, an association from the past was sparked."

"The accident involved Monsieur Lambert and it occurred on your boat. This is what you mean by association, *n'est-ce pas?*"

"Yes. I've looked at pictures of my husband, my parents, my friends, and there was no recognition whatsoever. Dr. Thirion thinks that because Michel is the only person familiar to me, he is the key to unlocking my memory."

"It seems, Mrs. Bass," Debray said, "that Monsieur Lambert is the key to many things."

"When my wife regains her memory," Carter said, "she'll confirm that what happened to Lambert was indeed an accident."

I glanced at Carter, surprised by his words. Why was he defending me? For the sake of his own pride, or for me?

"You may be right, monsieur," Debray said. "But we are not yet there, eh?" He cleared his throat. "If I may continue."

Carter shifted uneasily, but said nothing further.

"*Alors,*" Debray went on, "we have total amnesia, but we have a spark of familiarity in photographs of Monsieur Lambert and your sailboat."

"That's right."

"Is there nothing else you can add to enlighten us?"

"Well, I don't know if it's relevant, but I have a strong emotional reaction to the smell of roses. My perfume, Calèche, also does something for me when I smell it."

"Scents. You remember scents."

"My cat, Poof, is a comfort to me. She's familiar."

Debray glanced up at Carter. "What about monsieur?"

"No, not my husband. Nor my mother, either."

Again Debray pondered what I had just told him. Lepecheur scribbled on his pad. I had a feeling I was being set up for a momentous question, about the witnesses probably. My hands trembled as I clasped them together. Debray noticed.

"Mrs. Bass," the detective said, "has anything happened since you awoke that would give you an understanding of what might have occurred on the sailboat?"

I blanched. The dream I'd had of fighting with Michel instantly came to mind. But surely one wasn't obligated to share one's dreams with the police. Then it occurred to me that the detectives had spoken with Dr. Thirion. Did psychiatrists in France have the same obligations of confidentiality as in America? I didn't know.

"You are thinking, madame?" Debray said. The tiny smile at the corner of his mouth hinted at suspicion.

My heart began to thump. I sensed danger. The detectives waited. I took a deep breath, then made my decision. "No," I said. "There's nothing."

Lepecheur's pen scratched on his pad.

"Unfortunate," Debray said.

No one spoke. Both policemen stared at me.

I glanced up at Carter. My heart was still pounding. I took a deep breath, trying to calm myself. He put his hand on my shoulder. I pressed my cheek against his hand.

"Forgive me," the detective said, "for raising personal matters, but it seems, monsieur *et* madame, that you are on better terms than before the accident. We understood that you were estranged."

"I hardly see how that is relevant." Carter's voice had an edge.

"Mrs. Bass has amnesia," Debray said, his voice barely falling short of sarcasm, "but you, monsieur, have your memory, do you not?"

"Yes, of course."

"Perhaps we can draw on your recollections then, if you would be so kind."

"Sure. Ask me anything you want. But I was in London when the accident happened."

"Yes, we know this," the detective said. "Please, monsieur, did you know the victim, Michel Lambert?"

"Yes, unfortunately."

"Did you know him well?"

"Better than I'd have liked. I had no use for the bastard, but we talked on several occasions."

"Was one of these occasions not long before the unfortunate accident?"

"Yes," Carter said, glancing at me. "Lambert came to London to see me."

"Could you tell us what happened?"

I listened as Carter recounted the gist of their encounter. It was a relief to have the focus off me, even if I didn't like hearing again about Michel's demand that Carter divorce me. Unfortunately my reprieve didn't last long. Debray turned abruptly to me.

"And how did you feel about this meeting between Monsieur Lambert and your husband?"

I struggled to keep my voice calm. "Apparently I was upset by it. At least that is what I was told."

"By Monsieur Bass?"

"No," I said, "by my friend Lady Jane Nyland." I had a sinking feeling that I had just brought her into this mess unnecessarily.

"Ah," Debray said, gesturing for Lepecheur to make a note. He again engaged my eyes with the quiet look of a predator. "You say you were upset, Mrs. Bass. Do you mean very, very angry? Angry enough to kill?"

"Wait a minute," Carter said, interjecting again, "this is ridiculous. You can't make a case out of gossip. You're just fishing."

"Monsieur Bass," Debray said curtly, "I understand your desire to defend your wife, but in investigating a crime, motive is always of importance. For madame to be accused of murder she would need a motive to kill."

"If you have evidence of a crime, let's hear it," Carter shot back. "Otherwise, we don't need to talk about motive or anything else."

"Our obligation is to discover the truth, monsieur," Debray said pointedly.

"Well, I don't intend to have my wife subjected to un-founded charges and pointless innuendo."

Carter had gotten quite exercised. He was vigorously, even angrily, defending me. I was somewhat astounded by his fervor, even as it made me feel good. I reached up and took his hand. He squeezed my fingers.

Debray observed us. He rubbed his chin, unperturbed. "We have tried to be gentle, Mr. Bass, out of respect for ma-dame's recent illness. Perhaps brevity is as important as a gentle hand in this case. I will explain our dilemma."

"I wish you would," Carter said.

"*Tiens,*" Debray said. "We know that on the day of the accident Michel Lambert accompanied madame to the repair docks to pick up her sailboat. I am sorry to say, Mrs. Bass," he said, looking directly at me, "that three workers at the docks heard you argue. The disagreement turned violent. You were heard to tell Mr. Lambert that you wished to kill him."

"What?" Carter said incredulously.

"This is the account of the witnesses."

My heart went right to my throat. It was obvious what the police were doing. First they tried to find a motive, now they were bringing up the witnesses to establish my state of mind. My dream seemed even more terrifying.

"That doesn't prove anything, Debray," Carter said. "I threatened the bastard myself. People say a lot of things in the heat of anger."

"Yes, Mr. Bass, I am fully aware of this. Here, however, we have a situation where Mrs. Bass made her threat only a few

134

hours before monsieur was found dead, not far from madame's boat and with her still aboard."

"Nothing in that proves his death wasn't an accident."

Debray nodded solicitously. "To this point you are correct. But our investigation continues. We can also look forward to the day when Mrs. Bass regains her memory. It will be a most important day for us all."

I sat frozen. I felt as though slowly, gradually, I'd been hammered into the ground. Only Carter's touch kept me from breaking into tears. Both detectives were staring at me. My eyes flooded, despite my best efforts.

"Do you have any more questions, gentlemen?" Carter said. "If not, my wife needs to rest. She has been through more of an ordeal than any of us can fully appreciate."

"There is one small point I should like to clarify with you, Mr. Bass," Debray said.

"What's that?"

"You have told us about your meeting with Michel Lambert. Is it not the case that you also have met with Madame Claudine Lambert in recent months?"

Carter didn't say anything. I glanced up at him.

"Yes, I have," he finally said.

"Would you be so kind as to inform us of the purpose of your meetings?"

Carter scratched his ear. "Mrs. Lambert contacted me, actually. I saw her twice. Once in London. Once in Paris. The first time was in January, the second a month or so later."

"What did you discuss?"

"The affair," Carter said, shifting uncomfortably. "She was quite upset about it. Bitter. She had photographs of Hillary and Michel that a private detective had taken. She thought she was informing me of something I didn't already know."

"Was her intent to provoke you to take action?"

"I suppose so. She was looking for ways to hurt Michel.

She gave me some financial reports on his company, hoping, I guess, that I would somehow use them against him."

"Did you?"

"No, they were no good to me. I had no desire to ruin Lambert financially, even if I could."

Debray rubbed his chin again. "What *was* your intent, monsieur?"

Carter hesitated, glancing at me. "I didn't want to have to deal with it."

"Did you discuss Madame Lambert's visits with Mrs. Bass?"

"No."

"Why not?"

"There was no point. We had enough difficulties without adding that."

"I see." Debray seemed pleased to have embarrassed Carter.

No one said anything. Now I understood what this visit was really about. The police had suspicions, they had motive, they had intent, but not the essential piece of damning evidence they needed to hang me. Yet.

"Is there anything else?" Carter asked solemnly.

Debray turned to Lepecheur. The younger detective shook his head. *"Je n'ai pas de questions."*

"We have nothing more," Debray said.

"Well, I have a question for you," Carter said. "Yesterday my wife was verbally assaulted by a sleazeball reporter working for a couple of tabloids. He came in here asking about these witnesses of yours. I'd like to know where he got the information."

Debray lowered his eyes. *"Oui, monsieur,* we heard of this from the local officials. I can only say that this is a great embarrassment to us. We are investigating the matter."

"I hope you don't plan to conduct this investigation in the press."

"Of course not, monsieur."

"The incident proved a very trying one for Mrs. Bass," Carter said. "I'd be grateful if you could let me know just how this was leaked to the press."

"I will keep you informed, Mr. Bass," Debray said. Both policemen rose. Each shook my hand in turn.

I wanted to get up, but I had no strength. Carter led the men to the entry hall. I closed my eyes as a couple of tears seeped between my lids. I discreetly wiped them away. I heard the front door close, then Carter's footsteps as he returned.

He came to my chair and looked down at me. He didn't appear as shaken as I, but we both knew that matters were serious. He seemed ill at ease, as though he wasn't sure what to say.

"Thank you for taking my side, Carter. I'm grateful, but I don't understand why you did it."

"I didn't want them bullying you."

"Why?"

He gave me a look of consternation. "You're at a disadvantage right now and I feel sorry for you. Isn't that a good enough reason?"

"It didn't upset you when they said I was heard threatening Michel?"

"I threatened him myself."

"But you didn't threaten to kill him."

Carter didn't like my persistence. "No, but as I told the police, because you threatened him doesn't mean you actually did anything about it."

"How do you know? I myself can't say what I did that day."

"Hillary, whose side are you on?"

I bit my lip. "I'm scared. I don't know what happened and it frightens me."

Carter sat in the chair opposite me. He leaned toward me, staring intently into my eyes. "Until you get your memory back, no one will know what happened to Michel, so I suggest you leave it at that."

"But don't you want to know?" I said earnestly. "Aren't you concerned what kind of woman you married?"

"Of course. But all we can do is wait, Hillary. Until you recall what happened on the boat, there's nothing to be done."

I was appreciative of his attitude. Yet nothing had truly changed. Though he'd reached out to me in kindness, a chasm remained between us. I wondered if it would ever be breached.

"Tell me about Michel's wife," I said. "Does she hate me terribly? She must."

"There's no point in discussing her."

"Once my memory comes back I won't have any secrets from myself. I might as well learn all I can now."

"For what purpose? To torture yourself? Why wear a hair shirt?"

I thought at first Carter's motive was to spare me. Then it occurred to me he really didn't want to know the truth. He liked me better as I was now and probably wanted to preserve what he could. It was flattering to think that, but it hardly solved the problem. I couldn't run from who I truly was.

"Think of the lives affected by this," I said morosely. "It's not easy for me to put aside what I've done. I want to do something about it, yet I feel so helpless."

"There's nothing to be done," he said.

"I'm not so sure. As a minimum I could apologize to Michel's wife."

He grimaced. "That's ridiculous."

"I apologized to you. Why shouldn't I to her? Lord, I've ruined the woman's life."

"Michel did, not you."

"I want to see her, Carter. You know her. You can take me." I felt so anxious that I suddenly got to my feet. "Please do this for me," I begged. "Take me to see her."

Carter stared at me for a long moment, and when I began shaking with emotion, he stood up and took me into his arms. I was so relieved that my eyes flooded. He stroked my head as I quietly sobbed.

"God," he said, "this newfound virtue of yours has its down side. Things were at least less complicated before."

"Want me to change back?" I said, sniffling.

He laughed. "Good heavens, no!"

My chin on his shoulder, I smiled through my tears, feeling reassured by his affection. My eyes were still bleary, but when I glanced up I saw Polly. She was standing in the doorway. Realizing she'd been seen, she silently moved out of sight.

I

T TOOK A FEW hours, but Carter tracked down Claudine Lambert in a sanitarium outside Cannes. She'd checked in four days earlier, having suffered from nervous exhaustion. According to her son, she had taken Michel's death very hard.

The staff at the sanitarium was not encouraging when Carter asked about visitors. He again tried to dissuade me from seeing Claudine, but I was insistent, so he finally relented under the theory the drive would be pleasant and I could use an outing.

Antonio brought the Bentley around. Yvonne had prepared a cold lunch so that Carter and I could have a picnic along the coast. I didn't see Polly the rest of that morning, but Yvonne had seemed a bit warmer toward me. When I mentioned this to Carter, he said I shouldn't be surprised since I was so much more likable than before.

Antonio remained a source of embarrassment to me. I still wasn't sure what had gone on between us since his English wasn't good enough to convey the subtleties of what he meant when he'd claimed we'd been friends. But in spite of everything, there was no question that my greatest concern was Carter.

Our hot and cold relationship was very frustrating. I wanted a friend, someone in my corner who I could count on. That wasn't easy because little things kept cropping up—our business dealings, Polly's infatuation with him, his confrontation with Michel and his meetings with Claudine. Each was understandable, but added together they made me uneasy.

Antonio took us back along the route we'd followed from the clinic in Toulon. I studied the countryside, hoping to capture a sense of belonging, of familiarity. Nothing had changed.

"What do you think about Debray?" I asked Carter, hoping to get his take on the situation. "Was what happened this morning serious, or just a routine police matter?"

He turned from the window. "I think he's dead serious. The real question is if they have any evidence, or if it's posturing."

"Should we be concerned?"

"If they had what they needed, they'd have acted already. My guess is their case will turn on what you're able to tell them when you get your memory back."

"In other words, I'll have to hang myself?"

"You're the key, Hillary."

I watched the traffic on the twisting road as we headed east along the Mediterranean coast. "It's terrible, not knowing," I said. "If I was sure I was innocent, I wouldn't fear the truth. The way things are, I don't have anything to believe in, least of all myself."

141

"Let's assume it was an accident," he said softly. "There's nothing to be gained by thinking the worst." He turned to the window again and peered out, thinking. There was nothing he could say to reassure me, because he didn't know the truth himself.

After another half hour of driving, Carter had Antonio stop at a vista point overlooking the sea near a place called Val d'Esquières. The French were big at having picnics along the roadside, so we didn't bother to stray far from the car. Antonio stayed in the Bentley, though after he'd eaten he did get out to smoke a cigarette and watch the sea. From where Carter and I sat on our blanket, I could see Antonio leaning against the fender of the car, watching us.

I turned to face the blue-green waters of the Mediterranean. The air was warm and balmy and I could smell the tangy scent of Carter's cologne. It reminded me of our kiss. Though we didn't have that deep familiarity between spouses, I understood how I could have fallen in love with Carter Bass and married him. That gave me hope.

Yvonne had packed a half bottle of white Bordeaux to go with the ham, cheeses, bread, and fruit. As we drank, I enjoyed the sea air.

There were dozens of boats out, turning and dashing with the wind, it seemed, their sails ballooning over the gleaming water. We watched them for a while, taken by their dance.

"Am I actually able to sail like that?" I asked.

"Those are mostly small boats," he replied. "You handle the *Serenity* expertly all by yourself and she's a forty-five footer. You may not be world class, but you're a damned good sailor."

"Unless it's like riding a bicycle, I may have forgotten how to sail too. I haven't the slightest idea what one does on a boat."

142

"Actually, that isn't so surprising," Carter said. "If you were going to suppress anything, I would think it would be sailing, since that's at the heart of your trauma."

"Does that explain why I repressed you too?" I teased.

"No," he said, "I suspect you've repressed me just to be evenhanded."

"Sort of like forgetting the good with the bad?" I said, arching a brow.

"Something like that." He stared into my eyes a long time before looking away.

We watched the sailboats. They moved like swans gliding across a vast pond.

"You know," he said after a while, "this morning, when Debray was asking you about what happened on the *Serenity*, it occurred to me that we've been missing a bet."

"What's that?"

"Doesn't it make sense that if you visit the boat, maybe take her out for a while, it might spark something, some memory of the accident?"

I hadn't thought of that, though it seemed an obvious thing to do. "What you're talking about is returning to the scene of the crime," I said with a shiver.

"That is the objective, isn't it? To remember?"

The breeze swept my hair away from my face. I gazed out at the Mediterranean. Boats skimmed the water with such grace. The vista was so peaceful, yet Carter's suggestion struck terror in my heart. Apparently it showed.

He took my chin in his hand, rubbing my jaw with his thumb. "What's the matter, Hillary?"

I met Carter's eyes. "I'm not sure I'm ready to find out the truth," I said.

"Would you rather not go, then?"

"No, it's actually a good idea. Intellectually I understand that, though it frightens me." I chewed at my lip absently. "The boat's in Toulon now, is it?"

"Yes, at the marina. The police had it impounded in Nice, but once they'd completed their examination, they released it. You'd fired the B.N., so I had to find somebody else to bring it back to Toulon."

"What's a B.N.?"

Carter looked embarrassed. "Technically it stands for boat nigger, but nobody uses the term, just the initials."

I blinked. "I hate to sound prissy, but I think I'll find another term."

"Do as you wish." He paused. "You always have."

I reflected for a moment. "I have a theory about myself," I said.

"What's that?"

"I might have been a bitch at times, but I have a good side too. Jane liked me and I had other friends. And you married me, for heaven's sake. Maybe I repressed my better instincts and this experience has liberated whatever basic decency I have in me."

"You make it sound as if you were horrible all the time, Hillary. You weren't."

"Regardless, I'm determined to do better."

He reached over and pushed back my wind-blown hair, caressing my cheek. "You've made a good start."

I looked down, touched by his gesture. Once more we peered out to sea. The breeze was getting stiffer.

"Have you been out on the *Serenity* since the accident?" I asked.

Carter shook his head. "No, but I hired a new . . . an Englishwoman to look after her for you. Erica seems responsible and knowledgeable, but the decision as to whether you keep her or not is yours," Carter said.

"How did you find her?"

"Polly recommended her. She knows a number of Brits all up and down the Riviera."

That made me think. Why had Polly hesitated when I'd asked if she knew the woman? All she'd admitted was that they were acquainted.

"So," Carter said, "if you're willing to go out for a spin on the *Serenity*, I'd be glad to take you."

"You'd have to. I wouldn't know the first thing to do. Even the prospect of going aboard scares me."

Carter smiled. "You had a bad experience. But as you said, it's like riding a bike. If you fall, you get up and try again. Soon you'll be sailing like a pro. You'll see."

I watched him speak. I listened to his voice, observed his gentle manner. Carter was a kind and patient man. "You would have been a good father," I said. "You have a nice way."

Carter looked sad. He started putting the leftovers back in the basket. "So, what do you think," he said, clearly preferring the earlier topic, "want to give it a try tomorrow afternoon?"

"All right. Let's do it. I can't spend the rest of my life fearing the truth."

We returned to the car. Antonio dutifully held the door for us and we were soon back on our way to Cannes.

The sanitarium was in the hills above the city. To get to it we had to go up a long drive lined with Italian cypress trees. The main building, at the crest of the hill, had a tile roof and was Mediterranean in style. It was covered with flowering vines and appeared more residential than institutional. We stopped in the circular drive at the entrance.

"Maybe I should go in first and make your case for seeing Claudine," Carter said, putting his hand on mine.

It struck me as a curious suggestion and I briefly wondered if he was trying to keep anything from me. Then I decided he was merely being practical. "If you think that's best," I said.

Carter went inside and I was left with Antonio. I glanced at his eyes in the rearview mirror.

"You feel pretty good, eh, madame?" he said, taking immediate advantage of Carter's absence.

"Yes, I feel better."

"It is good you and Monsieur Bass are friends. He's pretty nice guy. More nice than Lambert," he went on. "I didn't like him so good."

Antonio seemed to be opinionated about the men in my life. Was that because I'd encouraged such talk in the past? I decided this was as good an opportunity as any to confront the issue head-on.

"Antonio, you described us as friends when we spoke the other day. What exactly did you mean?"

He turned around, smiling his boyish smile. "You like men, Madame Bass, *n'est-ce pas?* I am a man."

"That doesn't answer my question." I took a deep breath, knowing I had to be more direct. But how did you ask a man whether or not you'd had sex with him? It was so embarrassing. Finally, I just spit it out. "What I want to know is, have we ever slept together?"

Antonio grinned. "I must be honest. No, madame. We didn't."

"Thank God," I muttered under my breath. It was bad enough knowing I'd slept with both Michel and the boatman, Bob. But they, at least, were not around. It would have been mortifying to face Antonio every day, knowing he, too, had shared my favors.

"But if you ask do you like me," Antonio went on, "the answer is yes." He smiled confidently. "There is no harm in our friendship, *n'est-ce pas?*"

146

I was determined to sound firm. "There is no harm in being courteous to each other. But you might as well know that things are going to be different from now on. Completely different."

"What are you saying, madame?"

"I want you to do your job and keep it to that."

"Tell me, please," he said. "I say something to make you mad? We used to laugh. You tell me dirty jokes, I tell you dirty jokes. What's so bad about that?"

"Maybe nothing, but I'm not the same person anymore and you ought to know it. So, rather than have you misunderstand, I'm telling you very honestly and directly how I feel. I can't be more fair than that."

"It's the English," he said sullenly. "You talked to her, eh?"

"No, I didn't discuss you with Polly. But if you want to keep your job, you'll forget the past."

He stared at me, his expression slowly turning compliant. "*Oui, madame.* I don't want for me what happened to Bob."

"The best way then is to look after yourself, Antonio. Do you understand?"

He stared at me, then shrugged. "*Bien madame. Comme vous voulez.*" As you wish.

He'd made an attempt to sound resigned but I sensed he was unconvinced. Maybe it was his ego, maybe my warning was an idle gesture, but at least I'd done my duty. I could see, though, that reforming my life was not going to be easy.

Ten minutes went by without a sign of Carter, then fifteen. I decided there was no good reason to sit there with Antonio staring at me, so I got out of the car and went up the half-dozen steps to the front door. Girding myself, I went inside.

A receptionist sat behind a large antique desk graced with a crystal vase of summer flowers. She looked up as I walked toward her. There were Oriental carpets scattered across the marble floor. It seemed more a sophisticated pension than a sanitarium. I engaged the woman's eyes, smiling casually.

"*Bonjour, madame,*" she said, lifting her brows as if to ask my business.

"My husband, Carter Bass, came in a few minutes ago. I want to join him. Can you tell me where he is?"

"In the garden with Madame Lambert," she said, pointing toward the corridor behind her.

"Thank you." I headed for the corridor that led to a sort of sitting room-solarium that spanned the rear of the building. A number of French doors opened onto a lovely garden. Two elderly women attended by nurses were seated at the far end of the room, but it was otherwise deserted.

I peered out the wall of glass at the grounds. A man in a robe and pajamas was strolling with an orderly. Standing at the back of the garden was Carter with a dark-headed woman. My pulse quickened as I stared at my lover's wife.

Claudine was slender and petite. Despite the fact that she was dressed casually, she had a certain elegance and panache. She appeared to be in her late forties and obviously took good care of herself. Her hair and make-up were perfect. Evidently she was the kind of woman who devoted considerable time and resources to her appearance.

She and Carter were having a rather intense discussion. I saw emotion on her face. He seemed insistent and she was being adamant in her resistance to whatever it was he was saying.

I watched them for several minutes, marveling at their passion, until it occurred to me that I was watching the spouses of married lovers sharing a common humiliation. They both had every reason to hate me—the sole surviving wrongdoer.

I'd put Carter in a difficult situation by making him bring me here. Seeing him with Claudine brought home that fact. I felt so guilty about my selfishness, my callousness, that I was practically in tears by the time their conversation came to an

148

end. I wanted to turn away, run back to the car, but I made myself stay.

Carter offered Claudine his hand. She hesitated a moment before taking it. Then he turned and came back along the gravel path toward the building. As he opened the door, he saw me.

"Oh, Hillary," he said, surprised, "did you get tired of waiting?"

"Yes."

"I'm sorry to have taken so long. Claudine's doctor let me speak to her, but she was adamant about not wanting to see you."

"I noticed she was quite upset."

"Then you saw."

"Yes."

"I pleaded your case," he said, "but Claudine is very emotional about Michel."

I glanced out the window. Claudine Lambert was still sitting on the bench, unaware of my proximity. I could see her in profile. Her hands were clasped. She seemed unhappy, tense, tormented. Just looking at her made me feel guilty. "She bitterly hates me, doesn't she?"

"She doesn't want to see you. Let's leave it at that."

I wasn't prepared to walk away and forget things, though. I stared at her, agonizing. "What can I do?" I murmured.

"Nothing. Absolutely nothing."

"Carter, I feel terrible, wretched. Look at her. How upset she is. Even if Michel died by accident, this is still all my fault. I've ruined her life."

"She's bitter now, but she'll survive," he said.

"I can't just walk away as though nothing happened. I have to do something!"

Carter took me by the shoulders and made me look into

149

his eyes. "Hillary, you aren't helping matters by talking this way. What's done is done. You must look to the future."

"What about you? How do you feel?"

He gave me a gentle shake as if to emphasize his feelings. "I tried to impress upon Claudine that you're a changed person. She didn't care. She didn't want to give you the satisfaction of an apology, so we have to leave it at that. My happiness doesn't turn on her feelings and you can't let yours either."

He was speaking with genuine passion, making the case more adamantly than he had before. I was deeply touched.

"Do you really feel that way, Carter?"

His fingers tightened on me. His expression was serious, almost grim. "I've been wrestling with this for days, confused about who you are, why you're acting this way. One minute I tell myself you're too good to be true, the next I'm convinced you're totally sincere."

I couldn't help myself. I began to cry.

"Coming here has convinced me to accept you as you are, Hillary. If you stay like this, so much the better. If not, then we'll deal with it then. I can't worry about what might happen, and you shouldn't either."

My body shook and Carter gathered me close. I stared over his shoulder at the woman I'd hurt. She seemed a part of the statuary. I'd failed in my attempt to apologize, but some good had come of the visit. Carter and I had finally come to terms with each other.

He took my hand and led me toward the reception area. I wanted to freshen up before returning to the car and asked the receptionist to direct me to the ladies' room. By the time I returned, I'd regained my composure.

Carter was in better spirits too. He smiled as we stepped outside. Antonio was across the drive, seated on a bench and talking to a little blond nurse. The girl was giggling.

"Our chauffeur seems to have scored again," Carter quipped as we went down the stairs.

"Does he usually?" I asked.

"He's been known to fail," Carter said, "but he definitely has a way with women."

Antonio quickly hurried to the car. Carter had already helped me in back.

"*Je suis désolé, monsieur,*" he said, slipping into the driver's seat.

"*Vous avez eu assez de temps pour obtenir son numéro de téléphone?*" Carter said with a laugh.

"*Aucune importance, monsieur. Il y a assez des jolies filles à Toulon.*"

"What was that about?" I whispered as we started down the drive.

"I asked if he'd had time to get the girl's telephone number," Carter said under his breath.

"And what did he reply?"

"He said it didn't matter. There were enough pretty girls in Toulon."

I don't know if Antonio heard us, but he must have suspected what we were talking about. In any case, he beamed at me in the rearview mirror.

⁓

Carter suggested we dine in Cannes, but I was already tired so we decided to go directly home. If I felt up to it later, we could have dinner at one of the country inns near Montfaucon.

We didn't talk much on the drive back. I searched for safe topics, nothing too personal, that could be discussed in front of Antonio. I asked Carter about his parents and he told

151

me his father was a Virginia gentleman from the old school, a farmer and lawyer in the tradition of Jefferson. His mother was a beauty from an old-line Maryland family, an intelligent woman who was passionate about culture and education. Carter proudly proclaimed himself to be a mix-breed Yankee and Confederate.

"An identity crisis in the cradle?" I teased.

"Actually my parents got along quite well by never discussing the politics of North and South."

"It must have been difficult not to take the occasional swipe at each other."

"They have tremendous respect for each other. Something I've always admired and envied."

He didn't come right out and say it, but I assumed he was alluding to our shortcomings as a couple. I had failed my husband in so many ways. "Will you ever go home to the States?" I asked.

"One day, maybe," he replied. "I'm not quite an expatriate, and probably never will be. But I enjoy Europe."

"Why?"

"I like the life, even though I recognize that it will never truly be home."

"Would having children have made a difference?"

His expression indicated quiet disapproval. An admonishing response probably crossed his mind, but he settled on, "Maybe."

After a few minutes of silence I asked what his mother thought of me.

"She liked it that you were from the North. Mother thought that Southern belles were too frivolous for me. She wanted me to marry a sensible practical woman, especially since I'm not very traditional."

"Is that a tactful way of saying she didn't like me?"

"You never established any particular rapport."

I didn't have to ask what that meant. "Do we ever see them?"

"I get to the States fairly regularly. Once or twice a year I try to pop down to Virginia to spend a few days with them."

"Do they ever come to Europe?"

"Not since my father's health began to fail. They've stayed pretty close to home for the better part of five years."

I looked out at the sea where a lone sailboat plied the waters. "I think I'd like to get to know your parents better. Can I go with you the next time you have to go to the States?"

Carter was a bit surprised, but also pleased. "If you wish."

"I'd like to go see where I grew up too."

"You sound like you don't expect to regain your memory anytime soon."

"I've stopped wanting to regain it, to be honest. Despite all my problems, the present somehow seems more hospitable than the past."

"I'll tell you a secret, Hillary, I wouldn't mind if you never remembered." He rubbed the back of my knuckles with his thumb. Then he pulled my hand to his lips and kissed it.

The gesture was a simple act of affection, but it sent shivers down my spine. I looked into Carter's eyes and felt more strongly than ever that he truly was my husband.

This was the happiest I had been yet, though I was acutely aware that Carter and I were indulging ourselves. We might be willing to block out the past forever, but that didn't mean the rest of the world would. There was a time bomb ticking inside my head. When my memory returned, the bomb would go off and God only knew what would happen then.

After we got home I rested for an hour or so, enough to be refreshed. Poof, my steadfast companion, joined me on the bed and I fell asleep with her curled up against me. Before I'd gone upstairs Carter and I had discussed our plans for the evening. There was an inn on the outskirts of Montfaucon where we'd regularly dined in years past, and that was where we decided to go.

After I awoke, I changed and went downstairs. Polly was seated in a corner of the salon, quietly reading. Yvonne had taken the evening off and Antonio had left for town. According to Polly, Carter was in the orchard, inspecting the trees with the gardener who considered himself an arboriculturist.

I hadn't really spoken to my secretary since that first day, so I decided to take the opportunity to get a feel for her state of mind. I apologized for interrupting her as I pulled up a footstool. She closed her book and immediately offered me her chair, but I insisted she stay put.

"I may not have been very egalitarian before," I said, "but I am now."

Polly regarded me with a trace of skepticism. My past, I could see, refused to die easily.

"Mrs. Bass, I do have some information to pass along, if I may change the subject. I spoke with the administration at the clinic in Toulon this morning. They have no record of having received your personal effects from the hospital in Nice. They're sure it was a simple oversight and they're querying Nice about it. If they don't have news before the weekend, they promised to by the first of the week."

"Does Carter know?"

"Yes, ma'am. We discussed the matter while you were napping."

"He'll be more upset than I. I have no recollection of the ring, so I can't really miss it."

"It was quite lovely."

An uncomfortable silence hung between us. There were some things I needed to know, questions I wanted to ask, though Polly, I'd discovered, was not one to speak her mind readily. But I was determined to find out what I could about Antonio, so I decided to press her.

"You know," I said, "figuring out the chemistry in the household has been more difficult than I expected."

She looked at me curiously. "I'm not sure I understand, ma'am."

"I guess there's always a certain amount of intrigue and infighting in any group of people, but I gather there might be some hard feelings between you and Antonio."

Polly's brows rose slightly. "I don't know if I would describe them as hard feelings, Mrs. Bass."

"How would you describe your relationship?"

She was uncomfortable, but I'd backed her into a corner. "I don't believe either of us has a high personal regard for the other," she admitted.

"Why is that?"

"I can't really say, unless it's simply because I'm English. Some of the French have a thing about us, though not so much as for the Germans."

"You think that's all it is."

"I believe so, yes."

I nodded, thinking.

"If you don't mind me asking, Mrs. Bass, why are you concerned?"

"I want things to run smoothly. I don't want there to be back stabbing or ill feeling."

"As far as I'm concerned," Polly said, "Antonio and I get along well enough. He does his job and I do mine. I shouldn't think you'd have any reason for concern. Not as regards me anyway."

She was, I could see, adept at the political requirements

155

of her position. I considered asking who she'd met in Toulon the morning she picked me up at the clinic, but I decided that would only exacerbate the tension between her and Antonio since the information had to have come from him. "I'm sure I don't," I said. "But if there's anything you feel you need to discuss with me, I hope you won't hesitate."

"No, ma'am."

Just then I spied Carter on the terrace. He was with the gardener, a wizened old man in French blue work clothes and a few days' growth of beard frosting his jaw. They were discussing the potted plants. I watched Carter playing the role of patron. Polly turned and glanced out the window as well.

"Has Mr. Bass been behaving as he usually does when he visits?" I asked her.

She didn't appear happy with the question. "No, ma'am. He seems more relaxed."

Polly didn't add "and happier," but I gleaned the thought anyway. I was sorry to take pleasure in her disappointment, but my observation did confirm one thing—Antonio hadn't exaggerated when he'd said Polly was in love with my husband.

Where it was all leading I could hardly tell, but I was developing a sense of hope. That was good. I badly needed something I could cling to.

I rose from the footstool. "If you'll excuse me," I said to Polly, "I think I'll go out on the terrace."

I didn't gloat. I didn't smile triumphantly. I simply slipped out the French doors to join Carter. I could do nothing about Polly's hurt or resentment. She would have to find her own peace of mind. I had enough to worry about already.

I LEARNED WE KEPT a Jaguar at Montfaucon, though it was rarely driven because I apparently preferred to let Antonio chauffeur me around in the Bentley. But it was his night off, and Carter wanted to drive anyway, so we got into the Jag for the short trip down the hill to the village.

Each time I'd passed through Montfaucon it had been going to or from someplace else. I really hadn't seen much of the village, so Carter suggested we tour it on foot before strolling out to the inn where we planned to dine.

We parked in the tiny square in front of the church. The building was small, not much bigger than a chapel. When we ventured inside I saw that the interior was lit by devotional candles and the rays of the late afternoon sun coming in the stained-glass window. Apart from us, the church was deserted.

"It's sweet," I said.

"Sweet?"

"Like a grandmother's jewel box, I mean."

"You didn't used to like it. You said it was rather pedestrian. The Sacré Coeur was more your style."

Carter's words stung. Even if he hadn't intended it, he'd managed to disillusion me once again. It was becoming routine. "Well, I like it now. It makes me feel kind of spiritual."

Carter had long since stopped regarding me skeptically every time I said something that didn't square with the past. Even so, a sardonic smile flickered across his lips. "Come on, Mother Theresa," he said, "let's go eat. If you want to test your latent spirituality, I'll bring you to church next Sunday."

He took my hand and we strolled through the village. The few people we encountered greeted us, some more politely than others, almost all with a degree of surprise.

"How are we regarded by the locals?" I asked.

"As the Americans who own the big estate on the hill. In other words, we're tolerated. I try to do what I can for the community. I hire locally and make generous donations to local events and causes, and so forth. Like most things, we succeed some and fail some."

"You really mean you succeed and I fail, don't you?"

Carter turned to me. "Why do you say that?"

"Just a hunch," I said.

Carter squeezed my hand. An old man on a bicycle said, *"Bonsoir,"* as he peddled past. There were cooking smells coming from houses on the narrow street. A few people were sitting on their stoops, nodding and muttering a greeting as we passed.

"Bonsoir, Monsieur Bass," a smiling middle-aged woman called from her window over a flower box filled with red geraniums.

"Bonsoir, madame," he said with evident pleasure. The

woman was only a few feet from us and Carter stepped over, shaking her hand through the window. *"Et votre fils, ça va?"*

"Très bien, merci, monsieur. Grâce à vous, n'est-ce pas? Il va revenir la semaine prochaine. Tout le monde l'attend, surtout moi, sa maman. Je suis très contente. Merci." The woman was beaming at Carter. She turned to me. *"Bonsoir, madame. Très contente de vous voir."*

I smiled at her and nodded. She was genuinely happy about something. We bid her good-bye and moved on up the street.

"What was that about?" I asked.

"She's a widow and has a son who's a musical prodigy. He'd outgrown his teachers and a fund was established to send him to Paris to study. I put in about half the money needed."

"You are indeed lord of the manor, aren't you?" I said admiringly.

"My old man made a hobby of looking after the needy children in the neighborhood. I guess a little of it rubbed off on me."

I squeezed Carter's arm, feeling pride at his goodness.

The inn was a few hundred yards beyond the last house in the village, close enough that we could walk to it easily. Strolling along the lane, I felt a joy that must have been very rare in my life.

Dusk had fallen and lights were beginning to show in the farmhouses dotting the hillsides. Somewhere on the slopes sheep brayed. Across the valley a dog barked. I inhaled. The air was pungent with the dewy scent of hay. I gazed up at the sky. The quality of light was remarkable. We heard a whippoorwill calling from the hedgerow, but mostly there was stillness. The tranquility and timelessness of the moment moved me, and sharing it with Carter added a poignancy that made it very, very special.

"Was it like this between us when we were first married?" I asked, unable not to say what was on my mind.

A *vélo* putted up behind us. We stepped to the side of the lane to let it pass, the two boys riding it nodding as they went by. Carter took my hand as we resumed our walk, my question obviously still churning in his mind.

"Do you imagine it was this way?" he asked.

"Yes."

"I wish I could say it was, Hillary, but it really wasn't."

"That's too bad."

"Isn't it good enough that it's this way now?"

I smiled sadly. "I guess I don't trust this empty brain of mine."

"Don't think of it as empty," Carter said. "Think of it as purged."

The suggestion had a certain appeal.

We continued on until we came to the inn, once an old farmhouse. The original parlor and dining room had been combined into a single room, though it was still only large enough for eight tables.

The proprietress, Madame Coupat, was a heavyset woman with prematurely gray hair that hung in loose strands about her face. She pushed the hair off her brow with pudgy fingers as she greeted us. Her friendliness seemed genuine.

We were shown to a table next to an open window at the far end of the room. As Carter seated me I was immediately aware of the smell of roses.

I leaned over the sill. There was a small rose garden just outside the window. Judging by Carter's smile, I decided the choice of table had been calculated.

Madame Coupat said something to Carter about the wine, then disappeared. I inhaled the fragrant air, letting my eyes close as that same wonderful, but still incomprehensible emotion went through me. Then I looked at Carter.

160

"It's no accident, this window and the roses, is it?"

"Nope." There was a twinkle in his eyes.

I glanced around. Two other tables were occupied, both on the far side of the room. Seated at one was a fat man in a short-sleeved white shirt. He was reading a folded-up newspaper as a cigarette dangled from his lip. The other table was occupied by an elderly, prosperous-looking couple. They glanced our way and nodded. Carter said, *"Bonsoir."*

The restaurant was not elegant. Tables and chairs were mismatched. The wallpaper was flowered and overly ornate, the pictures were old, yellowish-brown prints with little to commend them but age. The sole distinctive piece in the room was a large mahogany sideboard against the rear wall. It was covered with plates of cheese, bowls of fruit, pastries, and a sheaf of baguettes.

"Your typical country inn," Carter said when I'd completed my visual inspection.

"I like it."

"I thought you might enjoy the rose garden. Madame Coupat is very proud of it. When I telephoned I told her you'd come to adore roses and we had to have the table by this window. I've already selected the food and wine. I hope that's okay."

"Sure. I'm the neophyte."

The proprietress returned with a bottle of wine. "And how is your health, madame?" she asked as she poured. "We were so sorry to learn of your accident."

"I'm much better, thank you. Getting stronger every day."

"C'est bien." That's good. "The entire village wishes you a speedy recovery."

"Thank you."

The dinner was superb. Carter had ordered lamb, saying I was especially fond of the way the chef prepared it at Madame

161

Coupat's. It was absolutely delicious, but it was Carter's company that made everything truly special.

After we'd had coffee and dessert, the proprietress took us out to her garden. We sat in lawn chairs by the roses, a low table between us, to have a glass of cognac. The night was full of sounds of the country—crickets, frogs, the faint clucking of chickens coming from somewhere back in the trees. Madame Coupat had left a short fat beeswax candle on the table. The light from it accentuated Carter's rugged good looks. We pondered each other as we sipped brandy.

"Is Montfaucon beginning to feel like home?" he asked.

"As much as it can to a person with amnesia."

"Things will change soon, Hillary. Visiting the boat might be just the thing that's needed."

I shuddered at the thought. The sailboat and my lover were at the heart of all that was bad and wrong in my life. And I was frightened of learning the truth. Yet I had to face it. I had to go on.

"Why do you look that way?" Carter asked.

"How do I look?"

"Worried."

"I don't know," I said dreamily. "Sometimes the past starts gnawing at me, playing games with my mind. I guess my subconscious is testing me, asking if I'm ready to hear the truth."

"Are you?"

"I don't know."

An old Deux Chevaux rattled past, its yellow headlights barely illuminating the way. When the sound finally died in the distance I looked at the roses, wanting to think about something else.

On the nearest bush was a bud on a long stem. I reached out and pulled it to me. Leaning over, I was able to sniff it.

"I wish I understood what it is about roses that affects me so."

"It's strange," Carter said, "especially considering they never particularly meant anything to you before."

I wanted to think the significance was somehow connected with Carter, but deep down I knew it wasn't. It went right to my core. I just didn't understand how or why I was so strongly affected.

After we finished our brandy, Carter settled the bill and we walked back to the village. The sounds of television sets had replaced the cooking smells. A few people were still sitting on their stoops, conversing or smoking. Words of greeting were exchanged. We moved quietly along the cobbled street, arm in arm.

The Jaguar was waiting in the deep shadow of the trees lining the square. Carter opened the passenger door for me, but before climbing in, I turned to face him. I reached up and took his cleanly shaven cheeks in my hands.

"This has been a lovely evening," I said. "One I'll always remember."

"I hope so."

I searched his eyes, barely able to read his expression. "If we let things take their natural course, we might end up in bed together tonight," I said hesitantly.

"Wouldn't you like that?"

"Yes, I would . . ."

"I hear qualification in your voice," he said.

I touched his lower lip with the tip of my finger, thinking about the last time we'd kissed. "I'm not sure that what I want and what's best for me are the same thing."

"Oh?"

"What I mean is, when I'm struggling so hard to sort things out, I'm not sure another complication is a good idea."

He smiled. "I've heard lovemaking called many things, but complication is a new one."

"Sex complicates any relationship."

"Yes, I suppose that's true." He brushed a strand of hair off my temple. "Even the relationship of a couple who've been married for eight years."

I pulled his face down to mine and kissed him. Carter's lips were soft and sensuous. I felt his emotion. I felt my own.

I gave myself up to the kiss, relaxing into his embrace, opening my mouth when Carter's tongue darted past my lips. I reveled in the feel of his mouth exploring mine, taking, giving, drawing me in deeper. The intensity of my feelings, the depth of my response, surprised me, catching me off guard.

Carter's fingers probed my skin through my dress. His thighs pressed against mine and I could feel the heat of his body.

Our mouths parted, and I pressed my face into his neck, filling my lungs with his scent, taking him in, any way I could. My heart pounded in my ears. "God," I murmured. "Are you sure we're really married?"

"A churchyard is not the most likely place to prove there's still a spark, is it?"

"A spark?"

Carter brushed his lips over mine. "This may be a complication," he said, "but as far as I'm concerned it's a damned nice one." He stroked my head and sighed. "I wish you wouldn't fight me, Hillary."

My eyes filled at his words. I was torn. I wanted him, but I was afraid of something—perhaps what I would discover.

"I want you in my bed," he whispered. "I want to make love with you."

"Oh, don't tempt me, Carter. Please."

"I'm not sure what you're afraid of, darling," he said, kissing my hair. "Isn't my love reassuring?"

I pulled back so I could see his face, at least what the

164

faint light in the square would allow. "The future frightens me," I said.

"Then don't dwell on it."

"Whenever I think about the *Serenity*, I get nervous. I sense something dramatic is going to happen tomorrow."

"But it won't change things, Hillary, if we don't let it."

"I'd like to believe that, but I can't."

Carter peered up at the dark boughs overhead. He was exasperated. "Why is it so impossible to argue with a woman?"

I laughed. "Because the things we say are built on a deeper truth than simple fact."

He pressed his cheek against my forehead. "That must be it."

I smiled, liking my husband very much.

"What if nothing happens tomorrow?" he said. "What if you go aboard and there's no catharsis, nothing?"

"Then I guess I'll just have to keep looking for the key."

He studied me critically. The light was good enough to see that. "I think at that point, we should turn to masculine logic."

"Meaning?"

"We accept the fact that our fears serve no constructive purpose. We concentrate on the good, the positive. We think about what we feel, not what it means."

"In other words, we make love."

Carter nodded, a wide grin on his face. "Now that's logic."

"You're incorrigible."

He gave me a final hug. "Come on, let's go home, even if it has to be to separate beds."

I took hold of his arms. "You aren't mad, are you?"

"I'm trying hard to be understanding."

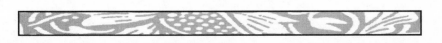

"You aren't answering my question."

He reflected a moment. "I'm not angry. Just frustrated. For years I had little feeling for you, and now I find I care very much."

I searched his eyes, my heart swelling. Then I kissed him. "It makes me happy to hear you say that," I whispered, holding him.

"That's what I want for you, Hillary," he said. "Happiness. It's what I want for us both."

THE NEXT MORN-
ing I awoke in good
spirits, feeling almost
joyful. Carter and I had
shared a pleasant evening—
maybe even a wonderful evening
—and all those good feelings
were still fresh in my mind. I lay
for a moment in my bed, savoring
the recollection of his kiss, wondering if we'd passed a turning
point.

When we'd gotten home the
night before I told Carter I
wanted to retire immediately. I
needed some distance from him to
sort out my feelings. Assuring me
he understood, he walked me to
my room, taking me into his arms
a final time before saying good-
night. Then he'd kissed me so
lovingly, so temptingly, that I
nearly lost my resolve.

But what about this morn-
ing? I wondered. Would the feelings we'd shared carry over to the

light of day? I didn't know. Carter was already behind closed doors, at work in his study. I was disappointed because I'd at least hoped to have coffee with him.

I resigned myself to eating breakfast alone. Yvonne served me a soft-boiled egg, telling me I liked them cooked that way. I accepted that piece of intelligence with more credulity than usual. The thought of a soft-boiled egg actually appealed to me. Perhaps my taste in food hadn't changed as much as I'd thought.

Yvonne was pouring my second cup of coffee when a vehicle entered the courtyard. She left to see who it was. Several minutes passed before she returned.

"It was a courier with a large envelope for Monsieur Bass," she explained, coming back to the dining room. "I gave it to him."

"He's still hard at work then?"

"Yes, madame. He makes the negotiations on the telephone all morning. He says to tell this to you. After lunch he will go with you to the marina in Toulon."

I invited Yvonne to join me at the table, a suggestion she received with surprise. But she soon got into the spirit of the moment and began gossiping. I learned that Antonio had driven Polly into Toulon to take care of some banking. I tried to get a sense of her feelings toward Polly, but she was very discreet. Yvonne apparently had learned the importance of avoiding internecine conflicts.

After she returned to the kitchen, I walked around the house, whiling away my time, examining knickknacks and paintings and books. Poof followed me for a while, but eventually lost interest in my small adventure. I passed Carter's office a couple of times and was tempted to stick my head in and say hello, but I resisted.

The day had started out hot so I'd put on a pair of

shorts and a thin cotton shirt that I'd tied at my midriff. It occurred to me that I might have unconsciously dressed that way to be enticing. That worried me. Was my libertine nature resurfacing? I hoped not. I told myself it was harmless. Carter was, after all, my husband, and I was simply starting to regard him as such.

When I ran out of things to inspect, I dropped into a chair in the salon. Like it or not, I couldn't stop thinking about Carter. I decided to see if he was still on the phone. At the door to his office I listened, but didn't hear a sound. After knocking softly, I opened the door a crack. Carter was at his desk, and he was on the telephone.

I started to close the door, but he gestured for me to come in. When I entered the room, he looked me over, pointedly checking out my legs. As soon as he had the opportunity, he covered the mouthpiece and said, "I'll be through in a few minutes, Hillary, if you want to wait." He nodded toward the easy chair opposite his desk.

"That's all right," I whispered, "I won't stay. I only came to say hello."

The notion seemed to please him, but he was drawn back to his call. "What's that, George? Say again, please." Again he pointed to the chair, insisting that I stay.

Giving in, I dropped onto the buttery leather cushion and crossed my legs. Carter smiled at me, even as he continued talking. I tried to act blasé, but my courage melted. As he went on and on about stock options, my eye fell on the unopened Federal Express package lying on the corner of his desk. Carter's tone with the caller became emphatic, and I looked at him again. He drummed the eraser end of a pencil on the desk as he spoke, but he was watching me. His mouth was saying one thing, his eyes another.

My heart was pounding at the subtle game we played.

Carter, if he wasn't mentally undressing me, was a master at giving that impression. I caught myself bouncing my leg and had to force myself to stop. I was self-conscious under his scrutiny. Why his gaze was so sexually provocative, I couldn't say, but the expression on his face told me he was enjoying the titillation and, heaven help me, so was I.

"Sure, go ahead and take it, George," Carter said, breaking my reverie. He gave me a devilish smile, something I hadn't seen before. "I'm on hold," he announced to me, his eyes drifting down my legs once again. "I haven't had such an enticing distraction during a business call since I don't know when," he said.

"Probably since your secretary last wore a mini skirt to work," I said.

"My secretary is fifty-five years old," he replied. "You look terrific, by the way."

"Thank you."

"Are the shorts intended to drive me crazy, or is that wishful thinking on my part?"

"I think you're a dirty old man, Carter." My leg started bouncing again and I had to make it stop.

"You haven't shown up in shorts before."

"It's hot this morning."

"Shall I pray for a heat wave?"

"Don't tease me or I'll leave."

"Frankly I was hoping you might come around and sit on my lap," he said, giving me a crooked smile. His caller came back on the line. "Yes, George," he said. "I'm here. No problem." He gave me a shrug and resumed his conversation.

I listened to him for a minute or two, undecided whether I should be encouraged by the sexual repartee or not. Carter was not a frivolous man. To the contrary he was very serious-minded. I certainly had been as well. And yet, I was relishing this lighthearted moment, even as I fought my misgivings.

A little playfulness was probably what we both needed. Even so, I found myself pulling back. The Hillary Bass of old was not known for her inhibitions, but I had scruples now. I decided it was time to make a getaway.

When I got to my feet, Carter asked his associate to hold. He put his hand over the phone. "You aren't leaving me, are you?"

"You're busy. I don't want to interfere."

"You might be distracting, Hillary, but I assure you, it's not interfering. I'm sorry this is taking so long."

"I'll go find something more productive to do. When you're done we can talk." I went to the door.

Carter watched me go, looking disappointed. Before I stepped out, he said, "Will you come again?"

I smiled. "Maybe." Then I silently closed the door.

I grinned all the way back to my room. Except for a few hours the night before, I hadn't felt this lighthearted since awakening at the clinic. The contrast to what I'd been going through was so pleasant that I was probably making more out of our game than was justified. But I couldn't help it. I liked what it had said about us.

The cheery sunshine drew me to the window. I don't know how long I sat there, running the best moments of the previous evening through my mind, before there was a knock at the door, braking my reverie. It was Carter with the telephone in his hand.

"Un coup de téléphone pour madame," he said on his way over to plug the phone.

"Who is it?"

"Huguette Cuvillier."

171

I looked blank.

"One of your very good friends, second only to Lady Jane," he said, going to the outlet to plug in the phone.

"Well, I don't know her from Adam. Does she speak English?"

"Perfectly. I brought her up-to-date on your condition. She had lots of questions, and she wants to speak with you."

I'd managed to talk to Jane Nyland without knowing much about her, but I couldn't connect this woman with any of the faces in the photo album. "It would be much easier if I knew something about her," I groused.

"In a nutshell," Carter said, "Huguette is a few years older than you, and married to a very old, very stuffy retired Parisian banker. Her claim to fame comes from leading a group to Marrakech each January on a sort of sex safari. You've gone at least twice that I know of. Both times, of course, before Michel."

"Thanks for that uplifting piece of news," I said dryly.

"Sorry, darling. But you asked."

"What can I say to her, Carter?"

"Tell her you now get all the sex you could possibly want at home," he said with a wry grin.

"I'll never visit your study again," I said, "so help me."

"This is payback time, my love," he said.

I went to the telephone, not altogether happy at having to talk to someone I didn't know.

"Hello?" I said, sitting down on the bed.

"Hillary, *ma chérie*, Car-tair told me everything. I'm so sorry. Total amnesia. How sad."

"It's not a lot of fun." Considering what Carter had just told me about Huguette Cuvillier, I was not particularly eager to reacquaint myself with her, but out of common decency I had to speak with her for a few minutes.

"I know just what's needed," Huguette said. "A bottle of champagne and two lovely boys, and we can make the world right, eh, Hillary?"

"I'm afraid lots has changed with the clunk I've had on the head."

"We were so worried for you, *ma chérie*. When you didn't wake up for so long, we were sure you would die. And poor Michel. He was such a charming man. You must be heartbroken, *non?*"

"I don't remember him, Huguette."

"Oh, *mais oui*. The *amnésie*. When I first heard poor Michel died near your boat and you were injured, I thought it was no accident. It must be Ro-bair. He is *méchant*, that one. He called me here in Paris, you know."

"Who?"

"The one with the big muscles and the beard. Your . . . what was it you always called him? B.N. or something?"

"Oh, him. But what are you suggesting?"

"I suggest nothing. But Ro-bair telephoned to me all upset because you made him quit the boat. He was very angry. He hated Michel for this because he knew that it was Michel who makes you do it."

"When was this, Huguette?"

"Maybe two days before your accident. I do not know. Ro-bair is friendly to me after I take him to Italy. He loved you, of course, but it is me he calls with the problems. I say to him, 'Forget this, Ro-bair. Hillary can do nothing to help you, so forget her. Find another beautiful woman who has a beautiful boat.' But he was very angry and did not want to listen."

I glanced up at Carter. He sat down next to me, wrapping his arm around my waist as he kissed my cheek. Evidently he'd been serious about paying me back. I decided to resist a little, so I tried to scoot away, but he began blowing softly in my

173

ear. Shivers went up and down my spine and I shifted the phone to the ear he was blowing in.

"Well, Huguette, I appreciate you telling me this. Everything I hear these days is news, you know."

"We must do another beauty treatment together and talk like we used to do before," she said.

"Yes, maybe we can get together the next time I'm in Paris."

Carter had leaned behind me and was kissing the back of my neck. He'd paint little patches with his tongue, then blow on them. I gasped.

"Hillary?" Huguette said. "What's wrong?"

"Oh, nothing," I said. "Just a pest that will soon go away I hope."

Carter chuckled and I had to remove his hand from my leg. I gave him a telling look, though I wasn't nearly as displeased by his teasing as I pretended.

"Comment?" Huguette said.

"Sorry," I said, "this isn't a good time for me to talk, Huguette. Can I call you when I expect to be in Paris?"

"Certainement. I won't keep you, *ma chérie.* I only wanted to give you my best wishes. You must be so upset by what's in the papers."

"What do you mean?"

"Didn't you see yesterday's *Le Beau Monde?* The article and picture of you?"

"No. I haven't seen any paper. What did it say?"

Carter patted my leg, got up and went to the door. He slipped from the room. I was glad because Huguette Cuvillier clearly had scandalous news, and I didn't want to hear about it with him titillating me.

"The picture of you in that bikini was very cute," she said. "It'll probably bring all your old beaus back for another chance."

174

"Bikini? What was in this article?"

"It says that the police have questioned you concerning Michel's death. That's the only statement of fact. The rest is innuendo and scandal. Exactly what you would expect. Sex, murder, infidelity. You know, it's what sells newspapers, *ma chérie.*"

I groaned. "Oh, great, just what Carter needs. Was he mentioned?"

"Of course, the cuckold is very important in such a story. Everyone must know."

I closed my eyes and shivered.

"It could be worse," Huguette said. "If you want my opinion, I think Claudine Lambert is behind the story. Her family has the connections to get that kind of information from the police. The whole thing is political, *ma chérie.* When fame and money are involved, the police become scrupulous to avoid appearance of *favoritisme.*"

Carter reappeared at the door. He had a Federal Express envelope in his hand. He sat down next to me as Huguette babbled on.

"We love you, Hillary," Huguette was saying, "and we don't want you to be upset. I've talked with a few people. When this is over, we'll have a big party, okay?"

"Well, not until I've recovered my memory."

"But why, *ma chérie?* Think how much more exciting it will be if we're all strangers."

"Let me think about that, Huguette, and I'll get back to you."

Huguette Cuvillier let me go, and as soon as I hung up I turned to Carter. "Dirty pool," I protested. "How am I supposed to talk while you're blowing in my ear?"

"Turnabout's fair play."

"What did I do that was so bad?" I demanded.

"You enticed me."

175

"I didn't mean to."

He kissed my neck. "Well, maybe I'm a dirty old man, like you said."

I scooted away. "Carter, there's bad news."

"You're a tabloid celebrity."

"How did you know?"

He picked up the Federal Express envelope and handed it to me. It had been opened. "I wasn't going to show this to you, but since Huguette called, I suppose I should. A friend sent it from New York. It came a little while ago."

I glanced at him warily and pulled a tabloid-sized newspaper from the envelope. It was the *New York Press Enquirer*.

"Oh, God," I said. "I'm in here too?"

"Page three. But don't let it bother you. Some people regard making the *Enquirer* a badge of honor."

I smiled faintly and turned to the article. The headline at the top of the page read, "Wife of American Financier Embroiled in Sex and Murder Intrigue in France." Under it were three photos—close-ups of Carter and Michel, captioned with their names. Between them was a picture of me in a bikini, probably from an old fashion spread, with the caption, "Hillary Bass, an affair gone awry?"

My eyes instantly brimmed with tears. I couldn't look at Carter, so I tried to read the story under Todd Halley's byline. A few paragraphs were all it took to see that Halley had managed to milk every ounce of scandal he could from the loose recitation of facts.

The police were quoted saying that foul play was suspected. There were a number of quotes from unnamed sources about my affair with Michel, as well as a tongue-in-cheek account of my amnesia. The article ended with the lines, "Why did Michel Lambert die? For love, for sex, or simply for money? Inspector Paul Debray, heading the investigation for the metro-

176

politan police in Nice, has promised to find the answer to that question."

"Oh, Carter," I said turning to him. "I feel horrible about this. You must be terribly humiliated. And you did nothing to deserve it . . . except marry me."

I sniffled and Carter put his arms around me. "Most guys have boring wives, Hillary. You're anything but boring."

"Quit trying to put it in a good light. You're as mortified by this as I am."

"It's more publicly scandalous than it's been in the past, admittedly."

"Will it ruin your business?"

"No, of course not. This has nothing to do with my work." He took my face in his hands and softly kissed my lips.

"I wish you wouldn't be so nice. It just makes me feel guiltier."

"What do you want me to do? Box you around?"

"No."

"Then?"

"Can't we sue? Do something to fight back?"

"It would only make it worse. Anyway, the truth is not easily denied, no matter how unfavorably it's presented. Forget about it, Hillary."

I stared down at the paper. "Do you think this will be the last of it?"

"Who knows? The same article was in a London rag too. I expect that if nothing new develops in the story, the worst may be behind us."

I shook my head. "I'm mortified." I was feeling such anguish I tried to get up and get away, but Carter held me.

"Listen to me, darling," he said. "I don't care about that crap."

Tears overflowed my lids and I gave Carter a big hug. He squeezed me back.

"So, everything's forgotten," he said. He slipped his hand under the hair at the back of my head and looked into my eyes. My resistance melted as he pulled my face to his and kissed me. "I'm trying to wring every advantage out of your contrition that I can," he muttered.

We sank back onto the bed. Carter brushed my neck with the tip of his tongue. I writhed against him and moaned. Then, as he moved to the base of my throat, his hand slid from my stomach to between my legs. I stopped him from caressing me. "You're a bastard for getting me so excited," I murmured. "And it doesn't change things that I used to be a rotten wife."

"Used to be?" he said.

"You aren't doing this for revenge, are you?"

"Sweet revenge."

I moaned. "You've got to stop," I said. I dug my fingers into his hair, though I couldn't make myself push him away. "We still have to go out on that damned sailboat."

He took my chin in his hand. "We can skip it."

I searched his eyes, trying to decide if he was simply thinking about sex, or if there was more on his mind. I couldn't tell, but I was aroused and sorely tempted. I tried to summon my resolve. "Don't you have business to tend to?"

"Yes, but right now I don't care about business."

"I wouldn't want you to hate me later," I said.

"I promise I won't."

I was backsliding again. When he began running his thumb around the edge of my navel, I sat up. "No, Carter, we're going sailing. I've got to see if getting on the boat brings my memory back."

He contemplated me thoughtfully. "I'm not so sure I want you to get it back."

178

"I am."

"Really?"

"I've got to know the truth. The uncertainty has been killing me."

"There are many truths, Hillary."

"But what I did was critical to so many things. Including us, our relationship."

"Not for me."

I took his face in my hands and touched my forehead to his. "Thank you," I whispered. "And thank you for being so sweet today and making me happy."

"Are you?"

I nodded.

"But you're thinking about the *Serenity.*"

"Yes."

"Then you give me no option but to take you to Toulon."

I nodded again and kissed him on the lips.

"I've got two more phone calls to make," he said. "Since you're being so moral, I suppose I ought to be responsible."

"I don't want us going bankrupt."

Carter chuckled. He caressed my thigh lovingly, then got up. "Maybe tonight, after sailing, we'll have cause to celebrate," he said.

"I hope so."

He winked at me and left the room.

S WE DROVE TO
the marina at Toulon,
Carter told me that the
French Riviera had
more pleasure craft per square
foot than any place in the world,
including Florida and Southern
California. Our contribution was
a Cambria 44—a 46-foot craft
with a 28,600-pound displace-
ment and 950 square feet of sail.
The *Serenity*, he said, was a
damned fine sailboat.

When I asked if he sailed
anymore, Carter replied that he
still had his uncle's boat back in
the States. "It's an old Hinckley,
Bermuda 40," he said. "I keep it
berthed at Oxford, on the East
Shore of Maryland, close to
where my mother's people were
from. Now *that* is a boat, Hillary," he said proudly. "One of
the last wooden ones made. My
mother's brother, Uncle Ben,
taught me to sail it when I was a
kid. When he died he left it to

me. Every time I take her out, it's like going home for Christmas."

There was a certain lilt in Carter's voice that told me he treasured certain experiences and pleasures that we didn't share. That made me sad.

"Have I ever been on your boat with you?" I asked.

"I think once or twice."

"Didn't I enjoy it?"

"It's hard to say what we enjoyed and what we didn't," he replied. "The good and bad ran together a lot with us."

It was the same old story, but no matter how many times I heard it, it hurt.

"But there's no point in discussing that," he said quickly. "We're going to concentrate on the present, remember?"

"Yes, I know that's what we agreed, but since sailing's an important part of both our lives, I want to hear what happened."

"All right. What do you want to know?"

"When we were in Maryland together, on the boat, what did I do that was so unpleasant?"

"You complained about everything. You didn't want me to buy another Hinckley for our use here in France, probably because you knew it was my first choice. You claimed you didn't like the wood or the engineering. It was stodgy, lacked sophistication, and it wasn't fast enough." Carter sighed. "When I told you the new B40s were the fastest thing with that waterline, you scoffed. 'A B40 might be quick on a beam reach,' you said, 'but on that point of sail a decent turn of the century, gaff-rigged Friendship sloop will beat it.' "

"I said that?"

Carter nodded. "I'm sure you heard some yacht broker mutter it sometime or another, but you did say it."

"I haven't the slightest idea what all that means."

181

"The point is I liked my Hinckley and you had to criticize her. And you combined your criticism of the boat with criticism of me, my uncle, and the East Shore. There wasn't a lot about me that you liked."

I felt dreadful and Carter noticed.

"You see why I didn't want to discuss it," he said.

"Yes, especially when everything you could say about me seems to be so negative."

"I'm not objective, Hillary. I deserve my share of the blame for what's gone wrong too. And since you can't defend yourself, it's much better if we concentrate on things we both know about."

"Like the present, you mean."

"Yes, like the present." He reached over and patted my arm. "Besides, maybe next time we buy a boat, I'll be able to talk you into a Hinckley."

"I'm sure you could."

"This tabula rasa business is beginning to appeal to me," he said with a laugh.

Carter was optimistic, I could see that. He wasn't nearly as nervous about going aboard the *Serenity* as I was. To me, it was all a terrible unknown and I was scared, more even than when we'd gone to see Claudine Lambert.

We entered the outskirts of Toulon. Some of what I saw looked familiar, but I didn't know if that was because my memory was coming back, or if my recollections were from the day I'd returned home from the clinic.

"Erica's going to meet us at the marina, by the way," Carter said. "I told her to have the boat ready. I also thought it would be a good time for you to meet her."

I was silent because I didn't know whether I should share my misgivings about Polly and the Englishwoman who was looking after the boat, or if by opening my mouth I'd simply sound grumpy or paranoid. Carter was trying to make this a positive experience, so I decided I should too.

We made our way through the heart of town. Carter left the Jag in a car park and we walked to the docks. I looked closely at the buildings, the people, absorbing what I could. There was a guard booth at the entrance to the marina, but it was empty. Carter waved to a man watching from a window in the building that housed the harbormaster.

"We'll see what kind of . . . how good Erica is," he said. "The jib should be on the deck and she should have the mainsail flaked on the boom."

"If you say so."

He laughed and put an arm around my shoulders, giving me a hardy squeeze. As we went out through the maze of naked masts, my stomach started to knot. The briny air was sharp with the smell of fish. Overhead a swarm of gulls soared and darted in a disharmonious ballet, vying for spoils in the jetsam floating in the harbor.

The sun was hot, though not the breeze. As we neared the end of a finger dock, I knew instantly which of the three boats ahead was the *Serenity*. She was stark white with teak decks and trim, her sails the color of unbleached muslin. She was a pretty boat, deceptively quiescent as she lay in the water.

I glanced at Carter. "Are things the way they're supposed to be?"

"Yes," he said, nodding with approval, "so far so good. Looks perfect."

He was pleased and I was pleased for him. The boat undoubtedly cost more than most houses, so it was no small matter. As we came alongside, a woman with a brownish-blond ponytail and wraparound sunglasses that completely hid her eyes rose from the cockpit at the stern of the boat.

"Hello," she said, walking up the deck to greet us.

183

Erica Maxwell, a sinewy, androgynous-looking woman of thirty-two or -three, scampered down the boarding ladder like a person well accustomed to her surroundings. She extended a large hand to Carter. "Afternoon, Mr. Bass." Then she turned to me, smiling, and offered her hand as Carter made the introductions.

"Sorry you met our boat before you met me," I offered.

"You've been through quite an ordeal, I understand, Mrs. Bass," Erica said. "I trust you're fully recovered."

"I'm nearly up to speed."

Erica smiled. She was one of those quintessential outdoor types—so thoroughly tanned she seemed to have lived exclusively in the elements. She wore no makeup and her clothes seemed a part of her. She had on a faded baby blue tank top, cutoff jeans, and white sneakers that had turned gray with age.

Erica Maxwell was an inch or so shorter than I, with broad shoulders, muscular arms, and hardly any bust. Only her hips betrayed her sex. She had a squarish, masculine face, though her mouth was quite attractive. She pushed her sunglasses up into her hair, squinting through gray, unremarkable eyes that were older than her years.

"You've a lovely boat, Mrs. Bass," she said. "I wasn't familiar with the Cambria before, but I've gotten a feel for her. These are ideal waters for her, I should think."

"No problems then?" Carter asked.

"No, sir. Nothing major. She seemed well cared for. Had a few weeks of grime on her surfaces, but that's to be expected then, isn't it?" Erica glanced at the boat proudly, dropping her glasses back onto her nose. "I'd say she's shipshape. No provisions aboard, though, sir."

"It doesn't matter. We won't be out long."

"Shall I come back this evening to put her to bed, Mr. Bass?"

"We'll have her back in two or three hours."

"Will there be anything else, sir?" She glanced at me. "Mrs. Bass?"

I deferred to Carter.

"I don't believe so, Erica," he said, looking at the sails.

"I'll be off then," she said brightly. "Have a good day. Cheerio!"

We watched her make her way back along the finger dock toward the entrance to the marina.

"She seems competent," I said to Carter. "And pleasant."

"Her references checked out."

We turned to the *Serenity* and all my trepidation came streaming back. My throat tightened, despite my will to maintain control. My husband's eyes were on me, but my full attention was on the sailboat. I looked her over carefully before I said, "I know this boat, Carter. I've been on it before."

"Of course you have. Hundreds of times."

"You don't understand. I'd slept in my bed before too, but it didn't feel like I had. It was the same with the house. And with you, for that matter. When we kissed, it was as though it was for the first time. The boat is different. I distinctly remember being on it."

Carter ran his eyes from the craft's bow to stern, then up her naked mast. "We're making progress then, aren't we?" He held out his hand. "Come on, darling, let's go aboard."

I thought I was ready, but my feet felt as though they'd been nailed to the dock. "I can't," I whispered. "I have this terrible, ominous feeling. To be honest, I think I'm going to be sick."

Carter seemed perplexed. "It's having that strong an effect on you?"

I nodded.

185

"Maybe we shouldn't take her out, then."

"No, I think it's important for me to try."

"Well, here, take my hand. We'll go aboard slowly."

I curled my clammy fingers around his. "I know I'm acting like a baby," I said, "but I really do feel ill."

"Whatever happened that day was obviously pretty traumatic," he said. "Maybe this is to be expected."

I climbed the boarding ladder, gingerly taking hold of the stanchions on either side of the gate. I glanced at the deck amidship. "That's where they found me, wasn't it?"

"You remember?"

"I don't recall what happened, but I have a sense of standing there when I was hit."

"By the boom, most likely," he said, pointing. "It was a rookie mistake, but the only one they could come up with. You'd been unconscious quite a while when you were found."

We went back to the cockpit. Carter suggested I sit. I glanced around at the padded seats, the wheel, the fittings. It all looked familiar. What a strange sensation it was to recognize something at last, to have a sense of having been there.

I sat still, trying to get control of my raging heart. "This is the weirdest sensation," I said, taking a shallow breath. "I feel as if my body's about to explode."

Carter eased down beside me. He took my hand. "You must be trying to get out whatever it is boiling inside," he said.

"I guess so." I kept glancing around, trying to pick out something seminal, something I could use to pop the balloon.

Waves were gently lapping at the hull of the boat, which bobbed ever so slightly in the water. My insides felt queasy. There was a quiet horror building inside me.

"What do you think?" Carter said. "Shall we try to take her out?"

I closed my eyes and swallowed. "Yes."

"You just sit here and relax."

Carter got up and began preparations to cast off. He made a circuit of the deck, then went below for several moments. He soon reappeared, but I was too busy fighting myself to pay a lot of attention to what he was doing. I felt useless and helpless too. For all I knew about sailing, this could have been an airplane.

When he was ready, Carter started the auxiliary engine and cast off. We pulled away from the dock and eased into the channel. My fingers gripped the cushion as I watched him standing at the wheel. He glanced back at me.

"How are you doing?"

I shook my head. "Not so good. I think I'm seasick."

"Are you serious? The water's as flat as a duck pond."

"I know, but I feel awful."

"Well, if you need to, hang your head over the stern. That's why God made gunwales."

We headed for the end of the breakwater and the open sea. The *Serenity* began rolling in the gentle swells. Every time Carter glanced at me I tried to buck up and be brave, but I felt dreadful. And it wasn't only physical. A storm was raging inside me, tearing me up.

We hit the open sea. Carter patiently explained what he was doing as he unfurled the jib and pulled on the halyards, raising the mainsail. Almost instantly, the *Serenity* rose like a spirited filly breaking into a gallop. The wind caught me full in the face and the beat of my heart lifted with the speed of the craft. I should have felt exhilaration, but instead it was terror.

For five minutes I fought myself. Then I couldn't stand it anymore. "Oh, Carter," I called over the rush of the wind, "I don't think I can do this. Can we go back?"

He looked a bit annoyed, then shrugged. "Sure, if that's what you want."

He brought the boat about, trimmed the sails, and headed back toward the entrance to the harbor. With everything under control, he turned and studied me.

"You look pale as a sheet," he said. "I thought maybe once we got out to sea you'd be okay."

"I could pass out right now."

"Are you seasick, or is it something else?"

"It's being on the boat."

"If it's not an inner ear problem, you can go below and lie down. But if it's seasickness, it'll only get worse if you can't see the horizon."

"I need to lie down."

Carter pointed to the companionway and I went below.

Entering the main salon was like walking into my home. The smell of it, the hardwood and leather, was shockingly familiar. I was so used to an alien world that the familiar was genuinely frightening. I glanced around, knowing with absolute certainty that I had been in this place. And it terrified me. Still, what recollections I had were hazy at best.

On the verge of passing out, I practically fell onto an upholstered bench against the wall. My ears began to ring. I heard screaming. Then I realized the sound was coming from within my head.

I clung to the bench, my breath coming in unsteady little spasms. That dream I'd had of Michel started replaying in my mind like a loop of film. I saw his anger. I saw my own rage as we struggled. Over and over I saw us, my arms flailing, our bodies perched precariously against the lifeline ringing the deck.

I began to sob uncontrollably, only vaguely aware of my surroundings. I don't know how long I went on that way, but I didn't stop until I felt someone lift me by the shoulders. I opened my eyes and Carter slipped down next to me and took me into his arms.

188

"I'm so sorry, darling," he whispered, "I had no idea it would be so bad."

I clung to him as he stroked my head, holding me until I grew calmer.

"Are we back?" I asked.

"Yes, tied up at the dock."

"Thank God."

He gazed into my bleary eyes. "Maybe you're going to have to take up skydiving," he teased. "I don't think sailing agrees with you anymore."

I sniffled. "No kidding."

"You going to be okay?"

"I'm so weak. It's like the whole thing happened again."

"What happened, Hillary? Tell me."

I looked at him woefully. "It was like the dream I had the other day. I saw myself fighting with Michel." I bit my lip. "I saw myself hitting him and . . ."

"And what?"

". . . trying to push him overboard." I broke down again.

Carter stroked my hair. "It's only a dream," he said. "It's just your imagination."

"But it was so real." I looked at him desperately. "I'm afraid I did it, Carter. I'm afraid I killed Michel."

"Don't be silly. You've gotten yourself worked up. Your imagination's out of control. That's all it is."

I put my arms around him. "I'm so afraid."

"Listen, I want you to rest here while I go get the car and bring it to the entrance of the marina. There's no point in making you walk any farther than necessary. Then I'll take you home."

"Don't leave me," I pleaded.

"It'll only take a few minutes. Once you're in the car I

189

can finish unrigging the boat. Erica won't be back for at least an hour."

I was too drained to argue. All I wanted was to go home.

"Why don't I take you into the master stateroom?" Carter said. "I think you'd be more comfortable there."

"Okay." I got up and staggered toward the door to the forecastle.

"No, babe, that's for the crew." Carter took my arm and led me aft.

The bed in the master stateroom looked so inviting I plopped right down. Carter sat beside me long enough to kiss me on the forehead.

"Will you be all right?"

"Yes, but please hurry."

Carter left. I lay there for a while, looking out the small port at the sky. What I'd just been through was not a product of my imagination. I was sure of that. I'd relived something that had really happened to me, though without the clarity of normal memory. I couldn't pull out the vivid recollections that reason told me had to be there. Something was holding it all in, something dark and sinister.

Panic welled in me and I got up from the bed and staggered back to the main salon. The screaming began all over again. I glanced out the port overlooking the deck and immediately began to shake. I don't know what I expected to see, but there was nothing there.

My panic intensified. I was under the control of a strange force. I felt a desperate need to get out of the cabin and off the boat. Though my legs were rubbery, I stumbled up the companionway and onto the deck.

The breeze felt cool and I realized I was perspiring. The cawing of the gulls overhead seemed raucous, even threatening. The desire to escape gripped me. I made my way to the boarding ladder and climbed down, nearly tripping on the dock. There wasn't a soul in sight. The rows of naked masts were as silent as tombstones. I started walking.

I don't know how far I'd gotten before it happened. Perhaps twenty-five or thirty yards. Suddenly it was like the end of the world. I couldn't say which I perceived first—the deafening explosion, or being thrown headlong onto the dock. But the next thing I knew I was flat on my face and debris was raining down all around me.

I lay stunned in an acrid cloud of smoke, my ears ringing like a thousand air raid sirens. All I could say for sure was that I was alive.

IT WAS A MINUTE or two before anybody showed up. The marina guard arrived first, but Carter was right behind him, nearly knocking the poor man down. I was still on my stomach and for some reason it struck me as odd that my husband was dressed in white, though of course he had been all along. He skidded to a stop beside me, pushing away a piece of debris as he dropped to his knees.

"Hillary. My God. Are you all right?"

"I don't know. I think so," I said, dazed.

The world had a curious surrealistic feel. I was removed from everything, though I observed what was happening around me. I had no particular sensation, except for the ringing in my ears, but even that seemed to be coming from outside my head. My body wasn't my own.

Carter was feeling my arms and legs, I guess to check for broken bones. I lifted my head and looked around, noticing the guard, a man in his fifties with a gray mustache and a jaunty cap. He stared at me, appearing as dazed as I.

"Let me turn you over," Carter said, taking me by the upper arms and rotating me slowly, as though I were an invalid.

My body responded to his prompting and I ended up sitting upright, facing the end of the dock. There wasn't a thing left of the *Serenity*. All I could see was a buckled stretch of dock tilted on its side. The nearest boat was listing at a forty-five-degree angle, its rigging entangled in the boat next to it.

The guard moved awkwardly toward the wreckage, but stopped after a few steps and glanced back at us, his expression bewildered.

"*Est-ce qu'il y a quelqu'un d'autre?*" Was there anyone else?

"*Non, personne.*" No, no one, Carter replied.

I stared at Carter and he stared at me. He looked frightened.

"What happened?" I mumbled.

"I don't know. The *Serenity* blew up. How did you get off?"

"I left. I was going to look for you, and the next thing I knew . . ." The reality of what had happened began to sink in and my eyes filled with tears.

Carter put his arms around me and held me tightly. "Hillary, you could have been killed."

I was beginning to understand that. If I hadn't panicked and left the boat, I would be in little pieces, just like the *Serenity*.

Two or three other people came running up the dock. Questions were asked and there were expressions of wonder and amazement. I didn't understand the babble of voices, but the meaning behind their tones was unmistakable. As more people

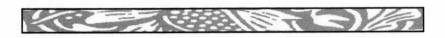

arrived, a circle of faces formed around me. Carter was still holding me.

"Est-ce que madame est blessée?" Is she hurt? *"Que s'est-il passé?"* What happened? *"Doit-on faire venir une ambulance?"* Should we call an ambulance?

Carter leaned close to my ear. "Do you want to get up, darling, or would you rather stay here?"

"I think I want to get up."

Carter and another man lifted me to my feet. I was numb and weak, but I felt no pain. Carter put his arm around my waist and we began walking toward the entrance to the marina. I could hear a siren. A policeman stopped to ask if there were others injured. Carter told him I was the only one and that I seemed to be okay.

As we reached our car a group of firemen made their way past us and out toward the site of the explosion. I was still so stunned that Carter had to help me into the passenger seat of the Jaguar. I knew I'd come within a whisker of being killed.

Carter got into the Jag with me and held my hand. "Do you want to go to the hospital?" he asked.

One of my elbows was a little sore and the heels of my hands were scraped where I landed on the dock, but the injuries were so minor I'd only then become aware of them. "I'm not hurt," I said. "Just a few scratches and a bruise or two."

"What happened? You didn't touch anything, did you?"

"No, I didn't do a thing." I put my hands to my ringing ears and shook my head. "Could it have been a gas leak?"

"Auxiliaries are always diesel, so that things like this don't happen. Did you smell gas?"

I shook my head.

"Hear anything, see anyone?"

"No, Carter, nothing unusual happened. I didn't feel well so I probably wasn't very observant. But I didn't see or smell anything suspicious."

He looked perplexed and worried, making me wonder what he was thinking. Quite a crowd had gathered at the entrance to the marina. I could hear the singsong wail of a siren and within seconds an ambulance arrived. The police began organizing the scene and the spectators who had made it out onto the docks were herded back.

"I'd better talk to the police," Carter said. "Will you be all right alone for a few minutes?"

"Yes, I'm fine."

Carter got out of the car and I stared at the crowd. I was having trouble understanding why I was alive when logic indicated that I should be dead. It was hard to accept that chance, simple happenstance, was the difference between life and death.

I could see Carter talking to a police official. The man was tall and lean and very erect in his bearing. He was in a crisp summer uniform, his *képi* square on his head. He came with Carter to the Jaguar. I opened the door.

"Madame," he said, leaning over to see me, "would you be so kind to come with me to the police van? It will be more comfortable to talk."

I got out and the officer introduced himself as Captain Marguet. He spoke very slowly, but his English was precise and, for the most part, correct. Strangely I was aware of his thin mustache moving on his lip as he talked. I glanced at Carter, who remained pensive and somber.

We went to the van. The captain noticed that my hand was bleeding. He had a medic clean the wound and bandage it. I was offered a glass of mineral water, which I sipped. Carter sat across from me, watching me with sad eyes and a furrowed brow.

Captain Marguet asked me to recount what had happened. I told him the story, and when I finished he asked if I would mind waiting for a while, unless I felt I needed to see a doctor. I told him that I would be all right.

Once he'd gone, Carter moved onto the seat next to me and held my hand in both of his. "I think they'll let me take you home soon," he said.

"I'm okay."

"Well, I'm not so sure I am. I've heard of boats blowing up like that, but I've never seen it." He caressed my fingers.

"Was it insured?" I asked.

"Yes."

"Maybe you can get that B40 or whatever it was, after all."

"It's a nice thought," he said, "but this wasn't quite the way I had in mind."

Only then did it occur to me that I was *supposed* to be dead, that someone might have *intended* for the boat to blow up. My hands trembled at the thought. "Do you think it was an accident, or did somebody try to do us in?" I asked.

"I don't know. They're trying to figure that out now," he said, tossing his head toward the growing army of officials and emergency workers outside the van. "It's surprising what damage a little bit of gas can do. A cup of the stuff packs a bigger wallop than a pound of TNT."

"I thought you said the engine was a diesel."

"It was, but there can be other sources of gasoline on a boat. At one time we stored the outboard for the zodiac and the fuel tank in the lazaretto. I'll have to ask Erica if it was still there." He ran his fingers back through his hair. "Another possibility is that Whitford brought a propane or gas cooking stove aboard. People will do that if they cook a lot. Alcohol stoves are safer, but nobody likes them because they don't burn hot."

"What would make something like that blow up? I thought things were made safe these days."

"Boats are especially vulnerable. Gas is heavier than air,

196

so it collects in the bilge eventually, regardless of where the spill occurred. Once a few cups of the stuff accumulate, all you need is a spark. The automatic bilge pump was supposed to be spark proof, but a short is always possible. Put the two together and poof, a quarter-of-a-million-dollar boat can go off like a one-ton bomb."

"It sounds like you're convinced it was an accident."

He looked into my eyes. "For the moment it's the most logical assumption."

I watched the hubbub outside the van for a minute, having trouble believing I was the one in the middle of it, that all this was revolving around me. I shivered. "I wonder if they'll ever figure out what happened."

"Marguet told me they've already got explosive experts and divers on the way from Marseille. Apparently even the smallest piece of debris can tell an awful lot. He's also trying to get hold of Inspector Debray in Nice," Carter said. "I told them what's been going on."

"You think this is somehow connected with Michel's death?" I asked.

"I'd like to think not."

I wasn't sure why Carter said that, but to me, in my paranoia, it made perfect sense. Perhaps my tragic journey had taken still another tragic turn.

He gave me a reassuring hug. "Maybe what you need, Hillary, is a change of scene. How would you like to go to Paris for the weekend?"

"Paris?"

"I have some business there and I'd prefer not to leave you alone. And if you come with me, I won't have to worry about you."

"Do you think I'm in danger?"

"Probably not," he said, "but I don't want to take any chances. Besides, it's nice having you around."

—

Twenty minutes later we were allowed to go home. During the drive I settled back into a somewhat more familiar reality, but I was shaken and knew I wouldn't be getting over what had happened immediately. By the time we arrived at Montfaucon I was not only emotionally drained, but I had a terrible headache. I went directly to my room to lie down.

Carter, who'd accompanied me upstairs, asked if I wanted Guy Lafon to examine me. The notion had some appeal because I felt an affinity for the kindhearted doctor, but there wasn't anything he could do that a couple of aspirin couldn't do just as well, so I declined.

"Is there anything I can get you?" he asked.

I sat on the bed and glanced around the room. "Where's Poof?"

"I don't know. Shall I find her for you?"

"I like petting her when I'm trying to fall asleep."

"I'll look for her then."

"You don't have to," I said.

Carter stroked my head. "I don't mind." He looked under the bed, then he went to my closet, calling her name. "She must be downstairs," he said, heading for the door.

After he'd left I stared blankly across the room. The ringing in my ears was practically gone. I became aware of the scent of blossoms and turned to look at the roses Carter had brought me. I got up to smell them, torturing myself with the surge of emotion they inevitably evoked.

But the memories that haunted me most were connected with the boat, those terrible images of my struggle with Michel.

That seemed so much more immediate, and threatening, than the anxiety I experienced when I smelled roses. I wondered if I was doomed to be haunted by terrifying visions the rest of my life.

Then an awful question crossed my mind. Was something else, even worse than my fight with Michel, hidden in my memory? Could that eerie vision have been only the beginning?

I heard Carter in the hallway. He entered the room with Poof in his arms. He was petting her as he approached. "She was in the kitchen," he said.

I touched her nose with my finger, feeling joy and love for her as Carter handed her over. "How long have I had Poof?" I asked.

"About five years, I guess. You got her in Switzerland. We were skiing at Gstaad. The mouser at the chalet we were renting had had a litter of kittens and Poof was the last one left. She reminded you of a cat you'd had as a girl and you decided you had to have her. You ended up smuggling her back into France in your purse."

I kissed her head. "That's one story about me I can believe."

Carter gave a sympathetic smile. He didn't look like he wanted to leave but I was beat and really wanted to lie down. "I'm sorry to be such a wimp," I said.

"After what you've been through, you deserve a rest," he said. "I'd say you've had enough excitement today to last the rest of the year."

I couldn't have agreed more. Carter left and I got a couple of aspirin from the bathroom. Then Poof and I lay on the bed for a nap.

I tried to relax, but I was wired. I took a deep breath and concentrated my thoughts. Only now, in the quiet of my room, did the afternoon's events start coming into focus. The horror of the explosion, the sensation of being knocked to the ground, played over and over in my head.

I went over those last moments that Carter and I were on the boat. He'd encouraged me to stay behind while he got the car. A chilling thought went through me. Had he known the boat was about to blow up?

The possibility that the blast had not been accidental struck at my heart. Carter was so sure the explosion had been caused by a gas leak. But what if it were a bomb? What if . . . he knew?

I couldn't believe my own husband would want to murder me. It was simply chance that he'd left minutes before the blast. Besides, even if he'd had the opportunity to set a bomb, that didn't mean he'd done it. I told myself it was insane to even consider the possibility.

Eventually I dozed off. I don't know what outrages tormented my sleep but I do know I awoke with two different nightmares burning in my brain. In one I was struggling with Michel; in the other I was hounded by Carter.

When Yvonne came to announce that dinner would be ready shortly I told her I wasn't feeling well. She offered to bring my meal to me, and I agreed. Poof had disappeared again so I was alone when Carter came to my room several minutes later.

"I understand you aren't feeling well," he said, appearing genuinely concerned.

"Everything sort of caught up with me, I guess."

He sat on the edge of the bed and took my hand. I tried to act as calm and natural as I could, but I wasn't successful. He read the anxiety in my eyes. "You seem really upset, Hillary."

I smiled weakly. "It's affected me more strongly than I expected."

"Do you want me to contact Dr. Thirion?"

"No, that won't be necessary. A good night's sleep and I'll be fine."

"Are you sure?"

I nodded my certainty.

He stroked my fingers and chills raced through my body. It was hard to look into Carter's eyes. I tried telling myself that the problem was with me, that he couldn't possibly have done anything to harm me. Yet I wasn't sure.

Yvonne came with my dinner. I thanked her and she left the room. Carter remained at my side.

"Aren't you going to eat?" I said nervously.

"I had a bite earlier. But I'll stay and have coffee with you, if you'd like the company."

"Certainly." I made a show of eating my soup, but I had no appetite. I still had trouble looking at him.

I told myself that I was paranoid, that there was no proof Carter had done anything wrong. To the contrary, that very morning he'd been playful and loving. He'd even tried to get me to skip going to the marina so that we could make love. That was hardly consistent with a desire to kill.

Besides, what possible motive could he have? Financial gain? He was already rich. And the possibility of doing it for revenge seemed ludicrous in light of the way he'd been treating me.

I had a few bites of the fillet of chicken breast and green beans, then I put my fork down. "I'm not hungry," I said with exasperation.

Carter took the tray and set it aside. He sat on the bed beside me again. As before, he took my hand. "Hillary, I have to tell you something," he said solemnly.

My heart practically stopped.

"Captain Marguet called while you were sleeping. He asked to come out to see us."

"What for?"

"He's fairly certain the explosion was caused by a bomb."

My mouth dropped open, not so much because of the news, which I'd suspected, but rather because I was hearing it from Carter's lips.

"A bomb?"

"Yes, they're questioning Erica Maxwell."

"Erica," I said vacantly. Of course! I hadn't even thought of her. She had been in charge of caring for the boat. It could have been her. For that matter, it might have been any number of people. Why had I jumped to the conclusion that my own husband was responsible? I engaged Carter's still solemn eyes. "Why would she want to blow up the boat?"

"Captain Marguet isn't saying that she did. But he feels she would know better than anyone what the condition of the boat was and if others had been around."

"Yes, of course."

"I figured I should tell you about Marguet's suspicions in advance, so you'll be prepared," he said.

"Thank you, Carter."

"There's something else," he said.

I waited.

He hesitated, then said, "I'm concerned what you might be thinking."

"What do you mean?"

He stared at me with the same contemplative silence as before. Then he said, "Did it bother you that I left the boat only minutes before the damn thing blew up?"

I was taken aback by his directness. "Are you asking if I'm suspicious of you?"

He shrugged. "It looks bad, doesn't it, that I left you behind, moments before the *Serenity* was blown to smithereens?"

I tried to sound incredulous. "Why would you want to kill me, Carter? That *is* what you're suggesting, isn't it?"

"I'm certainly not suggesting it. I'm concerned that you've questioned why I'd left when I did."

"I assumed it for the reason you gave me," I said evenly.

"Then it hasn't bothered you?"

"No." I lied.

He gave a sigh of relief, a burden lifted. He smiled.

I tried to act nonchalant, but I was still in a quandary. Had Carter just demonstrated his innocence, or had it been a ruse, a deception to hide the truth? I hated my suspicions. I needed a husband I could turn to for support, not one I doubted.

"To be honest, Hillary, I didn't like the way things looked myself," he said. "At first the possibility didn't even occur to me. Then, when Marguet called, I began thinking about it. I'm sorry now I didn't take you with me when I left."

He couldn't have been as sorry as I, but I wasn't about to say that. "Don't worry about it, Carter," I said. "I'm not."

He squeezed my fingers. "The last few days would have been a tragic waste in every way if my intentions were to kill you. I hope that's obvious."

I let his remark roll through my mind. I saw his logic. Why nurture love when hatred or greed is in your heart? "Well, at least we can be grateful that everything worked out for the best."

"Yes, things worked out okay," he conceded, "but I wish it had happened differently." He leaned over and kissed me. "Thank you for your trust. It's very important to me," he said.

I smiled, but in truth I felt miserable. Wretched. How could my life have been turned on its head again, just when I was beginning to feel hope? Were my sins so heinous that I deserved this fate? I understood how Job must have felt. Yet that was an inexact comparison. Job, at least, knew who he was and what he had done.

—

With Captain Marguet coming to see us, I changed into a soft cotton summer dress. Carter, who lingered in my room, asked if I wanted to play some cribbage while we waited.

"We played quite a lot when we were first married," he said. "It was one of the few things we enjoyed doing together."

"That's a sad commentary," I said. "How long since we've played?"

"Four or five years."

"Who won?"

"You did, mostly," he said.

Carter went to get the cribbage board and a deck of cards. I slowly paced, trying to get a grip on my feelings. I wandered to the open window. It was nearly dusk, another lovely evening. I looked down at my bandaged hand. Why did that damned explosion have to happen, just when things were starting to look up?

Carter returned and we sat at the table. We cut the cards to see who would deal. I won and began shuffling. I glanced up at him, recalling the fun we'd had that morning. I asked myself once more if he could have behaved that way only hours before attempting to blow me to kingdom come. I couldn't see how. The Carter Bass I had come to know didn't seem capable of such cruelty.

I dealt the cards. We each discarded and he cut the deck.

"I see you haven't forgotten how to play," he said. "Funny what you remember and what you don't, isn't it?"

I hadn't given it two thoughts, but he was right. I had forgotten all but a little French; my knowledge of wine had disappeared; I could no longer sail; but I could play cribbage. "Maybe this falls in the same category as being able to read and write," I said.

"Let's see how you do."

We played several hands and I developed a commanding lead.

"This is beginning to look familiar," Carter said with a laugh.

"Maybe the French, the wine, and the sailing I associated with Michel," I said. "Maybe I wanted to forget them."

"Yet you remember him and not me," he replied.

"I don't remember Michel fondly."

Carter rubbed the back of my hand. I looked down at his fingers. I yearned to trust him and had a sudden overwhelming desire to demand the truth, some measure of proof that he wasn't guilty. Then it occurred to me that the quickest way to exonerate him was to find another culprit.

As we played, I kept running the possible suspects through my mind. Erica Maxwell had struck me as nice enough, but she more than anyone had had the opportunity to secrete a bomb on board. And if she hadn't actually done it, why hadn't she been able to prevent it, or at least have noticed that something was amiss?

I wondered about Polly also. Antonio told me that she had met with some woman the day they'd come for me at the clinic. Could it have been Erica? And only that morning Polly had supposedly gone into Toulon to the bank. Could she have made a detour to the marina? Antonio probably could say, unless he was secretly in league with her and their mutual hostility was a cover-up.

And if it wasn't Erica or Polly or Antonio, maybe it was Claudine Lambert or Bob Whitford. Huguette had said Bob had been so furious with Michel he seemed capable of violence. If he felt that way toward Michel, why not toward me? The

205

same might be said of Claudine. And heaven only knew how many others might bear a grudge, as well.

"Your crib," Carter said, after I'd counted the points in my hand.

I picked up my cards. All four were hearts. "Look at that, a flush!" I said.

"Nope," Carter said, "turn card's a spade."

"But I get four points for the hearts."

He shook his head. "In the crib all five cards have to be the same suit for it to be a flush. If it was your hand, it would be different."

"Carter, that's not true. I get the points either way."

"No, Hillary. We had this argument when we first started playing. We checked the rule book and I was right. The rule is different when the flush is in the crib."

I gave him a stern, disapproving look.

"Don't you remember?"

"Of course I don't. How could I? I don't even remember *you!*"

He laughed.

"I think you're cheating me," I said.

"Want me to get the rule book?"

"No, I'm going to beat you by forty points anyway."

Carter rubbed his jaw, studying me. He had a rather whimsical expression on his face.

"What?" I said.

"It's interesting that you remember cribbage, but a version you played before we met. It's as if you blocked out the time in between."

"The other possibility is that you really are cheating," I chided.

"No, think about it, Hillary. This is very interesting. Three things you've learned during the course of our marriage —French, an expertise in wine, and sailing—have been wiped

206

completely from your mind. And the cribbage rules you know are the ones you played by before we met. Intriguing, don't you think?"

He was right. "What do you suppose it means?"

Carter shrugged. Then he beamed at me. "Would it be too self-serving to hypothesize that at a subconscious level you might want to be starting over?"

"It's a possibility," I allowed.

"One I rather like." He laughed good-naturedly.

We were still playing cribbage when Yvonne knocked on my door. She announced that Captain Marguet and another police officer had arrived.

"Whew, saved by the cops," he said. "Hillary, you're as merciless as ever."

Carter offered me his hand, and when I got up, I drifted into his arms. Yvonne had already disappeared down the hall, so I lingered in my husband's embrace, trying to make it seem right and safe.

"At least the police aren't here to accuse me of killing someone, like last time," I said. "This go-round, I'm the victim."

"I have a hunch you were the victim last time too," Carter replied.

"Do you really believe that, or are you just being nice?"

"I believe in you, Hillary. I've told you that."

Carter seemed so decent and genuine. I couldn't imagine that my suspicions had merit. My heart rebelled at the notion. But what hell it was to doubt.

We went downstairs. The authorities were waiting in the salon. It seemed a darkly ironic replay of the last visit by the police, though these were different men and their objective was the reverse of the detectives from Nice.

Captain Marguet greeted us with stiff formality, then introduced his associate, a stocky detective in civilian clothes

207

named Alliod. Marguet brought us up-to-date on the investigation.

"The technicians have determined that the bomb was a plastic explosive, most likely secreted near the fuel tank. The work of an expert."

Carter and I looked at each other. I saw nothing in his eyes that betrayed him.

"The speculation now," Marguet went on, "is that a timing device was activated when the engine was started. We think the intent was for the bomb to explode when the boat was at sea, but we cannot be certain at this point."

"You are saying the bomb blew up the while we were docked only because we returned early," Carter asked.

"That is a strong possibility," the captain said.

"Then it could have been intended for either of us."

Marguet shrugged. "It is impossible to say if the assassin knew you would be on board, monsieur."

Alliod, who spoke little English, had some questions for Carter about Erica Maxwell. I was able to understand only bits and pieces, but I gathered the circumstances of her hiring were the main line of inquiry.

"Is Erica a suspect?" I asked Marguet.

"As you undoubtedly know, Mrs. Bass, in these matters everyone is a suspect."

The officers asked Carter a number of questions about his business, but I gave up trying to follow the conversation. Marguet reviewed with me the events leading up to the explosion, asking where, exactly, Carter and I were at all times during our sojourn on the *Serenity*.

Then Alliod began questioning Carter about some of the same things. As they talked, Captain Marguet leaned over to me and said, "Madame, perhaps we could step outside for a few minutes. The air is very pleasant this evening."

We headed for the French doors. I noticed Carter's brow furrowing. He knew and I knew that Marguet wanted to speak with me in private. The captain slowly strolled toward the edge of the terrace. For a moment he stood there, staring out at the night and listening to the crickets, his hands clasped behind his back. He did not look at me.

"Madame," he said with evident uneasiness, "are you aware of any reason why your husband might wish to murder you?"

I'd known it was coming, but I hadn't expected him to be so direct. "No," I said, trying to sound positive. "I can't think of any reason."

"Are you quite sure?"

"I have amnesia, as you know, Captain, so I'm at a disadvantage. But I can think of no reason."

Captain Marguet contemplated the night.

I grew more and more anxious as he let the silence hang. "Do you suspect Mr. Bass?" I finally blurted.

"We must consider every possibility."

"But why him? Didn't you say the bomb was a timed device, set to explode out at sea? But for my getting sick, Carter would have been killed too."

"That is one possibility. The other is that before leaving the boat Mr. Bass activated the device so that it would explode in five or ten minutes. You said you weren't sure where he was in the final minutes before he departed, is this not so?"

"Yes, but that doesn't mean he was setting a bomb."

"The bomb could have been in place already, madame. It merely needed to be activated. The technicians tell me this might even have been accomplished from a remote location."

"That means any number of people could have done it," I said.

Marguet finally turned to look at me, smoothing his mustache with the knuckle of one finger. "You seem very sure of Monsieur Bass's innocence."

"Unless you have proof to the contrary, I'd prefer to think he *is* innocent."

"Then let me ask you this. Are there large sums of insurance on your life?"

I'd asked myself whether Carter had anything to gain by my death and had dismissed the possibility. But on the lips of the policeman, the question gave me pause. "I have no idea," I said, trying to remain unruffled.

"I understand you are co-owners of a business. In the event of your death, madame, who would receive your interest?"

"I don't know the answer to that either."

"We will be making inquiries," he said.

I did not like the implications. I did not like hearing Carter accused, and yet I was more than a little curious about the answer myself. My heart had told me that my husband was innocent, but was I fooling myself? "I hope it turns out to be a waste of time," I said.

"Please understand, Mrs. Bass, I accuse no one. I have spoken to you in private because it is entirely possible you yourself had suspicions."

I drew an uneven breath, but remained silent. We listened to the crickets together.

"You must have other suspects," I said after a long silence.

"There are people we are questioning. The investigation will continue, I assure you."

I pondered the situation. "Carter wants me to go with him to Paris this weekend," I said. "He's concerned for my safety."

"I understand," Marguet said. "But this bombing was not a casual attempt at murder. If indeed it was planned to occur

210

at sea, it is likely no one ever would have known the cause. You would have been dead with no reason to assume murder."

"Are you saying it's unlikely someone will try to shoot me down in the street, Captain Marguet?"

"Let me put it this way, madame. There was one attempt to be subtle. The future, of course, cannot be predicted." Marguet held his wrist up to the light coming from the house to read his watch. "It is late. If my colleague is finished with monsieur, we must go."

We walked slowly toward the house. "I know you're only doing your job," I said, "but your visit hasn't reassured me. Now I'll be looking over my shoulder all the time."

He nodded in understanding. "Unfortunately, this is the world in which we live, madame. It is not always a happy place."

ARTER SHOWED
Captain Marguet and
Inspector Alliod to the
door while I waited in
the salon. I was very tense when
Carter returned. He looked care-
worn, much as he had that first
day I'd seen him at the clinic. He
sat down across from me.

"So," he said, getting right
to the point, "am I a suspect?"

"Everybody is," I replied
solemnly.

"What did you say when
Marguet asked if I had reason to
kill you?"

Carter's bluntness took me
aback. I told him I couldn't think
of any reason. He did not look as
pleased as I'd have expected. He
calculated my answer.

"I was right, wasn't I?" I
said when he didn't respond.

He was bemused by the
question. "Of course you were."

"Then we don't have any-
thing to worry about."

"As between us, no," Carter said, "but somebody wanted one or both of us dead. That can't be ignored."

"So what do we do?"

"I still think it would be a good idea for us to leave here, if only for a couple of days—long enough to clear our heads and get a perspective on things." He saw my hesitation. "Don't you like the idea?"

"I'm not sure," I replied. "I feel safe here even though it's only been home to me for a few days. It's all I have."

"I won't pressure you to go to Paris," he said, "so if you feel more comfortable staying here, I understand. Or maybe you'd like to visit Jane. I don't mean to force myself on you."

I could see Carter was somewhat insecure about me, and that wasn't what I wanted. "When would you want to leave?"

"I thought tomorrow. The press will probably start swarming around here again and I'd just as soon avoid them. I have business in Cannes I have to tend to in the morning. We could leave afterward."

He wanted a decision, but I wasn't sure what to do. Captain Marguet's suspicions had shaken my resolve. "Can I decide in the morning?" I hedged. "I'm not thinking very clearly right now."

"Yes, of course. I don't want to pressure you. Just the opposite. I want you to feel as secure and safe as possible. You've been through another ordeal."

"It's starting to be a way of life," I said, trying to sound lighthearted about my tribulations. "First the hunter, now the hunted."

"I'll look after you," he said, his voice heavy with emotion.

I nodded in response, wanting with all my heart to believe that he cared. I needed him. It had been bad enough before, when I didn't know if I myself was a killer. Now the

213

danger had shifted to me. There was someone, somewhere, who badly wanted me dead.

—

Polly awoke me the next morning. As she stood at the open door, I squinted back at her, then looked over at the bedside clock, rubbing my eyes. It was after nine.

"If you hadn't awakened me, I'd have slept all day," I mumbled.

"Mr. Bass said to let you sleep, but not too late. He's booked an early afternoon flight to Paris and wants to know if you want to go."

"Has he left for Cannes already?" I asked.

"Yes, ma'am. Before the newspeople started showing up."

"They're here?"

"The police are keeping them off the property, but there've been calls. Mr. Bass left instructions not to speak with them."

"When's Carter going to be back?"

"He said he'd call around eleven to see what you wished to do."

I felt a bit like a pampered child. Carter obviously felt the need to coddle me, probably because I'd seemed so confused and unsure. Unfortunately, a good night's sleep hadn't changed that.

I glanced at Polly, who was waiting. She wore a white blouse, navy skirt, and pumps, just as she had the day I'd first seen her at the clinic.

My secretary was hardly a sinister figure, but still I questioned whether she might somehow have been behind the bombing. I knew it was unreasonable to doubt everyone in my life, and yet I did, especially after my conversation with Captain Marguet.

"Will you be wanting to pack, Mrs. Bass?" Polly asked.

"I'll decide after I get cleaned up and have breakfast."

"Where will you take your breakfast?"

"I'll come down."

"Yes, ma'am." She started to turn away.

"Before you go, Polly, I have a few questions. Close the door, please." I sat up in bed, propping the pillows behind me.

Polly warily shut the door and stood with her hands clasped, waiting.

"We haven't discussed my estate very much and there are some things I'd like to know," I said. "Are there insurance policies on my life?"

"Several, ma'am."

"Totaling?"

"I would have to check to be sure, but in the aggregate of a million dollars, U.S., I believe."

"Who's the beneficiary?"

"Mr. Bass. Originally a large policy was purchased for the benefit of your mother, but with her death it went to Mr. Bass as secondary beneficiary."

"What about my interest in the company?"

"The same, ma'am. Your will provides that the interest now goes to your husband."

There was nothing surprising about either piece of news. For all intents and purposes, I had no one but Carter. Still, the inference was inescapable. "Thank you, Polly," I said.

"We have a copy of your will here in the files. Would you care to see it?"

"Sometime, yes, but there's no rush."

"Yes, ma'am."

"I'll be down for breakfast in half an hour."

Polly left and I stared at the sunshine streaming in the window. I was not especially upset by what I'd just heard. Nothing had changed except that my faith in Carter was still being tested.

—

I finished breakfast—café au lait, bread, and my soft-boiled egg—and had just gotten back to my room when Jane Nyland called from England. Polly brought the telephone up and plugged it in for me before stepping from the room. Jane was as ebullient and outspoken as before.

"God, Hill, what next?" she said.

"Are we talking about my boat?"

"It was in all the papers this morning," she said. "How do your nerves stand it?"

"If I'd stayed aboard fifteen seconds longer, I wouldn't have had any nerves to worry about. I guess I'm lucky to be alive."

"You poor darling. My heart goes out to you."

"Thank you, it's good to hear a sympathetic voice," I said. Even though my memory went back only a few days, I felt a real rapport with Jane. I guess her engaging personality was as hard to resist now as it had been when we'd first met.

"They obviously don't know who did it," she said.

"No."

"Who do *you* think is behind it?"

"I don't have the slightest idea," I said. But there was equivocation in my voice. I heard it myself.

"No one's made threats or anything?"

"No. I guess whoever it is believes that action speaks louder than words."

Jane didn't say anything.

"Am I sounding glib?" I asked.

"You sound stressed out," she said.

"Then it shows."

Another pause.

"Hill, what's wrong? I know you're afraid, but is that all it is? Or is there something more?"

I didn't want to be disloyal to Carter, yet at the same time I needed the opinion of someone who could give me perspective, bolster my confidence in my own judgment. "I'm afraid I've turned completely paranoid," I ventured.

"What do you mean?"

I agonized for a long moment before it all came spilling out. I told her about the timing of the explosion, how Carter had left me behind, how I'd been spared only by chance. I told her about my conversations with Carter and Captain Marguet and about Carter's invitation to go with him to Paris.

"Dear Lord," she said when I'd finished, "you have always had a knack for adventure, love, but this time you've outdone yourself."

"You know Carter. Is he capable of murdering me?"

"Good God, what a question." She took a second before answering. "Honestly, I'd have to say no, he isn't. At least I don't think so. But you're there in the midst of it all. Surely you have a gut instinct, a feeling about him."

She was right. I did. I believed Carter was starting to love me again. I was nearly positive that he cared deeply. Yet I was afraid to trust my judgment. My life, as I remembered it, was scarcely a week old, and I was dealing with a world of strangers, not the least of whom was my husband.

"All the unknowns have me off-balance. What I need is to gain some equilibrium, some perspective."

"Well, if that's the case, then why don't you get your ass out of Montfaucon and come stay with me here at Bakesly Court. Tell Carter you need some rest. You can pass a few quiet days in the country while you decide what you want to do.

You'd be out of harm's way here, love. It's so beastly dull, no self-respecting assassin would deign to come round."

"Where's Bakesly Court?"

"Oh, shit, I keep forgetting about your amnesia. It's James's mummy's place in the Cotswolds. I should say it *was* hers. The old girl died before I came along. Apart from smelling the flowers and the manure, there's not much to do up here but screw. Which is why James and I come here every fortnight or so. He believes in sexual binges followed by periods of abstinence, which is fine for him, considering he's nearly sixty. But being on the sunny side of forty, Lady Jane insists on the occasional quickie in Paris or London, or Lord Nyland will be forced to share her ladyship with an accommodating Frog." Jane took a long breath. "So, having thus explained not only Bakesly Court but Lord and Lady Nyland's sex life, would you, Hillary dear, care to fly up and join me? James will be leaving Sunday evening, so you and I shall have the run of the place. The only servant's a nearsighted old love who barely totters, so we can skinny-dip to our heart's content. What do you think?"

"It's a wonderful offer, Jane," I said, amused. "A very generous one, but I'm afraid I'd only be running from my problems. I think I should go to Paris with Carter. It's what I want, deep down. I just needed someone to open my eyes to the fact."

"Surely you aren't planning a conjugal romp with your own husband? Not the Hillary Bass I know and love."

"Until the damned sailboat blew up, I would have said anything was possible. Now it will probably just be an opportunity to get away and regroup. We both have some confidence rebuilding to do."

"Hillary, you're sounding like a woman who wants to be in love."

"I'm not sure about that part of it. But the time has

definitely come for me to start taking charge," I said, feeling a sudden resolution. "I can't sit around waiting to be a victim."

"Bravo!" she said. "That spirit is you, Hill. I only hope it doesn't backfire." Jane paused for a moment, then went on. "But tell me, will you still be needing my services down there the first of the week, or shall I plan on going home to Paris?"

"I'd still like to see you," I said.

"Super! Where are we least likely to have our car machine-gunned, there or someplace else?"

"Why don't we talk Sunday evening and decide then," I suggested.

"Capital idea. Will you be staying at your flat in Paris?"

"I guess so."

"I'll ring you there."

"Sounds good."

"Oh, by the way, Hill," Jane said, "has Huguette Cuvillier telephoned you, by any chance?"

"Yes, we spoke briefly. She wanted to tell me about the valentine from Todd Halley in *Le Beau Monde.*"

"Huguette loves scandal."

"She did make one interesting point. She said she thought Claudine Lambert was behind the story and that there's politics involved. What do you think?"

"Huguette could be right. Claudine's family's awfully well connected. She has a brother who's a deputy minister of something or other."

"Just what Carter and I need," I said with a sigh.

"Best thing to do, Hill, is to put it from your mind. You've survived scandal in the past—even thrived on it—you shall again."

"I know. And you're a real friend to say so."

"That cheers me, love. Thanks. But I must tell you something. At first I was a little unsure how to take the new you, but I'll admit you're growing on me. I'm not the same person I was before I married James. I've mellowed as well. Perhaps it's for the better, a sign we're growing up."

"I'd like to think so."

"Perhaps we'll become even closer than before," she said.

"That would be nice, Jane."

"Well, on that syrupy note I must run, ducks."

"Talk to you soon."

"Ciao!"

I was about to put down the receiver, but before I did I heard a click on the line. My first thought was of Polly. I blushed to think she might have been eavesdropping.

I had to talk to her about packing anyway, so I went off to find her. She was in Carter's study, working on some files. His telephone was sitting on the corner of the desk. She looked up at me innocently.

"Yes, Mrs. Bass?"

She was so controlled, I couldn't be certain whether she'd been listening in or not. "I've decided to go to Paris," I told her. "I'll need to pack, after all."

"Shall I help you now?" she asked, rising.

"Yes, if you would. Please."

Polly went with me to my room. We briefly discussed what clothing I would need and I started making selections. She went off to get my suitcases and I went to the bath to gather my cosmetics. While I stood at the medicine cabinet Poof came in, meowing as she looked up at me.

I picked her up, realizing that I would be leaving her for a few days. The prospect saddened me because I'd grown as attached to Poof as anything I'd encountered in this new life of mine. I was standing at the door, holding her, when Polly returned with the suitcases.

"I hope kitty doesn't carry on during your absence like she did when you were in hospital, Mrs. Bass," Polly said.

"Was she in a bad mood?"

"I was gone much of the time, but Yvonne said Poof was an absolute pest. She must have missed you because she spent her days staring longingly at the door. Oddly enough she's still doing it some. Otherwise, she seems content enough now that you're home.

I blew at Poof's face, teasing her. "Did you suffer a loss of memory right along with Mommy?" I said to her.

"Cats like order the same as people, I suppose," Polly said.

I put Poof down and watched her scamper out the door. "Maybe so."

The telephone rang and Polly went to answer it. "For you, ma'am," she said. "It's Mr. Bass."

I walked to where Polly stood.

"Shall I leave?" she asked.

"No, I don't think it's necessary." I took the receiver.

Carter sounded in good spirits. "How are you feeling, darling?"

Happiness flowed through me at the sound of his voice. Maybe I had finally laid my fears to rest.

"Did you hear me, Hillary?"

"Oh yes. Sorry. I'm fine. Much better. I had a good night's sleep. It's made all the difference."

"Does that mean a weekend in Paris is in the cards?"

"If you still want to go," I said.

"I do. I have the reservations. All I need is your go-ahead."

"Are you coming back soon?" I glanced at Polly, who was folding clothes and putting them in the open suitcase. I could tell she was listening closely.

221

"I thought I'd have Antonio drop you off here at the brokerage, if you don't mind. That will allow me time to finish my work."

"Whatever you wish."

"Hillary, I'm really pleased you're going with me. It means a lot more than you might think."

His words made me happy. I prayed I was doing the right thing. At a certain point in a relationship trust becomes the issue, and that's where I was with Carter.

We said good-bye and I hung up. Polly's expression was serene, but I was certain she was suffering. There was a touch of extra color in her cheeks.

"Maybe I'm taking too many things for a weekend," I said.

"You always like having several choices, Mrs. Bass. Better too much than too little. That's what you always said."

I nodded, seeing that in some areas it was easier to accept the past than to change it.

"Incidentally, ma'am, did Yvonne speak with you at breakfast?"

"No," I replied. "Did she wish to?"

"No, ma'am, it's not that. I thought she might have told you Paul Debray and Jacques Lepecheur came to the house yesterday, while you and Mr. Bass were in town."

"The detectives from Nice?"

"Yes, ma'am. They interviewed Yvonne, Antonio, and myself. I told Mr. Bass about it this morning before he left. He asked me to mention it to you."

I wasn't quite sure what to make of the news. "What was the purpose of the interviews?"

"I suppose it was routine. Everything with the police is routine to hear them tell it. Mainly they wanted to know about your relationship with Mr. Lambert, particularly what happened just prior to your trip to Nice."

I realized that our past conversations regarding Michel had been general. I didn't have the vaguest idea what had occurred during those last couple of days before the accident. I sat on the bed, studying Polly's expressionless face.

"May I ask what you told the police?"

I discerned a trace of smugness. Polly knew she had an advantage over me when it came to Michel. "There wasn't a great deal to tell, Mrs. Bass. You'd spoken to Mr. Lambert once or twice before you left for Nice. I remember one instance clearly because I answered when he rang up. I didn't hear your conversation, but you seemed upset afterward."

"I didn't discuss my intentions with you, then?"

"No, ma'am. You were going to Nice to pick up your boat at the repair docks. Your boatman had taken it there a few weeks earlier and you'd discharged him in the interim, so you had to fetch it yourself."

In my first conversation with Jane, she'd claimed I'd intended to give Michel a piece of my mind because I was going to be in Nice on business anyway. But Jane didn't know what that other business was, and neither did I. "Was getting the boat my main reason for going to Nice?" I asked Polly.

"You said you were going to meet someone, though you never said who. Monsieur Debray pressed me on the matter, but I'm certain you never told me what your plans were or who you were meeting. Antonio drove you, so he may be able to enlighten you further. The police spoke with him, but I have no idea what he told them."

"I see."

I watched Polly as she worked, pondering this latest piece of information. Who, besides Michel, could I have been meeting in Nice?

Once the suitcase was packed, Polly gave me a pleasant if insincere look. "Shall I carry your case down to the entry, ma'am?"

"If you don't mind."

"Will there be anything else?"

"You might keep an eye on the case to make sure no one tries to slip a bomb in it."

"A bomb?"

"They tried once, a second time wouldn't be surprising," I said.

Polly appeared thoroughly perplexed. "What are you saying, Mrs. Bass?"

"You knew the *Serenity* blew up yesterday afternoon?"

"I was aware of the explosion, but I understood it was due to a gas leak. That's what Mr. Bass said when you got home."

"Then you haven't heard the latest. Last night the police informed us that a plastic explosive with a timed device had been put on the boat. Someone tried to kill me, and maybe Carter as well. It was only by chance that we were both off the boat when it went up."

Polly blanched. Her fingers went to her mouth. "I had no idea," she mumbled. "How terrible . . . horrible."

"It was in all the papers. That's why Jane called me this morning."

Polly seemed to be in shock. *"The Guardian* comes a day late and I haven't seen the local papers yet. Mr. Bass didn't say anything this morning, but perhaps he assumed I knew." Her eyes were still round. "I'm so sorry."

Her reaction surprised me. I wouldn't have expected her to gloat, but she seemed genuinely disturbed.

"Your friend, Erica Maxwell, is being questioned by the police," I said. "She more than anyone had control of what happened on the boat, given her position."

Polly sat on the corner of the bed. "Are they sure it was a bomb?" she intoned.

"Yes."

She looked genuinely aghast.

"Carter says that until whoever is responsible is caught, we can't be sure what's going to happen. My concern is that others are in danger because of me."

"I shouldn't think you need worry about that," she said vacantly.

"Polly, if you don't mind me asking, why did you give me the impression you didn't know Erica Maxwell very well? Carter said you were the one who recommended her in the first place."

She looked embarrassed. "I didn't mean to give that impression, ma'am."

"Do you have any reason to think Erica might want to see me harmed?" I asked.

"No, not in the least." Polly abruptly got to her feet. "Shall I take your case down then, ma'am?"

I had no idea what to make of her strange behavior. "That would be fine, thank you."

She hurried from the room, her expression grave. The bombing had clearly upset her, and I didn't understand why, unless it was the realization that Carter had nearly been killed.

I finished the overnight case myself, gathered my purse, and headed downstairs. Halfway down I saw Polly going out the front door. Yvonne wandered into the entry.

"Where was Polly going?" I asked.

"I don't know, madame. She told me she had some business and that she would be back in an hour."

We heard an automobile moving quickly in the gravel. "She has a car?" I asked.

"Yes, a small one for her personal use."

I glanced at the door. "Did she seem upset?"

"*Oui, madame.*"

"I wonder what about."

"*Je ne sais pas.*"

225

I checked my watch. "I guess I'd better be going."

"You want that I call Antonio to bring the car?"

"Please."

Yvonne went off and I went to the front door, opened it and looked out at the array of summer flowers. The air was fragrant. A minute later Antonio brought the Bentley around. Yvonne bid me good-bye. The chauffeur carried my bag to the car, placing it in the trunk.

"Beautiful day, eh, madame?" he said, as we circled the tree.

"Very beautiful."

We headed through the gate and down the drive. At the entrance to the property there was a solitary *gendarme* who saluted when we passed. No members of the press were in sight. Antonio smiled at me in the rearview mirror.

"What happened to the English?" he said. "She seemed in a big hurry, *non?*"

"I don't know what's wrong with her," I replied.

As we went through Montfaucon, I glanced nostalgically at the little church, remembering my lovely evening with Carter. I recalled his kiss, the way he held me, and I felt good. I could not conceive of him acting that way the night before he intended to kill me. No. It wasn't Carter behind the bombing, I was sure of it.

We'd gone a few more miles before I decided it was time to question Antonio. "I understand the police visited yesterday while we were in Toulon," I said to him.

"Yes, they asked about you and Monsieur Lambert."

"Polly said you drove me to Nice the day of the accident."

"Yes, madame, the English is right."

"Did I tell you what I intended to do there?"

"Well, you were getting your boat. That's why I was not waiting there to bring you back to Montfaucon. You were going to sail to Toulon, and when you call to me at the marina, I was to go for you in the car."

"I didn't mention anything else?"

"Yes, I took you to Nice a day before the boat she was ready because you had to get somebody at the airport."

"At the airport? Who?"

"I don't know, but that is where I take you. Not to the town, not to the apartment, not to Monsieur Lambert's. I take you to the airport."

"You drove me there, but you didn't see who I was meeting?"

"No. You tell me to go home. You say you will take the taxi. And I say, 'Why? I am here with the car.' And you say, 'Do what I say, *mon chou*.'" He grinned at me in the mirror. "You call me *mon chou* for the joke, *n'est-ce pas?* It is our little game. So anyway, I say, 'Is there a secret?' and you say, 'Yes, there is a secret.'"

"How strange. I wonder who I was picking up? Could it have been Michel?"

"No, madame. Monsieur was already in Nice. You said this to me."

I was thoroughly perplexed. The missing piece of information could be significant. My secretiveness on the issue made me uncomfortable. It was a chilling thought, but I wondered if I might not have had still another lover beside Michel. Maybe that was what Michel and I fought about. Maybe it had nothing to do with Carter at all.

Still, I wondered what that could possibly have to do with the bombing, if anything. As time went on, things were getting more complicated rather than less. And Polly's behavior that morning had added to the confusion.

"Antonio," I said, "yesterday morning you drove Polly into Toulon, didn't you?"

"*Oui, madame,*" he said, watching me in the mirror.

227

"Where did you take her?"

"To the bank."

"Anywhere else?"

"No, madame."

"She was in the bank the whole time?"

"Yes, I believe it. Of course, I did not go with her. I was in the car in the street."

"Was she inside for long?"

"Maybe twenty minutes. I am not sure."

"Then you came home?"

"Yes, madame."

Antonio hadn't given me anything that was helpful—assuming that raising more doubt about Polly was desired. Had he reported she'd met with Erica Maxwell, I might have had greater cause to suspect her. My sleuthing wasn't very productive.

We arrived in Cannes and Antonio soon pulled up in front of a distinguished old building in the commercial part of town. It being Saturday, the streets were relatively quiet.

Antonio went round to open my door and I stepped out onto the sidewalk. No sooner had I alighted than Carter came out of the building, briefcase in hand.

"Hello, darling." He embraced me briefly. Then to Antonio he said, "No problems on the drive down, I take it."

"*Non, monsieur. Rien de tout.*"

Carter nodded. "I'm not sure of our return plans, Antonio, but the Jaguar will be at the airport. If you're needed, we'll call."

"*Oui, monsieur.* What about madame's valise?"

"I'll take it."

Antonio got the suitcase from the trunk and placed it on the sidewalk. He saluted us and went round to the driver's seat.

Carter took my suitcase and his briefcase in one hand,

and my arm with the other. We started up the street as Antonio drove off.

"I hope you weren't disturbed by the press this morning," he said.

"No, there weren't any calls that I was aware of."

"Good. I told Polly to screen them. I fielded one myself before I left. You've become quite the story in Paris and London, Hillary."

"Not the sort of publicity I aspire to."

"Being a victim might bring you a little sympathy, though."

"I don't care what people think," I said. "I just want everything resolved." I looked at my husband, hoping we would be able to recapture the closeness I'd started to feel before the damn boat exploded. We'd both become tentative and I didn't like that nearly as much as the way things had been.

"Want your memory back too?" Carter asked.

He didn't intend the question to raise all the other dark issues I faced—foremost among them Michel's death—but it did. "Yes," I replied. "Despite all that's happened, I think I can handle even that. I want this over with."

We went to a nearby garage and waited while the Jaguar was brought around. I told Carter about Polly's bizarre behavior that morning, expecting him to make light of it, but he surprised me, responding with a grave, ominous look.

"I'll speak to her about it the next chance I get," he said, attempting to put my mind at ease.

But it was too late, his concern was apparent. "What do you suppose it means?"

"I don't know," he said, putting his arm around me. "I've come to realize nothing should be taken for granted in this business." Carter was the soberest I'd seen him.

"Should I be more worried than I am?" I asked.

229

Carter looked into my eyes as the attendant pulled up with the car. "I don't want to upset you unnecessarily," he replied, "but I believe I was followed this morning after leaving Montfaucon."

"By whom?"

"I haven't the slightest idea. I'm not absolutely sure I was actually being followed, because the car disappeared after a while. But I called the house and told Antonio to be alert when he brought you."

"That's why you asked him if there had been any problems."

"Yes. Apparently he didn't notice anything strange."

I took an anxious breath. The little surge of fear in my heart was the worst since the bombing. I was reminded again that the danger was still there.

The attendant was holding the passenger door open for me and I climbed in. Carter paid the man and came round to the driver's side. After he'd buckled himself in, we looked at each other for a brief moment.

"It won't go away, will it?" Carter said.

I shook my head.

"I'm not even sure what they're after," he said wearily. "It might not be you."

"Are you saying the bomber was really after you?"

"I have no idea. Either way it will be good for us to get out of here. I'm glad we're going to Paris."

"Jane called this morning and suggested I might want to visit her in the country," I told him.

"What did you tell her?"

"That I had a better offer."

Smiling, Carter leaned over and kissed me on the lips. "You do, darling. You do."

He put the car in gear and drove out of the garage.

Moments later we were hurrying along the boulevard, headed for the airport.

That joy Carter gave me was back again. I was glad I was with him, glad we were going to Paris. Maybe we could put everything behind us and rediscover our love. Maybe the nightmare would finally come to an end.

CARTER SEEMED distracted during the drive to the airport. He checked the rearview mirror quite often, and I glanced back a time or two myself.

"Is anyone following us?" I finally asked.

"No, I don't think so."

"But you're concerned?"

"I'm being cautious, darling."

A feeling of despair came over me. What a way to live—always looking over your shoulder, wondering when the next attempt on your life would be made. "I'm sorry you have to suffer through this too, Carter. It isn't fair."

"It's you I'm concerned about," he said.

Carter was clearly on my side, and that heartened me. I told myself it was important to get into a more positive frame of mind, for both our sakes, so I turned my thoughts to Paris. Our trip would be an adventure, an opportunity to renew our relationship, and maybe our love. I wanted everything to go well. I wanted to find happiness again.

Being at the Nice airport turned out to be a little like going aboard the *Serenity*. I'm not sure when the strange unsettled feeling first came over me—if it was as we approached the terminal building, or when I was standing at the curb out front —but the instant I saw her, an emotional storm welled up.

She was small and frail and very old, sitting under a large umbrella amid her buckets of flowers. Her face was so familiar, yet I couldn't say who she was or why I knew her. She was seated on a stool and wearing a black dress, her gray hair gathered in an untidy knot at the back of her head.

She did not see me right away, but as I walked toward her, her black eyes shifted to mine. She did not smile, but she did look at me intensely, perhaps because of the way I stared at her.

"Des fleurs, madame? Vous voudriez des roses?" As she spoke, she pulled a long-stemmed red rose from the bucket by her knee. The bud trembled in her gnarled, arthritic hand.

I shook with emotion as I peered into her eyes. I took the rosebud and pressed it to my nose. It was as though a powerful drug had been shot into my veins. The only sensation I could recall that had been more intense was the feeling I'd had on the *Serenity*, the dread that had gripped me as Carter had taken me up the boarding ladder.

"Elle est belle, n'est-ce pas?" she said. *"Très belle."*

I nodded as I stared at her, the bud still at my nose.

"Combien en voulez-vous, madame? Une douzaine?"

I realized then that I was merely a customer to her. She'd asked how many roses I wanted, not whether we knew each other, or why I was looking at her so strangely. "Just one," I replied. "How much? *Combien de francs?*"

233

She did not seem pleased that so much theater should result in a request for only a single bud. *"Dix,"* she said. *"Dix francs."*

I fumbled through my purse, but the next thing I knew Carter was giving the flower vendor a ten-franc note. "Is one all you want?" he said to me.

I was watching the woman, trying to fathom the bizarre emotion she had evoked. "Yes." He took my elbow to go, but I said, "Wait a second. Would you ask her something for me? I want to know if she's ever seen me before."

He translated my question. I listened to her response, but didn't understand it.

"She says you look familiar. Even though she sees many hundreds of people every day, you are quite pretty and not easily forgotten." Carter grinned. "I certainly can vouch for that."

"Has she ever sold me flowers before?"

Carter translated. The woman pondered the question, then gave her response. "She says you bought a single flower from her, perhaps a month ago. It was a red rose, just as now."

The news excited me. It was almost like remembering it myself. Carter watched me, a quizzical expression on his face.

"I wonder why you would have been at the airport a month ago. That would have been just before the accident. Could you have been flying somewhere? Or maybe returning?"

"Antonio told me he brought me here to pick up someone. That must have been the occasion."

I turned to the old woman. Here was someone I recognized and who recognized me. Until now, there had only been Michel. How odd. Why this woman?

"Carter, ask her if I was with anyone when she saw me."

He asked the question. The woman replied that I was alone. My heart dropped. I stared at her, searching my mind for a spark—something, anything, that would trip my memory.

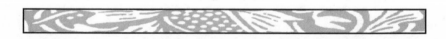

Another customer came up. She turned away. *"Merci, madame,"* I said. I took Carter's arm, and we headed to where a porter waited with our bags. "I know her," I told him. "She is very familiar."

"I've often seen her myself," he said. "She's been around for a long time."

"Yes, but she's the first living human being I can say that about. I recognized *her*, but not my own mother, not you!"

Carter glanced back, sobered by my comment. "That makes no sense. Why her?"

"Wouldn't I like to know."

"If you were meeting someone, maybe you bought the flower for whoever it was," he said.

That possibility occurred to me as well. "Carter, do you think I might have had another lover, someone besides Michel?"

"Do *you* think so?"

"I have no idea. But that would explain why I'd fought with Michel."

Carter listened solemnly as we followed the porter toward the ticket counter. "But you have no recollection of anyone," he said.

"None."

"Let's take that as a good sign and not borrow trouble."

I glanced at him. He stared straight ahead.

"I'm sorry if I upset you," I said.

"Like all the rest of it, Hillary, you're better off if you try to forget the past."

"That's exactly what I've done. I've forgotten it completely."

He smiled at the irony. "Maybe what I'm saying is you should not try so hard to remember."

"The truth, Carter, is you don't ever want me to remember."

235

We'd come to the ticket counter. He paused to analyze what I'd said. "I don't know if that's true, but I'll admit you've got me wondering what I really do want," he said.

While he paid the porter I glanced around and immediately noticed two men approaching us. They were the detectives, Paul Debray and Jacques Lepecheur. Debray was in the lead and striding purposefully. His hair seemed to be particularly shiny, almost wet.

"*Bonjour, monsieur, madame,*" he said, his unruly brows arching. His friendliness was clearly perfunctory.

Carter had not seen them and turned at the sound of the detective's voice. "Well, messieurs," he said, sizing them up, "what a pleasant surprise."

"I regret the intrusion," Debray said easily, "but we learned from your housekeeper you were on the way to Paris and we thought we might intercept you before you begin your voyage."

"For what purpose?" Carter asked.

"Only for some conversation. It saves the trip to Toulon later, *non?*"

Carter glanced at his watch.

"It will only take a few minutes," Debray assured him. "They tell me there is time."

"Let me at least check us in," Carter said.

After he'd finished with the ticket agent, Carter said we had no more than fifteen minutes to spare. Debray assured him we would make our flight. He led us to an employee lounge where we could talk in private. Carter and I sat down on one badly worn Naugahyde couch, the policemen took another one across from us.

Debray eyed my rose, then glanced down at the low coffee table between us. It was littered with dog-eared magazines and empty foam cups. In a fit of tidiness, the detective stacked

236

the cups and set them to the side. Then he leaned forward, his elbows on his knees, and peered at me.

"First, Mrs. Bass, my regrets for the tragedy of the loss of your boat. A most shocking event."

"Thank you," I said tremulously. I glanced at Carter for reassurance. I was more than wary. Debray frightened me, as much because of his forced politeness as his words.

"A terrible loss, monsieur," Debray said to Carter.

"Hillary came within an eyelash of being killed, Debray. The boat's not important."

"Quite right, monsieur." The detective straightened the magazines on the table. "We are in close contact with Captain Marguet in Toulon, so I am aware of the details."

"Surely you didn't come out here to tell us that," Carter said.

"No, we have other matters to discuss," Debray allowed. He gave a sideward glance at Lepecheur. The younger policeman stroked his beard, his notebook at the ready, though he remained mute. Debray cleared his throat. "Marguet has no evidence pointing to a particular suspect. Do you have any theories?" he asked.

The detective looked at me when he asked the question, so I responded. "We have no idea who was behind it," I said. "If we did, we certainly would have told Captain Marguet. But I have a question for you, Monsieur Debray. Do you think the bombing was connected to what happened to Michel?"

Debray seemed suddenly ill at ease. "We have no indications of it," he replied, "but one must consider that anything is possible." He contemplated his nails. "There are various ways one can connect them. The most obvious, of course, is that the bombing was revenge for Monsieur Lambert's death. But it could be that the same person wanted both you and Lambert dead. Another possibility is that whoever blew up your boat did not wish to chance that you would recover your memory." He contemplated both me and Carter. "This last, I think, is a most intriguing possibility."

"But why would that be important?" I asked.

"If I knew the answer, I would also know the identity of the culprit."

"We can't even be sure the bomb was intended for Hillary," Carter said. "They might have been after me."

"Perhaps, monsieur. I have discussed this with Captain Marguet. But this possibility is troubling to both of us. The assassin would have to know you would be on the boat that day, whereas since it was madame's boat, she could be expected to take it out anytime. Let me ask you, Mr. Bass. How many people knew you would be with madame that afternoon?"

"Hardly anyone outside the household. Erica Maxwell is the only one I told personally."

"She is the person most central, it is true," Debray said flatly.

"Do you seriously suspect her?" I asked.

Debray rubbed his chin. "With no apparent motive, a person in such an obvious position to kill is not likely to do so in such an obvious fashion. Not a rational person, and I understand Mademoiselle Maxwell is quite rational."

"Then you don't believe Erica was behind the bombing," Carter said.

"I eliminate no one, monsieur, but I personally have serious reservations about the probability of her guilt. Also, she has been questioned thoroughly and nothing, I am told, has turned up in these conversations."

"Where does that leave things, then?" Carter asked.

Debray's eyes shifted to me. "It leaves us as dependent as ever on madame's memory. May I ask, Mrs. Bass, has there been any improvement? Have you been able to recall any more than the last time we spoke?"

"Nothing about Michel. Nothing about what happened that day."

There must have been equivocation in my voice because Debray stared at me for a moment, then said, "Are you sure?"

I sighed and looked at Carter. Then I met the detective's gaze. "I still have no clear memory, but when I was aboard the *Serenity* I did have a terrible feeling and visions of myself—"

"Hillary," Carter interjected, "there's no need to go into that. Bad dreams, visions, or whatever the hell it was that you had, are not evidence of a crime."

I looked at my husband, aware of what he was thinking, what he feared. But I had a strong desire to unburden myself. I bit my lip and turned to Debray.

"What was your terrible feeling, Mrs. Bass?" he said.

"I pictured myself struggling with Michel."

"That doesn't prove anything," Carter said. "It could have been in self-defense."

Debray ignored him. "What else, madame?"

"I knew the boat quite well. I have recollections of being on it. It was familiar to me, unlike so many other things."

"Hillary," Carter protested.

"It's the truth, Carter," I said. "I have no desire to hide it."

"These guys aren't playing games. This is serious business," he shot back. "The flower vendor out front seemed familiar to you too, so your vague memories are obviously random." He shifted his attention to Debray. "Don't you see, her emotions, these half-baked visions she keeps having, are meaningless?"

Still Debray did not look at Carter. "What is this about the flower vendor, Mrs. Bass?"

I explained what had happened outside the terminal building. Lepecheur scribbled a few notes.

239

"This is ridiculous," Carter said. "It's all meaningless. I don't know why you bother, Hillary." He shifted uncomfortably. "Anyway, we have a flight to catch."

"Monsieur is right," Debray said. "We don't want you to miss your plane." He got to his feet and so did we. "But I am not so pessimistic as your husband regarding the importance of your visions."

I glanced at Carter somberly. "If it turns out I'm guilty of something, I would just as soon know," I said. "And I won't be hiding the truth when I do recall what happened, no matter the consequences."

My husband was not pleased, but he didn't say any more. We went to the door, where Debray hesitated. "There is one other thing. I'm afraid we do owe you an apology regarding the incident with the reporter, Monsieur Halley. I have learned that the information of our investigation was leaked by an official in the Ministry of the Interior to a relative of Madame Lambert. The family then passed it to the press, we assume to discredit you, Mrs. Bass. In any case, we are deeply embarrassed and extend our apologies to you both."

"Your candor is admirable," Carter said.

"We work in the interests of justice," Debray replied. "But we are human. We make mistakes." He opened the door and Carter and I went out of the lounge and headed for the gate. Carter took my hand as we walked. I still had my rose, and I inhaled its scent.

"You were very clever," my husband said to me. "At first I thought you were being foolish telling Debray so much, but then I saw what you were up to. You wanted him to think you were being a hundred percent up-front with him so that he won't doubt you."

"I *was* being a hundred percent up-front with him, Carter. And I will be in the future. I don't intend to hold anything back. I've thought about it. If I did kill Michel—if I wake up one of these days and remember that—I'll confess. I wouldn't be able to live with myself otherwise."

Carter stopped and stared at me with disbelief. Then, without saying anything, he took my hand again and we continued along.

As we reached the gate, they were calling our flight for boarding. Carter pulled me aside, not far from a young couple who'd embraced and were saying good-bye. He took my face in his hands and said, "Hillary, in my entire life I've never been so confused about what's real and what's not. But I want you to know one thing. I'm falling in love with you all over again."

I smiled as he kissed my lips. All the torment I'd been through suddenly seemed worthwhile.

THE MOMENT THE plane was airborne I felt a sense of relief. I hadn't left all my troubles behind, but at least Carter and I were getting a change of scene, a respite from the anxiety and danger of the past few days. But our escape was only part of the reason for my happiness. When Carter confessed that he was falling in love with me again I'd felt not only joy, but a sense of hope.

Since boarding the plane neither of us had said much, though Carter had held my hand continuously. That, perhaps, was an eloquent statement in itself.

As I leaned close to him, he rolled his head my way. I suspected we were having many of the same thoughts. Soon we would be lovers again. Without pretense. Without apology. But not, unfortunately, without some measure of uncertainty. My husband might love me, but in so many ways he remained a stranger. I didn't know his body, or the way he made love. That was partly what this trip was about —rediscovery.

The rose he had bought me was lying on my lap. I picked it up and inhaled its scent. Roses were becoming an addiction, a symbol of my obsession with that nebulous vision locked in my head. I closed my eyes and snippets of the mystery woman in the rose garden played through my mind. She was so tenacious, this woman. Even now she seemed to be imploring me. But I could see no connection between her and the flower vendor. The woman from my dream was different somehow. She was fired with a deeper passion—one I vicariously shared.

The flight attendant came round offering drinks. Carter suggested a glass of wine. It sounded good. I was ready to kick back a little.

The wine was served in individual carafes, large enough for two glasses. I drank my first rather quickly while we chatted. Carter talked about his regular commute between London and Paris, and the fact that he hadn't made the trip to the south of France much in recent months. I asked about his life in London and he contrasted it to our lifestyle at Montfaucon.

We were proceeding as new lovers might, cautiously testing each other, going from one step to the next so long as what was happening felt good. Yet there was more to it than that —another dimension that couldn't be ignored. For me, at least, love was uncharted territory. I had no memory of previous experience to fall back on, no fond recollections. And yet, I was a sexual being. When kissed I'd become aroused. I'd known what to do and what I liked.

Carter had been watching me reflect. "You have the most fascinating expression on your face. Dare I ask what you're thinking?"

I laughed. He was bemused by my reaction.

"That good?" he teased.

"Am I blushing?"

"Now you've got me really intrigued."

I leaned close to him, and in a low voice said, "I was thinking about sex."

That brought a smile. "Something any gentleman would be pleased to hear."

"Don't jump to conclusions, Carter. It's a problem for me."

"You're afraid you've forgotten how?"

"Not exactly. But imagine if you were in my shoes and couldn't remember having done it."

He tried not to laugh, but he was clearly amused. I gave him a jab with my elbow. "It's not funny," I said.

We'd been talking softly, but Carter lowered his voice even more. "Would you like for me to enlighten you, darling? I'd be pleased to tell you anything you want to know."

Color stained my cheeks. "I'm not sure this is the proper time," I said, unable to hide my embarrassment.

"You raised the issue."

I took a long sip of wine. Dutch courage. "True."

"So, are you interested or not?" He drew my hand to his lips and kissed it, I suppose as a gesture of reassurance.

I considered his offer. The objective wasn't unworthy. How else was I going to find out about our sex life?

"I'm not interested in the X-rated version," I said, barely above a whisper, "but I am curious how things were when we first met . . . what I was like, what we were like together."

"Where shall I begin? We met in Paris, as you know. Your father called from New York, asking if I would check up on you. He and your mother hadn't been able to reach you for several days and they were worried. I phoned the flat where you were staying, but we never connected. Finally I decided to drop by and happened to catch you in.

244

"You'd been living the high life—partying all night, going off on wild jaunts. You'd come home to change clothes and answered the door in your slip. When I explained my purpose in coming, you were terribly amused."

"Amused?"

"Yes, you asked me what I expected to find. I told you I wanted to make sure you weren't on the verge of starvation. And you, cheeky little thing that you were, asked what I'd have done if you were starving to death. I told you I'd probably have to force-feed you."

"And what did I say?"

"That I ought to take you out to dinner if I was so concerned. But it had to be a three-star restaurant because you only let strangers take you out if the meal was first-rate."

"I didn't lack for gumption, did I?"

"No, Hillary, that was never your problem. Anyway, you dressed while I waited and by the time we left I was completely smitten. You were the most beautiful woman I'd ever seen."

"So, it was love at first sight."

"I was smart enough to know you weren't at all my type, that you were frivolous, self-possessed and insincere, but that didn't matter. I couldn't resist you. I rationalized that under my steadying influence you'd come around."

"You were going to reform me, in other words."

"I was going to save you, Hillary."

"You wanted to play rescuer," I said, "but what did I want, a free meal?"

"You were attracted to me, but not as much as you were drawn to the illicitness of it all. Later you confessed that you were fascinated with the idea of having a fling with your father's business partner."

"Nice attitude."

"You've always enjoyed being outrageous. I don't believe you were as naughty as you liked to pretend, but you put on a good show. But to continue the story, we left for dinner and weren't in the taxi two minutes before you wanted to know if I kept champagne in my refrigerator. I asked if you were suggesting we go to my place and you said, 'Bass, you're a quick study.' "

"I *was* a cheeky little bitch, wasn't I? We never made it to dinner, I take it."

"No, the champagne course is as far as we got."

I covered my face. "I'm not sure I want to hear the rest."

"It was quite a nice evening, actually."

"I bet it was."

"We got to my flat and, alas, I was out of champagne. Ever the patient one, you sent me out for some. When I returned, you had disappeared. I assumed you'd left until I found you in my tub, up to your chin in bubbles. To make a long story short, you drank your half of the champagne in the bathtub, and I had my half sitting on the bidet."

"I'm afraid to ask what happened next."

Carter's grin was faintly diabolical. "You invited me to join you. Not being one to pass up a golden opportunity, I stripped down. You claimed you liked watching a man undress. Most women, you said, didn't appreciate the potential in that, but you did."

"Quite a first date," I mumbled.

"You don't want to hear the rest?"

"I have a feeling you're going to tell me."

"Not if you don't want me to," he said.

I glanced around, satisfying myself that no one was listening. "All right, so what happened?"

"You wanted me to rub you down with body lotion. Being a bachelor, I didn't have any. But I found a shaving balm and we massaged each other with it. You insisted on doing me

246

first. After I did you, we made love, right there, right then, on the bathroom floor."

My insides were quivering. I can't say whether Carter had intended for the account to sound so erotic, or if it was the circumstances in which I was hearing it, but I was getting turned on, no doubt about it. I drew a calming breath. "It's safe to say I'm not shy."

"No one can accuse you of that, Hillary."

I drank more wine, then stared at my glass, turning it slowly by the stem. The obvious question was on the tip of my tongue, so I gathered my courage and asked it. "So, how was the sex? Good or bad?"

"It was good. First times aren't always."

"Good for me?"

"You told me you liked wild, frenzied sex, and that's what we had. You also admitted that half the excitement came from the taboo, the fact that I worked with your father."

That shocked me. "Did you feel I was using you?"

"Not really. We used each other. But I was an idealist. I'd fallen hard for you and believed there was a germ of love buried somewhere in our relationship. I wasn't entirely wrong. We had a functional, if not blissful, marriage, at least until we were overwhelmed by its shortcomings."

"Hearing that doesn't give me much hope for the future," I said.

"There's no reason to feel that way. A lot of things have changed. I get different vibrations from you now, Hillary. I hear different words when you speak. No matter how skeptical and suspicious I've been this past week, you've yet to disappoint me."

The whine of the engines changed pitch and there was a jolt as the pilot let down the flaps. I peered out the window, considering what Carter had said. Could this be a new beginning for us? We were returning to where it had all started, but we

247

were different people now. We were older, wiser. We both wanted to make it work.

The flight attendant came by and I handed her my wine glass, as did Carter. We put up our trays. Carter leaned over and kissed my ear. "I don't want you to be nervous," he whispered. "I know how emotional this trip is for you. I hope that knowing I care, that I love you, will make it easier."

I touched his cheek. I wanted to tell him that I loved him too, but how could I? Love without trust was meaningless, and before I could put any trust in our relationship, I had to be able to trust myself. Unfortunately, there was nothing Carter could do about that. It was totally beyond his control.

—

I watched Paris unfolding through the window of a taxi and it was like seeing it for the first time. In the early evening the City of Light had a dreamy quality, a mellowness amid the vibrancy. Holding Carter's hand, I was content.

I had glimpses of the Eiffel Tower now and then as we made our way along the Seine. Carter had told me that our apartment was not far from the parc du Champ, where the tower was located, so I could tell we were getting close.

The Seventh Arrondissement was bourgeois, a little stuffy and quite expensive, but it was central and Carter assured me that the flat itself was quite nice, a pied-à-terre that served our purposes well. Since it had become neutral territory, I hoped it would prove to be a suitable place to lay our hostilities to rest once and for all.

By the time our taxi entered the Quai de Grenelle, I was starting to get nervous. Being alone with Carter would be still another test—not only of my memory, but of me as a woman. I was now in the unenviable position of having to compete with myself.

Carter must have sensed my anxiety because he kept up a stream of conversation. As we went up the Avenue Bosquet, he pointed out places that had had meaning to me at one time. I hardly heard him. I was having a crisis of confidence.

He pressed my hand to his cheek and said, "You really feel clammy. Are you okay?"

"Just a little nervous."

"Relax," he said. "You handled it well the first time I brought you here, and you were only twenty-two then."

"That's what's been bothering me—then versus now."

The taxi made two quick turns on side streets and abruptly came to a halt. I peered up at what must have once been a rather grand townhouse. It was three stories, with an apartment on each level. Our flat was the middle one.

I didn't recognize the building. That had become a given. We got out. I glanced up and down the quiet street, trying to picture myself alighting here almost a decade earlier. I was a high-living model at that time, hungering for seduction and adventure. Now I was thirty, ignorant of my own sexuality and shaking in my boots.

Carter supervised the unloading of our luggage, then we went inside. The entry smelled somewhat like a grand old hotel that had had many years of care. I suspected it must have struck me the same those eight-odd years ago. What had been going through my mind that evening? I wondered. Had I carried a secret fear that Carter hadn't gleaned? Had my outrageousness been a mask to cover my insecurities?

We went up the stairs while the driver brought up the rear with our suitcases. I ran my hand along the highly polished banister as I climbed. It occurred to me then that part of my fear was that I might disappoint Carter. What if this didn't work out? What if our big romantic weekend was a failure? And most frightening of all—what if I started to remember, and didn't like what I discovered?

249

The door to our flat was very tall and heavy. Carter unlocked it, and I stepped inside while he paid the driver. I entered with reverence and wonder, just as I had at the villa that first day.

The scent of leather, fine wood, and roses filled the salon. The room was large and formal. A bay window over-looked the street. There were two dozen pink roses on an an-tique marquetry table in front of the window. I walked across the enormous Oriental carpet, drawn to the flowers. I smelled the buds. They were fresh, doubtlessly placed there at Carter's instructions.

I was still carrying the rose I'd gotten at the airport in Nice. It looked weary, so I slipped it into the vase to give it a drink. A single red bud among the pink.

I peered out the window. In the street below, I saw the driver climb into his taxi and drive off. An elderly man walked his schnauzer on the sidewalk across the way. I could hear the hum of traffic on the nearby boulevard, but the neighborhood was otherwise quiet.

I turned to see Carter standing on the far side of the room, watching me. He didn't speak, nor did I. I fancied that on that first occasion I'd filled the room with outrageous prattle, all the while flaunting myself, daring Carter to do something overt. I suspected that back then I'd been trying to define my own limits. Now I quailed because I didn't know what those limits were. Moderation, it seemed, was coming to me late in life.

"What do you think of it?" Carter asked.

"The apartment?"

He nodded.

I glanced around, noticing the art—two Impressionist paintings, a somewhat older landscape, and a few miniatures. "It's formal," I said, "but not cold. I like it."

"The flowers are for you, by the way. I took the risk you'd feel more at home with roses around."

I sniffed a bud. "Thank you. That's very considerate."

Carter turned on a lamp in the far corner of the room. He walked to a Louis XVI armchair—most likely a replica—and sat down, crossing his legs. I stayed at the bay window, watching him.

"Where I live, really, is at the house in Kensington," he said. "If you judge me, it should be by that."

"I bet you didn't say anything like that the first time you brought me here," I chided.

"No, how you felt about my lifestyle was probably the least of my concerns. Once we'd arrived I was focused on one thing."

"Sex?"

"Sex."

We stared at each other.

"What happened when we first got here? What did I think of the flat?

He reflected. "You pronounced it very stuffy, suitable for fucking Frenchwomen. You said both I and my house needed loosening up."

"I'm surprised you didn't pitch me out."

"Being impertinent was part of your persona, Hillary. You liked provoking me and fighting was foreplay as far as you were concerned. I'm glad to see that's no longer the case, incidentally."

"What a difference a few weeks of unconsciousness makes," I said.

Carter smiled.

"But don't get too used to it," I warned. "I can't make any guarantees."

He raised his brows but didn't comment directly.

"Would you like something to drink or eat? I've had the place stocked."

"Are you having anything?"

"I'm considering champagne."

"Haven't I heard that someplace before?" I said with a laugh.

"Does that mean you'd rather not?"

I shook my head. "Actually it sounds good, in spite of the associations."

"It's the people, not the drink, that matters, Hillary. I don't think either of us are the same now as then." He got up. "I'll just take the suitcases back, then I'll get the champagne."

Carter left the room. I took a deep breath, drawing in myriad scents, dominated by the roses. I peered out the window at the opaque sky and heard a siren somewhere off in the direction of the Seine. The sound reminded me of the chaos at the marina following the explosion, and I shivered as I recalled once more how close I'd come to death.

Something drew my eye to a car parked up the street, facing the apartment. There was a man seated inside and he seemed to be looking directly at our flat. The notion that someone might be spying on us disturbed me. Was it my imagination? My paranoia? I saw a puff of cigarette smoke emanate from a window of the car. There was nothing unusual about a man in a car on a city street, I told myself. Maybe he was simply smoking while he waited for someone.

Still I couldn't dispel my suspicions. For the minute or two I stood there, I felt I was being watched. The trance was broken when Carter returned with an ice bucket, the champagne, and glasses.

He'd taken off his sport coat and was in a tie and shirtsleeves. He looked relaxed, and confident, and very sexy. I wanted to be near him, so I went over.

"Carter, do you think we're safe here in Paris?"

"Safe? What do you mean?"

"I don't know. I guess I'm gun-shy. I keep imagining people are following us."

"I shouldn't have told you I thought I'd been followed this morning," he said as he removed the wire keeper from the bottle.

"It's not your fault. I'm probably just jumpy."

"Considering what happened at the marina, you're entitled. But I don't want you to think about any of that. Concentrate on Paris, on being with me, and having a good time."

I pressed my cheek against his shoulder. "You're right. It doesn't help to worry."

Carter put his free arm around me and gave me a hug. "What you need is a nice glass of champagne," he said, pouring some into one of the flutes. He handed it to me, then filled a glass for himself.

We faced each other. "Welcome to Paris," he said, saluting me.

I smiled and so did he. We drank.

"Listen," he said, "would you like a tour? You haven't really seen the apartment yet."

"Sure."

We took our glasses with us and Carter led the way to an intimate dining room. There was an antique sideboard against the far wall with an ornate gold framed mirror above it. It looked valuable. I could picture us eating at the table by candlelight.

The kitchen was enormous. It had been modernized, but between the high ceilings and the tile, it still had an Old World charm.

I joined Carter at the refrigerator. Neatly wrapped and carefully labeled provisions had been stacked on the shelves. There were also fresh vegetables, milk, some sort of creamed

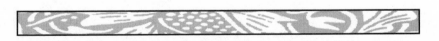

pastry in a plastic container, and three more bottles of Laurent Perrier.

"Is the apartment always ready?" I asked.

"There's a woman who keeps it up," he said, closing the refrigerator door. "We notify her when we're coming and she stocks the kitchen and makes sure the linens are fresh. One or the other of us is here a third of the time," he said.

We'd moved to the middle of the room and were facing each other. I sipped my champagne, watching him over the rim of the glass. "Do I cook?" I asked.

"Not nearly so well as you play cribbage," he teased. "Puttering in the kitchen comes far down the list of your indulgences."

I didn't even bother to ask.

We went back through the apartment. "The bath," he said, reaching into the room to turn on the light.

"The infamous bath," I said.

"Yes, the infamous one."

From the hall I could see an expanse of white tile. "I'll want to visit it shortly," I said.

"Let me show you the bedrooms."

We looked in on the small guest room first. It was tidy, functional. The master suite consisted of a large bedroom-sitting room arrangement, as well as a dressing room. The decor was less formal than the salon, but not especially homey.

The bed caught my eye. It was high off the floor, typically European, and it had an unusual gilt wood headboard. It was very beautiful. If I let myself I could picture naked bodies on the bed—mine, Carter's. The thought aroused me.

He'd swung open the window to let in some fresh air. I joined him and saw that there was a small garden in back, lush with flowering shrubs and beds. It had been an overcast day, and with twilight approaching, the quality of light was rather remarkable.

Beyond the nearby rooftops I could see the upper half of the Eiffel Tower rising into the darkening sky. I must have looked at this view a thousand times, but I knew I could look at it a thousand more and never fail to appreciate the romance of it all.

Carter took a sip of his champagne. "Paris is yours, my love."

I watched the blinking lights on the tower. "It's lovely. Very romantic."

In the evening light Carter's eyes seemed darker, a deeper richer blue. His thick brownish blond hair swept across his forehead, softening the contours of his face. Watching him, I thought of strength and masculinity and a kind of controlled sexiness that I wanted to test.

"You're so lovely," he whispered.

My throat tightened. I had to force myself to draw a breath. Carter set our champagne flutes on the chest behind him. Then he gathered me close. I slipped my arms around his neck and our lips met. His tongue slid over the edges of my teeth. The kiss deepened.

He explored my mouth—cajoling me not to hold back, to give more and give again. I responded immediately, surprising myself at how eagerly I accepted his affection, how quickly my fear had turned into desire. When the kiss finally ended I took a deep breath, drawing in his tangy scent and the fragrances from the garden. I felt shaky, almost weak. I started to speak, but there were no words.

Carter's breath washed over my neck as he gave me a final kiss, just below my ear. "Sorry if I got carried away," he murmured.

"People who are married as long as we've been aren't supposed to feel like this, are they?" I said.

255

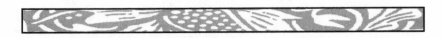

"Supposedly not. But I assure you, I'm not pretending." He held me protectively. I felt loved and safe. For the moment, all my demons had been vanquished.

After a minute or two I slipped away. "I think I'd like to freshen up," I said. I looked around the room. "Is my overnight case here?"

"Yes," he said. "But before you go, I'd like to give you something." He went to the dressing room. I heard him opening closet doors. Then he came back with a package wrapped in clear plastic. He handed it to me.

"I got this in Japan for you a year or so ago. I never gave it to you, but I'd like you to have it now."

"How sweet." I removed the wrapping. It was a white silk kimono with a black ibis embroidered on the back. "Oh, it's lovely, Carter," I said. "Thank you. I'll put it on."

He took my jaw in his hand and brushed his lips across mine. I wanted to prolong the caress, to put my arms around him and kiss him again as we had kissed before. But I held back, knowing that if I didn't leave then, I never would.

Taking the kimono with me, I headed for the bath. My heart was still pounding when I got there. I closed the door and leaned against it, hoping to calm myself.

Eventually I became aware of my surroundings. The infamous bathroom, as we'd called it, was quite large. In the European tradition the water closet was separate, the next door down the hall. My eye went to the tub. It was oversized, gleaming white. I had a vivid image of myself in it, buried to my chin in bubbles as Carter and I drank our champagne, titillating each other.

I knew it wasn't an actual memory, because until I'd seen the bathroom, I'd pictured it differently. But now, standing there, I visualized myself provocatively lifting my leg from the bubbles to arouse him.

I glanced down at the tile floor, imagining the cold feel

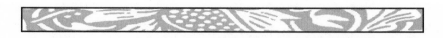

of it against my back. I pictured myself lying there, my skin flush and alive, with Carter standing over me. I imagined opening my legs to him as he knelt between them.

I played the fictional memory over in my mind. It excited me. I struggled to recall the actual sensation of Carter entering me. I knew his kiss, his tongue, but not his sex. That part of him remained a mystery.

I literally trembled with need. I stared at the floor, imagining us writhing on the tile. Trying to get control of myself, I stepped to the basin to splash cold water against my cheeks. My heart grew calmer.

I undressed then and sponged myself off before putting on my kimono. The silk felt cool and sensuous against my skin. The wickedness of being naked under it appealed to me. That made me wonder if I was about to return to my old hedonistic ways.

I decided not to worry about it. I was Hillary Bass either way, whether I regained my memory or not. I'd been living her life, sleeping in her bed, and I was on the verge of making love with her husband. That was as it should be. Carter wanted me. And right then, I wanted him. That was all that mattered.

ARTER WAS AT
the window, in the
midst of closing the
heavy draperies, when I
opened the bedroom door. He
froze at the sight of me.

"You look lovely," he said.
"Truly lovely."

I smiled, touching my hair
self-consciously. I was aware of
the cool silk of the kimono rubbing against my skin. I remained
at the door, more uncertain than
afraid.

He finished closing the
drapes. As they came together I
had a last glimpse of the Eiffel
Tower lit against the deep blue
sky. The room smelled of humid
evening air and the floral scents of
the garden. The only light now
came from a small lamp in the sitting area. The warm glow cast tenebrous shadows across the suite.

Carter walked toward me.
My lips slightly parted as the image of us making love rolled

through my mind. The man who'd pleasured me on that tile floor in the bathroom so many years ago had come to life.

He had removed his tie and unfastened the top few buttons of his shirt. I became aware of the dusky mat of hair covering his chest. I imagined the feel of it against my breasts. There were no words in my head, only awareness.

Carter did not speak either. I sensed he understood it was important for me to have this silent connection, this moment of communion. Yet I knew he wanted us to have more than that too, much more.

As if on cue he put his hands on my waist. The flow of energy between us coalesced as he drew me into his embrace and kissed me. The tip of his tongue brushed mine. Now that I was in his arms, my awareness of him became acute. I sensed his need, his desire, and I knew my ardor matched his.

When he pulled back, he left me trembling. I felt weak.

"Carter," I murmured, "please make love to me."

His eyes darkened. He slowly and deliberately reached out and untied my kimono. The gown opened, exposing my breasts—and more—but he didn't look down. He continued to gaze into my eyes. The power in that made me shudder.

Carter slid the kimono from my shoulders and let it drop to the floor. I stood naked before him.

He lifted me into his arms then, and carried me to the bed. I lay there, stunned by the suddenness of it all. Only an hour before I'd been fearful of making love again, now I was yearning for it, eager for my husband's touch. Carter sat down next to me and took my hand, the one I'd scraped falling on the dock. He ran the tip of his finger around the edge of the bandage.

When he glanced at me I saw a tinge of uncertainty on his face. "Are you sure this is what you want?" he asked.

I nodded. "Yes. I'm very sure."

He took my hand. I was touched by his gentleness. The

gesture was deceptive, though, because when he drew his tongue across my palm, the effect was so electric, so completely unexpected, it took my breath away.

Carter had known in advance I would like that. I could see the power of knowledge in his eyes. There was nothing tentative about the way he'd approached me. He had a lover's mastery. A longtime lover.

"You know more about my body than I do, don't you?" I said.

He smiled in response.

"Are you going to take advantage of your knowledge?" I asked.

"Would you like me to?"

It was a strangely compelling question. Carter would know my responses before I made them. He knew what I liked, whereas I didn't. And yet that had to be every woman's fantasy —being with a lover who knew exactly what she wanted and needed without her having to say a word.

"Yes," I whispered, "show me what I like."

He took my little finger in his mouth and drew his lips along the shaft, wetting the skin. I closed my eyes as he sucked every finger that way. Each time he did it made me shiver.

"You enjoy this, don't you?" he said.

"Oh, yes."

"Bring back any memories?"

It didn't. But that hardly mattered. It was wonderful.

"Carter . . ."

He turned my hand over and kissed the back of my wrist again. "Yes?"

"Is this what I like best?"

"There are certain rituals you enjoy but you like everything."

"What do you mean by everything?"

In response he only smiled.

"That isn't fair," I said, as he moved his mouth up the inside of my arm. "If this is my fantasy, I must know it too."

"Ah, but think of the excitement in not knowing what's coming. This is the only time it can ever be like this. Next time you'll know what to expect."

He licked the middle finger of his right hand, then lightly touched the tip of my nipples. I moaned. "Do you really mean everything?" I asked breathlessly. *"Everything?"*

He nodded. He put his hand on the flat of my belly. The heat from his skin radiated right through me. Knowing he was going to do with me as he wished, I closed my eyes. Carter had his own agenda. We would be doing things his way, at his pace. I almost forgot to breathe, waiting to find out what would happen next.

I didn't have to wait long. When he moved to the foot of the bed and began kissing my toes, my eyes flew open. I watched him poke his tongue into the gap between each toe until I couldn't watch anymore. Instead I stared at the ceiling, finding the blind discovery of his actions even more stimulating.

He drew his tongue up my instep. I groaned.

"You like this even better than when I kiss your hands, don't you?" he asked.

I made a fist, as if to recapture the feeling on my palm. It was true. What he was doing to my feet turned me on even more. "Yes," I muttered.

Carter's lips moved up my leg. He began kissing the insides of my knees, crossing back and forth, from leg to leg, as he made his way up my thighs.

"Oh my Lord." I couldn't help myself; I lifted my head to see what he was doing. "You'd better stop," I said, grasping myself between the legs. "I can't take much more."

"Hillary, the part you like best is yet to come."

Now I understood what he meant when he'd said everything. There was no limit, there were no bounds.

261

Carter resumed caressing my thighs, moving closer to the juncture of my legs. I could feel the heat of his breath on the back of my hands where I clutched myself.

The anticipation was excruciating. I could hardly wait, but Carter held back. He toyed with me. Teased me.

When he finally pulled my hands away, I grabbed the bedspread, knotting it in my fists. I felt his cheek brush my curls. I felt his breath. Then he pushed my legs farther apart and I felt his tongue graze my nub. I gasped.

"Oh, Carter! Oh, my God!"

He flicked his tongue across me, once, twice, then he pulled back just enough to blow on me. A charge went clear to the ends of my fingers. My body throbbed, wanting more. I scooted toward him, just a bit, and opened my legs even wider.

When he slipped his finger inside my opening, all the while making love to me with his mouth, I cried out. It was too much pleasure.

"Stop, oh stop!" I pleaded.

Carter pulled back. The air felt cool every place he had touched me. "Hillary . . . darling . . . Hillary," he said over and over.

I was oblivious to everything but my pleasure. How could ecstasy such as this ever have escaped my mind? I would never forget this night. No matter what.

Two or three minutes passed before Carter lifted his head. "You liked that, didn't you?"

I laughed. "How could I not?" I ran my fingers through his hair.

"There's only one problem. You weren't supposed to come yet," he said. "You were supposed to tell me when you were on the edge."

"You didn't let me know. Not that it would have made any difference. But now I want you in me. Please."

262

He got up from the bed and began unbuttoning his shirt. He did not hurry. The very deliberateness with which he moved was a statement in itself.

As Carter removed his trousers I saw that he was more muscular than I had realized. He was a beautifully made man. He joined me on the bed, lying on his side, his body touching mine. His skin felt hot. I hadn't realized I was cold until then.

The perfume of some aromatic flower in the garden pervaded the room. The fragrance was distinctive and erotic. It mingled with Carter's scent.

"Have you recovered?" he asked softly.

"I don't think I'll ever be the same again."

He rubbed a slow circle on my stomach with his palm. "Maybe you'll find this even better."

This time I wanted to pleasure him too, to give back a measure of what he'd given me. I began by caressing his chest but I quickly learned that I didn't have the patience Carter had. I couldn't wait. I moved my hand between his legs and took him.

Carter felt very smooth and hard and full. He stiffened at my touch. The thought of having him in me became all-consuming. Even if he was willing to wait, to let me play out the same game he'd played with me, I wasn't.

"Take me now," I whispered, "right now."

He moved between my knees and I guided him into me. And when he began, I discovered that here too, he knew how to pleasure. He teased, cajoled, almost giving me what I craved. Then he denied me, making my desire keener.

When I couldn't stand the torment any longer, I arched, lifting my hips to get more. He thrust into me again and again. Our excitement rose. We were almost there.

Once, twice, three times he thrust into me. And then it happened. He surrendered to me as I surrendered to him.

Several long luxurious moments passed. I stroked his head. There were no words to express my feelings.

"I love you, Hillary," he whispered. "I love you very much."

I opened my mouth to respond. The words "I love you" were on my lips when another man's name popped into my head. Roger. I'd nearly called him Roger—not Michel or Bob or even Antonio, but Roger! I didn't know anyone by that name. Or did I? A shudder went through me.

Carter, thank God, didn't notice. He didn't question.

"Tonight is a new beginning for us," he said.

I felt wretched, horrible. I was glad the faint light didn't allow him to see my expression.

"How about you, darling?" he asked, running his finger over my shoulder. "Was it completely new to you? Nothing at all familiar?"

"It was wonderful," I said, "but so far as I'm concerned it was the first time."

He sighed. "Well, no memories are better than bad ones."

Once again I appreciated how unequal our situations were. Carter knew me in two different contexts—the Hillary before and the Hillary after. I knew him in only one. In my memory we'd made love just once.

I wanted to believe that it would always be as it was tonight, but it was difficult to refute history. That other Hillary, the woman who'd abandoned Carter for the excitement of other men, must have had her reasons for acting the way she did. One day soon I would understand her. But nothing could ever erase the beauty of what we'd shared.

"I want to ask you something," I said, putting my hand

on his chest. "Tell me honestly. Was it any different tonight? Did I seem the same?"

"No, not at all."

"How was I different?"

"Hillary, I've already told you, we've been unhappy for years."

"I know in recent months nothing between us has been right," I said. "But what about in the early days when we still cared for each other?"

"This was much better, darling. It's never been like this."

"You said the sex was terrific at first. What about the bubble bath and making love on the floor? Wasn't that wonderful too?"

Carter lifted himself onto his elbow and studied me. "Why are you so anxious? Don't you believe me?"

I bit my lip, realizing my emotions were about to rage out of control. "I'm trying to understand myself," I said. "I'm trying to understand our relationship."

"We had great sex in the beginning," he said, "but it was just sex. This was different. This was something more." He grimaced. "Didn't you feel it? Or was it all in my head?"

"No, I felt it was special too. Of course, I did."

"Then I don't understand."

"Oh, never mind."

"No," he said, "there's something bothering you. We should talk about it."

"I'm worried."

"About what?"

"About . . . us," I said.

He smiled indulgently. "If a night like this is cause for worry, Hillary, you're destined for a bad case of ulcers. I think you've got to learn to enjoy what you've got. I couldn't feel better about you than I do right now."

His words were too much to bear, given my anguish. I swung my legs off the bed and sat up. Then I went over and picked the kimono up and slipped it on, cinching the belt at my waist. Carter was watching me.

I didn't know what to say. I went to the window and opened the drapes a crack, inhaling the pungent air from the garden. The Eiffel Tower was a dramatic sight, one that had brought joy to my heart earlier. Now I was filled with a sadness and desperation. Tears flooded my eyes.

"Hillary," Carter said, "why are you upset?"

I turned to face him, knowing I owed him the truth. "Something awful almost happened," I said.

"What?"

"When you told me you loved me, I opened my mouth to tell you I loved you too. But—"

"But what?"

"I almost called you by another name," I blurted.

There was a terrible silence, then he said, "Michel?"

"No. Roger. I almost called you Roger. And I don't even know who he is!"

Carter was silent again.

"Do *you* know who Roger is?" I asked.

He shook his head. "No, I don't."

I left the window, walking across the room before turning and walking back to where I'd started. "Do you see how upsetting that is?"

"It doesn't necessarily mean anything," he said, sounding only halfway convinced. "You've been having strange dreams and visions . . . you've got amnesia. How can you make something of a name popping into your head at random?"

"Things don't pop into my head at random," I countered. "Everything means something. The question is what?"

"Maybe you're making too much of it."

"What if Roger is my lover? What if he was the one I was meeting at the airport in Nice when I saw that flower vendor?"

"Do you remember anything specific?" His voice had an edge to it. I could tell he was starting to see the implications.

"No," I said, "but I was meeting someone. And judging by the way Antonio described the day, it wasn't something I wanted publicized. It sounded like a secret rendezvous, to be blunt."

"Antonio's a boy. He likes to play games with you."

"No, this was different. I was involved in something clandestine. I'm sure of it."

"I think you're making some pretty big assumptions, Hillary. It's speculation at best."

"But Michel and I were very upset with each other. It makes perfect sense that there was another man in the picture, especially when the name Roger pops into my mind right in the middle of our . . . when he did."

Carter studied me. "You aren't suggesting I should be jealous, are you?" I heard the doubt in his voice. He was definitely having second thoughts. I hated myself for doing this to him.

"Well, I was certainly not thinking of Roger, whoever he is, while we were making love. I was thinking of you, Carter. Only you."

He held out his hand, inviting me to go to him. "I'm not going to worry about what's going on in your subconscious," he said. "As long as it was me you were making love to this evening, I'll find a way to handle the rest of it. Michel is dead in more ways than one, as far as I'm concerned. And the same is true of Roger and all the rest of them."

I looked down at my hands. "You're a very tolerant husband."

"I can hardly blame you for things you can't control, even when they don't please me. I love you, Hillary. Concentrate on what is, not what was. Okay?"

I nodded.

"Now I don't know about you, but I'm starving. Shall we get cleaned up and go out for dinner, or do you want to make do with a home-cooked meal?"

His good spirits made me smile. "You decide."

"I'm inclined to stay in. Something really erotic might happen at the dinner table."

"Don't tell we we've made love on the dining room table."

Carter grinned. "You know, I just realized something. I can define our sex life any way I want, can't I?"

I shook my head. "I might have amnesia, but I'm not completely gullible. Anyway, if something we do doesn't feel good, I'll notice."

Carter laughed. "You've given me a real challenge, darling. But I've got one large advantage. I'll know for sure and you won't."

He went off to find a robe and I went to the bath. Realizing my brush was in my purse, I went to look for it.

I found it on a chair in the front room. The air was chilly and I noticed the curtains billowing at the window. I went over, and as I reached out to swing it closed, I glanced down at the street. It was too dark to tell if the vehicle below was the one I'd seen earlier, but something I saw troubled me. A red glow flared behind the windshield. Somebody was in the car, smoking a cigarette.

Two or three hours had passed. Was it the same car, the same man? Shivering, I locked the window and closed the drapes. A quiet terror went through me. What did it mean? Should I be concerned?

Carter called out. "Where'd you disappear to, Hillary?"

"I'm coming," I said.

Should I tell him about the man in the car? Or was this just another crazy fabrication of my mind? I had so many demons to contend with that it was becoming difficult to tell the good from the bad, the real from the unreal. Despite my new-found joy, it was beginning to seem that my trials would never end.

IT WAS NINE IN the morning and the flat was full of cooking smells when I woke up. I hadn't gotten to sleep until the small hours, but once I finally dropped off, I'd slept like the dead.

I put on the kimono Carter had given me and went to the bathroom. When I returned he was in the bedroom, waiting for me.

"Glad to see you're up!" he said cheerily. "I was afraid you might have slipped into another coma."

"Perish the thought."

"I've made brunch. Salmon, scrambled eggs, fresh squeezed orange juice, croissants, kumquat jam, café au lait."

"Sounds like a veritable feast."

Carter came over to me and took me lovingly into his arms. "How about if I serve you breakfast in bed, Mrs. Bass? Could you stand the pampering?"

"I guess I could try."

He gave me a quick kiss, then went off. I fluffed some pillows and sat on the bed to wait. I glanced out the window and saw that the gray clouds of the day before were gone, replaced by a pale blue sky and sunshine. I sighed contentedly.

Our lovemaking had lasted for hours. Eventually we'd eaten a light meal and then we'd gone off to bed and made love again and again. Each time had been a little different. Sometimes it was tender and slow, and once it had been so frenzied and wild that I lost all control.

If we'd been estranged the past year, we had done our best to make up for it. By the time we fell asleep in each other's arms, thoroughly exhausted, Carter had become my husband, in fact as well as in name. As between us, my amnesia no longer mattered.

During those languid, sensuous hours we were together, I hadn't stopped to analyze what was happening outside our bed, or to question how our growing love fit into the larger picture. It was enough that we were together. Now that morning had come, I found myself still optimistic, though deep inside I knew the world hadn't changed, only my marriage.

Carter returned with an impressive meal. He brought a tray for himself and pulled a chair by the bed to be near me. He seemed as content as I.

"You seem especially pleased with yourself," I said. "What's the reason? Your cooking prowess or your skill as a lover?"

"Glad to see you haven't forgotten. I'd hate to think it was all for naught," he teased.

"My memory since recovering from the coma is perfect," I said. "I recall every single detail vividly." I tore off a piece of croissant. "So don't get the idea you can pull one over on me."

271

Carter didn't say anything; he just smiled, looking as happy as any man could on a morning after. For my part, I was grateful that the day was turning out to be as agreeable as the night before. But wonderful as Paris had been so far, it was not without its riddles.

"I don't want to put a damper on the mood," I told him, "but I noticed something last night that concerns me a little."

His brow furrowed. "What's that, Hillary?"

I explained about the man in the car. He listened gravely, and when I'd finished he marched from the room. A few minutes later he returned. "There doesn't seem to be anyone out there now." He stroked his chin. "I wish you'd said something last night. I could have called the police."

"We were having such a nice time," I said, "I didn't want to spoil it. Anyway, I was sure it was my paranoia. Do you think there's reason to be concerned?"

Carter shook his head. Then he leaned over and gave me a kiss. "No, I don't think so. If someone was out there now, though, I would feel differently."

Carter returned to his chair and resumed eating. As he spread jam on his croissant, he gave me a reassuring smile. I took a sip of the delicious coffee he'd made, wondering whether he was trying to shield me, or if he truly wasn't concerned. I decided to take him at his word. "What's the plan for today?"

"If it were up to me, I'd lie around the apartment all day, making love. But since you've yet to see Paris, I ought to show you some of it, I suppose."

"We don't have to do it all in one day. I expect to be back."

"Well, I'll take you out for a nice lunch, regardless. We can decide what we want to do after that."

"That's just as well," I teased. "Another day of love-making and I'll probably be ready for a new guy."

272

Carter shook an admonishing finger as the telephone rang in the other room. "That's not very funny, my darling," he said wryly. "It strikes a little close to home."

"You're right," I conceded. "Loose morals aren't the stuff of jokes."

He winked and went off to answer the phone. He was back in a few minutes. "It's Paul Debray."

"He's calling from Paris?"

"No, from Nice. He had a question for me, but now he wants to speak with you."

Carter lifted the tray off my lap and I got up. He went with me to the salon. I warily picked up the phone.

"Hello?"

"Mrs. Bass, my apologies for disturbing you," Debray said, "but I have a few questions, if you don't mind."

"Not at all."

"First, a point of information. I understand you are trying to recover a ring you felt had been removed at the hospital in Nice. I have been checking into the matter and I thought you might wish to know that you had no ring on when you were brought to the emergency room. I have talked with the *police maritime*, the ambulance services, and everyone who came in contact with you that day. No one recalls seeing a ring. We cannot be sure someone is not lying. There may have been a theft, but for the moment those are the facts."

"I'm sorry to hear that, but I think my husband will be even more upset. The ring was a gift from him. I have no memory of it myself." I glanced at Carter, who listened soberly.

"Quite," the detective said. "The clothing you were wearing at the time of your rescue was in the possession of the hospital in Nice. It has been sent on to Toulon. Our technicians examined the items and were unable to find anything that might help explain what happened that day on the sailboat."

"I'm sorry to hear that too, Mr. Debray."

273

"Am I correct in assuming you have not regained any memory?"

"Yes, that's right. My condition is the same."

"Pity," he said.

"Did you have some questions for me?"

"Yes, may I ask if you are in the habit of carrying American dollars with you when you are about?"

"I have no idea. Why do you ask?"

"I spoke to Mademoiselle Frampton about the matter. She told me you often carry pound sterling in addition to French francs because you are so often in Britain, but you do not normally carry dollars."

"Polly would undoubtedly know. What's the significance?"

"After we spoke at the airport in Nice, I interviewed the old woman, the flower vendor."

"And?"

"She confirmed your story, but remembered another detail. She sold you a rose, but you paid for it in dollars. Apparently you had no French currency with you. This struck me as curious. Can you think of an explanation, madame?"

I pondered the question. "No, I can't."

Debray let the silence hang. "Well, it's a bit more to add to your memory bank, Mrs. Bass. One never knows what little item might set off a chain reaction of memories. That is how it happens, *n'est-ce pas?*"

"That's what my doctor suggested."

"I won't keep you any longer, madame. Enjoy your holiday."

"Thank you."

"*O, pardon.* I nearly forgot. I spoke with Captain Marguet last evening. He told me the technicians are virtually certain the bomb was detonated by a very sophisticated timing device that was activated by the ignition of the auxiliary engine.

274

They feel the explosion was intended to occur at sea. They also believe the bombing was the work of a highly skilled professional. In other words, someone with considerable resources meant to kill you, Mrs. Bass."

I glanced at Carter. "I don't know whether that's good or bad," I said to the detective. "On the plus side, it almost certainly means my husband wasn't involved because he was on the boat with me."

"So it would appear," Debray said.

"I don't suppose you or Captain Marguet have come up with any suspects, have you?"

"We have no important indications, madame."

I thought of the man last night in the car outside the apartment. "Would you say I'm still in danger?"

"Those responsible know you are alive. And I'm sorry to say that one who finds the courage to kill once often finds the courage to try a second time. I advise you to be cautious, Mrs. Bass."

"Can I assume you aren't so convinced now that I'm responsible for Michel Lambert's death?" I asked.

"I wish I could say yes, Mrs. Bass. Unfortunately the connection between the two incidents is not clear."

"When can I expect that this will be resolved?" I asked impatiently. "Surely this won't go on for months."

"Let us hope not," Debray said. "But at the moment I think our best hope is that you will regain your memory. Surely you yourself hold the answer to our many questions."

I sighed. "I wish I could say you're wrong, Monsieur Debray. But I can't."

"*Tiens.* I wish you Godspeed, madame. *Au revoir.*"

I put the phone down and looked at Carter. "Next time we go someplace, let's make it one without telephones."

"Was it bad?"

I shook my head. "No, just more of the same."

"Debray had only one question for me," Carter said. "He asked if I had any idea where Bob might be. Captain Marguet wants to question him and they've heard Whitford's in Paris."

"Why here?"

"I have no idea. I don't know thing one about his personal life, but his friends told the authorities he came here after he was fired." Carter shrugged. "What did Debray have to say to you? I heard you mention the ring."

I related the gist of the conversation.

Carter stoically listened. After I'd finished, he took my hands. "At least maybe you won't suspect me anymore. Is that a safe assumption?"

I chortled. "Considering last night, I figured you might be willing to reconsider any plan you had to bump me off."

He pinched my cheek. "You're right about that, my love. Just think what a dull weekend I'd be having if you'd gone up with the boat!"

———

Carter and I showered together. We playfully soaped each other down, tantalizing each other just enough to maintain our expectations for later.

"What we need, my dear," he told me, "is some fresh air, some exercise, and a nice lunch. I know a nice little Algerian place in the Fifth, just off the Saint Germain that makes great couscous."

"Sold," I said.

We dressed. Carter suggested we take a stroll in the Parc du Champ de Mars for a close-up look at the Eiffel Tower. As we descended the stairs I felt so full of energy, and so carefree, that I was ready to run with the wind in my hair.

When we entered the street, I suddenly became apprehensive. I remembered the man from the night before and began studying every parked car along the way. But I found nothing alarming. Carter was alert too, though he was more subtle than I was. I decided he was more concerned than he'd let on. Still, he chided me when I glanced behind us every minute or two to see who might be following.

He rubbed the back of my hand. "Are you really scared, Hillary?"

"More apprehensive. The world has been a little rough on me of late."

"Your feelings are understandable, considering. But I'd like to think you're safe with me."

"So long as you don't leave me on any boats, you mean."

It was black humor, but we both managed to smile. I resolved to forget everything except Carter.

It was a mild day. Big fluffy clouds had sailed in from the Atlantic. The park was only a few blocks from the apartment. It was alive with people—families, tourists, young couples, old ladies, and old gentlemen sitting on benches. I had hold of Carter's arm as I stared at the Eiffel Tower, gracefully looming over us.

He bought me an ice cream from a street vendor and then a red balloon that he tied on my wrist. We sat on a bench while I finished my cone. My balloon swayed and bobbed in the breeze. "What a lovely day," I said wistfully. I didn't know why I was suddenly feeling so nostalgic, unless it was because I'd spent another summer day like it and was half remembering.

A small troop of preschoolers came along, herded by three nuns. They stopped at an adjacent bench, and as I watched them, a strong, unsettling emotion welled up inside me.

There were about a dozen of them, all chattering with excitement, the officious voices of the nuns rising above the general din, keeping precarious order. I remembered the vision

I'd had on my walk at Montfaucon, the sounds of children at play that I'd imagined hearing.

The longer I observed the preschoolers, the more intense my affinity for them became. Carter was watching me watch them, my eyes glistening. I found myself wanting to take one of them into my arms. There was a dark-headed girl at the edge of the group who was particularly cute. I thought she was staring at me, then realized she was looking at my balloon.

"Does all that clatter bother you?" Carter asked.

"No, they're angels. Especially that little girl looking at us. See her?"

"That angelic expression might be avarice," he said.

"Oh, don't be so cynical," I scolded. "She's just a baby."

The girl began moving toward us and had gotten almost within reach when the clarion call of one of the nuns rang out. "Sophie! *Viens ici! Tout de suite!*"

Carter signaled that the child wasn't disturbing us. I reached out to touch her little hand. *"Bonjour, petite,"* I said.

She regarded me shyly from under her brows, but it was evident the balloon was a good deal more fascinating than my smile. I pulled the string down and let her hold it, which brought an immediate smile.

"Isn't she darling?" I said.

"If this were a year ago, Hillary, you'd already be a block away."

"Oh, don't remind me." I pushed a wisp of dark hair off her chubby face, but she was too enamored with the balloon to notice the affection. "Here, Carter," I said, "untie the string so I can give it to her. It'll do a lot more good on her wrist than mine."

Carter obliged, but when the nun saw what I intended, she wagged her finger disapprovingly, calling something out I didn't understand.

278

"She says you can't give her the balloon, because the others don't have one and there'll be a second storming of the Bastille."

I shrugged. "I can certainly understand that."

The little face before me began to crumble.

"Oh, dear," I said to Carter. "There's only one solution. We need eleven more balloons."

He rolled his eyes.

"I thought you liked kids," I scolded.

"I thought you didn't."

"Well, in case you haven't noticed, I've changed."

Carter looked around until he spotted the balloon man across the plaza. "You hold down the fort," he said, getting up, "and I'll play Santa. If you spot me drifting off into the clouds, I want you to know this has been a hell of a weekend."

"Oh, go on, before we have tears."

He grinned and headed off for the balloons.

"Anyway, the weekend won't be over until tonight," I called after him.

Carter turned to face me, walking backward. "Does that mean I might get lucky again?"

"Carter!" I glanced at the nuns.

"Don't worry," he said with a laugh, "the idiom doesn't translate easily."

I gave him a dismissing wave. Meanwhile Sophie had begun tugging on the string of the balloon. After a glance at the sister, I picked the child up and set her on my knee, pulling the balloon down so she could touch it.

"Aren't you an angel?" I cooed.

She laughed gleefully.

Knowing more favors were on the way, the nun didn't object when I tied the string on Sophie's wrist. She giggled.

"*Qu'est-ce que tu dis?*" the sister called out. "*Dis, merci.*"

I put the girl down so she could romp around with her

279

prize. But I was so taken with her joy that unable to help myself, I leaned down to kiss her cheek.

My lips no sooner touched her skin than there was a loud pop, almost an explosion. I jerked, thinking the balloon had burst. Sophie had been frightened too, and she shrieked.

Then I realized the sound had come from behind me. I turned and saw the top board of the bench had shattered. The nun wailed hysterically and came running across the gravel, snatching up the screaming child.

I looked around in confusion. An old man nearby was shouting something and pointing up the concourse with his cane. A large man was running away. There was a gun in his hand. I'd been shot at!

I got to my feet and saw Carter hurrying across the plaza, a handful of balloons trailing behind him. I looked again at the fleeing man. He was a hundred yards away by now, but he turned to look at me before dashing into traffic. He had a beard.

I was shaking as Carter came racing up, breathlessly. "What happened?"

I pointed at the shattered bench. "Somebody tried to shoot me. He ran up that way."

"Oh my God." There was fear in Carter's voice.

The nuns were herding the children away. Carter dashed over and handed the balloons to one of the sisters. Then he came back. My knees were beginning to shake so badly I had to sit down.

Carter sat beside me, his breath coming in jerks. Babies seemed to be crying everywhere. Curious people started gathering. It was like the marina at Toulon all over again.

Carter kept looking around. "Where are the goddamn police when you need them?" Then he took me by the arm and pulled me to my feet. "The hell with it. Let's get out of here."

We hurried past the children and the nuns, toward the

closest street. I had a glimpse of Sophie as we ran by, her plump cheeks streaked with tears. I felt terrible knowing she'd nearly been hurt. I understood now that the evil haunting me would spare no one, even the innocent.

The terrible truth was that I wasn't safe anywhere. I couldn't afford the false security of Carter's love. If I was to survive, no place and no one could be trusted.

ARTER HAD THE taxi driver take us to the nearest police station. We were there only forty-five minutes—long enough to give statements and explain what had been going on—before we returned to the park in the company of half a dozen policemen. Three officers on foot patrol were already at the scene. Two witnesses had been interrogated. They had confirmed that the gunman wore a beard, but no one had had a good look at him.

Two policemen accompanied us back to the apartment. While I went to lie down, Carter called a security agency to arrange for bodyguards. I wasn't as upset as I'd been last time, though I was discouraged and depressed. The danger seemed unrelenting. I wasn't even safe while on a romantic weekend with my husband.

After getting off the phone Carter came back to the bedroom and sat on the edge of the bed, looking sad and sympathetic. I'd been sitting up, paging through some old fashion magazines I found in a drawer. I set them aside.

"There's a manhunt on for Bob Whitford," he said glumly.

"Is that who they think it was?"

"He's a suspect, let me put it that way. Between the beard and Marguet wanting to talk to him anyway, they decided to arrest him, if they can find him."

"I only saw one or two pictures of Bob," I said. "And that man today was too far away to tell if it was him." I sighed, feeling more than a little desperate. "One of these days my luck is going to run out."

"Don't talk that way, darling. Maybe it'll turn out to be Whitford. Once they have a name, the police are pretty good at finding people, especially foreigners."

"Maybe, but it's still hard to believe someone would try to kill me just because he got fired. Bob wasn't a hot-tempered psychopath, was he?"

"No, he was pretty easygoing, as a matter of fact. But let's let the police worry about that. From here on out you're not going anywhere without an armed bodyguard. I told you that you were safe with me here in Paris. I obviously miscalculated. I'm not going to make that mistake again."

"That won't stop a determined killer," I said darkly.

"Maybe not, but we're going to make it as hard for them as we can."

I smiled sadly. "I bet years ago, when you showed up at my apartment that first time, you never expected this."

"I didn't expect this three days ago." He took my hand. "But I don't want you to worry, darling. We'll be safe here until the bodyguards arrive. And from now on they'll accompany you everywhere . . . if we go out to eat, on the trip back to Mont-faucon, everywhere."

"At least we won't be prisoners in our own house."

"There's one small problem," Carter said. "I had a call a short while ago. The Belgian acquisition I've been working on with George Dunphy is supposed to come together at a summit meeting in London tomorrow. I may be able to put it off, but so many other things are riding on it, it'll be tough."

"Go to your meeting, Carter, by all means. I'm sure I'll be fine."

"You could come with me."

"That's silly. I'd just be in the way. Besides, I'm supposed to meet Jane. We were going to talk this evening about what we'd do and where we'd go. I'm not so sure I'm the most desirable company at the moment, though. I'll have to let her know about the shooting attempt."

"You'll be safe once the bodyguards arrive. And I plan to take as late a flight as I can, in order to stay with you. Unfortunately there are some things I should do this evening in London to prepare for the meeting."

"Do what you have to do," I told him.

"Well, at least let's go out to dinner this evening and afterward we can pick up Jane. If she's still amenable, she can stay here with you. You can go down to Montfaucon tomorrow or you can stay in Paris or come to London. It's up to you."

"I think I'd like to go back to Montfaucon." I toyed with Carter's fingers, staring down at them. "Will you be returning to Montfaucon, or do you have to stay in London?"

"I'll be back Tuesday, if I can. Wednesday at the latest."

I nodded, accepting the fact, though I wished it had worked out differently.

"This deal is happening at the worst possible time," he

said. "I'd feel so much better if you'd come with me to London."

"No, I really want to see Jane. You don't have to worry about me."

Carter scooted closer to me so we could kiss. His lips lightly grazed mine. Then he pulled me firmly against him. The kiss turned hard and I ran my fingers through his hair.

"If I'm going to die," I said, "maybe it should be in bed."

"Yes," he agreed, "you never know how long this mutual attraction will last."

Minutes later we were undressed. But this time there was a melancholy undertone to our lovemaking—the poignancy of lovers about to part.

I was staring into Carter's eyes when I came. I arched against him, moaning, my mouth sagging open. He thrust a final time just as I went limp. Then he covered my mouth with his, murmuring that he loved me.

"Do you really, Carter?"

"More than ever," he said, his eyes shimmering.

"You don't feel sorry for me, do you? That's not what it is?"

"No," he said, "I love you because you're you."

Tears streamed from my eyes. "How can life be so wonderful and so horrible at the same time?" I asked.

"I don't know. I guess you're just lucky."

The buzzer sounded in the salon. Carter rolled onto his back. "Shit, that must be the security people."

"At least they waited until we were finished."

Carter shook his head. "As soon as this is over, you and I are getting on the first plane for Tahiti. No bombs, no gunmen, no newspaper people. Just you and me, Hillary. Just you and me."

While Carter dealt with the security men, I took a shower and changed. When I joined them in the salon, they were having coffee. Carter introduced me.

Marcel Ucciani was forty, half French and half Italian. He was a tad under six feet, broad-shouldered, and stocky. His partner, Bruno Cecconi, was Italian and spoke French with a heavy accent. He was a bull of a man with a flat nose and hard black eyes. His arms were bigger around than my thighs.

Both men—but Bruno in particular—looked as though they belonged in the Mafia. Perhaps there'd been a connection once. I couldn't complain about the way they treated me. They were friendly and very solicitous.

Marcel spoke the best English. "We will disturb you as little as possible, Madame Bass," he said, holding my hand with both of his like a devoted knight. "If you don't mind, we want to inspect the apartment. It is important to know the territory. *Vous comprenez?*"

I told them to make themselves at home. They went off. I sat on the sofa next to Carter.

"They seem intimidating enough to scare off any bad guys," I said.

"That's the general idea. Marcel comes very highly recommended. A third guy will be joining them tomorrow. Marcel says round-the-clock protection works best with at least three people."

"This must be costing a fortune," I said.

"The cargo's rather precious to me," he replied.

I leaned over and kissed him on the cheek.

"I took the liberty of calling Jane," he said. "She was pretty distressed and wanted to come over right away, but I convinced her to wait until after we'd had dinner. I hope that's okay."

"Fine."

"The two of you can decide what you want to do tonight. The boys are prepared to go with you wherever you want."

"Sounds like a fun party," I said dryly.

"It's not too late to come with me to London."

"Yeah," I joked, "maybe I can take notes at the meeting. Marcel and Bruno can be my assistants." I patted his hand. "Honestly, being in my own house and in my own bed is best."

"I understand."

"But I'll be looking forward to when you get home. Playing bridge with Jane and Marcel and Bruno will probably get old real fast."

"You play bridge now, Hillary?"

"Don't I?"

"Not to my knowledge."

I thought about it. I definitely knew the game. The conventions rolled through my mind. I patted Carter's knee. "Maybe I learned on one of my trips to Marrakech."

The security men returned. "Not too bad," Marcel said. "The curtains have to stay closed in the day and in the night, but otherwise it's okay. The top floor is better, but this we can defend. *Pas de problems.*"

"Does that mean I'll live to see morning?" I asked.

Marcel chuckled; he sounded like a horse whinnying. "You don't worry, madame. Before they kill you, they got to kill me."

"I don't know how pleased your insurance company will be to hear that."

Marcel laughed and nudged Bruno with his elbow. "Madame Bass, she is very funny."

Bruno rubbed his flat nose with his paw. *"Oui, d'accord,* Marcel."

I smiled sweetly at Carter. "I think I already know who'll end up as my bridge partner."

—

Marcel and Bruno drove us in their armor-plated Citroen to the Algerian restaurant Carter had intended to take me to for lunch. Marcel knew the place and liked the setup. It also had the advantage of being near the Ile St Louis, where Jane's house was located. Carter brought his suitcase along so that he could go directly to the airport.

When we left the flat, I got a real dose of what it meant to be under a death threat. Bruno went out first to bring the car around and check out the street. Marcel led the way down the steps, whisking me and Carter into the backseat of the sedan.

"So this is what it's like to be president," I said as we sped across the Esplanade des Invalides, headed for the Boulevard St Germain.

"No, this is what it's like to go out to dinner with a madman lurking about. Point is, presidents can't get a bunker mentality, and neither can you."

Carter held my hand as we sat shoulder to shoulder in our battle wagon. I glanced out at Paris, knowing in my heart I really belonged somewhere else. This couldn't be my life.

The restaurant, Chez Ali, proved to be a cozy little place fifty feet off the boulevard with red tablecloths, drippy candles, and the lusty smell of lamb. Marcel checked inside before he ushered us through the door. After we were shown to our table, he waited there until Bruno returned five minutes later. Then Bruno guarded the door and Marcel sat at a table adjacent to ours.

"Nice of them to take a separate table," I whispered to

Carter. "They're sweet and all that, but I hope they don't insist on looking under my bed every night."

"I think the trick is to ignore their existence. They're paid to do the worrying."

It was easier said than done, but after a while I managed to forget our companions, though whenever I happened to notice poor Bruno standing at the door I worried that his feet were aching. Most of the time, though, my mind was on Carter. He did his best to keep things lighthearted, but his worry lines were deeper than I had ever seen before.

The couscous was wonderful. I enjoyed the Algerian wine. The waiter never let my glass get close to empty.

"What do you think of the idea of a trip to the States?" Carter said, sopping the sauce from his plate with a chunk of bread.

"When?"

"As soon as I wrap up this Belgian deal. Probably in a week."

"What about Tahiti?" I said.

"That's for after the police have this stalker behind bars. I'd like to take you to the States regardless."

"Where would you want to go?"

"I thought we could visit my parents in Virginia, maybe do some sailing on the Chesapeake. You mentioned you'd like to go to New York. We could check out the neighborhood where you grew up."

The idea sounded awfully good to me. "I'd like that, Carter. But do you think Paul Debray would let me cross the Atlantic?"

"He hasn't got a case, Hillary. You wouldn't be sitting here if he did."

"But he knows and I know that one of these days I'll remember what happened."

"When that day comes we'll talk to a lawyer before we

talk to Debray. We might also decide to move to Maryland and spend our days sailing."

"What about our nights?" I asked, sipping my bottomless glass of wine.

"I'll leave that to your imagination," he said with a wink.

It was then I thought about how much had changed in the course of only a few days. We had gone from being completely estranged to having near marital bliss. Was I being naive? I couldn't help wondering.

"My life the past few years has gotten lots of attention," I said, "but I haven't heard a lot about yours."

He looked directly into my eyes before commenting. "You obviously have a question."

"I'm wondering how you spent your nights before I woke up with amnesia. I bet you have a sweet little English girl in London who keeps you company, and you're unwilling to admit it."

Carter nodded toward my empty plate. "Ready for some dessert?"

I gave him a look. "I thought so." Then I shook my finger at him. "If I ever do visit you in London, there'd better not be any trace of her in the house."

He grinned and signaled for the waiter. "You do the suspicious wife bit pretty well," he said to me. "When did you learn that?"

"There are certain things a woman instinctively knows."

We had a pastry soaked in honey for dessert. When Carter finished his coffee he consulted his watch and said, "I'm beginning to run a little late. I'd better head for the airport soon."

"Aren't we going to take you?"

"No, I'll have the boys drop me at a taxi stand, then they can drive you on over to Jane's."

It started sinking in that we'd be parting soon. I began missing my husband already. Ever since awakening in the hospital, I'd had trouble thinking of myself as married. But since we'd made love, marriage was beginning to feel natural.

While he settled the bill, Bruno went for the car. When it pulled up in front we went out under Marcel's watchful eye. In seconds we were comfortably behind the armor plating and headed down a side street toward the Seine.

Bruno pulled up at a taxi stand on the Quai de la Tournelle, then got out to retrieve Carter's suitcase from the trunk. Marcel kept an eye on the foot traffic as well as the street.

Carter took both my hands. We were seated close, our knees pressed together. A sad feeling came over me and my eyes started to glisten.

"I'll call you as soon as I get to London," he said.

"If it's convenient, but don't worry if a phone isn't handy."

"Do what these fellows say, Hillary. They know their business."

"Yes, Father."

He gave my chin a squeeze. "And call me immediately if there's a problem of any kind. I don't care when it is, day or night. In the daytime my secretary will always be able to reach me. Her name's Kate. Polly can give you the numbers."

I looked at him, trying to keep my emotions in check. "Kate's not the one, is she?"

"What one?"

It annoyed me that he made me say it. "Your girlfriend."

"No, silly." He hesitated. "Listen, Hillary, I don't want you thinking—"

I put my finger to his lips, stopping him in midsentence.

"Silence is better than lies. I won't press you on things you don't want to talk about, if you won't lie to me."

Carter shook his head in disbelief.

I glanced out the window. "Bruno's waiting."

He took me in his arms and kissed me fervently. "Take care of yourself, darling," he said.

"You too."

"I love you."

He was gone and I was relieved, even though I felt wrenched inside. Bruno got back in the car, but I asked him not to leave until Carter was safely in a taxi. When the cab drove off, we pulled away too, turning onto the bridge that led to the Ile St Louis.

—

When we stopped in front of Jane's elegant but ancient townhouse, I told Marcel I wished to go in alone. He said he would accompany me to the door.

As I stood with the bodyguard at the arched entry, waiting for the bell to be answered, I breathed in the evening air and the musty smell of stone and ivy. When the door finally swung open a plump but pretty girl in her twenties appeared.

"Good evening, Mrs. Bass," she said in a light French accent. "Please come in."

I bid Marcel good-bye with a nod of my head and stepped into the entry hall of the Nyland home.

"I am Sylvie," the girl said, "the domestic for monsieur and madame. Lady Nyland is just about ready. Won't you please come up to the salon?"

I followed Sylvie up half a flight of marble stairs to a drawing room dominated at the far end by a large stone fireplace. The furnishings were a mix of antiques and comfortable modern pieces. There were books and magazines, photos and various mementos strewn about. The room looked well used and inviting. I imagined a fire burning brightly on a winter night and how pleasant it must be to be curled up in front of it.

"Please sit down, Mrs. Bass," Sylvie said. "I'll tell Lady Nyland you're here."

I sat on a fat yellow silk sofa and looked about curiously. On the coffee table in front of me were a number of magazines and albums. There was also a stack of art books. The one on the top had a picture of the Golden Gate Bridge on the dust cover. When I saw it, my heart lurched and a deep sense of familiarity shot through me. The reaction was similar to what I'd felt when I smelled roses, though not so vague and ambiguous. San Francisco!

I turned the pages of the book, my heart pounding with an excitement I couldn't explain. Why did the place seem so familiar?

"Hillary, love, I'm so sorry. You know me, always running half an hour late." Jane swept into the room, her arms outstretched.

I stood, matching her smile with my own. Jane was the woman I'd seen in my photo albums, handsome without being pretty, and stylishly put-together. Her dark hair was pulled back and her eyes were well made-up. She was in a navy and gold and orange Hermès silk blouse with navy silk pants. Jane was three inches shorter than I, but seemed tall somehow.

We embraced and it felt almost natural. I'd come to know her in our telephone conversations, even though she was no more familiar in person than she'd been in the photos.

She took my face in her hands and looked at me with delight, the smile lines crinkling at the corners of her eyes, her diamond and gold studs twinkling. Then her brow furrowed and she looked palpably sad. "Hill," she said, "what have you done to deserve all this misery?"

I rolled my eyes. "God, I don't know."

293

Her fingers were still pressed to my cheeks. They were warm. Jane was studying my eyes closely, a question forming somewhere in the back of her mind. But she dismissed whatever it was with a tiny smile. Then she scrutinized my face. She took the ends of my hair between her fingertips, the furrow in her brow becoming definitive. "When did you cut your hair?"

"Polly and I decided it must have been when I went to Nice, just before the accident."

"Nice? Why in God's name would you have your hair cut there? Kurt's done it for years."

I shook my head. "I can't explain it."

She looked at me critically. I suppose it wasn't unusual for her to examine me so closely. She'd marketed modeling talent for many years, and it had been part of her job.

"You look good, Hill," she pronounced. "Younger. I think it's younger that I see. Definitely different. Is it that nice long sleep you had in the hospital, or is it love?"

"I don't know," I said, blushing. "I think I am falling in love with Carter."

"Well, I must say, that's convenient because he's most definitely in love with you. I heard it in his voice. 'Jane,' he told me with that businessman's voice of his, 'I'm counting on you to look after her while I'm in London. Go wherever you want. It's on me. Just don't take any chances.' "

"Carter said that?"

Jane gave me a look and shook her head. "This *affaire de coeur* is really serious, isn't it? I mean, it's not one of your flings."

"Jane, he *is* my husband."

She took my hand and we sat on the sofa. "We must talk more about this later. Sylvie and I are in the middle of packing, but she can't finish until I know what we're going to do. What'll it be?"

"First, I don't want you doing anything unless you

294

really want to," I said. "I'm not the safest person to be around these days."

"Rubbish."

"Whoever wants me dead is damned serious," I insisted. "If I wasn't so lucky, I'd be dead already and you'd be talking about going to my funeral."

Jane gave me a stern look. "Pardon the personal question, but did you and Carter have sex?"

I blushed again.

"That's what I thought. And was it good?"

"Fabulous."

Jane nodded, apparently expecting that answer. "Danger. Works every time. I've never seen it fail."

"Danger?"

"Does wonders for your sex life. I nearly bought the farm, as you Yanks say, years ago in an IRA bombing in London. I staggered out of the tube with this chappie. We were clinging to each other, gasping for air. To make a long story short, I went with him to his flat in Mayfair and we had super sex, the best bloody orgasm of my life. Never saw the bloke again. I'm sure it would have been ghastly if I had. It was all adrenaline, Hill. Nothing more."

"So what's the bottom line?"

"The bottom line is, why should I let you have all the fun?" Jane threw her head back and laughed.

"Want to go to Montfaucon with me tomorrow?" I asked.

"Whatever you fancy, love. I'm game for anything."

"Carter made reservations on an eleven o'clock flight."

"Super. I'll tell Sylvie it's the south," she said, getting up. "I won't be a moment."

While Jane stepped out of the room, I flipped through the pages of the San Francisco photo book. Something was churning inside me and I wondered if my memory wasn't about to snap into place. I gazed at a picture of Coit Tower rising out of the fog, and shivered. I could almost smell the wet salty air.

Jane came back. I glanced up at her. "Does San Francisco mean anything special to me? Are you aware of a particular connection of any kind?"

She shook her head. "Not to my knowledge."

"Have I ever gone there? Do you know?"

"I'm sure you must have done. Why?"

"I've been looking at this book and I've got this incredibly strange feeling. A strong emotion. I know San Francisco, Jane. I know it well."

"How very odd."

I closed the book and tapped the cover with a nail, staring at it, trying to pull from my mind what was almost there, just under the surface.

"Hold on," Jane said. "Now that I think about it, once last winter you and Michel popped over for a brandy one evening. James and I had had this dreadful little tiff and I was having my period. The two of you came by to cheer me up. You and Michel were sitting here on the chesterfield and you picked up that book and said something about us all going away for some sun. 'Let's go to California,' you said. Michel laughed, saying you were daft. 'San Francisco's no place to go for sun,' he said."

"That's it?"

"There might have been more, but that's all I recall."

I shook my head. "Something's strange, Jane. I couldn't have said that." I peered down at the book. "I know this place."

Her brows danced mischievously. "Won't we have loads of fun sorting it out, though!"

"I do have tons of questions for you," I allowed.

"Such as?"

"We can talk when we get back to the apartment. You are coming home with me tonight, aren't you?"

296

"If you like."

"Good, because I don't want to be alone."

"Aren't Carter's gorillas charming enough for you?"

"They're nice, but definitely not my type," I said.

"Nor mine, I expect. But I've given up the wayward life. No outside men until further notice. James and I had a smashing weekend, by the way. Sexually speaking."

"Good for you."

Sylvie came in and set Jane's case at the top of the stairs. "All ready, ma'am," she said sweetly.

"Let me grab a cardigan and my purse, Hill," Jane said. "Then I'm ready." She was off again.

I waited at the top of the stairs with Sylvie. When Jane returned, the three of us slowly descended the steps.

"Jane, have you ever known me to play bridge?" I asked.

"Bridge? Heavens no. I play occasionally and offered to teach you once. You categorically refused. Why do you ask?"

We stopped at the door. I felt shaken. My mind started to spin. "Have I ever had a lover named Roger?"

"No, you never mentioned anyone by that name. Nor Ro-zhay, either," she said, pronouncing the name the French way. "Why these questions?"

"Jane," I said, taking her arm, "are you absolutely sure? Could I have taken another lover at the end, just before Michel died? Might there have been someone you weren't aware of?"

"Well, I suppose it's possible," Jane said, "but I wouldn't wager you did. You tell me absolutely everything, ducks. We have no secrets. Not you and I."

I was stunned. I played bridge, I knew I did. There had been a Roger at some point in my life, and he was important to me. And San Francisco was much more to me than a bunch of photographs in a book. What was going on?

Sylvie opened the door and Marcel Ucciani, who'd

297

been leaning on the fender of the Citroen, hurried to greet us. He took one look at my ashen face.

"Are you okay, madame?" he asked.

The answer was no. There was something terribly, terribly wrong. I think Jane was aware, but she said nothing. I simply nodded to Marcel and said, "Yes, I'm fine."

JANE NYLAND AND I talked until two o'clock that morning, sitting on my bed like a couple of thirteen-year-olds, though we were sipping cognac instead of munching on pepperoni pizza. I confided everything, listing all the things that had struck me as familiar since awakening and all the things that were totally alien.

Jane asked a question from time to time, but mostly she listened—listened and pondered, peering at me with those observant eyes of hers, dissecting me, comparing what she saw with what she knew.

I expressed my fears about what had happened between Michel and me on the sailboat that day. Jane was reassuring as she had been the first time we'd talked.

"I had a telephone call earlier from a police inspector in Nice," she said. "Paul Debray."

"What did he want?"

"He was very interested in talking to me about you. I told him I didn't know a damn thing, but he was insistent. When I said I expected to be down there the first of the week, he asked me to call when I arrived. I may have to do that, Hill."

"Lord, I don't see that it makes any difference. You can't tell him anything you haven't told me, can you?"

Jane shook her head.

Carter had called from London around eleven. He'd spoken with the Paris police. "Good news and bad news, Hillary," he said soberly. "They arrested Bob Whitford tonight at the Gare St Lazare, trying to board a train. The bad news is he was with his girlfriend and two other couples. The six of them had spent the entire day roller-skating in the Bois de Boulogne. The police are keeping him overnight to check further into the alibi, but it looks like he's not our man."

I tried to decide how I felt about the news. "Somehow I'm glad," I said.

"It's good for Bob, but it means the bad guy with the beard is still on the loose."

"Don't worry, M & B are taking good care of me."

"I wish you were with me," he said simply.

We chatted for a few minutes longer, then Carter signed off with an unusual comment. He said, "Give my love to Jane." When I told her that, she laughed and shook her head.

"The world's gone mad, Hill, I truly believe it has."

Morning turned into a hectic rush. Bruno had spent the night on the sofa. Marcel and the third member of their gang, a bulldog of a man named Pierre, arrived to pick us up around nine. Pierre was fairer, but he had cauliflower ears and was obviously cut from the same mold as his compatriots.

Jane spent the morning running around the flat in nothing but the silk robe she'd gotten from my closet, ignoring Bruno as if he were a piece of furniture. I'd made the poor man some breakfast, though he'd humbly told me it wasn't necessary. Then, while Jane showered, the soft-spoken bruiser and I had a cup of coffee together. In his broken English Bruno told me he had a wife, five kids, and a girlfriend who was pregnant with his child. I listened politely but did not congratulate him on his accomplishments.

Jane was still dressing when the telephone rang in the sitting room. I ran to get it, thinking that it might be Carter. "Hillary," came the masculine voice with the strong American accent. "How's it goin'?" It took me a second to realize it was Todd Halley.

"I have no desire to talk to you, Mr. Halley."

"I can understand that," he said, "but it could be in your interest."

I was tempted to slam down the receiver, but my curiosity got the best of me. Halley was counting on that and he won. "How so?" I said.

"I've been investigating the Michel Lambert murder and I've turned up some interesting info. I'd like to get your reaction."

"I have no intention of saying anything to you."

"Yeah, yeah, objection noted. But what would you think if I were to tell you that your husband and Lambert were mixed up in a business deal—an acrimonious business deal—about the time Lambert got aced?"

I was stunned. Halley let the silence hang. "I wouldn't believe you," I finally said.

"Because of what I said, or because it's coming from me?"

"Both."

"Well, if I told you Lambert had been blocking a deal your husband was trying to put together, and I could prove it, what would you say then?"

"That you're a liar."

301

He sighed. "Were you aware of the trouble the two of them were having?"

"No. And if you're on a fishing expedition, Mr. Halley, you won't find anything here. You're wasting your time."

I hung up, angry, and at the same time concerned. Muckrakers like Todd Halley thrived on gossip, falsehood, and innuendo. But there was usually some grain of truth in what they said, and that bothered me. I was still trying to come up with a perfectly reasonable explanation to Halley's question when Jane was finally ready and we left the apartment.

Between the five of us and the luggage, it was crowded in the Citroen as we sped across Paris for the airport. Marcel sat in back with Jane and me, so we didn't have an opportunity to talk in private until we were several thousand feet above Fontainebleau.

Jane reclined her seat as far as it would go and said, "Hill, I want to talk to you."

I glanced at her. "Yes?"

"This is from the heart. Please don't go in a blue funk, but I agree with what you said last night. There *is* something wrong about this situation." She took my hand, looking as if she'd just come from a funeral.

"What's the matter, Jane?"

"You are a dear love, but—Lord, how do I say this?— you are not Hillary Bass. At least you're not the one I've known for nearly a decade."

I stared at her. Jane was dead serious.

"Last night I studied your face closely," she said. "You're almost a perfect copy, but not quite. The bones are virtually identical, but the skin is different—it's younger, and the sun damage has dissipated. Not everybody would notice, perhaps no one who wasn't looking for it."

I was in shock. Stunned. "Jane, how can you say that?"

"I know it's brutal to hear it like this, but it's the truth. Your skin is not the same. That I'm very sure of."

"You don't think I could have had some sort of treatment?"

Jane shrugged. "I've listened closely to your speech too. Your voice is the same—timber, pitch, so on—but you use it differently. Before, even when you spoke English, you'd inflect like the French at times. And you'd use French words. English-speaking people do when they live here for extended periods."

"That's easy enough to explain. I've forgotten French. The psychiatrist said I've rejected my whole European experience because I want to go back to my past."

"It's been the better part of ten years, Hill, but I don't recall you sounding quite this way when you first got off the boat. There was a touch of New York in your speech back then. You don't have it now."

I could feel a dark tension building within. "How can that be?"

Again Jane shrugged. "I don't know. I'm only telling you what I see and hear."

I bit my lip, thinking, wondering, fearing. It was as though this world I'd been struggling to accept had been suddenly turned on its head. Could Jane be right? Or was this more madness?

I studied her eyes. There was no doubt she was sincere. Yet how could I believe her? A week ago I didn't want to accept the fact that I was Hillary Bass, now it frightened me to think I wasn't.

I thought of Carter. Good Lord, what if Jane were right? It would mean he wasn't my husband after all! And this life I'd been leading, the people I'd gotten to know and who knew me—was she saying none of that was real? I shook my head. "You're asking for a gigantic leap of faith, Jane. If I'm not Hillary Bass, who am I and where did I come from?"

"The truth can be the truth without one understanding it," she said.

"You're telling me Carter isn't my husband."

"Does he seem like someone you were married to? I mean, deep in your soul?"

"I have amnesia, for God's sakes. How can I answer a question like that?" I heard my voice turn shrill, but I couldn't help it.

"I'm not thinking of memories. I'm thinking of intimate things that might touch your soul. Was there anything?"

I considered the question, trying to search my heart and answer honestly. "No," I said at last. "It was wonderful, but not at all familiar."

Jane smiled knowingly.

"But if you're right, why didn't Carter pick up on it?"

"He knows you're a changed person. Besides, I'm sure Carter sees what he wants to see. Men do, in case you haven't noticed. James and I were dining at Le Gavroche in Mayfair several months ago. He was in the middle of his mousseline of lobster when he looked up and said, 'You're certainly looking lovely tonight, Jane. New dress, is it?' Hill, I'd worn the bloody dress in his presence at least twice, but that morning I'd had my hair lightened and four inches chopped off. Men are clueless when it comes to observation. They sense a change, but can't say what it is."

"I suppose you're right." I looked out the window at the fluffy clouds. "That brings us back to the same old question. If I'm not Hillary Bass, who am I? A twin who coalesced out of thin air?"

Jane shook her head. "It's not easily explained, I know. Perhaps we should do a little detective work of our own. Dental charts and fingerprints ought to settle the matter."

I closed my eyes and tried to gather my thoughts. Jane had understood my doubts, she'd even shared them. But I had

304

to have come from somewhere. I must have had a life. What had happened to *my* past? And where was the real Hillary Bass, if I was a fake? No, Jane might be sincere, but this made no sense at all. It was much more likely that I was Carter's wife, albeit a reformed one, than a dead ringer who'd appeared out of nowhere.

—

Carter had arranged for Antonio to pick us up at the Nice airport. Marcel organized a convoy. He rode with Antonio in the front seat of the Bentley, Jane and I were in back. Bruno and Pierre followed in a rental car.

As we left the terminal building I looked for the flower vendor, but the old woman wasn't in sight. I had a sinking feeling. I sensed my life was about to unravel, yet I was no closer to regaining my memory than before. That, I realized, was still the key. If only I could remember, all our questions could be answered.

Antonio had been briefed on the situation, but didn't like taking instructions from Marcel. The men exchanged a few pointed words. I wasn't sure what their tiff was about, but Jane seemed amused by it.

"I think the day is coming when women will rule the world," she said, leaning close to whisper. "Testosterone has seen its day."

I smiled, wondering if testosterone had been part of the problem between Michel and me. Then a thought occurred—if I wasn't Hillary Bass, did that mean I wasn't a murderer? But before I could take heart from that notion, I recalled that I'd seen myself struggling with Michel. If I was truly innocent, why had I had that vision?

And whether I was Hillary Bass or not, *I* was the one they'd found on the *Serenity* and it was *my* head that had been

305

clunked. And how could I have gotten on Hillary's boat, in her place, without the world knowing? Then I had a chilling thought. A shiver went up my spine.

"Jane," I said under my breath, "do you suppose whoever is trying to kill me is doing it because they think I'm Hillary Bass, or because they know I'm not?"

She looked at me queerly. "Hill, that's a ruddy good question. I hadn't given that aspect a thought."

A wave of fear washed over me. My situation, whatever it was, seemed to be getting more and more complicated. All these loose strings had to be connected, but how?

"Here's another dotty thought," Jane said after a moment's reflection. "What if the killer stalking you is desperate to see you dead before you can regain your memory?"

"It wouldn't surprise me," I said blackly. "Nothing does anymore."

We arrived at Montfaucon to find an unfamiliar vehicle in the courtyard. I immediately thought of Todd Halley, but realized this wasn't the same car. Another reporter perhaps?

Marcel Ucciani had been vigilant as we wound through the hills, and he asked about the car the moment Antonio pulled up behind it. I could tell by the chauffeur's reaction that he didn't know. Marcel glanced back at us.

"I think it might be an unmarked police car, Madame Bass," he said. "Are you expecting them?"

"No, but that doesn't mean anything, Marcel. They're very interested in me these days."

At his insistence we waited in the Bentley until he verified that the visitor was Paul Debray. The detective greeted us at the door.

"What an unexpected pleasure," I said, shaking his hand. "Are you here to see me or Lady Nyland?" I introduced Jane.

"A pleasure, madame," he said, shaking her hand. "I am here to speak with you both, mesdames, if I may."

We went inside while Marcel and company began their inspection of the premises. I led the way into the salon. "To what do we owe your visit, Monsieur Debray?" I asked.

"When I learned you were returning from Paris this afternoon, I took the liberty of coming uninvited. I hope you will forgive me." Debray's wild brows twitched provocatively, giving the impression there was more to his words than what he actually said.

I was getting used to the man. Even though I knew intellectually that he was a danger to me, something about Debray made me want to help him. "You wouldn't come all this way if it wasn't important," I observed.

"Indeed, madame."

Jane and I sat together on the sofa. Debray took one of the wing-backed chairs. Jacques Lepecheur, the mute sidekick, was nowhere to be seen.

Once we were settled, the detective leaned forward, his elbows on his knees. He shifted his eyes to Jane, then back to me. "I will speak with Lady Nyland later in private, if you will allow me," he said politely. "But I have news of interest to you both, I am sure. May I assume you wish to discuss matters in the presence of your friend, Madame Bass?"

"Yes, Lady Nyland and I have no secrets."

"*Alors*, Mrs. Bass," Debray said, "The news is good. There has been an arrest. We've caught the man who we believe tried to assassinate you in the park."

"Really?"

"*Oui, madame.*"

"That's marvelous!" I said, elated. "Who is he?"

"The name is August Jonker. He is Dutch, a hired killer. Jonker was wanted in this country in connection with another homicide several years ago. The man is a professional,

307

an expert in munitions. We caught him very much by accident when he was crossing the Belgian frontier, a fluke as you say."

"Then you think he is also responsible for the bombing?"

"That is our belief."

"Oh, thank goodness!" I felt such relief. I glanced at Jane who, to my complete surprise, didn't seem to share my joy. She was pondering the news.

"Inspector, if the man is a paid assassin," she said, "who is his patron?"

"Aha! That is the key question, is it not? I am happy to report in that regard we have had good fortune as well. There has been a second arrest." Debray paused for dramatic effect, his eyes moving back and forth between us.

My heart was pounding. I was eager, yet afraid to hear the answer.

Debray cleared his throat. "Jonker named Emile Lambert, the younger son of Monsieur Michel Lambert, as his employer."

"I don't know him," I said. I turned to Jane. "Do I?"

She shrugged. "Perhaps you've met him, love, but I'm certain you don't know him well."

"Are you sure there's no mistake?" I asked Debray.

"I am advised the confession was made this morning in Paris."

I felt anguish rather than relief or joy. "He must hate me very much."

"The motive is apparently revenge, madame. Lambert holds you responsible for his father's death, for the end of his parents' marriage, and for the emotional breakdown of his mother."

I felt sick. The affair had caused so much pain, so much heartache. It was a terrible mess and becoming worse by the minute. And innocent people had been affected. Carter would have been blown to bits if the *Serenity* had been at sea when the bomb went off. And that little girl in the park, Sophie, could have been killed by a bullet meant for me.

Debray let me agonize for a moment before he said, "The authorities in Paris feel that only the two men were involved in the conspiracy. But of course, one never knows with absolute certainty."

"Then I can't assume the danger is over?"

"The probability is that it is over," he replied. "But I make no guarantees."

"Do you consider the investigation complete, Inspector?" Jane asked.

Debray gave her a wily look. "There is a death that remains unresolved, Lady Nyland."

"Michel's," I said flatly.

"Oui, madame. And I must ask you now whether this latest development might have sparked some recollection, some further piece of information that might help us understand Monsieur Lambert's death."

"Hillary would be a bloody fool to give you anything, even if she knew," Jane said snidely. "You are trying to place the blame for Michel's death on her, are you not?"

"You may assume so, madame, but the truth is I would welcome any useful information, even if it does not incriminate Mrs. Bass."

"I can save you both the trouble," I said. "I don't have a thing to add to what I've already told you."

Debray contemplated me. "Then you can tell me nothing more of Monsieur Michel Lambert's affairs that might shed light on the situation?"

Todd Halley's telephone call that morning crossed my mind, but that was hardly information from my own knowledge. I was sure it was untrue. Anyway, to repeat what the reporter said would only cause needless trouble for Carter. "No, Monsieur Debray," I told the detective, "I have nothing more to add." He lifted his shoulders in a Gallic shrug. "Well then, Lady Nyland, might I impose on you with a few questions?"

Jane glanced at me. "Yes, Inspector, if you wish."

"Perhaps you will walk with me to my car."

"Gladly."

I said good-bye to Debray and told Jane I was going to have a word with Polly. She said she'd go upstairs to unpack after she'd finished talking to the inspector.

I went looking for my secretary. I wanted to get Carter's telephone number in London. I found Polly in her room. She was seated in an antique needlepoint chair, staring stoically out the window. When I rapped on the door frame, she had a start and jumped to her feet.

"Oh, Mrs. Bass. I wasn't aware you'd returned."

"May I come in?"

Polly was sort of looking down and away. When I got closer, I could see she had a terrible bruise on her cheek and her eye was badly swollen.

"Good heavens, what happened to you?"

"I fell, ma'am. It's nothing really."

"Nothing?" I said, lifting her chin for a better look. "That's a real shiner."

Polly looked both embarrassed and upset. I didn't know whether to press her or let it pass.

"There's news," I told her. "You'd heard someone tried to shoot me, didn't you?"

"Yes, Mr. Bass informed us when he telephoned to make arrangements for your return."

"Well, the police have arrested the men who've been trying to kill me."

Polly's eyes rounded. "They did?"

"Yes. One was a hired killer from Holland. The other

310

was Michel's son Emile. The police feel they were also responsible for the bombing."

She frowned, as though the news perplexed her. But then she recovered and smiled. "It's wonderful they've been captured, ma'am. Lovely! I'm so pleased!" But her mind was working as though she was trying to sort something out.

"Now maybe things can get back to normal," I said. "Whatever normal is."

"Indeed," she said absently. "So, do the police consider the investigation concluded?"

"That part of it, the attempts on my life, yes. The investigation of Michel's death is continuing."

"I see."

Polly did not look at me. She was pondering something. Her reaction seemed strange, a trifle off.

"There is something you can do for me," I said.

She turned her attention back to me. "Certainly, Mrs. Bass."

"I need Carter's office number in London. He said you could give it to me."

"Yes," she said, "I have it right here." She went to her desk and jotted something down on a piece of paper. "Dial the numbers in this sequence, just as I've written them."

"Thank you."

"Oh, Mrs. Bass." She hesitated. "I'm truly delighted things have turned out so well."

"Yes, but only part of my problems are over," I said. "I still have to contend with what happened on the sailboat."

"I'm certain it will all work out satisfactorily, ma'am."

I smiled and turned to go, but thought of something else I wanted to ask. "Polly, can you think of anyone I might know by the name of Roger?"

"You mean with the Christian name Roger?"

"Yes."

She thought. "No one comes to mind right off, Mrs. Bass. Oh . . . just a moment. There is a chap at the solicitors in London called Roger, now that I think about it. You've talked to him on occasion."

I agonized. "Let me put it this way. To your knowledge, have I had much contact with this Roger you're referring to?"

Polly looked surprised. "I shouldn't think so, Mrs. Bass. I can't think when you'd see him, though you do speak with him from time to time."

"It must be a different person, then," I mumbled.

Her mind was turning, but she was reluctant to ask for an explanation. I saw no point in giving her one.

"Never mind," I said. "It's not important." I nodded and left the room.

In the entry hall I encountered Yvonne, looking distraught. "Madame," she seethed, "these men, they are going through the house like locust. *Mon Dieu!* Can nothing be done?"

"Yes, perhaps so, Yvonne. I don't think we'll be needing them anymore. I'm going to talk to Mr. Bass about it."

"I hope so. They are in my kitchen, in the dining room. They are in the soup, *alors!*"

She stomped off, and I went to the study and immediately dialed London. Carter's secretary, Kate, answered. We chatted for a minute and I was relieved that she did, in fact, sound like a mature woman. I realized that it was silly to feel jealous—after all, my husband had assured me he wasn't having an affair with her—but my insecurities were running so rampant that I was no longer sure of anything. Kate told me that Carter was still in his meeting but that she'd pass on the message that I'd called.

I found Marcel Ucciani outside, in back, checking the windows, and told him about the arrests. He looked dubious.

"Where there is one hired assassin, Madame Bass, there can be two, *n'est-ce pas?*"

"But with Emile Lambert under arrest too, I prefer to think any others who may be out there will consider discretion the better part of valor."

"Madame?"

"I don't think there's much danger now," I explained. "I assume you and Carter have your agreement regarding compensation, and I'll be talking to him about what to do, but you might want to start making plans to return to Paris."

Marcel shrugged. "What matters in the end, I suppose, is that when I leave you are alive and well."

"I have felt safer because of you," I told him. "And I'm grateful."

He seemed pleased. "I will telephone the airlines to learn our options."

I went round the house, wondering if Jane was still talking to Paul Debray, but the policeman's car was gone. There was no sign of her, so I assumed she was upstairs unpacking.

I headed for the door. Poof bounded up to me. She purred and rubbed up against my leg. I picked her up.

"So, kitty," I said nuzzling her, "did you miss me?"

She meowed and I hugged her. Poof had been an emotional anchor, raising my spirits every time I held her. But at the same time I was feeling a great emptiness. My conversation with Jane had put my very identity in doubt.

On the surface the notion that I was not Hillary Bass seemed absurd. How could I have been transplanted into her life without a soul noticing? And what, for heaven's sake, was I doing on the *Serenity* with Michel Lambert, if I was not Hillary? I couldn't have dropped from the sky.

And yet, even as I dismissed Jane's claim, a part of me was still skeptical. Hillary Bass had been an anathema from the beginning. I'd never truly related to her or her life. So which

313

truth was greater? In the end, Jane was right, science would provide the answer. We could settle the matter with a visit to my dentist.

I carried Poof back inside. We found Jane in the guest room, sitting on the bed, a half unpacked suitcase at her feet. She was in good spirits. "Inspector Debray is looking for proof of your motive for killing Michel," she said blithely. "Of course, I gave him nothing useful whatsoever."

Her cavalier manner made me smile. And I was grateful she hadn't made me ask about Debray. "I hope you gave him nothing because there *was* nothing," I said.

Jane laughed. "Don't be daft, love. What woman doesn't want to kill a husband or lover from time to time? But that bit of wisdom is for women to share with one another, not the police."

"But since you're convinced I'm not Hillary, what she might have done or not done hardly matters, does it?"

Jane laid a finger on her jaw. "There's an interesting metaphysical problem at play, I grant you. I said nothing to Debray about my suspicions, of course, but we must give this some thought. When it comes to Michel, are you better off as Hillary or someone else?"

"I am who I am, Jane. I still have to worry about what happened on that boat, regardless." Poof had gotten tired of being held so I put her down. She scampered from the room. "But I'd rather not think about your misgivings just now. Let's table the matter until I can have an exam or whatever."

"I understand, Hillary. Who could feel comfortable having their very identity drawn into question?"

"Thank you for calling me Hillary," I said.

A naughty smile crossed her face. "You are she, love, until proven otherwise. I promise."

She patted the bed next to her, inviting me to sit. I did. She put a friendly arm around my shoulders. "Let's consider the

314

good news. They've captured the would-be assassins and you're out of harm's way. I must say, though, I was rather surprised when the copper named Emile Lambert."

"Debray could have said it was the hunchback of Notre Dame and I wouldn't have known the difference."

She laughed.

"To tell you the truth, Jane, I feel kind of embarrassed. You can't imagine all the people I suspected of trying to do me in—even Carter at one point."

"It's hardly a lark to have people trying to blow you to pieces or shoot you down in cold blood."

"No, definitely not my idea of fun."

I saw that questioning look in her eye, the expression that said, "Who are you? Why are you wearing my friend's clothes and living in my friend's house? What has happened to her? Where is she?

I was not the only one touched by this insane situation. So many people were affected by who I really was, Carter foremost. I had a sudden urge to cry, but I held back my emotion.

Sensing my turmoil, Jane patted my knee. "I don't know about you, ducks, but I'm famished. Do you suppose we can talk that housekeeper of yours into feeding us?"

I appreciated her attempt to be cheerful. "I'm sure it can be arranged. What would you like? I'll go put in the order."

"I'll come along. Two hungry mouths might bring quicker action."

We went downstairs together, Jane slipping her arm in mine. What a life I led. How many people had to ring up their dentist to ask if they were who they thought they were? I wasn't sure that I was emotionally ready for the answer, no matter what it was. On the other hand, what alternative did I have? The truth had a weight and a momentum of its own.

315

JANE AND I ATE on the terrace, enjoying the view. The silences between us were far more eloquent than the things we actually said. Considering I had no other identity to cling to, it was awkward trying to avoid talking as though I were Hillary Bass. Until everything was resolved, my life seemed destined to be one frustration after another.

After we finished lunch Polly came out with an armful of file folders. "I'm awfully sorry to disturb you, ma'am," she said, "but could I ask you to take a few minutes to sign some checks? There's quite a backlog and some items are overdue."

I glanced at Jane. "Life goes on."

"If this is a bad time . . ." Polly said apologetically.

"No, no. Let's take care of it. You have your work to do." I noticed that Polly had applied a considerable amount of makeup to her bruised cheek. The poor thing. I hoped I hadn't embarrassed her.

Polly put the checks in front of me. She explained the purpose of the first item and handed me a pen. As I prepared to sign my name, I realized this was the first time since awakening that I'd had to write. I put pen to the paper, wondering if my subconscious would show me the way. But nothing magical happened. There were no revelations. I simply wrote out my name in longhand.

Polly glanced at the check and did a doubletake. She looked at me.

"It's not my signature, is it?" I said.

She shook her head. "No, Mrs. Bass."

Jane reached over, took the check from me, and examined it. "It's *not* your signature." She leaned back in her chair, giving me a meaningful look.

None of us said anything. I stared at the stack of checks. I felt as though I'd been driving along a road and it abruptly came to an end in the middle of nowhere. I shivered, putting down the pen.

"What's the point in signing these?" I said. "The bank won't honor the signature."

Polly appeared shaken. Jane did not.

"Hillary," she said, "have you studied your handwriting at all since you've been back?"

I shook my head. "No."

"Would you care to?" She was asking if I was willing to risk raising still another doubt about my identity.

"We're all here. Why not?" My words were more courageous than my feelings, but it seemed pointless to resist.

"Let's do an experiment, love. Have a blank piece of paper with you?" she asked Polly.

Paper was produced and Jane had me write out some limericks and nonsense. She and Polly studied the result. Both

317

agreed my handwriting was decidedly different from the way it had been before.

"It could be a product of the amnesia," I said, feeling the same defensiveness as before. "I've heard that handwriting reflects a person's personality, so if I've changed, why wouldn't my handwriting?"

"I think you're groping," Jane said. "If you don't mind a candid view."

Polly seemed thoroughly confused.

"You might as well know," I said to her. "Lady Nyland is positive that I am not Hillary Bass. She's tried to convince me I'm her double."

Polly put her hand to her mouth and gasped.

"You've been around Mrs. Bass a great deal over the years," Jane said, "and spent more time with her than all but a few people. Don't you agree she's not the same woman—if you *really* look at her closely and open your mind?"

"Well . . . I . . . that is, I hadn't really thought of . . ." Polly drew a long breath. "Of course she's much changed, Lady Nyland. We've known that from the beginning. We've all assumed it was because of the amnesia. But . . ."

"The skin's the giveaway," Jane said. "It's far less sun-damaged. This is not Hillary Bass's skin."

"Have I had some sort of treatments?" I asked Polly. "Something in the past few months that Lady Nyland might not have known about?"

"No, ma'am. Not that I'm aware of. I took care of your appointments, paid the bills for everything. I can't imagine how you'd have had work done without me knowing."

"You see," Jane said.

I was shaken. The handwriting business probably wasn't any more damning than all the other curious things—my inability to speak French or to sail, my new speech patterns, the

318

knowledge I'd lost about wine, my changing taste in food—and yet the accumulation of evidence was beginning to weigh on me. I'd definitely lost my confidence.

"I hate this," I said, closing my eyes. "I wish to hell I'd just remember. Even if it means discovering something horrible about myself."

"If you want my advice, love," Jane said, "make an appointment with the bloody dentist and find out once and for all. If those aren't Hillary's teeth in your mouth, you'd do well to know it."

Jane was right. The time had come. "Polly, is there a dentist nearby I see regularly? Someone who might have X rays?"

"Yes, ma'am. Dr. Gernigon in Cannes."

"Would you call and make an appointment, please? The earliest possible."

"Yes, Mrs. Bass."

Polly went off. I noticed she looked unusually pale, shaken. I glanced over at Jane, feeling on the verge of tears. "This is going to drive me crazy yet, if it hasn't already. Somebody has to know who I am and where I came from. Why haven't they come forward?"

"That's not a bad question. You didn't spring fully formed from the head of Zeus," she replied. "That's for sure."

"Thanks, Jane, but that doesn't help."

"Hillary must have known you, ducks. After all, you were on her sailboat."

There was a certain logic to that, but it explained nothing. If Hillary knew me, then why hadn't Jane heard about me, or Carter? Jane, in particular, seemed to know everything else. Why not something as important as this? I was left again with a deep sense of frustration. "I'm going to tell Carter about my misgivings," I said.

319

"Who do you intend to tell him you are? Madame X?"

"I'll tell him the truth, that I don't know."

"Lovely. But do us both a turn and don't mention me in the same breath."

"I've had my doubts from the very beginning, Jane. It's not like I haven't wondered."

"Then you agree with me that you're not Hillary Bass?"

"I agree there are a lot of questions that need to be resolved. But, yes, you've added to my uncertainty."

We each lingered in our private thoughts until Polly came back to tell me that Carter was calling from London.

With a look at Jane I got up and hurried to the house, my sense of urgency coming from my emotions. Polly walked with me.

"I spoke with the dentist's office, ma'am," she told me. "The earliest he can see you is day after tomorrow."

"All right, that will be fine."

I knew the visit to the dentist would be pivotal, but at the moment Carter concerned me more. I couldn't get the thought out of my mind that we had been living as a married couple, when it fact we might be complete strangers.

I took the call in the study, slipping into his chair, feeling anxious, unsure of myself, and not knowing for certain what I would say.

"Darling," Carter said, his voice sounding painfully far away, "is everything all right?"

I fought the bubble of emotion in my throat, wishing I could look into his eyes and see his reaction to my words. "Yes, fine," I said. "Well . . . fine and not fine. Have you heard the news about the arrests?"

"No," he said. "Tell me."

I told him about the arrests of August Jonker and Emile Lambert. Carter was silent.

"Did you hear me?" I asked.

"Yes, darling. I'm stunned, that's all. Shocked."

"I suppose I can rest easier now," I said. "I'd like to dismiss the bodyguards, if that's okay with you."

Carter seemed distracted. "Yes, let them go, if you want," he said. "The retainer has more than compensated them for the time they've put in. I'm sure having them around has been a nuisance."

"They've been nice enough, but I was hoping you'd say that. Yvonne is upset, and if there's no need for them . . ."

"Tell them they can go back to Paris."

"Okay, I'll take care of it."

Carter hesitated, then he said, "Hillary, you're still upset about something. I can hear it in your voice. What's wrong?"

All the things Jane and I had talked about were bursting to get out of me. But there were other concerns as well. That call from Todd Halley affected me. I considered mentioning it, just to get it off my chest, but I didn't want to put Carter on the defensive. There would be time to talk about that later. But how could I ignore the doubts I had about my very identity?

"Carter," I said, summoning my resolve, "can I make a confession?"

"What kind of confession?"

The wariness in his voice put me on guard. Yet the words had to be said. I wanted everything out in the open. I wanted Carter to know. "I'm having doubts," I said tentatively.

"About us?"

"No, about me. I'm not so sure I'm your wife. I'm not so sure I'm Hillary Bass."

Another silence followed. I imagined displeasure in it, maybe even anger. "Jane's behind this," he said after several moments.

"Only in a way. She is convinced I'm not Hillary, that's true. But Jane's not the reason for my doubts. There are just too many things that have happened."

"Like what?"

"I've mentioned some things before. But . . ." I paused, gathering the courage to spit it out. "Carter, I went to sign some checks for Polly, and my signature has changed. My handwriting is completely different now."

"A lot has changed. You couldn't sail a boat either."

"That's the point. Don't you see? It's all adding up to an inescapable conclusion. I mean, how much proof do we need?"

I guess the angst in my voice was convincing, because Carter said, "I'm getting on the next plane out of here."

"No," I said resolutely. "I don't want you to leave your meeting. That isn't why I brought this up. I only wanted you to know how I feel . . . and that I'm . . . scared."

"I appreciate your consideration," he said. "But I'm coming home anyway. With luck I'll be there in time for dinner."

"Carter—"

"No arguments, Hillary. About some things I can get pretty dictatorial."

I was secretly glad. Even though I had serious doubts that Carter was my husband, my growing love for him couldn't be denied. And at the moment, that mattered more than anything.

—

Jane took the news of Carter's change of plans stoically. I don't think her misgivings about him were nearly as great as his about her. I suspected that if they gave each other a chance, things could be different.

322

"Perhaps I should hop on a plane to Paris," she said. "That way I shan't muck things up here."

"No, I'd like for you to stay. I'd like your help in getting Carter to consider everything with an open mind."

"At this stage my conviction is a matter of faith, and that's not easily transferred. Your trip to the dentist ought to decide the matter once and for all. The end's in sight."

The comment should have been reassuring, but it wasn't. I was still torn and confused.

Jane, I discovered, was not one to lie around. She proposed a jaunt into Toulon or a drive along the coast. I would have accommodated her, but I was exhausted, emotionally spent. So when I opted for a nap instead, Jane happily went off on her own, promising to be back in time for dinner. Antonio was to drive her in the Bentley.

Before I went upstairs Marcel, Bruno, and Pierre announced that they'd booked a flight to Paris. We said good-bye in the salon. I shook each of their hands in turn, thanking them for their effort.

"The only thing better would be to have captured the *canaille* myself," Marcel said. "But it is good the police have him. You will sleep better."

Once the bodyguards had driven off in their rental car I was alone with Yvonne.

"Amazing how quiet it suddenly is," I said to her.

"*Grâce à Dieu, madame,*" she said. "It was not so bad when the Germans were in my native village during the war. But now we can have our life again."

I smiled at the irony of that remark. I had no idea what life to reclaim. I was a woman without an identity—no past and an uncertain future.

I climbed the stairs, suddenly very, very tired. I felt bloated and vaguely crampy, as if my period was due. Then it occurred to me—if I did get a period it would be proof positive that I wasn't Hillary Bass. That couldn't be ignored . . . even by Carter.

I lay on my bed and tried to relax. Despite my fatigue, I didn't fall asleep. I played over in my mind everything I'd learned during the past several days, trying to make sense of my random flashes of memory, the mounting evidence that I wasn't really Carter's wife.

I tried to imagine myself with another life. Where did I live? What was my name? Ann? Carolyn? Meredith? And what the hell was I doing here in France?

I took inventory of all the things that had deeply affected me. There were the roses, of course, and the woman in my dream, plus the familiarity of the sailboat and Michel. Why would I have fought with him, if Hillary was his mistress, and I the stranger?

I recalled the flower vendor at the airport, those pictures of San Francisco in the book at Jane's. And children. I'd heard children's voices. Then it occurred to me—what if I had children of my own? What if I was married . . . to a man named Roger? What if I had another life filled with people who cared about me, people who loved me? The notion was so bewildering that I shuddered.

I no longer knew what to think, what to believe. The answers to all my questions were hidden where I couldn't get to them. They were locked inside my head.

THE SMELL OF roses infiltrated my brain like a fog pushing its moist fingers along the streets of a city, oozing over rooftops until every neighborhood had been blanketed. I inhaled deeply, sucking in the fragrance. The scent was very strong. I'd been asleep and only then blinked awake. Carter was sitting on the bed beside me.

"Hello, darling," he said softly. He leaned over and kissed my lips.

"Carter," I murmured, putting my arms around his neck. I hugged him fiercely. Then I let go of him so I could see his face. It was dusk and the only illumination was the evening light coming through the window. "How'd you get here so fast?"

"I chartered a plane. It still took a few hours. Yvonne tells me you slept for a long time."

I peered at the clock. It was after eight.

"Dinner will be ready in half an hour," he said. "I thought I ought to wake you."

It was then I noticed the long-stemmed red rose in his hand. He gave it to me. I pressed the blossom to my nose.

"I think I smelled this in my sleep. It was in my dream."

"The same dream as before?"

"I think so. The rose garden. But this time there was fog too. Rose-scented fog."

"That's a novel twist, even for a dream."

"I was in a city—maybe San Francisco."

"You remember San Francisco?"

I blinked again. "Have we been there before?"

"Yes, I took you four or five years ago. We were in New York, you were visiting your mother and I was working on a deal. I had to fly out to the coast to meet with a venture capital firm and you decided to go with me. We were only there a few days. It was summer, but really cold. You liked the town, but not the weather."

"Is that the only time I was there?"

"As far as I know. Although you and a few friends went to Thailand a couple of years ago and you may have come back via the States and San Francisco. I don't recall."

I wondered if that could have been the basis for my reaction to the book at Jane's. Once again I felt whipsawed by two competing truths. "I'm glad you're home," I told him.

"It was a mistake to go to London. I never should have left you."

"No," I said. "No harm's been done. I've been safe. Jane and I have gotten along well."

"So I gather," he said, a hint of pique in his voice.

"I like her," I told him. "She's nice. A little nutty at times, but nice." I glanced toward the door. "Is she back? She went to Toulon this afternoon."

"That's what I understand. But no, she's not back yet. Jane, as you may already have discovered, has many virtues, but punctuality is not among them. I expect she'll be rolling in any time though." Carter stroked my face, looking at me lovingly. "What do you think? Want to get up and get dressed?"

"Yes, I suppose I should."

Carter helped me up and when I was on my feet he deftly gathered me into his arms. He felt good, and I liked to be held by him. I hugged him tightly and he hugged me. Neither of us seemed willing to let go.

"I missed you," he said.

"Did you?"

"Yes, and I worried about you too. When I got that call I was afraid you'd gone round the bend."

"I'm not sure I didn't." I looked into his eyes. "Oh, Carter, so I'm afraid."

He pulled his head back. "Of what?"

"I'm afraid of what's going to happen."

Carter took my face in his hands. "Hillary, we've got each other. What else do we need?"

"What if we don't have each other? What if I'm not your wife?"

He looked equally distressed and annoyed. "You're really taking Jane's bullshit seriously, aren't you? I was hoping by the time I got here you'd have come to your senses."

"What if it's true? What if she's right?"

"Then I guess I'll have to start calling you by your other name."

"You're making fun of me," I said. "I'm being serious."

"Okay," he said, "what do you want me to say?"

I didn't answer.

"That I love you anyway?"

"I don't want you to say it unless you mean it," I groused.

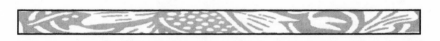

"Well, I do mean it," Carter said. "I love you, Hillary . . . or whoever you are. So you see, it really doesn't matter."

"You're saying nice things, but underneath you're making fun of me. You don't believe a word I'm saying."

"If you're asking whether I believe this theory you and Jane have concocted, you're right, the answer is no. But that doesn't mean I don't love you, whether you're crazy or not."

"I hope we are crazy."

Carter laughed and held me close. I smiled, but what I'd said was true. I wished I were crazy and that all the doubts I had would go away. "I'd better get dressed."

"Need any help?" he asked.

"Somehow, I think you're more proficient at undressing a woman than dressing one."

Carter followed me to the closet. "Now how would you know?"

I turned on the light and slipped off my silk wrap as I walked along the long row of dresses in my bra and panties. "It's an educated guess," I said. I examined a few outfits. "Have any suggestions?"

"Something bare and short," he said.

I chuckled. "What's that—the glandular approach to fashion?"

"I'm the one who'll be looking at you."

"So will Jane."

"I don't think she cares."

I inspected a few more garments, finally holding up a silky peach sleeveless dress that had a very short skirt. "Is this titillating enough?"

"Very nice," he said. But Carter was looking at my legs and hips as much as the dress. His provocative expression told me he was thinking of later, when we'd be going to bed.

"Don't you have to go change shirts or something?" I said, holding the dress in front of me like a shield.

"Are you trying to get rid of me?"

I stared at him, my mind still churning. "If I'm not your wife," I said, "you know what that means, don't you?"

"That we've been committing adultery."

"Exactly. And it also means that somebody else is Hillary."

Carter put his hands on his hips and came toward me. I backed away until I bumped against the wall. I held the dress between us as his body came up against mine. He peered down at me. "You know, darling, this is one time adultery seems like a damned good idea." He kissed me on the lips.

"There's only one problem," I murmured.

"What's that?"

"What if my husband isn't so keen on the idea?"

Carter smiled. "Then I guess we'll have to get rid of him too."

It was a joke. And it would have been funny if I hadn't been in such torment over the possibility that it might be true. I managed to smile though, and Carter seemed not to notice my anguish.

He kissed me again, then he said, "I think I'll go change shirts. See you at dinner."

⸺

We were seated at the dinner table, me in my silky peach number that was more befitting a twenty-two-year-old than a woman of thirty, and Carter in a fresh white shirt that he'd left open at the neck. I'd freshened up my makeup, putting on coral lip pencil and blush. He had showered and smelled of fresh cologne that I detected all the way from the other end of the table. There were two tall candles between us, the same as that first night we'd dined together at Montfaucon. The French doors were open, admitting the pungent and warm evening air. Jane's place sat empty.

"She's used to missing the soup course, I'm sure," Carter said, taking his napkin. "I think we've waited long enough to be polite."

"I suppose she'd have called if there was anything wrong."

"Jane is Jane."

"All right," I said, glancing toward Yvonne, who stood at the door, her hands folded, "let's have our soup, then."

The housekeeper immediately picked up the Limoges tureen to serve us. We'd just taken our soup spoons when we heard a vehicle in the courtyard.

"Lady Jane might get her soup, after all," Carter said.

Moments later we heard the front door open, followed by footsteps in the entry, then Jane in the doorway, breathless, her arms filled with plastic shopping bags, a lank of hair across her forehead. She looked hot and harried. "Good, loves, you didn't wait dinner."

"We waited for a while," I said apologetically.

"If you'd let me ruin Yvonne's cooking, I'd never have forgiven you, Hill." She made her way to the sideboard, passing behind my chair. "Carter, darling, how are you?" she said, dumping her things. "Please don't be cross with me. There's a lovely silk tie in this mess for you."

"I'm never cross with anyone, Jane, you know that."

She made her way directly to him, kissing him on the cheek. "You're a bloody liar, but we forgive you." She went to her place.

Yvonne, who'd heard Jane's entrance, returned to the dining room and served her soup.

Once the housekeeper had gone Jane said, *"Bon appétit,"* and picked up her soup spoon. "So, Carter, how is business? Did you make another million?"

"I'm working on it."

The conversation soon lagged and the only sound was the tinkle of silver and china. I was aware of the warm air wafting in from outside and the smell of hay and blossoms.

"Looks like you had a busy afternoon shopping," I said, trying to help the situation.

"I *love* to spend money," she said. "I don't care what they say, it *does* make up for the deprivations of youth."

"You're lucky to have such an accommodating husband," Carter said. "Lord Nyland must get off on it as much as you."

"Don't be dim, dear boy. James gets off on my body and me. I get off on his money and him. That's the way God designed things. It makes for maximum pleasure all round and propagates the species along the way."

I chuckled.

"You see, Hill," Jane went on, punctuating her remarks with sips of broth, "that's why my husband is superior to yours. James thinks primarily in terms of sexual satisfaction, making him scads easier to deal with, whereas you must deal with a man who takes himself far too seriously. Carter's a dear, don't get me wrong, but infinitely more difficult to contend with."

"Evidently you're not a woman who likes a challenge," Carter said.

"I'm lazy by instinct, true," Jane admitted. "Now, this woman on the other hand," she said, gesturing toward me, "is a horse of a different color. Like you, she's serious-minded, but she's kind, thoughtful, and decent as well—the perfect woman for you, Carter."

"I'm relieved you think so," he said.

Jane dabbed her lips with her napkin. "Well then, have we determined yet just who she might be?"

An awkward silence followed in which eyes moved back and forth between us.

331

"We won't be able to enjoy our meal until we get this behind us," Jane said, justifying her sally.

"You're probably right about that," I admitted. I glanced down the table at Carter, who did not look as displeased as I expected. He even gave me a little smile.

"Who do *you* think she is, Lady Nyland?" he asked nonchalantly.

"I haven't the least idea." She spooned her soup. "I only know who she isn't."

"Proving a negative isn't easy," Carter said.

"Quite right," Jane said. "That's why women are forced to fall back on their intuition. Science knows only a fraction of truth anyway. All the really important things in life aren't quantifiable."

"Except money," Carter said.

She seemed amused by the observation. "The exception that proves the rule."

Carter gave me another self-satisfied smile, as if to say, "See, I can scrap with your friend nicely." I appreciated that, but the scrapping didn't concern me so much as the topic.

"Since money is quantifiable," I said, "maybe we should talk about that. Who I really happen to be seems a bit too personal for dinner conversation."

"You mustn't be selfish, Hill," Jane said.

"No," Carter agreed, "I want to know who I'll be going to bed with tonight and Jane wants to know where in her celestial firmament of feminine intuition you really reside."

"Now don't go bloody-minded on us, dear," Jane admonished. "Men are so much more attractive when they aren't snide, especially since it's such a disagreeable and annoying trait."

"Is logic equally offensive, my lady?" Carter said, arching his brow playfully.

"You're a sod, Carter, aren't you though? But I love you," Jane said. "Come on then, let's hear your logic." She turned to me. "You don't mind, do you, ducks? This is terribly important."

"Heavens no," I said. "Who am I to spoil your fun?" She was a bit taken aback, making me wonder if there'd been more of an edge to my voice than I thought.

"Are you angry with us?" she said contritely.

"No," I said, dismissing the question, "I'm enjoying this. I really am. Anyway, I want to hear Carter's analysis. And I want you to hear it too. Honestly."

Yvonne came in and cleared the soup plates. We waited to pursue the conversation until the roast lamb was served and the housekeeper had gone. Yvonne had forgotten the wine, so Carter retrieved the bottle that had been breathing on the sideboard. He poured some for Jane, then for me.

"We don't have to discuss this if you don't want," he said, kissing my temple.

"No, I intended it, to tell the truth. I just had a little crisis of confidence. That's all."

He returned to his place and Jane and I waited. Carter began by taking his glass for a toast. "Which shall it be? To truth or tolerance?"

"To both, by all means," Jane said.

"Then to truth *and* tolerance."

We all sipped our wine, Carter taking a particularly healthy quaff.

"First, we have to consider the possibilities," he began. "The lady at the other end of the table is either my wife, the woman I married eight years ago, or she's a perfect double or identical twin. Correct?"

Jane and I exchanged looks. We both nodded. "So far we're with you, love," she said.

333

"I don't know what the odds are of two unrelated human beings looking so much alike, but I would think they're nil, particularly when the avowed double turns up on Hillary's sailboat with Hillary's lover."

Jane agreed. "There's a certain logic to that."

"All right," Carter said, "it seems to me the greater probability is that we're dealing with identical twins."

"I would say so," Jane concurred.

"For that to be the case, you'll have to convince me that I could live with a woman for eight years and you, Jane, could be her friend for—nine?—without her once mentioning to either of us that she had a twin."

"You're assuming Hillary knew," Jane said.

"Quite right," he returned. "It's not likely that she could have known without telling us, without letting it slip, without her parents having tipped it off, et cetera. Can we agree to that?"

"Yes."

"Okay, that leaves us with the proposition that Hillary's twin was unknown to her, at least until very recently."

"Yes, I agree," Jane said.

"To believe that, we would have to accept the fact that Hillary's parents either gave her twin away at birth, or that Hillary was in fact adopted, a secret that was kept from her for thirty years."

I tried to listen dispassionately, but the more Carter went on, the more anxious I became.

"That *does* happen, you know," Jane said.

"Granted, but it's hard for me to believe it in this case. I can't picture Hillary's parents having given away a child in a million years. But let's assume for the moment it's true, or the alternative that they adopted Hillary and she had a twin. There would be evidence of that somewhere, but it's never turned up. I was one of the executors for both estates. I never found any

334

papers that so much as hinted that Hillary wasn't their natural child, or that they'd had another who they'd given away.

"However, for the sake of argument, let's assume I'm wrong and Hillary does have a twin. For her sister to wind up here, with us tonight, something had to happen that caused the two of them to change places."

He gave each of us a searching look. "It may be possible to fake amnesia, but you sure as hell can't predict it. Yet you're saying that not only did this other woman materialize on board the *Serenity* at the same time Michel was there, but that the real Hillary was able to arrange for her to have a convenient case of amnesia. Is this what you really want to believe, ladies?"

"You make it sound farfetched," I said, "but you have to admit nothing you said is impossible."

"True, but look at the implications. The twin, presumably, would have agreed to this switch, since we've already come to the conclusion that the amnesia couldn't be predicted. To what end would she do such a thing? Remember, the other woman was almost certainly a stranger, otherwise we'd have heard about her before now. What motive could she possibly have for going along with a switch? For that matter, what motive could Hillary have had? And most importantly, where is the real Hillary now, if you are her twin?

"Let's look at the facts we have," he went on. "Hillary was here in the house a few days before the accident. She went to Nice. The day of the accident Hillary and Michel were heard arguing by witnesses at the repair docks, right? Jane, you tell me. What language did Hillary and Michel speak when they were together?"

"French mostly."

"French. So, they were heard by French workers arguing. The workmen not only heard harsh tones, they heard and understood words constituting a death threat. I would say that's a pretty good indication it was our old Hillary with Michel on

335

the *Serenity* that day, not this supposed twin, who, as we know, would have difficulty ordering a meal in French.

"Yes, I know," Carter said, holding up his hand before Jane could speak, "Hillary can no longer speak fluent French, and therefore she isn't Hillary. But it's coming back to you, isn't it, darling?"

I nodded. "Yes, it's coming back some. I can understand better than I could at first."

"And I'll bet that if you give me a day or two with her on a sailboat, she'll be sailing like the master she was. It's true she's changed. She's another woman now, a different woman. And I thank God for that. Maybe it's a miracle. Or maybe it's the result of a severe blow to the head. But if I had to bet my life on what happened, I'd take the miracle following the blow to the head over the immaculate materialization of an identical twin."

Neither Jane nor I said anything for a long moment. I'm not sure about her, but I felt chastened, like a fool. We looked at each other, sensing a common humiliation.

"Have you ever noticed, Hillary," Jane said, "how men wield logic like it was an extension of their bloody penises? We know the truth, yet we're made to think we don't know shit."

"I wasn't trying to put anyone down," Carter said. "You asked why I felt as I do, and I told you my reasons."

"Don't be defensive, love, I'm merely making an observation, not a criticism. If there's a flaw, it's in hormonal balance, not you in particular."

"Maybe my reasoning is faulty," he said. "Shoot it down."

"I can't argue with your logic, Carter," Jane said. "My approach to truth follows a different path altogether."

"How so?"

"Let me put it this way. I don't think all the facts are in. But the result I see clearly. It's a matter of faith."

"What about you, Hillary?" he asked. "Where does your feminine soul stand?"

I put down my knife and fork. "I would like to believe you're right," I said.

"Why?"

"Because the alternative scares me. Jane can be facile whereas I can't, because it's my life. I'm like the mother who knows her missing child is not dead. I have convictions without being able to explain or justify them."

"Hill, I'm so sorry," Jane said. "We've been insensitive."

"No, you haven't."

"Yes, we've been blithely going on as though you were a piece of furniture. And it's my fault. I shouldn't have forced the issue."

I looked up at Carter, my eyes suddenly filling, my emotions clawing at me. He looked sorry too, contrite. "Jane and I might disagree on who you are," he said softly, "but we both still love you. And frankly, it doesn't make a damned bit of difference who's right. Not a damned bit of difference."

I laughed as tears seeped from my eyes. "You're sweet to say that."

"Hear! Hear!" Jane chimed in. "Well said, Carter. It truly doesn't make a damn bit of difference who you are."

I wiped my eyes and smiled at them both. They were being very kind. The irony was that it *did* matter. Who I really was mattered to me a great deal. "Now that we've established that, let's finish our dinner, shall we?"

"Should we tell Carter about your appointment day after tomorrow?" Jane whispered to me, though loud enough for him to hear.

I peered up the table at him. "I'm going to the dentist on Wednesday to see if the teeth in my head are Hillary's or someone else's."

"The mystery will be resolved then," he said.

"Five hundred pounds says I'm right," Jane whispered to Carter, pretending not to let me hear.

"Make it a thousand and you're on," he replied.

"Done."

"You two are incorrigible," I said, "trading on my misery."

"Well, somebody ought to profit," Jane said. "Care to put some money up yourself, ducks?"

It was black humor and I was almost, but not quite, amused. "If I had to bet, I'd say I'm going to wake up in Kansas."

They both laughed.

"Wouldn't that be dreadful," Jane said. "No tin man, no lion, no husband, no best friend."

"The way you two are going on, it just might not be so bad."

"Pour this dolly-bird some more wine, Carter," Jane said, "we need to get her tanked up."

"No thank you," I said primly. "I want to remember every minute of this evening. After all, how many times does a girl from Kansas get to visit the Land of Oz?"

I T WAS SUCH A warm and pleasant night that we decided to take a walk after dinner, ending up in the village. Jane had gotten a little tipsy on the wine, though with her, outrageousness was a matter of degree. Carter was forbearing and I was pleased by that, though I knew he wanted to be alone with me.

I wanted to be alone with him too, but there was something about the languorous pace of the evening that appealed to me. It heightened my anticipation. Carter touched me when he could, his hand rubbing my skin through the silky fabric of my dress, our thighs brushing when the three of us crowded onto a bench in the town square. We sat there for a while, listening to the cicada singing in the trees. Jane talked nostalgically about her father who'd been a land agent in Bournemouth where she'd grown up eating peas from the garden, as she put it, and her mother's lovely French sauces.

Jane insisted on a cognac, so we went to the sole café in the village and Carter bought her a drink. I had a lemonade and luxuriated in the swirling air under the ceiling fan. Carter squeezed my knee under the table as Jane got progressively more giddy. When she finished her second cognac, Carter hired a man to drive us back to the house.

"I really can walk, dear boy," she said as Carter helped her into the car. "All you're doing is embarrassing me in front of the village."

"I don't want to have to carry you," he gently chided. "Think of it as a kindness to my back."

On the drive up the hill Jane babbled in French. Carter gave the driver a couple of twenty-franc notes and then the two of us virtually carried Jane to the guest room. "Screw all night, if you must," she said, "but please don't be too vocal. I'm bloody randy enough as it is."

I got her undressed and in bed. While I was saying good night Jane took my face in her hands and pulled me close to her. "Don't tell your sexy husband, ducks, but he's going to lose our wager. He may have logic on his side, but I have right . . . and truth . . ." She kissed my cheek, lay back on the pillow and was asleep before I left the room.

Carter was at the window, contemplating the lights dotting the hillsides, when I entered the master suite. "Wonderful night, isn't it?"

"Perfect," I said, going to him.

"Jane okay?"

"Sleeping like a baby."

"The two of you used to get snockered all the time. She, especially, could get pretty rowdy. I have to admit though, she's softened a lot."

340

"I think she's worried about me, Carter. Friends do that, they get upset vicariously."

"And what about lovers?" he said, taking my face in his large warm hands.

"I guess they just worry about love."

He kissed the end of my nose. "That sounds good to me."

I didn't like the uncertainty I felt. It was so much better when I'd still believed we were husband and wife. Yet my feelings for Carter hadn't diminished in any way. If anything, I felt a new sense of urgency, a desire to make love with him now, while I still could, before Fate took him away.

"I'd like a shower before bed," I told him.

"Do you need any help?"

"Is that an indecent proposal?" I asked.

"I guess that depends on what happens once we're in the shower."

I was already shampooing my hair when Carter stepped into the shower. He hugged me as the water pummelled us. His body felt so good, familiar in the way a husband's body should.

All day I'd worried that I might not be Hillary Bass, but right now it didn't matter who I was. Reality was our being together as a torrent of water streamed over our bodies.

I could feel Carter's sex rise against my belly. He caressed me and my skin came alive under the dual sensations of the water and his touch. He slid his slippery chest back and forth across my breasts, making my nipples hard, arousing me.

"I've got to finish my hair before the hot water runs out," I said. "You'd better stop."

Carter was reluctant to quit. He sucked my breasts as the water washed over us. I almost asked him to take me right then, but before I could suggest it he began rinsing the suds from my hair. After we'd dried off he kissed my forehead and told me he loved me.

341

"The last few days have been rough," he said. "And yet I feel so close to you."

"You say that because you're positive that I'm your wife. But I'm not sure I want to see your face when you find out I'm not, that I have another life with other people in it."

"It will all work out, darling, even if you end up having to divorce your husband and abandon your kids."

He kissed me deeply then, arousing me so much that I hated my doubts, hated my fears. I wanted nothing other than to be his wife.

Carter insisted on drying my hair. It struck me as a very intimate thing for him to do. When he was done he kissed my shoulder and hugged me from behind, his arms wrapped around my chest. We peered at our reflections in the mirror. "How's that?"

"It'll do," I said, "but don't give up investment banking to open up a hair salon."

We continued to observe each other. Carter cupped my breasts, making the nipples hard again, making me throb.

"Do I really look like the woman you've been married to all these years?" I asked. "You don't see even the slightest difference?"

Carter turned me around, holding me by the shoulders, and looked me up and down. "Scars," he said thoughtfully. "Let's see, did you have any scars?"

He took my hands and examined them carefully, then my elbows and arms. He made me turn around slowly. He had me giggling as he pushed and probed, finally finding a faint half-inch scar on the inside of one knee.

"Here's something," he said thoughtfully. "But the question is, was that there before?"

"Don't you know?"

He shook his head. "Never really inspected you this closely."

"Some help you are!"

"With all this perfection, who'd bother looking for flaws?"

"Jane said my skin is younger, not as sun-damaged as it was."

Carter took my face in his hands and examined me closely. "Could be."

I put my hands over his eyes. "All right," I said, "what color are my eyes?"

"Uh . . . blue, light blue."

I removed my hands from his eyes and looked at him with disgust. "They're gray."

He peered into them. "I see some blue. Not much, but there are specks of blue."

I examined my eyes in the mirror. "They're gray."

"Doesn't matter, Hillary, it's your inner beauty that attracts me. It's the person I love."

"You slipped out of that one nicely," I admitted. "But your credibility is shot to hell. An alien wouldn't have any trouble slipping a phony past you."

"Sounds to me you're siding with Jane. Thinking of putting a hundred pounds of your own on that dental visit?"

"Yes, I just might."

Carter took me in his arms again. "I sure hope I win the bet."

"Why?"

"I don't want to have to court you all over again."

"It's not that. You're afraid my husband is a six-foot-six truck driver."

He kissed me. "I wouldn't like that at all. Not one little bit."

We went to the bedroom and Carter stretched out on the bed. The moon had come up, illuminating the room with dusty light. I sat beside him, my legs drawn up to my chest, my arms wrapped around them.

"I'll be glad when this is over," I said wistfully.

"So will I."

"What'll we do if I'm not Hillary?"

"We could pretend you were."

"No," I said, "that would never do. I'd have to find out who I was. Having doubts about your identity is a wrenching experience, believe me."

"Then we'd keep at it until we figured out who you are. Whatever it takes to make you happy."

I stroked his chest. "You aren't worried, are you?"

He rolled his head back and forth on the pillow. "No."

I sighed and Carter reached up and pulled me on top of him. He was hard almost instantly. We made love again and again, the first time with a poignant urgency. There was a desperation in our lovemaking—the mutual acknowledgment of a threatened love. I was afraid I'd be losing him soon, that I would be going back to another life, if not another man.

We'd joked about the possibility of me having another husband, but if true I knew it would be too awful to bear. How could I love anyone else and also love Carter the way I did? How would I ever forget these incredible hours with him, these hours in which I was his wife?

The last time we made love it was one or two in the morning. It was slow, languorous. I started out on top, straddling him, filled by him as I slowly undulated my hips. Carter caressed my breasts and I felt creamy and calm. We made love that way for a long time, until it was impossible to hold back. Then we rolled over and he took me beautifully, my legs wrapped around him, my body convulsing, my nails digging into his flesh as he thrust into me.

We turned onto our side, our bodies still united as we kissed. Though it was late, the air coming in the window had

hardly cooled. Our bodies were bathed in perspiration and smelled of sex. Carter was exhausted, but he held my hand, our fingers entwined. I listened to his breathing, wanting to believe I would always be with him.

My mind went back over the day. It had been a long eventful one, seeming more like a week than a single rotation of the earth. How many more would Carter and I have together? The question kept going through my mind. I wasn't as confident as he was about the way things would come out. That much was certain.

At least I was better off now than when I'd awakened that morning. My tormentors were in jail and I no longer had to worry about getting killed. Then I recalled the phone call from Todd Halley. His sole intent had been to create trouble between Carter and me. The evil of half truths.

I hadn't really thought much about what the reporter had said. Suggesting that Carter and Michel had been mixed up in an acrimonious business deal was tantamount to saying that my husband might have somehow been involved in my lover's death.

Just then I felt Carter slip out of me. A twinge of loss, deprivation, shot through me. I felt so much more complete with him in me. I pulled my head back to see his face. His eyes were closed, but his breathing didn't sound attenuated, like a person who was asleep.

"Are you awake?" I whispered.

He squeezed my fingers. "Yes."

"I'm tired," I said, "but I don't think I'll be able to sleep. My mind keeps turning."

"Over what?"

"The same old things. I'm still worried about Michel and what the police are going to do."

"I really don't think there's anything to worry about, darling."

345

I sighed and listened to the lulling sounds of the night —crickets in the distance, a dove cooing. "Carter, is there anything about Michel that I'm not aware of—something that might help explain what happened?"

He turned toward me. "Like what?"

"I'm not sure. But there must have been more involved in his death than a lovers' quarrel. Could he have been upset about something else?"

"You'd know that better than I, absent the amnesia, I mean."

I didn't come right out and tell him what Todd Halley had said because I wanted to give Carter a chance to volunteer the information, assuming it was even true. "Could Michel have been mad at you?" I asked.

"I'm your husband, Hillary. By definition I couldn't have been one of his favorite people."

"But there wasn't anything else going on? Nothing at all?"

"Darling, I hate to sound peevish, but is this a time to be talking about Michel?"

I hugged him. "I'm sorry, my mind was churning, and as always, I'm concerned."

He kissed my shoulder. "Things will work out, Hillary, I'm sure of it. They'll work out just fine."

—

I didn't sleep, though Carter did, his sonorous breathing giving him away. I lay beside him, so tired and yet so awake.

Finally I got up and slipped on a silk wrap and went downstairs. I decided to find a book, anything to take my mind off Paul Debray's investigation and my impending visit to the dentist.

The house was dark, but the moon provided ample light

346

to move around. There was a superabundance of books in the study so I went there first, turning on the lamp on Carter's desk. I picked out a volume of nineteenth-century English poetry and went to the reading chair in the corner. Carter's briefcase was lying on it, open, and I picked it up and carefully set it on the table beside the chair.

Idly, almost unconsciously, I peered in at the files in the case. There were half a dozen, all color-coded the same. Each was marked "Vermaut-Drouet, S.A.," presumably the name of the Belgian firm Carter had been trying to acquire. Most of the files had sub-headings. One was marked "George Dunphy"—I assumed he was the George whom Carter had spoken with that time I'd come into the office. I was about to close the briefcase when the sub-heading on one of the files caught my eye. It said simply "Lambert."

My heart went to my throat. Todd Halley's nasty laugh rang in my ears as though he were standing there, watching. Another shock, another blow. I felt sick.

My pulse raced. I wondered if a business file concerning Michel could possibly be innocent. I desperately wanted to find a reason it could be, but I knew that wasn't likely. Had Carter lied? Was the reporter right after all?

There was no way I could let this pass without getting to the bottom of it. I had to know if I could trust Carter or not. Without trust, what did we have?

I opened the thin file folder. It contained correspondence between Carter and George Dunphy. The subject of each letter was Michel Lambert. There were photocopies of letters between Michel and Dunphy. I skimmed through the correspondence. A lot of the business gobbledygook I didn't understand, but the gist of the situation became evident. Michel owned a substantial minority interest in Vermaut-Drouet, S.A., and he was trying to prevent the acquisition by Carter. Quite simply, Michel was a thorn in Carter's side.

I closed my eyes, feeling sicker than before. The man I'd just slept with, who I'd made love with, hadn't been honest with me. He'd betrayed me. Tears welled as I agonized. Was nothing sacred?

Suddenly I sensed a presence. Looking up, I saw someone standing in the doorway, an apparition garbed in white from head to toe. I gasped. But then I made out her face as she stepped into the circle of lamplight. It was Polly.

"Oh . . . you scared me to death," I said. The file had fallen to my lap and my hands were clutched at my chest.

"I'm terribly sorry, Mrs. Bass. I didn't mean to startle you. I was sitting in the salon because I couldn't sleep. I saw you come down the stairs."

Polly was wearing a simple white cotton robe. Her bruised cheek shone bluish-green in the faint light. I thought about her sitting in the salon by an open window. It would have been directly under the master suite. I wondered if she'd heard our lovemaking.

"I couldn't sleep, either," I said, "and thought I'd look for something to read." The volume of poetry had slipped down in the chair beside me and I picked it up, setting it on the file.

Polly seemed neither concerned nor curious about what I was doing. I'm not even sure it registered that I was going through Carter's briefcase. Her eyes were fixed on mine.

"I won't disturb you for long, ma'am, but may I just say one thing?"

"Sure. What is it?"

Polly lowered her head, seeming unsure of herself, perhaps having second thoughts. "Mrs. Bass . . . I wish you hadn't dismissed the bodyguards."

"Why?"

"I . . . have a feeling . . . there's still reason to be cautious. That you may be facing more danger."

348

I was caught totally off guard by the remark. "Why do you say that? I told you about the arrests. The police have the men who tried to kill me."

She wrung her hands. "There must be others who want you dead. I can't believe Monsieur Lambert was alone in this."

I studied her. "Is this intuition speaking, or do you have some particular knowledge?"

Her face twisted. She was on the verge of tears. "I'm just concerned for you, ma'am. I don't want you to be hurt. Truly I don't. Please don't let down your guard. Be careful. Please!" Polly turned then, without giving me another chance to speak, and slipped back into the hallway.

I sat motionless for a long time, not knowing what to think. Had the goblins of night gotten to Polly or was she aware of something concrete and was afraid to talk about it?

Somehow I was sure that she knew something she couldn't bring herself to tell me. She'd been acting strangely for some time, perhaps longer than I'd realized. In the past I'd attributed it to jealousy over Carter. Once or twice I'd asked myself if she and Erica Maxwell might not have been involved in the bombing. The police had squelched that suspicion, but now I began wondering all over again. What did Polly know that she was afraid to talk about?

My first thought was to discuss it with Carter, but his betrayal had undermined my trust. Every time I thought I'd found solid ground, it turned to quicksand.

I put the files back in the briefcase, got up, and began pacing back and forth, not knowing what to do, what to think. The only thing I knew for sure was that I would not return to that bed with Carter.

What I felt like doing was running away. If it had been within my power, I would have gotten on a plane that very instant and headed for home—wherever that might be. For the moment, though, there was nothing I could do but wait until morning. Then I'd *make* Polly tell me what was up. I'd *demand* that Carter explain his lies.

As my nervous energy drained away, I was overcome by an overwhelming fatigue. There was a small leather couch by the wall opposite the desk. I turned off the lamp and crawled onto the buttery soft cushions. Tears welled in my eyes. I cried silently for a long while until I finally fell asleep.

—

The morning sun angled through the bougainvillea outside the study window, striking me in the face, warming my skin, making my nose tickle. I squinted through my lashes and saw Carter, fully dressed, his back to me, looking in his briefcase, as though he wanted to make sure everything was in place. I drew a startled breath and sat upright, suddenly afraid.

Carter turned. I stared at him, fearing his wrath. To my surprise, he smiled. "Good morning, Hillary. I'm glad you're awake."

I was still numb from sleep and somewhat disoriented, but I was all too aware of Carter and the impending confrontation.

He stepped over and sat next to me on the couch, putting an arm around my shoulders. "You didn't tell me you walked in your sleep," he teased. "It took me ten minutes to find you this morning."

"Oh," I mumbled, "I came in here to borrow a book. I read a few poems and I guess I fell asleep."

"You looked so peaceful I didn't want to awaken you. I had breakfast alone. But I'm leaving now and I wanted to tell you good-bye."

"Where are you going?"

"Apparently there's been an important development in Nice. Debray wants to see me immediately."

"What happened?"

"They found your ring, Hillary. The diamond."

I rubbed my face, trying to clear my head. "Where was it?"

"I don't know. Debray wouldn't tell me. But he did say it's urgent that I get over there. He even sent a car for me. The policeman is waiting out front. I've got to go."

I glanced at the briefcase, which Carter had put back on the chair where I'd found it. "Why does Debray want to talk to you and not me?" I asked.

"I don't know, but that was the message he sent."

Carter sounded so innocent that I suddenly feared for him. If Todd Halley had found out about the trouble he was having with Michel, surely Paul Debray had as well. Maybe Carter wasn't even aware that his duplicity had been uncovered and he was under suspicion.

"When will you be back?" I asked.

"I don't know. I can't imagine it will be long."

I didn't know what to think. I'd intended to confront him about his dealings with Michel, but now I found myself fearing for him. I was terribly confused.

"I'm sorry I have to run off like this, but whatever Debray's got, it's obviously important. Judging by the way the policeman outside was talking, there seems to have been a breakthrough in the case. I'm sure you're as eager to know as I am."

I nodded. "Yes, I am."

I had a terrible sense of foreboding. I wasn't sure whether to fear for Carter or myself. I couldn't imagine how Debray would think he was involved in Michel's death, though. Everybody knew that Carter was in London at the time. But then nothing was at it seemed. Nothing made sense.

351

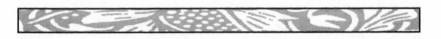

He kissed my cheek and got up. I stared past him at the briefcase. When he stood motionless, not moving, I glanced up at him, looking into his eyes, knowing that he knew.

That moment may have been one of the low points in my life—as bad as those first minutes following the explosion of the *Serenity*, when I didn't know whether I'd been left alone by chance or design. I stared into Carter's eyes, my soul aching.

"You read my files, didn't you?" he said matter-of-factly.

"Yes."

He hesitated. "We'll talk about it when I get home."

I lowered my eyes. "I think that might be a good idea."

He touched my face with his fingers. I tried not to quail.

"It sounds facile for me to say this, I know," he said, "but please don't let what you saw upset you."

I did not respond. I couldn't look at him.

"I love you, Hillary," he said. Then he left the room.

I heard him go out the front door. I heard a car start in the courtyard. I heard it drive away. I listened until I couldn't hear it anymore.

CARTER HAD BEEN gone for several minutes before I left the study. Yvonne was in the hall. She made no comment about the tragic look on my face or where I'd spent the night. Though she had to have wondered, she greeted me cheerfully.

"Has Lady Nyland been down for breakfast?" I asked.

"No, madame."

"She may not be getting up for a while. We'll just let her sleep in."

"*Comme vous voulez.*"

"I'm going to shower and get dressed. Would you tell Polly I'd like to see her in, say, forty-five minutes?"

"Mademoiselle went to the clinic in Toulon to retrieve your clothes and personal effects. Antonio drove her. I don't think they will be back before an hour."

"Then I'll talk to her as soon as she returns."

"Oui, madame."

I went upstairs and decided to look in on Jane. She was twisted in her sheets, sleeping like the dead, her breathing bordering on a snore. By the looks of her, there would be a hangover that lasted till dinnertime.

I had my shower, anguishing at the thought that scarcely ten hours earlier I'd stood there with Carter, soaping him down while he was caressing me. How quickly the fortunes of love changed.

I thought about the things he'd said just before he'd left. I couldn't decide if he was a slick operator who had deftly squirmed out of a sticky situation, or if things weren't as bad as they'd appeared. There was no doubt, though, that Carter had anticipated that I would be put off by what I'd found. That file was damning, at the very least.

I tried to convince myself that there would be time enough for accusation and explanation when he got back. Assuming, of course, that Debray let him come home. The detective had sent a policeman to pick Carter up—that could mean that something ominous had happened.

I told myself I couldn't do anything about that right now, but I could find out why Polly was so sure I was in danger. I had so many worries, it seemed there was always something I needed to do in my battle to survive.

When I dried off, I discovered that I was spotting. Lord, was I having a period? Or was the blood from an abrasion from our night of vigorous sex? Time would tell, but one thing was certain—if I was menstruating, I wasn't Hillary Bass. *If.*

Yvonne had breakfast waiting in the dining room. There was no sign of Polly. I felt the deep anxiety of being out of control and vulnerable, sort of like a leaf floating helplessly down a petulant brook.

I'd finished breakfast, and was sitting at the table, agonizing over my problems, when Jane finally put in an appear-

354

ance. She paused at the entrance and leaned against the door frame. It was evident she had some misery of her own to contend with.

Jane groaned and said, "Apart from absinthe and maybe ouzo, cognac is the worst bloody drink known to man."

"Or woman," I said.

"*Especially* woman."

Jane had showered and dressed, but hadn't bothered to dry her hair. There were bags under her eyes and her color was terrible. She sat at her place, her head cradled in her hands.

"What would you like for breakfast?" I asked.

"A decapitation would be the kindest thing you could offer," she moaned, "but I'd settle for café au lait."

"How about a croissant and butter?"

"Not if you cherish your tablecloth, ducks."

I waited for Jane to get down half her coffee before I broke the news about Carter and related what Polly had said in our middle of the night conversation. Jane shook her head before letting it sink into her hands again. "You might do with a decapitation yourself. How do you succeed in finding difficulties at every turn, Hill?"

"I suppose it's bad karma."

"This might be a time to run away from home," she said.

"Believe me, I considered it."

"You could come home with me to Paris. And if that's not far enough from harm's way, we could go to Bakesly Court. Better still, James has a distant cousin with a lodge on one of the northernmost isles of Scotland. It's a dreary place and depressing as hell, unless you're into the poetry of desolation."

"Let's keep that option in reserve."

"Where in bloody hell do you suppose they found your ring?" Jane asked out of the blue. "And why, if it's yours, do they wish to discuss it with Carter rather than you?"

355

"Maybe it's because I'm not me and they know it."

"You're a convert, are you, then?"

"The evidence is mounting. I think I'm about to have a period."

Jane became alert for the first time that morning. "That's something Hillary Bass couldn't pull off, my dear."

"Not according to what I've been told."

She studied me, slowly nodding. "We aren't surprised, are we?"

"I'm not positive that's what it is, but it's looking more and more like you're going to win your bet."

"Tra la!" Jane said cheerily. "Won't Carter be galled? Undone by a woman's period!"

"Maybe."

When Yvonne came in to clear the table, we left the dining room for the salon. We'd no sooner settled down when we heard a car enter the courtyard.

"That can't be Carter already," I said.

"Perhaps it's Polly."

Jane turned out to be right. My secretary came hurrying in with a large and a small plastic bag. She seemed agitated. "I retrieved your things from the clinic, ma'am," she said breathlessly.

"What's wrong?"

"They're not yours. The clothes and jewelry belong to somebody else."

"There may have been a mistake, a mix-up."

"I don't believe so. The inventory taken at the emergency hospital in Nice perfectly matches what was sent this morning. If there was a mistake, it could only have been made then, at the time you were admitted."

Jane and I exchanged looks.

"I'll wager the stuff in those sacks is yours, ducks," she said. "If you know what I mean."

356

"Let's see it," I said, gesturing.

Polly emptied the contents of the larger sack onto the coffee table. Out tumbled a bra and bikini panties, some khaki shorts, a pair of sneakers, a white blouse, and a white sweatshirt with a picture of the Golden Gate Bridge and the words "San Francisco" across it.

My mouth sagged open. I picked up the sweatshirt, my hands trembling. It reminded me of the photo book I'd seen at Jane's townhouse. I glanced up at her. She smiled knowingly.

"Well?" Jane said.

"These are my things," I replied somberly.

"I know all your clothing, Mrs. Bass," Polly said. "I'm certain I've never seen any of this before."

"Slip on the plimsolls, Hill," Jane said. "See if they fit."

I put on the sneakers. They fit perfectly. Even the slightly frayed lace on the left foot seemed right. These were definitely my things.

Jane picked up the smaller plastic sack and dumped the contents onto the table. There was a sports watch, fat gold hoop earrings, a punched bus ticket from the Nice Department of Public Transportation, a ten-franc note, a five-dollar bill, three ones, and several French coins. I picked up the watch.

"This is mine too. And the earrings." I could not say how or why they were familiar, but they were. My instinct was to put the watch on.

"Polly's right," Jane said, looking over the items. "These are not Hillary Bass's things. They're simply not her style. A sports watch?" she asked rhetorically. "The underwear, the blouse, and the sweatshirt are all American made. And why would Hillary have a bus ticket? And small denomination American bills? If Hillary carried anything, it was hundred-franc notes."

"Oh my lord," I said, beginning to tremble. There was

357

a flicker of light in the recesses of my memory. It told me that Jane had been right.

The telephone rang. Polly hesitated momentarily, then went off to the study to answer it.

I gazed at the items on the table. I fingered the watch. Strong feelings, not easily described, swirled inside me. I was at war with myself. My brain struggled to bring it all into focus, but it wasn't working.

"You're looking at the real you," Jane said softly.

"I know," I said, my eyes turning glossy, "but I still can't remember. It's right at the edge of my mind, almost within reach, but I can't quite pull it out."

Jane put a hand on my arm. Then we heard another vehicle outside.

"What now?" I muttered. I thought it might be Carter and I wasn't sure I wanted to see him just then. My emotions were so muddled I couldn't think.

The doorbell rang and I realized it had to be someone else. I heard Yvonne in the entry and the door opened. A woman's voice carried through the house. From the corner of my eye I saw Jane brace. Then Yvonne came to the entrance to the room, a dark foreboding look on her face.

"Madame," she said, "you have a visitor."

"Who?"

"It is *the wife*, Madame Lambert."

The way Yvonne said it, "the wife," sent a chill down my spine. I hadn't expected this.

"What in God's name could *she* want?" Jane said.

My heart stopped beating. I didn't breathe. With a clarity of vision that comes with absolute certainty I knew that Claudine Lambert had come to even up the score. The irony was she'd come looking for Hillary Bass at virtually the moment I'd concluded that I was another woman. What a time to have to deal with Hillary's sins!

358

"What shall I say?" Yvonne asked when no comment from me was forthcoming.

I looked at Jane. "What do we tell her? That Hillary's not here and we haven't the slightest idea what happened to her?"

"It wouldn't do to tell her to buzz off, I suppose."

I shook my head. I knew it was up to me to do something. I had to take charge. "Tell Madame Lambert I'll see her," I said to Yvonne.

"*Oui, madame.*" The housekeeper withdrew. In half a dozen ticks of the clock she was back with Claudine Lambert at her heels.

I stood, as did Jane. Michel's widow appraised me as I appraised her. She was as I remembered her from the asylum—short and slender, dark-headed. She was surprisingly chic in a striking white and black Chanel suit. She carried a quilted shoulder bag.

It was evident from her expression that her intent was not friendly. Finally, she spoke.

"I understand, Madame Bass," she said, "that you came to the asylum in Cannes some days ago and tried to see me."

"Yes, that's true." I looked at Jane, realizing that despite my bewilderment, the social niceties were up to me. "Do you know my friend, Lady Nyland?" I asked Claudine.

"I believe we've met," the Frenchwoman said perfunctorily.

"It's good to see you, Madame Lambert," Jane said.

I gestured toward the chair opposite us. "Won't you sit down?"

Claudine took several steps in our direction, her eyes never quitting mine. I was uncomfortable under her gaze. Behind Claudine, I saw Polly appear at the entrance to the room. Her mouth sagged open.

Jane busied herself by gathering the things scattered

over the coffee table and stuffing them in the plastic bag. Claudine rested her hand on the chair I'd indicated, but did not sit. She was controlled, but under the cool veneer a fire was simmering. I could see it in her eyes.

"Let me be frank," she said. "I did not come here for a social visit, Madame Bass. I wish to speak with you. In private."

Jane looked at me. I nodded.

"There's a bottle of aspirin upstairs that's been calling my name," Jane said. "If you'll excuse me, mesdames, I think I'll retire to my boudoir."

Claudine watched her go. As Jane skirted past Polly, I saw a look pass between Claudine and my secretary. Polly was clearly distressed, even terror-stricken. Claudine herself did not appear happy at the sight of Polly.

"Foutez le camp!" she commanded angrily. *"Allez-vous en!"*

I could only assume Claudine was ordering Polly to leave, because Jane, who was going out the door, glanced back at Claudine with surprise.

"No, Madame Lambert," Polly cried. "You don't understand. There's been a terrible, terrible mistake. This is not Hillary Bass!" She came toward us, virtually in tears.

I was completely befuddled. Claudine and Polly were getting exercised over something I didn't understand.

"There was a call just now from Mr. Bass," Polly said, her voice beseeching. "The police have discovered a body with Mrs. Bass's ring on it. The real Mrs. Bass is dead, Madame Lambert, drowned like your husband."

Polly's words shocked me. I looked at Jane, who was coming back from the hall. She was dumbfounded too.

No one spoke until Claudine threw back her head and laughed. "You take me for a fool? You think I believe such nonsense?"

"It's true, madame," Polly said. "I swear it."

"You are lying!" Claudine's tone turned ugly. "You know why I am here." With that she dug into her purse and removed a revolver.

There were gasps all over the room. The loudest may have been mine. I stared at the gleaming nickel-plated weapon, its muzzle leveled at my heart. My insides turned to liquid.

"No, no!" Polly screamed. "This is Mrs. Bass's sister, madame! Her twin! She is the wrong woman. Don't do it!"

Claudine's face was florid. Her eyes burned with hatred. "You!" she shouted at me. "You, *salope*, will pay for what you've done!"

I was stunned, frozen. My knees began shaking. Jane screamed something in French, but Claudine ignored her too.

"You have killed my husband," Claudine railed. "My son is in prison, and it is all because of you. I wanted you dead. I wanted you and your damned sailboat in a million pieces. You escaped them, but you cannot escape *me!*"

Polly hurled herself in front of me, nearly knocking me on the sofa. "Don't you understand," she cried. "This is the wrong woman!"

"Out of the way, idiot!" Claudine shrieked.

Polly reached for Claudine's gun hand. The weapon went off, knocking Polly against me. We tumbled backward onto the sofa, Polly on top of me.

I looked up at Claudine. She was a madwoman. She fired again. The bullet pierced the back of the sofa, just above my head. Jane screamed. Still another shot rang out. This one hit Polly, making her limp body jerk.

Claudine's hand was shaking so violently that the next shot whizzed above my head, exploding in the wall behind us. In the midst of the shooting I heard a man's voice and saw Antonio rushing across the room. He hurled himself into Claudine, knocking her to the floor.

Jane came over and helped me slide out from under

361

Polly's body. "Oh God, oh God," she kept saying as she took hold of Polly's face.

I was on my knees by the sofa. Blood was everywhere. Behind us Claudine was raising a ruckus, but she finally stopped shrieking as Antonio subdued her.

Polly moaned and her eyes rolled in her head. Her limbs twitched every few moments, telling me she was still alive.

"Yvonne," Jane cried, *"vas appeler une ambulance!"*

"La police, aussi!" Antonio added. He had Claudine by the shoulders and half led, half dragged her from the room.

Jane and I got Polly straightened out on the sofa. Her upper right chest, just below the shoulder, was soaked with blood. So was her left side at the waist.

"We have to stop the bleeding," I said.

"I'll go find some cloths," Jane said. "Stay with her." She ran off. I watched Polly carefully, fearful that at any moment she'd stop breathing.

Her eyes fluttered. "Relax," I said. "Help will be here soon."

She seemed to recognize me. "Madame Lambert didn't shoot you?" she murmured.

I shook my head. "Thanks to you."

Polly stared at the ceiling, her breathing labored. Blood oozed from her wounds, soaking her clothing. I was astounded by how serene she seemed.

After a few moments passed, she turned her head to me. "It's true," she said with an airy voice. "The body they've found is Mrs. Bass. She's . . . dead." Polly coughed, wincing in pain for the first time.

"Don't talk," I said, stroking her brow. "We'll sort it all out later."

Jane rushed back with a handful of towels that we used to make compresses. Both bullets seemed to have gone clean through Polly. As best we could tell no critical organ had been damaged, but the bleeding was the danger.

Soon we heard sirens in the distance. Polly coughed a lot and her body trembled from time to time, but we'd stopped the worst of the bleeding. The paramedics quickly got her stabilized. I held her hand, and when they prepared to take her to the ambulance, she begged me to ride with her to the hospital. I agreed without hesitation.

"It's my fault this happened," she said as they wheeled her to the ambulance.

"Nonsense," I said. "You're not to blame." I wanted to say *we* were. But who did I mean by "we"? Hillary and I?

The realization that I was not Hillary Bass was beginning to sink in. If Polly's news was accurate, Hillary was dead. The unreality of it all was greater than the horror.

Jane had followed along behind and I turned to hug her while they put the stretcher in the ambulance. The police were there too. Claudine Lambert was sitting in a police car, staring at me. Antonio was beside the car, talking to the gendarmes.

Jane took my face in her hands. "We'll get it all sorted out, love. Don't worry."

I nodded, too emotional to speak.

"As soon as Antonio's free, I'll send him after you to bring you back from hospital."

"Thank you."

The paramedics were ready. One helped me into the back of the ambulance. I sat next to Polly and held her hand.

As we pulled out of the courtyard I saw that Polly's eyes were shimmering. She was trying not to cry. "I'm so sorry," she said. "I had no idea it would turn out like this. When I found out they wanted to kill you, I almost went to the police."

"Polly, what are you saying?"

"Madame Lambert paid me to spy on you. I bitterly

resented you. . . ." She stopped, catching herself, half laughing, half sobbing. "What am I saying? I mean I resented your sister. I wanted to put her in her place. She was so cruel to Mr. Bass, you see. But I thought they only meant to humiliate her. When the sailboat was bombed I realized what was happening and I objected."

"That's how you got your black eye, isn't it?"

"Yes. They threatened me. I felt better when I saw you were protected, but when I realized they hadn't arrested Madame Lambert, I knew you were still in danger." She held my hand tightly. "I was so afraid, I didn't know what to do. I almost told you everything." She coughed. "I regret now that I didn't."

Polly started to cry and the paramedic intervened. He didn't want her to talk and asked me to move away.

Once we arrived at the emergency hospital in Toulon, Polly was whisked away. I was informed that she had sustained no major damage and was expected to recover. When I went outside, I found Antonio waiting for me. He was quick to relate that Claudine Lambert had been taken away by the police.

"You saved my life, Antonio," I said as we walked to the Bentley. "You and Polly both. I can't tell you how grateful I am."

"It's okay, eh?" he said, beaming. He opened the door and I climbed in the backseat. Antonio went round to the driver's side. When he was in, he turned and looked at me. "It's true you are the twin sister of Mrs. Bass?" he said.

"I guess it is, Antonio."

He laughed and started the car. We drove for a while and I asked if there'd been any further word from Mr. Bass.

"They say he's going to Montfaucon. Before I come, Madame Nyland say she talked to him and he's coming soon. Maybe he will be there when we arrive, *n'est-ce pas?*"

As we headed home, I tried to sort through the jumble

in my brain. It was difficult to comprehend the reality of who I wasn't, let alone the reality of who I was.

But now that I knew the truth—or at least part of it—it seemed I ought to be able to remember the rest. But I couldn't. Nothing was turning on the light in my brain, nothing was starting that chain reaction of remembrance.

My thoughts turned to Carter. He'd left home that morning under a cloud of suspicion. I'd thought the worst of him—even wondering if he might have somehow been involved in Michel's death. There was no question of that now, but what about his lies?

I hated to think that in all the excitement, all the tragedy and near tragedy, there could be yet another loss—one that would hurt more than any other—but that's exactly what had happened. I was not Carter's wife. I was someone else, a woman with another life.

I shuddered at the thought of having a husband and children, that someone named Roger could be a central figure in my life. Did the discovery of my dead sister mean everything that Carter and I had shared was an illusion? Did another reality belie that love?

I felt sorry for that woman in the San Francisco sweat-shirt, the gold hoop earrings, and sports watch who'd been found unconscious on board the *Serenity*. I felt sorry for her because I suspected she was an innocent victim of a large and very dark tragedy.

I knew I should feel sorry for Hillary Bass too. She was, after all, my sister. I suspected though, that she was a stranger to me—no more loved or understood than the dark side of my own soul.

Of all the questions remaining to be answered, the one that stood out was the one that I had wrestled with from the moment I'd awakened in the clinic in Toulon—who was I?

ARTER WAS WAITing at the front door when the Bentley pulled into the courtyard. I climbed out of the car without waiting for Antonio. Carter came to where I stood, looking as if he wanted to embrace me, but he held back. We stared at each other in silence until I said, "Well, I guess you lost your bet with Jane."

He nodded.

"Do you know who I am yet?"

"Yes."

As the weight of his answer settled into my brain, I studied his face. Neither of us moved. Antonio had the presence of mind to go off somewhere.

"Do you recall the last thing I said to you before I left this morning?" he asked.

I did not respond.

"I told you I loved you." He waited, then added, "And it's true. As true now as it's ever been."

I bit my lip to keep from crying. So much was at stake. I was standing at the threshold of my life, my future.

"What's my name?"

He sighed. "I called Dr. Thirion and asked how we should do this. He suggested it was best if you made the discovery on your own. We found your things in Hillary's apartment in Nice. You'd evidently been staying there."

I could conjure up a vague image of that—of me as a separate person, visiting my sister. But having lived in her stead, I knew her better than I knew myself, and that was frightening.

Carter stepped forward and pushed the car door closed. Then he took my arm. "Jane's waiting in the salon. We have your purse, your passport, everything."

On the surface I was calm, but actually I felt more numb than in control. The truth that was waiting for me seemed overwhelming. At the front door I stopped and faced Carter.

"I know you won't believe this," I said, "but I'm almost afraid to find out."

"Dr. Thirion said you might get pretty emotional, but Jane and I will be with you every step of the way, unless you'd prefer we didn't. It's up to you."

I drew a shaky breath. "No, it's fine that you're with me."

Carter brushed my cheek with his knuckles. "I understand now why I fell in love with you," he said. "You seemed different because you *were* different."

His words gave me courage. They were a vote of confidence. I could only hope that whatever I discovered inside, things would somehow be all right between us.

We went to the salon where Jane gave me a big hug. "Courage, ducks," she whispered in my ear.

"Polly's going to be all right," I told her, my eyes shimmering.

"Yes, I know. We telephoned the hospital."

She took my hand and the two of us went to the sofa. On the chair opposite was my suitcase, a brown leather and cloth affair that I recognized immediately. My purse, a shoulder bag I'd had for years, was sitting on the coffee table. I was seeing old friends. The only thing was, I couldn't quite remember their names.

Opening my purse was like opening the door to my house. A worn but familiar wallet was on top. My hairbrush was there, a small package of tissue, a camera, two or three tampons, a bottle of Advil, a key ring containing four keys and the letter J on a leather tab, a partially used roll of breath mints, and a French-English pocket dictionary.

In the zippered side pocket I found my American passport. I held it for a second, rubbing my thumb over the shiny blue cover, knowing that it held the secret to my identity. Jane slipped her arm around my shoulder to bolster me. My fingers trembled as I opened the passport. My likeness was there, smiling back at me, familiar in a way that Hillary's photos never were. I was wearing a plain white blouse and a gold chain, my smile more innocent than devilish. My eyes slid to the name printed next to the picture. Jessica Payton.

I glanced up at Carter who watched silently, but with concern. My eyes shimmered and I managed to smile. "Jessica," I said.

"Yes, darling," he said. "Jessica."

I stared again at the passport. The birth date was my birth date, one that felt comfortable and familiar. The place of birth indicated was California, U.S.A., the issuing authority was the Passport Agency in San Francisco, the city I called home. I studied the picture. It was me, all right. I was somebody named Jessica Payton. Yes, that was my name.

Remembrance, understanding, awareness welled inside me. A sense of myself started coalescing. Feelings came to me rather than facts or events, but I knew I had found myself, and I began to cry.

Jane took my hand. Carter came round and sat on the other side of me.

"Are you okay?" he asked.

I shook my head. "No, I'm really sad."

"Why? What's the matter?"

"I don't know." I started sobbing, my whole body shaking.

Jane rubbed my hand. "Do you want to rest for a while, love?"

I nodded. Carter gave me his handkerchief and helped me to my feet.

"I'll take her upstairs," he said to Jane.

I went with him to the entry hall. Carter put his arm around my waist as we climbed the stairs. We went to my room —Hillary's room. I lay on the bed and Carter sat beside me.

"I'm so sorry," I sobbed. "I don't know what's wrong."

He stroked my head. "Dr. Thirion said it could be rough. He suggested you might want professional help. Shall I call him?"

"No, I'll be okay."

I heard a meow then, and the next thing I knew Poof had jumped onto the bed. She insinuated herself between us, looking at me with sleepy eyes. As I petted her, I realized she wasn't even mine.

I wept, staring at Carter through a blur of tears. I wanted to care for him. I wanted everything to be all right between us. But there was something holding me back.

"I've got to ask you a question," I said. "It's very important, so please don't lie to me."

His expression was somber. "You want to ask about my dealings with Michel."

"I want to know why you didn't tell me the truth. I gave

369

you every opportunity to say what was going on between the two of you, and you acted as though there was nothing."

"At the time I took the question to mean anything of a personal nature. It wasn't until this morning, when I looked at those files through your eyes, that I saw them differently. The acquisition wasn't that important to me, Jessica. It was just another deal. In fact, I let George Dunphy handle most of the negotiations, simply to avoid undue complications. Anyway, I'd discussed all this with Debray several days ago."

"You mean the police knew about your dealings with Michel?"

"Yes, when I heard the press was poking around, I called Debray from London. That's partly why I didn't want to make an issue of it with you. Besides, with a gunman stalking you, I felt you had plenty on your mind and didn't need more to puzzle over."

I shook my head. "I was sure there was something sinister going on. I even wondered if that policeman had been sent to arrest you."

"No, no," he said, shaking his head. "I was summoned to Nice because of the ring. Physical identification of the body wasn't possible. For that they needed dental charts, which I authorized immediately. Debray was insistent on getting a positive identification before he came to speak with you again."

I shivered. "That must have been awful, having to do that."

"It was. And I can't tell you how bizarre I felt, going to Nice to confirm Hillary's death, while knowing you were alive and well here at Montfaucon. It was a surrealistic experience. Not to mention painful."

Poof moved to the end of the bed and curled up. I put my hand on Carter's arm. Though intellectually I knew this was my sister we'd been talking about, the reality hadn't fully sunk in yet.

"Jane told me what happened here," Carter said. "Believe me, Polly and Antonio are both getting hefty bonuses." He sighed. "At least the worst is behind us."

The worst, perhaps. But what I faced still seemed daunting. So much had happened. I needed time to adjust to the fact that I'd lost my sister and the chance of ever getting to know her. And I was still in the process of rediscovering myself. Many critical questions remained—not only about the past, but the future as well.

"If you don't mind, Carter, I'd like to rest a few minutes and let everything sink in."

He nodded. "Of course." Then he kissed my cheek and left the room.

My mind began spinning. Jessica Payton's life was somewhat obscure, but at least she was real. I closed my eyes as a strange peacefulness settled over me.

I could see myself in San Francisco. I was going out the front door of an apartment building. I went to my car, a blue VW Bug, and moments later I was headed for the Bay Bridge. As I crossed the cantilever section I could see sailboats off to the north, toward Berkeley.

Berkeley, yes, that's where I was headed. I was afraid, nervous. In my purse was a paper with her address. Once in Berkeley I drove to the north side of the campus. I followed Euclid Avenue into the hills. She'd said the house was just beyond the Rose Garden.

I climbed the stairs to the old brown shingled house, half overgrown with vines. I rang the bell and turned to look out at the view. The waters of the bay gleamed in the afternoon sun like a vat of mercury. San Francisco and the Golden Gate Bridge were barely visible through the haze.

I turned at the sound of the door opening. An old man with a white beard and full belly peered at me over half-frame reading glasses.

"You must be Jessica," he said. "Madeline's nurse took her to the Rose Garden. She loves to spend an hour or two there when the weather's nice. It's just a few steps down the road. You'll find them easy enough. You'll see the wheelchair."

I went to the garden. It sloped down the hillside from the street. Standing at the gate I was able to see a woman in a wheelchair. A uniformed nurse sat beside her on a bench. I made my way there, and when the woman in the wheelchair saw me, she began to cry.

The nurse stepped away and I took her place on the bench. I searched Madeline Johnson's gray eyes that were so very much like my own. She took both my hands in hers. "I promised myself I wouldn't get emotional," she said, "but look at me."

Tears were streaming down my cheeks too. I'd known I was adopted from the time I was a small child, but I hadn't learned my birth mother lived so near until my parents had driven up from Fresno to tell me they'd heard from her and that she wanted badly to see me. She was seriously ill and wouldn't live more than a few months.

We'd exchanged letters and one phone call, then I'd agreed to come to Berkeley. The smell of the roses was overwhelming. Hundreds of rosebushes were in full bloom. For fifteen minutes we hardly spoke. We smiled and we cried a great deal.

Then this woman, the birth mother I'd never known, told me something that shocked me profoundly. "Jessica," she said, "there's something I want you to know, something not even your parents are aware of."

I waited, my insides twisted with emotion. "You have a twin sister who was adopted by a couple in New York," she said. "Her parents never told her she wasn't their natural child, and like your parents, they didn't know there were two of you. I wrote to her mother asking if she would allow me to contact my daughter, but she resisted. All I got was a letter from her lawyer saying she didn't want anything to do with me."

I listened, stunned. Only minutes earlier I'd met my birth mother. Now I was learning I had a twin I'd never known existed.

"Jessica," Madeline said, "I don't want to burden you, but it's clear I'll never see your sister. I hired a detective at very great expense to track her down. I wrote to her three times before I got a reply. She has no desire to meet me. I didn't tell her about you, but I didn't want to die with the secret. I have her address. I thought if someday you wanted to see her, you could." She reached into her pocket and pulled out a slip of paper. "What you do with this, dear, is up to you."

Hillary Bass, Montfaucon, France. My sister. My *twin* sister.

—

I must have fallen asleep, because when I awoke, completely disoriented, Dr. Thirion was at my side. The sight of his white hair and feral eyes was unexpected, and startled me. But then he smiled, putting me somewhat at ease.

"Good afternoon, Jessica," he said. "It is Jessica now, isn't it?"

I nodded, feeling like a child in the presence of some gray eminence. I touched my face, which felt cool and clammy, and tried to sit up.

"Please relax for a few minutes," he said, gently putting his hand on my shoulder. "There's no urgency. Slow is sometimes better."

I sank back on the pillow.

"Mr. Bass telephoned me," the psychiatrist said. "He was concerned and thought I might be able to assist you. It's not easy to bring back a whole life, is it?"

"No."

"How are you feeling?"

"Like I've been in a deep sleep."

"What can you tell me about yourself?"

"I understand the woman in my dreams now, and the roses. She was my mother." The episode in the rose garden came to me again. "And Hillary is my twin sister."

"Hillary is gone now and you're here in her home in France. Do you recall how that happened?"

I thought for a moment, closing my eyes and trying to bring it back. "I think so, but . . ."

"There's no need to rush, Jessica, if it upsets you," Dr. Thirion assured me. "Would you rather tell me about yourself first?"

I took a deep breath, trying to focus my thoughts. My memories were all there, just waiting for me to pluck them. "I live in San Francisco, on Filbert Street in Cow Hollow," I said. "In a one-bedroom apartment."

"Do you live alone?"

"No, I have a black cat named Sable. She's . . . oh my God, she's been at the vet for weeks. The bill is going to be enormous." I was horrified. How could I have forgotten my cat?

I looked at Dr. Thirion and he patted my hand. "Let's talk about your life in California," he said. "What work do you do, Jessica?"

"I'm an associate professor of education at San Francisco State. My specialty is elementary education." When I thought about it I could see my cramped little office on the campus. My friend Margie had the office next door. The view out my window was often shrouded in fog. On my desk I had a picture of my parents. I could see their faces. There was also a polaroid of Sable that Roger had taken. "Roger!" I said aloud.

"*Pardon?*" Dr. Thirion said. The psychiatrist was watching me, his finger pressed against his jaw.

"Roger's my . . ." I looked around the room, seeing no one. "Where's Carter?"

"Mr. Bass has given us a few minutes alone, mademoiselle."

Mademoiselle. I was no longer *madame.* How strange it felt, knowing who I was.

"You were speaking of Roger," the doctor said.

"My boyfriend. We've dated for nearly a year." Dr. Thirion listened without judgment. "Roger's a geologist. He went to Hawaii for the summer. I was coming to see my sister . . . and he was going to the islands."

"How do you feel about this Roger now?"

"We've been close, but we both wanted this time apart . . . a kind of trial separation before we decide . . ."

"Decide what?"

"If we want to get married." That thought was immediately followed by recollections of Carter—our weekend in Paris, the love we'd shared. "My God. I can't believe the things I've been doing. Doctor . . ." I said, my voice beseeching.

He patted my hand again. "You cannot be hard on yourself, Jessica. There is nothing that can be done about the past."

I managed to calm myself. As I lay there, Jessica Payton rose from the wellspring of my soul and became me. Hillary Bass was now somebody else, a role I'd once played.

Dr. Thirion continued to ask me questions and I answered them. My recollections marched steadfastly toward the present as I related what had happened in the Berkeley Rose Garden and in the weeks following.

"What brought you here, Jessica?" he asked. "Why did you come to France?"

"After our birth mother died I wrote to Hillary, telling her about myself. I sent a picture, hoping she'd agree to see me. She wrote back that her life was very complicated just then, but that at some time in the future we might get together.

"When the school term was coming to an end, I wrote that I was planning a trip to Europe. I asked once more if she would see me. She agreed, saying she would meet me in Nice late in June. She said I could stay at her apartment there and she offered to pick me up at the airport. I could tell by the tone of her letter that she wasn't truly enthusiastic, but apparently her curiosity had gotten to her."

"What were your feelings toward your sister at that point?"

"Meeting my birth mother had been very emotional. I saw her three more times before she died. The poor thing anguished about Hillary's refusal to see her. And as she was dying, she made me promise to explain why we'd been given up for adoption, why she had considered it an act of love. By the time I left for Europe, I felt I was on a mission."

"Your trip was very emotional then?"

"I don't think I slept for a week before I left. That first time I'd seen my mother had been so traumatic. I dreamed about her every night, always seeing her amid the roses."

"Tell me about your meeting with Hillary."

"My flight arrived early and she was a little late picking me up. As I wandered around the terminal building, I saw that old lady selling flowers. I bought a rose for Hillary as a kind of symbol of our mother, and the message of love I was bringing.

"When Hillary finally arrived, I wanted to throw my arms around her. But she was distant, very formal, and clearly upset by our meeting. She was dressed elegantly, though she had on large sunglasses and a big hat, almost as if she was trying to disguise herself. She hustled me into a taxi, and on the way into town, she told me she was in the midst of a big emotional problem involving a friend. I tried to rationalize the reception I'd gotten, but I knew deep down my existence did not please her."

"Did she tell you that?"

"Not in so many words, but her feelings were evident. We went directly to her apartment. It was uncanny how much alike we looked. That didn't appeal to Hillary at all. She kept saying things like, 'This is so incredible, it's frightening. Don't you feel violated?' She must have said it three or four times, making me feel as though I'd somehow robbed her of something."

"Then what happened?"

"I tried to tell her about our mother, but she didn't want to listen. She drank a lot. I could see she was insecure. I had no desire to upset her, so I offered to leave. I guess that made her feel guilty because she insisted she wanted me to stay for another day at least.

"We spent the night in the apartment and ate there as well. I realized then that Hillary didn't want to be seen in public with me. At first she talked very little about her personal life, except to say that her relationship with her husband was distant. When she got drunk, she told me about Michel and how upset she was with him, though she didn't say why."

"How is it you ended up on the boat?"

I looked at Dr. Thirion, my eyes suddenly filling with tears.

"Would you rather not talk about it now?" he asked.

"No, I want to get it out. I think this is what has been eating at me . . . this and . . . our mother."

The psychiatrist took both my hands. "Jessica, Paul Debray and Jacques Lepecheur are downstairs. Debray wishes to interview you about what happened aboard the sailboat. I told him I wasn't sure you were emotionally ready for such a step, but it occurs to me you may wish to tell the story only once. What is your preference?"

"Have them come now. I want to get it over with."

"Very well." He got to his feet, but before he left he said, "Mr. Bass is most eager to speak with you also. Would you allow a few words from him while I fetch Debray and Lepecheur?"

"Oh yes, I'd like that."

The psychiatrist stepped from the room. I watched the curtains billowing as they had that evening when Carter and I had first dined together. There was a light rap at the door. Carter entered, slowly walking to the bed. He sat beside me and held my hand.

It seemed so very natural for him to do that, though it was impossible to say what ought to be natural between us. He rubbed the back of my hand with his thumb. He still hadn't said anything.

"I guess twins . . . even twins separated at birth . . . have a lot in common," I said. "Hillary and I both chose the same perfume. We both liked cats. We both fell in love with you."

"There were also some very important differences, Jessica. Believe me. I should know."

"In Paris, after we made love, I was sure I was your wife." Tears filled my eyes. "But you were my brother-in-law, Carter. My sister's husband!"

"Darling, everything that happened, happened because of our feelings for each other. Don't think for a moment that isn't true. Just because we were wrong about who you were, doesn't change how we felt."

"But now I know who I am. I have a whole life I wasn't aware of before. I have a boyfriend, Carter, a man I'm considering marrying."

He was taken aback. His expression grew somber. "Roger?"

"Yes."

"Do you love him?"

"I remember caring for him. But I don't feel the same about him now, not since I've been with you."

Carter allowed himself a relieved smile. He leaned over to kiss me but there was a knock at the door.

"*O, pardon, monsieur, madame.*" It was Dr. Thirion.

Carter got to his feet as the psychiatrist entered. Paul Debray and Jacques Lepecheur were right behind him.

As they came in, I sat upright on the bed. Carter helped fluff a pillow behind me. Debray stepped forward and extended his hand.

"Mademoiselle Payton, I appreciate your cooperation. I understand that this is a very difficult time. My sincere regrets at the loss of your sister."

I acknowledged his words with a nod. It was so bizarre to be receiving condolences over Hillary's death. If madness was anything like the world I had been living in, then I understood what it was to be mad.

Carter had brought a chair for Debray. Lepecheur went to the table, his ever-present notebook at the ready. Carter sat at the foot of the bed. Dr. Thirion stood behind Debray.

"Mademoiselle," the detective began, stroking his chin, "we are most anxious to learn what occurred on the sailboat *Serenity* the day of the accident. I trust you can relate to us the facts."

"Yes," I said, my voice trembling.

"I understand you were staying with Madame Bass at her apartment in Nice. Begin with what happened that morning, if you would."

"Hillary awoke late. She was in a big hurry to leave the apartment, saying she had some business to take care of before she picked up her sailboat. She had suggested we go sailing that afternoon, I guess because it was something we could do together that wasn't too public. I was apprehensive because the only time I'd been on a boat I'd gotten sick. But I agreed."

"She had other business, which is why you did not accompany her when she left the apartment?"

"Yes."

"Did she say what that business was?"

"No, but I had the impression it had to do with Michel."

"I see," Debray said. "Please continue, mademoiselle."

"Hillary gave me directions to the marina before she left. Since we would be out on the water, I decided not to take my purse. Somehow I pictured a little sailboat and thought we would be in life jackets. I dressed accordingly.

"Anyway, I stuffed some money in my pocket and took the bus downtown. After I walked around, window shopping, I went to the marina and waited where Hillary had told me. I knew she was bringing the boat from the repair docks, but I hadn't expected Michel to be with her."

"What did Monsieur Lambert say when he saw you?"

"Hillary had told him about me, but he was surprised at how much alike we were. Frankly, I think he found it amusing. He made a big ceremony, kissed my hand and all that. It was obvious he was trying to get Hillary's goat."

"Why do you say that?"

"Because it was pretty clear that they'd been fighting. They were very hostile, hardly speaking with each other at first."

"Do you know what they were fighting about?"

"No."

"Please continue."

"Well, once I was aboard and Hillary was ready to set sail, she told Michel to go ashore. He refused to leave. They shouted at each other, but I couldn't understand because it was mainly in French. I'd studied the language in high school, but their conversation was over my head.

"I wasn't sure what the problem was, but they were both livid. I felt my presence wasn't helping matters any, so I volunteered to leave. But Hillary said we were going sailing no matter what. Finally she cast off with Michel aboard.

"We no sooner were under way when I started feeling queasy. I went below, but when we hit the open sea I got really sick. I could hear Hillary and Michel up on the deck going at it. Once I looked out the window and saw her slap him. He slapped her back."

"Blows were actually struck?"

"Yes. I was horrified because I wasn't used to violence. There had never been any in my home growing up."

"Did their fighting continue?"

"I don't know for sure. Things were quiet for a while. Meanwhile I was feeling so ill I thought I'd die. I decided I needed some air so I went up on the deck—crawled up, actually. When I got to the top of the stairs, I heard Hillary scream. There was nobody at the wheel. Then I saw her hitting Michel and he was hitting her back. They were like a couple of wild animals."

Tears streamed down my cheeks and Carter handed me his handkerchief. I wiped my eyes and glanced at Debray and Dr. Thirion. After a minute I regained my composure.

"I know this is difficult, mademoiselle," the detective said. "But it is most important that we know exactly what happened. Did either monsieur or madame have a weapon of any kind?"

"No, they were striking each other with their fists. Finally Michel grabbed Hillary, I think to keep her from hitting him, but she continued to fight. They were at the rail, and when the boat shifted suddenly, they were thrown overboard. It all happened so fast. One moment they were there, the next they were in the water."

"What did you do?"

"I ran to the rail. Hillary screamed something about bringing the boat around, but I didn't have a chance to get to the wheel. The next thing I knew the boom swung and clunked me on the head."

Debray, who'd been rubbing his chin, gazed at me. Finally he leaned back in his chair. "A simple accident," he murmured. "Little more than that."

"But for Mademoiselle Payton it was a good deal more than that," Dr. Thirion said. "You see, she came to France in a highly emotional state. She was not well received, and at the tragic moment when she saw her sister and lover thrown into the sea, mademoiselle was struck on the head. The amnesia is not surprising under such circumstances."

Debray nodded. "The fact that she has no identification and is the perfect double of her sister puts her in the unfortunate woman's shoes, and consequently makes her a victim too."

"No one is to blame," I said. "I'm just glad it's over and that we know what happened."

"To my mind, mademoiselle, that was always our only hope," Debray said. "But of course, when I thought this, I had no idea that there were two of you."

We all laughed. Then Carter's gaze met mine. I sighed. I was drained, weary.

"Is there anything more you need, Monsieur Debray?" Carter said, getting to his feet.

"We would like a formal statement from mademoiselle,

but there is no rush. Anytime in the next few days will do. I do not mean to say it is unimportant, of course." He looked directly at me. "Once we have your statement, Miss Payton, you are free to leave France." He got to his feet.

Across the room Lepecheur closed his notebook and joined Debray. They shook hands all round and left the room. Dr. Thirion invited me to come see him if I felt I needed his assistance, then he, too, left.

Carter and I were alone. He stood at the end of the bed, his hands in his pockets, staring at me. Curiously I was seeing him just as he had been that first day he'd come to the clinic. His expression was not quite as stern, but there was consternation on his face.

"How do I convince you to stay here in Europe with me?" he said.

I looked off toward the window and saw the afternoon sun streaming in. At last the mystery of who I was and why I was here had been solved. All that remained was to decide whether this was where I wanted to be.

"I can't simply abandon my past," I told him. "I have a life of my own, parents, friends, a cat, a job. I can't just take Hillary's place and forget who I am."

"You think that's what I want?"

My voice quavered as I said, "I've lost a sister and you've lost a wife. We can't forget that."

"In both cases the loss occurred a long, long time ago." He sounded a touch wistful, though very sure of his words.

"I have to go home," I said. "I just have to."

Carter came around the bed and sat beside me. "Then I'll go with you. I want to see where you live and where you work. I want to meet your parents and friends. But I already know you better than you think, Jessica. A lot better."

He intertwined his fingers with mine. I was seeing him

through the eyes of Jessica Payton, but he was the same man—
the one I'd been falling in love with from that first day at the
clinic. My heart hadn't changed.

"I'm not the expatriate type, a jet setter like my sister," I
said.

"I understand that."

"It's beautiful here, but I might not want to spend
twelve months out of every year in Europe."

"I understand that too."

"My career is important to me. I need to teach, or at
least get deeply involved in something I care about."

"I wouldn't expect less."

I ran my fingers over the back of his hand. "Why are
you being so agreeable?"

"That's an easy one. It's because I want to be with you.
Always."

GETTING MY LIFE back together took time. Carter and I debated where Hillary should be laid to rest and finally decided it should be in New York, with her parents. In remembrance of her we erected a monument on the grounds at Montfaucon. It is not far from that bench where I usually sit when I take a walk. There are identical red rosebushes on either side of the marker.

Carter and I spent the month of September in San Francisco. We needed that time together—time to heal, and time for him to get to know the real me. But even before we left France, we knew that he wouldn't be returning to Europe alone.

For many months, Hillary continued to possess both of

us. My sister was a tragic figure, but to me she will always be a reminder that love and goodness can prevail. That was our mother's belief, the one she had wanted me to pass along.

I'd come to Europe with her message of love. I hadn't managed to convey it to my sister, but I had succeeded in creating a different kind of happiness, in a way I never would have imagined. I think Madeline Johnson would have been heartened that at least one of her children had been able to realize the dream she'd had for us both.

Whenever I stroll down by Hillary's monument I think of her. We missed so much, she and I. We never truly experienced each other, and yet our fates were bound together even before our birth.

Carter and I were married at that little church in the village of Montfaucon on Christmas Eve. All four of our parents flew over for the ceremony. In the two years since then we have made a home at Carter's farm in Virginia. I teach classes at the university each fall. We divide the rest of the year between London, Paris, and the south of France. I no longer feel that Montfaucon is Hillary's home— it became mine the day I married Carter. And the memories here are happy ones now, memories we've made together.

We are a two-cat family these days. Poof and Sable learned to be friends and they go with us back and forth across the Atlantic. Yvonne and Antonio are still in our employ, though Polly returned to England after her recovery. I didn't hire another secretary, but we will be looking for a nanny soon because I'm pregnant. Carter is hoping for twins—to make up for lost time, he says—but the doctor assures me I'm having only one. That's fine with me.

Jane and I have remained friends and she and Carter

have grown closer. Jane has mellowed the past couple of years, though she is still the character she always was. Whenever I'm with her, a part of me is transformed and the spirit of Hillary Bass lives again. I do not feel guilty about that. I think my sister might even have been proud.

R. J. Kaiser is the pseudonym for the husband-and-wife writing team of Ronn Kaiser and Janice Sutcliffe. Ronn is a published mystery writer, and Janice, under the name Janice Kaiser, is the bestselling author of over twenty novels of romantic fiction and is published in thirty-one countries.